NO NAME
ON THE BULLET

DON GRAHAM

No
Name on
the Bullet

A BIOGRAPHY OF
AUDIE MURPHY

VIKING

VIKING
Published by the Penguin Group
Viking Penguin, a division of Penguin Books USA Inc.,
40 West 23rd Street, New York, New York 10010, U.S.A.
Penguin Books Ltd, 27 Wrights Lane, London W8 5TZ, England
Penguin Books Australia Ltd, Ringwood, Victoria, Australia
Penguin Books Canada Ltd, 2801 John Street,
Markham, Ontario, Canada L3R 1B4
Penguin Books (N.Z.) Ltd, 182–190 Wairau Road,
Auckland 10, New Zealand

Penguin Books Ltd, Registered Offices:
Harmondsworth, Middlesex, England

First published in 1989 by Viking Penguin,
a division of Penguin Books USA Inc.

1 2 3 4 5 6 7 8 9 10

Library of Congress Cataloging in Publication Data
Graham, Don.
   No name on the bullet.
   Includes index.
   1. Murphy, Audie, 1924–1971.   2. Soldiers—United
States—Biography.   3. United States Army—Biography.
4. Motion picture actors and actresses—United States—
Biography.   5. World War, 1939–1945—Campaigns—Western.
6. Medal of Honor—Biography.   I. Title.
U53.M87G73   1989   355'.0092'4   [B]   88-40286
ISBN 0-670-81511-X

Printed in the United States of America
Set in Plantin Light.   Designed by Ann Gold.

TO BETSY BERRY

"We admire most the courage to face death; we give such valor our highest and most constant adoration; it moves us deeply in our hearts because we have doubts about how brave we ourselves would be. When we see a man bravely facing his own extinction we rehearse the greatest victory we can imagine. And so the hero has been the center of human honor and acclaim since probably the beginning of specifically human evolution. But even before that our primate ancestors deferred to others who were extrapowerful and courageous and ignored those who were cowardly. Man has elevated animal courage into a cult."

—Ernest Becker, *The Denial of Death*

"I never liked being called the *'most decorated'* Soldier. There were so many guys who should have gotten medals and never did—guys who were killed."

—Audie Murphy

"The essential American soul is hard, isolate, stoic, and a killer."

—D. H. Lawrence, *Studies in Classic American Literature*

PREFACE

F.M. 69 is a two-lane blacktop that runs straight from Greenville to Kingston and Celeste, where it bends through town and then on north to Leonard. You can drive as fast as you like on this road because the police mostly patrol the main arteries flowing into Greenville, the county seat of Hunt County, Texas. One March day in 1985 I drove along F.M. 69 well within the speed limit because I was looking for something. To the left of the road and parallel to it runs a railroad track; to the right is a bar ditch, a line of fence, and beyond, set well off the road two or three hundred yards distant, are houses, mostly brick ranch-style. The terrain is flat and grassy and a few cattle graze here and there. Behind the houses, another hundred or so yards away, there is a line of trees. Already, in midspring, the heat is pronounced and it will remain that way for the long summer ahead that stretches into late October, unless it's an unusual year and fall comes early with its mild weather to relieve everybody's spirits.

About four miles north of Greenville I saw the sign announcing "Historical Marker Ahead." A mile further there it was. The hollow cast-iron pipe that supported the plaque lay propped against the barbed-wire fence. Somebody had either snapped the pole accidentally or had meant to steal the marker and been scared away. The plaque could still be read though, and what it said is that here, in a field east of where I was standing, on June 20, 1924, Audie Leon Murphy was born.

Later that day I was talking with one of the local reporters at the Greenville newspaper and happened to mention that the Murphy marker was in disarray. Somebody was dispatched to repair it; this wasn't the first time the marker had been defaced. Later still, I spent the better part of an hour with an old and quite ailing man whose chief pride and memory lay in the fact that he had spearheaded the effort to get the marker established and afterwards helped keep it intact and safe from vandals. Not long after the marker was put in place, in 1973, vandals had painted it black. The old man guessed it was roughnecks jealous of Audie, but it seemed to me more likely that the black was meant to symbolize somebody's disapproval of a war hero. Another time the plaque was removed and thrown into a ditch about a mile away.

It seemed curious to me that I had not until now visited Audie Murphy's birthplace. Raised in Collin County, southwest and adjacent to Hunt County, I had always known about the legend of Audie Murphy, from the end of the war on. Bonnie and Clyde and Audie Murphy—those were the great heroes of my time and place, rural, southward-looking Texas in the 1940s. Three young people with guns: two outlaws and a legitimate hero.

In McKinney, thirty miles west of Greenville, where my father worked during the late 1940s, Audie Murphy was a familiar sight. He used to stop in at a greasy spoon for a cup of coffee with his friend Everett Brandon, a highway patrolman. On one such occasion my father met Audie and shook his hand. He never forgot Audie's quiet good manners, his modesty.

Audie Murphy used to be a legend in Texas and still is among those old enough to remember World War II and the postwar decade. A hero equal to any that the Alamo has to offer, he has suffered, the way heroes sometimes do, from a shift in the modern consciousness. For all the public schools in Texas named after Travis, Crockett, and Bowie, there is not a single school named after Audie Murphy.

Young people today hardly know who Audie Murphy was. Pressed, they think maybe he's Eddie Murphy's brother. But then they don't know much about World War II, either. It all happened so long ago, and in a culture where Madonna is confused with Marilyn Monroe and history was daily misrepresented by a President who spent the entire war in Burbank but believed he was in Germany when the death camps were opened, in such an amnesiac culture we ought not to be surprised that Audie Murphy is less recognizable than rock stars or game-show hosts.

Audie died in 1971, in a plane crash, at the height of the Vietnam War. Since Vietnam, Americans have had trouble believing or honoring the kind of warrior that Murphy represented. We prefer video fantasy—*Rambo*—a kind of MTV celebration of American machismo in which the nation wins that unpopular war it never should have fought and which, of course, it lost. Audie Murphy could have had Sylvester Stallone for breakfast. Audie Murphy was the real thing, not some pumped-up, aerobicized celluloid palooka. And the real thing is always more interesting, more human, more tragic, more blood-and-death-ridden than the made up, the phony. It was that real hero, the man behind the bronzed statuary, that I had come to find.

ACKNOWLEDGMENTS

From 1985 when I began research on this book in earnest until its completion in 1988, I received help from a number of people. Without their assistance the going would have been much more difficult. I wish to thank them one and all, and I only hope that I've left nobody out. First, the staffs at certain libraries deserve much credit: Dawn Lowell, Gail Slater, Bobbie Day, and Edna Carraway of the W. Walworth Harrison Library, Greenville, Texas; Carol Cullen and the late Carol Epstein of the Margaret Herrick Library, Academy of Motion Picture Arts and Sciences, Beverly Hills, California; Ned Comstock of the Special Collections of the Doheny Library, University of Southern California, Los Angeles, California; Ralph Elder of the Barker Texas History Center, University of Texas, Austin, Texas; and Kent Keeth of the Texas Collection, Baylor University, Waco, Texas.

There were many others who offered tips, leads, hints, advice, and various kinds of help, including Charles Bowden, Frances Mallard, Emilie White, Vincent Flores, Barbara Bordelon, Mickey Francis, Mrs. Ray Woods, Ikey Parkey, Tom Pilkington, James W. Lee, Hank Tester, Lance Bertelsen, Tom Schatz, Horace Newcomb, Fred and Mimi Berry, John Joseph, Mrs. Caroline Ryan, Colista Bird,

Sarah Bird, Harbert S. Byers, Al McGuire, Joann Burns, Kathleen Bailey and the late Lillian Bailey of the Audie Leon Murphy Memorial Fan Club, John Medill, Claudette and Garnette Harris, Ray Merlock, Bob Compton, Karen McCormick, James Ayres, Bill and Sally Graham, Joe Slate, Jean Vache, Fred and Tina Berry, Rolando Hinojosa, John H. Lenihan, Jim Magnuson, Mark Busby, Roger Spiller, Ed Muhl, Raymund Paredes, Betty Sue Flowers, Harry Wilmer, Claudio Segre, William Barnard, Harold Simpson, Paul Fussell, Bob Compton, Kent Biffle, and Joyce Graham.

In my early visits to Los Angeles, former colleague and friend Lynda Boose generously provided me with accommodations and helped me find my way around the City of Angels. Later, my research assistant, Betsy Berry, served as driver, adviser, companion, and coconspirator in the search for Audie Murphy. She helped with several interviews and was solely responsible for an important interview with a call girl. Without Betsy, the research would have been less complete and a whole lot less fun. In addition, her editorial suggestions for my final draft were invaluable.

I also wish to thank the University Research Institute of the University of Texas for two Special Research Grants, which provided funds for renting films.

And of course I want to thank the folks in New York: John Wright, the best of agents, wise, funny, and supportive; Gerald Howard, a superb editor who shepherded the book from first draft to last and knew what I should keep and what I shouldn't; and Dan Frank, who took over with grace and efficiency after Gerry moved on.

CONTENTS

NO NAME
ON THE BULLET

1.
YOU HAVE SEEN
THEIR FACES

"I can't remember ever being *young* in my life."
—*Audie Murphy, 1956*

The world Audie Murphy was born into in 1924 seems to us now impossibly remote. Woodrow Wilson and V. I. Lenin died that year, two titanic figures whose moment lay in the previous decade. New leaders were just off stage waiting for *their* big moments. Benito Mussolini's Fascist Party garnered 65 percent of the votes in Italy; Adolf Hitler was released from prison after serving eight months of a five-year sentence for leading what proved to be an abortive Beer Hall *Putsch* against the state of Bavaria. There he had had time to brood and begin writing a book called *Mein Kampf*. Half a world away, a small island empire was showing increasing signs of imperialistic belligerence, and that same year, 1924, a new U.S. immigration law went into effect that excluded all Japanese.

In the United States Calvin Coolidge succeeded Warren G. Harding midway through a decade of unparalleled prosperity. But the Roaring Twenties, asplash in bathtub gin, soaring stock prices, and a credit-based corporate economy, didn't roar very loudly in

1

the boondocks, in Hunt County, Texas. Anglo civilization was still very thin there. The county was less than a century old, and both the frontier experience and the War Between the States were still a part of the living memory of the oldest family members. The first Anglo settler had fetched up in what was to become Hunt County in 1839, just three years after the fall of the Alamo and the Texas victory at San Jacinto. Caddos and the Kiowas, led by their chiefs Blackcat and Cowleach, still inhabited the area. The first Anglo residency was established in 1843, and by 1846, the year after Texas entered the Union, the town of Greenville had been designated the county seat. In 1920, a few years before Audie's birth, the county contained a population of 50,350.

In the 1920s Hunt County was part of a vast and remote state that insistently regarded itself as different from the rest of the country, but still had ties with the South that were quite strong. Hunt County was a provincial backwash of the last wave of Southern cotton culture as it lapped on the flatter, barren shores of the beginning of the edge of the Great Plains, a hundred, two hundred miles on. It was cotton country and entirely different from the Texas of legend. Here there were no vast ranches, no long-horned cattle grazing on the lowly jimson weed, and, as yet, no oil. (There never would be much.) Life in Hunt County in the twenties and thirties was scarcely distinguishable from that of any rural society in the Deep South stretching all the way from Texas to South Carolina. Protestantism, hard work, temperance, and cotton were what mattered most. Men wore overalls and brogans and followed mules up and down rows of cotton and corn; many wouldn't own tractors for another fifteen years. Their wives and children worked in the fields beside the men, sharing the load, sharing the poverty.

Into this impoverished agrarian society Audie Murphy was born on June 20, 1924, in a tenant farmer's meager house in the middle of a cotton field. His daddy was a sharecropper, and in the South, where cotton was still king, that meant living a life in the perpetual shadow of the American Dream. Franklin D. Roosevelt made history in the next decade when he described America as a place where one third of the nation was ill-housed, ill-fed, and ill-clothed, but tenant farmers, white and black, knew all about that; they were on the cutting edge of retrograde poverty in the booming America of the twenties. The Murphy family could have posed for any of the documentary photographers of the thirties: Walker

Evans, Dorothea Lange, Margaret Bourke-White. You have seen
their faces.

Cotton was a chancy crop at best. Farmers tended to live on
dreams of past glories and futures that never happened. World
War I had sparked cotton production, driven prices up, and provided
a couple of bonanza years. War was good for cotton. Cotton clothed
the soldiers, formed an essential component in the manufacture of
ammunition, and was equally necessary for bandages, gauzes, and
other medical paraphernalia to repair the damage caused by the
shells. There were no big wars in the twenties, though, and the
market fell. But Hunt County, like every county in the rich black
waxy prairie that stretched from northeast Texas all the way to the
Gulf Coast, four hundred miles south, was inextricably wedded to
cotton. Certainly the Murphys were. Their succession of rent houses
floated in a sea of cotton. But somebody else's, never their own,
neither houses nor cotton.

All during the years the Murphys tried to live by cotton, the
tenant farmer system was proving increasingly unworkable. Cotton
production records in Hunt County provide a cruel picture of the
ironies of this way of life. When prices were high, production was
low. When prices were low, production was high. The peak year of
cotton production in Hunt County was 1931, in the wake of the
onrushing Depression. Audie's father stood a better chance of making money playing dominoes than he did farming cotton under the
tenancy system. A cotton field, wrote novelist Edward Everett Davis
in *The White Scourge* (1940), was "the great open air slum of the
South, a perennial Hades of poverty, ignorance, and social
depravity."

As tenant farmers, the Murphys of course didn't own their
house. They didn't own anything to speak of. They owned one milk
cow. The house where they were living when Audie was born belonged to S. F. Boles, a prominent landowner. So did the farm it
sat on. Audie's father's job, and his mother's, was to plant Mr.
Boles's cotton, tend it (that meant hoeing it), and pick it. For his
labors and those of his wife and such children as were old enough
to help him in the fields, he received a percentage of the income
derived from the cotton's value after it was ginned in the fall. The
owner might get rich, but the sharecropper never would. More often
than not, the owner just managed to get by, and even in the best of
times the sharecropper only scraped by, picking up such odd jobs

as he could in the off season or during slack periods when the cotton didn't require daily attention. The children didn't have to be very old before they were sent to the fields: age four or five if they were healthy.

The day Audie Murphy was born was a bright hot dazzling blue June day. The temperature hit the mid-90s in the afternoon and hung on, the way it does in Texas, right through the early part of the evening. It would have still been very hot when Dr. P. S. Pearson, the local country doctor, arrived in time to deliver the baby around 7:00 P.M. In rural communities in those days most babies were delivered at home (and most people died at home, too; a few months before Audie was born in that house, his grandfather, George Washington Murphy, died there). They named him Audie after a neighbor, and Leon because the oldest daughter, Corinne, liked it. For most of his early life he went by Leon. Outside the South, that name had too much of a hillbilly flavor ("Take it away, Leon," sang Bob Wills), and once in the Army, Audie never went by Leon again.

The house was a simple wood-frame affair with a brick chimney and four rooms: two bedrooms, a kitchen, and another smaller all-purpose room. Not much space for a family like the Murphys, which already had eight members. Out back by one corner was a cistern for catching rainwater. This June, it didn't look like there'd be any to catch. The Dallas *Morning News* carried a front-page cartoon that day that depicted a farmer gazing at a stunted crop in a field with deep cracks already beginning to show in the soil. He was singing, "Oh, ain't it gonna rain no mo'?"

A barn stood nearby, and an outhouse. Electricity, bathrooms, and other such luxuries were unknown to rural Texas in 1924. The house, which faced south, sat well back from the road, which was little more than a country lane. Beyond the road was the railroad track. The Katy was one of twenty-six railroad lines that connected Hunt County to the larger world. People boarding the train in Greenville could ride all the way to Chicago. Some local folks ate their first blueberries in the dining car of the Chicago train. The Murphy kids rode the train now and then, hopping on slow freights making the run from Greenville to Celeste, and jumping off a couple of miles down the line. Later, the Murphys had a more poignant relation with the railroad. On two different occasions they lived in a boxcar.

Where the Murphys lived was about three miles south of Kingston, which wasn't big enough to be called a town. It was what people called a community, or, less elegantly, a wide spot in the road. Kingston had missed its single chance to grow when the citizens let Celeste, to the north, cater to the railroads. Celeste wound up with two railroads passing through, the Santa Fe and the Katy, and Kingston withered. To the south of Kingston was Greenville. It was a pretty big place, population two thousand or so, the hub of the county, a minor magnet attracting all the surrounding farmers and their children. Farther to the south and slightly to the west was Dallas, the capital of East Texas. To landlocked provincial farm families it might as well have been the capital of the world.

Audie was the seventh child and third son born to Emmett Murphy and his wife Josie Bell Murphy. Apparently they perpetuated the pattern of their own background without thinking much about it. Emmett came from a family of twelve children himself, and his wife from one of thirteen. Such large families made more sense in the nineteenth century than they do now. As a grown man Audie looked back on his family's size with a kind of contempt—directed at his father, not his mother. Of his father he said, "Every time my old man couldn't feed the kids he had, he got him another one."

Not much is known about Audie's immediate forebears. His father's father, George Washington Murphy, came from Louisiana, of Irish descent, and moved to Texas in 1872 and married Virginia Berry. Of the Berrys, however, a great deal is known. Virginia Berry's family tree included such men as Audie's great-grandfather John Berry and several great half uncles all of whom fought when called upon, from the War of 1812 to San Jacinto in 1836 to the Mier Expedition in 1842, one of several ill-fated Texan excursions into Mexico. There were also six forebears who fought in the Civil War—all for the Confederate cause, naturally—and three of Audie's uncles on his father's side fought in World War I, as did two of his mother's. Audie's mother, Josie Bell Killian, came from equally strong Southern roots. Her father bore the name of Jefferson Davis Killian. A North Carolinian, he came to Hunt County, Texas, with his wife, Sarah Elizabeth Gill, in 1888. Their daughter, Audie's mother, was born there three years later. In sum the Murphys—Emmett and Josie Bell—were very much of a piece with the dominant strands of emigration that led white southerners to Texas all during the nineteenth century.

The Murphy line in 1924 didn't look too promising. Poorly

educated, the large family was hanging on from year to year without any real prospects for improvement. By the time Audie was sixteen, the family had all but unraveled, father gone, mother dead, some children scattered and married, some children placed in an orphanage south of Greenville, the Boles Home, named after the very family on whose land Audie's family was living and working when he was born.

Emmett Murphy wasn't a very good provider. He might have worked hard at times in his life—there were neighbors who said he was a good worker (but many more who said he wasn't)—but what he did never seemed to amount to much in the long run. Or the short run either, for that matter. He liked to go to town and play dominoes, and he didn't mind gambling a little bit if he had any walk-around money, which most of the time he didn't. After the war, Audie wrote that his father "was not lazy, but he had a genius for not considering the future."

Emmett Murphy, or Pat as some people called him, was short and heavyset. He had very little education and could just barely read. Some neighbors didn't think much of Pat Murphy. He dressed shabby, they said, and always wore a pair of black rubber boots. When he hired out, you had to keep an eye on him if you wanted the work to get done. A neighbor woman remembered one time when he was hired to work in her garden. She said she had to stand over him to make sure the work was done right and he didn't slip off to town. Another neighbor remembered how Pat always seemed to visit their house at dinnertime. (Dinner meant the noon meal. Supper was at night. There was no cocktail hour.) He came there to get his hair cut, but he always came exactly at dinnertime and got a free meal to boot.

One thing Pat did stuck in a neighbor woman's craw for the rest of her life. It was the custom to slaughter hogs when it got cold the first time in the fall, and one Thanksgiving weekend Pat helped a neighbor kill the hogs, boil the hair off them, and turn the meat into sausage. The final step was to plunge your hands into the rich hot meat and press the mixture into tubes for storing. What got the neighbor family was that the next week they found out that Pat Murphy had had the "itch"—as scabies was commonly called—when he was helping them put up that sausage. Scabies was not a respectable thing to have; it was a mark of what in that time and place was known as white trash. Nobody would have said it, but they would have thought it.

Like most people, Pat Murphy had other sides to his character. He loved his children, though probably not in any useful way. He always preferred the last-born. One neighbor remembered something that set Pat apart from most men of that time. On two occasions at least, he stayed in the room with his wife when she was giving birth. When one child was born, he was on his knees, beside the bed, holding his wife's hands. After the event he said, "It's a girl." His wife asked, "How do you know?" "Because she's stopped to paint and powder." This glimpse into the secret life of these two parents suggests a more complicated picture than any account of external facts can convey. It would be sentimental, however, to think that such warm, intimate moments overcame the bleakness brought on by the continuous poverty of the Murphy family.

Whatever Pat Murphy might have been like in private, he seemed unable to set or keep the family on a successful course in any direction. They lived in a succession of houses on a succession of tenant farms: two years on the Boles farm south of Kingston; a few years near Hogeye, east of Celeste; another stint on a farm near White Rock, south of Hogeye; and still another one near Lane, west of Celeste. Life on these farms varied little. The food was the same, the meals made up of the familiar staples of poor Southern fare: lots of cornbread, gravy, and molasses. There was meat when pork was available, or small game such as rabbits, squirrels, doves, and fish. The work was grinding and repetitive, stoop labor at its worst. The prospects for getting ahead were nil. While still an infant, Audie was, he later recalled, "strapped like a papoose in a yard swing" while his mother hoed weeds in a nearby field. As a very young child Audie was given chores. One was gathering wood for the wood-burning stove; the other was massaging his mother's hands after a day of work in the fields. Very early in his life, too, when he was five, he took his place among the cotton rows, hoeing and picking according to the season. The tenant farmer life shared by Audie and his family was no different from that experienced by thousands of Southern farm families in this period.

There's nothing that will set a boy to dreaming faster than working one's slow way up and down a cotton field on a blazing, endless summer day in Texas. So it was that Audie, hoeing alongside one or another of his uncles who'd fought in the Great War, heard tales of combat and dreamed of becoming a soldier himself. The uncle coughed, a lingering condition from being gassed, and told him, "If you want to fight, start fightin' these weeds."

In a signed 1956 article Audie wrote of those years, comparing his early life to war: "People know me for my record as a soldier. But the truth is I must have done some of my best fighting in a war I was in long before I joined the Army. You might say there never was a 'peace time' in my life, a time when things were good. . . . I never had just 'fun.' I am one Texan boy who never had a pair of cowboy boots. I am one native-born and native-bred American male who actually doesn't know the rules of our national pastime—baseball. I never had time to play or the paraphernalia you play it with. I never had a bike. It was a full-time job just existing."

In large, chaotic families as in small, tidy ones, children compete for the affections of their parents. In a family like the Murphys the competition must have been particularly fierce. Audie received direct care from his mother for only about two years. One of his earliest memories, he wrote later, was of his mother as a "sad-eyed, silent woman" who "toiled eternally." In 1926 a brother was born and in 1928 another brother came along. With each new baby the mother had necessarily to redirect her attentions toward the newest demands upon her time and affections. When the first child after Audie was born, the responsibility for taking care of Audie, now two, fell to Corinne, the oldest child, who was sixteen. Corinne must have been much like her mother. In later life she certainly looked like her. Both were women with round faces and dark straight hair who, like many farm women overburdened by work, childbearing, and a starchy diet, ran to overweight.

Corinne took to Audie from the first because, like her, he alone among the other Murphys had blue eyes. To Corinne, Audie was a laughing, lovable youngster who loved to tease everybody. In a letter she recalled a scene from his early childhood: "I use to stand him on a box and have him saying little speeches one was

> *Roses on my shoulder*
> *shoesis on my feet*
> *I am momma little darling*
> *dont you think I sweet."*

Already he showed a stubborn streak. He had to have cream gravy for breakfast or he wouldn't eat. When Corinne tried to spank him, he would grab her hand and stick it in his mouth to keep her from punishing him.

But Corinne's surrogate mothering didn't last long. When she was eighteen and Audie five, she moved away from home to live with her grandparents in Farmersville. Soon she was married and had a child of her own.

In 1933 the Murphys moved closer to Celeste, the little town within a few miles of all the surrounding farms on which they had lived. Celeste had a school, and if the kids were going to get any schooling, they needed to be nearer to where the school was. In the beginning the Murphys lived in a boxcar south of town, near the Katy tracks. Such cars were sometimes set aside to provide housing for indigent workers. Living in a boxcar was the most desperate form of shelter available to the poorest of the poor. That's where the Joads lived when they reached the Promised Land in California. The Joads went to California; the Murphys stayed in Texas.

After a short time the Murphys moved into Celeste proper. The town sported then, and still does, a sign trumpeting itself as "Heaven—Texas Style." Heaven was and is small; the population today stands at 716. Celeste was scarcely distinct from the surrounding rural environment in some respects. People kept cows in town, planted gardens, and hung slaughtered hogs up to drip in carports. The Murphys didn't do any of these things; they just existed. They moved into a run-down house on Second Street, two blocks off the commercial district, which amounted to one main street with a few side streets. According to one townsman, the house they lived in hardly qualified by that name: "You wouldn't call the place they lived in a house. It was a *shack*. They were in bad shape." Like the house Audie was born in, this one had just four rooms. It was T-shaped, with a porch, two rooms across the front, and two smaller rooms in the stem of the T, with another porch on one side of the stem. An outhouse stood at the back of the lot, and a cistern near the side porch. A brick fireplace was in the center. The house had electricity but no gas or plumbing. Light fixtures consisted of a single drop from each ceiling, a bulb with a string attached hanging starkly in each room.

The Murphy home possessed no amenities, no screens, no nothing, remembers a boyhood friend of Audie's. There were no radios, no books, no magazines, no amusements for the children. The Murphys lived in the kind of absolute poverty that sends children into the streets and into friendly neighbors' homes to find something to do.

Pat Murphy took a WPA job in Celeste but wasn't able to hold on to it. Here was another indication of almost total lack of sufficiency. The rent on the Celeste house was $4 a month, but it was not generally paid. The fact is, Pat Murphy drank. Drank and just lay around. Sometimes he got arrested for drinking and spent the night in jail. Jailing a man was one way that kindly authorities could get poor families on the welfare rolls. A man in jail couldn't look after his family, and so they were eligible then for relief, often a necessity during the bitter years of the Depression. Pat Murphy would have been poor in any era, but the Depression was enough to knock the drive out of more ambitious men. Some gave up; some hung on till World War II came along and kicked the economy into high gear; a few turned outlaw. Pat Murphy did in the thirties what he had done in the twenties: he depended on the kindness of charitable neighbors.

Josie Murphy struck those who knew her as very quiet. She never complained, at least not to any of the neighbors. She was part Indian, and there were neighbors ready to attribute her taciturnity to that fact. She was a devout churchgoer, a Baptist, and sometimes played the piano for local churches. She liked the old hymns best: "Rock of Ages," "The Old Rugged Cross," "What a Friend We Have in Jesus."

Childbearing took a heavy toll on her. Neighbors described her as sickly. Said to have been pretty once, she had aged fast. Bearing twelve children and living dirt poor all that time, she had plenty of reason to turn to Jesus for solace. When the good ladies of the Methodist Church brought the Murphys blankets and quilts, Josie Murphy accepted the charity but didn't say a word. What one church woman attributed to bad manners may have been embarrassed pride.

Some people in Hunt County who remember the Murphys from the thirties are unwilling to discuss the family. One lady explained why: "There's nothing good to be said." Then she adds, "The Murphys didn't know what water was," and, "The father never worked a day in his life." Neighbors of better economic standing— and that included just about everybody—saw the Murphys as a family inured to sloth and headed nowhere. Some families forbade their children from playing with the Murphy kids because of the difference in social class.

A neighbor from that time remembers one of the Murphy girls who worked as a domestic in his family's Celeste household. She seemed to have picked up the vast inertia of her family's ways. Every time she came to work, the lady of the house made her take a bath first. And she didn't work much when she was there. She'd wear a hole in the floor sweeping in one spot. Most days when she finished up, the lady would give her a sack of groceries to take home.

One day when the Murphy girl came to work, she mentioned sort of offhandedly that one of the Murphy babies had fallen in the fireplace. The lady's family sent for a doctor, but he didn't want to go inside the Murphy house. It would be dirty and he wouldn't ever be paid. The lady's family made him go anyway.

Against such a backdrop of poverty, shiftlessness, and inertia, young Audie stood in sharp relief. He was eager and full of drive. He wanted to be somebody. In places where there were books and magazines, he was enthralled. The drugstore was everybody's library in those days, and the local druggist in Celeste remembered Audie's coming into his store to read the magazines and comic books. Any world beyond his family's repetitive shabbiness of ill fortune and irresolute habits seemed better. Audie was one of those children determined to have a life different from the one he'd been dealt by his family. The only question was what form that drive would take.

Although Audie cared deeply about his mother, he kept looking for other maternal figures. During the Celeste years his sister Corinne, a mother now herself, would take the dinkey, a little two-coach train, over from Farmersville and visit them. Audie enjoyed these visits and still liked to tease her. One time when they were eating, he flipped a pat of butter across the table that landed on Corinne's nose. Everybody laughed.

When Audie entered the first grade in 1933, he was two years older than was customary for beginners. The school at Celeste was a two-story brick building on the other side of town from where the Murphys lived. Compared to the small rural schools of that time, it was a full-scale operation. Smaller schools often had one teacher for the first eight grades, but Celeste had individual teachers for each grade.

The only surviving report card shows that Audie was a good student. In the second grade, 1934–35, he made a B average in reading, numbers, writing, spelling, language, phonics, and art. He was absent a lot: 46 days out of 178. Such attendance was not uncommon among poor families in the Depression. There were times when a boy even that young was required for duties at home. There were also probably some illness and truancy, too.

Besides the rudiments of academic subjects, Audie learned other things at school. He learned something about social classes, about exactly where his family stood in the scale of things. If he hadn't known it before, he would surely have begun to see now how poor his family was. He had one pair of overalls and as he grew they began to ride up high on his legs. The other kids called him "Little Britches," a name certain to make him angry. A lot of things made him angry. He didn't like being called Pat or Little Pat after his father, but for the first three or four grades that's what he was called. Later, he didn't like his first name, Audie, because it sounded like a girl's. Leon was what he preferred, until he went into the Army. In the Army he was Murph to his buddies, as he was later in Hollywood.

Audie's second-grade teacher remembered him vividly. He did well in class, was eager to learn, and liked to stay after class to help her clean the erasers. He liked to walk home with her. The order and cleanliness and purpose of the classroom must have struck a chord in the child, who found few of these qualities outside it. All the teachers were aware of how poor he was, and they tried to find ways to help Audie fit in. During one class project, a course in manners, they made sure Audie had the same things the others did. One child would bring the food, and others would sit with the provider and discuss approved subjects. One kid defined the boundaries of what was permissible by saying that you shouldn't talk about dead horses at the table. When it was Audie's turn to supply the food, one of the teachers always made sure to bring some for him so he would be able to participate and not be embarrassed. There were many days when Audie had little food for himself. His second-grade teacher would sometimes rush home in the afternoon starved to death because she had given her lunch to Audie.

For poor children, Christmas is the hardest season of all. The school at Celeste had a Christmas party and tree every year, and all the parents brought gifts for their children. Audie's teacher knew there would be no gift from his parents. So she bought a football for him and had it wrapped and placed under the tree, and Audie got a gift like everybody else.

On another Christmas Audie, the smallest kid, was chosen to play Santa Claus. With a red suit and a big pillow for girth, Audie gave out with a ho-ho-ho and turned as red as his suit. He was a sharp kid, and he probably didn't believe in Santa Claus for long, if he ever did.

His third-grade teacher remembered him as an inveterate tease. That Christmas everybody exchanged names, and Audie's gift to the teacher whose name he drew was a pair of white mice. Another time, for teasing a girl, he was punished by being sent to the cloakroom. He got even by cutting a triangle in another student's raincoat. The paddling he received for this misdemeanor really made him mad. He stayed away from school for two days and said he didn't like the teacher, said he was never coming back. But he did, the next Monday, and brought her a gift of two powder puffs.

Outside the classroom, Audie kept getting into fights on the playground. "I was a mean kid," he said later. His second-grade teacher said he had a chip on his shoulder. She thought of him affectionately, sadly, as her "Fighting Irishman." Looking back over the years, she summed up his childhood as "always a struggle against many odds, but he was intelligent, industrious, quick to anger, but very loyal and devoted to the ones he loved."

One good thing about living in Celeste was the Murphys' next-door neighbors, John and Willie Cawthon. Audie became much attached to them. John was the town's only barber; he cut hair in Celeste for fifty years. The Cawthons had three sons, all of whom palled around with Audie. Something about the Cawthon family drew Audie to them; Mrs. Cawthon was a big part of it. A warm, gregarious woman, long since widowed, she lives in the same house now over fifty years later. (The Murphy rent house, next door, was torn down long ago.) The local expert on Audie Murphy's childhood, she enjoys talking about Audie. She says she "kinda took the Murphy kids under her wing." Audie seemed to stay at the Cawthons more than he did at home. The barber, as Audie called Mr. Cawthon, gave him and his own sons money whenever they wanted to go to a movie. Audie liked to see westerns, anything with shooting in it. He liked Gary Cooper westerns the best.

One time when a carnival came to town, Audie won a box of peanuts with a prize in it, a string of pearls. He brought the pearls to Mrs. Cawthon. Touched by the gesture, she said it wasn't her place to accept such a gift. He should offer them first to his mother. When he did, she said to go ahead and give them to Mrs. Cawthon, they would just get broken and scattered in the Murphy household.

Audie showed his affection for the Cawthons in other ways. When Mrs. Cawthon had an operation and was unable to do her usual tasks, Audie pitched in. This was later, when he was about fifteen. He made supper from scratch, dressing himself up in an apron that fell "plumb to his ankles" and a chef's hat he'd made out of paper. He chicken-fried a steak, made creamed gravy and creamed potatoes, and for dessert a chocolate cake with icing. Mrs. Cawthon said Audie seemed always to have known how to cook. Then, proud of his work, he set the table and covered it; everybody had to wait till the barber came home from the barber shop. It was a "nice-looking table," Mrs. Cawthon remembers.

The barber's sons didn't share their father's passion for hunting and fishing, but Audie did. He'd beg Mr. Cawthon to take him hunting, which the barber often did. One time during dove season, in the fall, they went dove hunting. Mr. Cawthon stationed Audie under a tree and told him to stay there while he went over the hill looking for doves. Out of Audie's sight he could hear the shotgun going bang every few minutes. The boy was shooting up a storm, it sounded like, and when Mr. Cawthon returned there stood Audie surrounded by doves he'd shot. He had far exceeded the legal limit. The barber figured he'd be thrown under the jail if the law caught them. Mrs. Cawthon cooked the birds and made biscuits; doves and biscuits were a great delicacy. She used the dove feathers to stuff a pillow.

Outside school was the rough-and-tumble world of boys at play. There were the usual boyhood fights—with rocks, brickbats, watermelons, and fists. There was a fight over girls with a bunch of boys in Leonard, a little town north of Celeste. The Leonard boys didn't like the Celeste boys coming up there to court their girls. Audie picked a fight with the biggest Leonard boy. In most fights Audie was physically outmanned, but he never backed down: he thrived on challenge. There was something fierce about him. Like his teachers, his friends felt he had a chip on his shoulder. Said one of them later, "Pat was little but couldn't be pushed around."

The play often involved danger of one sort or another. Audie, never a good swimmer, took risks wading across dangerous creeks or diving into treacherous water tanks. But the biggest risks had to do with firearms. The boys played hair-raising games with guns. One boy would hold an object in his hands; the other would shoot it out. One time it might be cigarettes; another it might be "Big Little Books." Other times boys would put bottles on their heads and take turns shooting them off. Though none of these adventures resulted in harm, some were on the scary side. One of Audie's

brothers remembered Audie and another brother, Buck, actually
trying to shoot a glass marble out of each other's lips. Once when
Audie and a friend were hunting, Audie fired a .12-gauge shotgun
between his friend's feet, spraying mud on his clothes.

Firecrackers and guns offered irresistible pleasures. Audie
dropped firecrackers down the chimney of the barber shop, blowing
the front door open. He had to clean up the mess. There were .22
fire fights among friends, the boys darting behind trees for cover.

There was also one instance of quick thinking on Audie's part.
Coming home from school one day, he stopped by the feed store to
say hello to a man who worked there. But when there was no answer,
Audie went in to see where he was. There the man lay, entangled
in a conveyor belt, bleeding and in serious trouble. Audie ran for
help, the man was saved, and the local newspaper carried a story
about it, the first time Audie landed in the news.

Many of the pranks and harassments were directed at Negroes,
who were considered fair game in those days. Socially at the bottom
of the ladder, they were an easy mark for poor white boys who
wanted to feel better off than somebody. North-Central Texas, settled by southerners, was Jim Crow country. Drinking fountains in
all public places, including courthouses, were designated "Colored"
and "White." Headlines in the sports pages of the local paper were
blatantly racist: NIGGER LUCK WINS GAME FOR TROJANS. The society
was completely segregated. Hunt County had a very active Ku Klux
Klan during the 1920s. The night before Audie was born, back in
1924, the Klan held a rally in Celeste that drew four thousand people.
During the twenties the Grand Kleagle of the Klan was a Dallas
dentist. In Greenville a famous banner was strung over Lee Street
(for Robert E. Lee) in 1926, when Audie was a baby. It said:

The	GREENVILLE	The
Blackest	WELCOME	Whitest
Land		People

Local people then and now swear the sign signified nothing racial.
"White" simply meant decent. People said, "Why, that's mighty
white of you," when they wanted to praise a good action.

Audie, completely of his time and place, took part in a general
pattern of "agitating the black community," remembers a pal from
those days. Audie and his buddies concealed firecrackers inside cig-

arettes and gave them to Negroes. The Negroes took a knife after the boys. Or he would pack firecrackers in mud balls and throw them on the porches of Negro houses. Once, from the vantage point of the Celeste water tower, he rained shots down on the tin roof of a Negro establishment, causing the people inside to pour out of the building in flight.

In a society where most boys learned to use firearms early and had the run of the countryside, incidents sometimes occurred. One day east of town, near the railroad tracks, Audie and his pals ran into a group of Negroes who asked to go hunting with the white boys. Audie said no, and the Negroes snapped off a shot in his direction. Audie, using a .22-caliber automatic that he'd borrowed from Mr. Cawthon, fired back. The Negroes scattered.

Another incident involved a Negro man who came across Audie one day when the boy was hunting. The man laughed and kicked Audie's dog. Audie didn't forget. Later, on another outing in the woods with one of his buddies, Audie spotted the black fellow. The buddy was carrying a shotgun, and Audie said, "Hand me the shotgun; I see a blackbird." He shot him in the seat of the pants, from far enough away that the pellets only stung the man.

The language of that era was so color-coded that even a familiar kind of hunting itself had a racial cast to it. Audie started out hunting with a slingshot, or nigger-shooter, as it was called in those days. This weapon came in two forms: home-made and machine-made. The home-made kind has a Y-shaped stock made from a sturdy fork of a tree branch. A blocked Y cut on a lathe made an even better stock. The best rubber came from inner tubes, and the best pouch for holding the rock missile from shoe leather. The best missile, rare but deadly, was a ball bearing. A good slingshot can propel a rock with deadly force, but hitting a creature like a rabbit with one is an incredible feat. Boyhood friends swear that Audie killed rabbits with this weapon.

He certainly killed plenty with a .22. One summer day a neighbor boy from an upper-middle-class family, home on vacation from SMU, saw Audie coming up the street headed for the woods. He had a nigger-shooter in his hand; he was going hunting. The boy asked him if he wanted to borrow his .22. Of course he did; what boy wouldn't? It was a single-shot .22, and the SMU student gave Audie eight shells. Some hours later Audie returned carrying four rabbits. He gave the boy the remaining four shells. The SMU student never forgot it.

All of Audie's outdoor skills came together in the act of hunting. He had "eyes like a hawk," remembered one old friend, and could spot squirrels in the bushiest trees. He was also an expert at "still" hunting—waiting silently until a squirrel exposed itself. He could hear a squirrel moving about in the branches or scratching its claws on the bark. There is no evidence that he could grin a squirrel out of a tree the way legend said Davy Crockett could a coon, but if one was within range of sight or sound it was doomed. He hunted with both shotgun and .22. With a .22 he could hit darting rabbits from a car, no mean feat. Shells were cheap, but even so, shots counted, and Audie, by all accounts, rarely missed. He couldn't afford to, went the legend.

Audie's formal education didn't last long. It was over about as quick as his childhood. He completed four grades at Celeste and the fifth grade at Floyd, a little community west of Greenville. By then family needs were so imperative that an able-bodied lad like Audie couldn't afford to stay in school. The last Murphy child, a boy, was born in 1935. That made twelve, though three had not survived. Nine children, then. Audie had five younger brothers and sisters pushing him out of his childhood.

"When you grow up in the country, you grow up mighty fast," goes a song by a Texas songwriter. So it was with Audie. He lost his virginity at age twelve to a farm wife, he told an old friend in Hollywood.

The Celeste period ended in 1937 when the Murphys left the house on Second Street and moved once again into a boxcar south of town. The family was beginning its final fragmentation. Buck, the oldest boy, had left home; Corinne and June, the second-oldest girl, had both left; soon Audie would follow. He stayed out of school in 1937–38. He worked for a couple of building contractors in Farmersville, in neighboring Collin County, and as a hired hand on a farm near Celeste. Though small, he did a man's work. Every employer during these years praised the teenager's capacity for sustained work. In 1938–39 Audie returned to school for his last year, the fifth grade. He was fourteen years old, and the disparity between age and grade level must have begun to be noticeable, though he was small and looked younger than his age.

Then, in the summer of 1939, Audie, like his brothers and sisters before him, departed from what was left of home. He lived from hand to mouth, taking room and board with a farm family for a time, then living in a garage apartment in Greenville. School was over for keeps. To a dispossessed boy like Audie, education must have seemed an irrelevant luxury now. The family's needs were as urgent as ever, but any hope of improvement lay elsewhere than with Pat Murphy. The Murphys were living on a farm near Farmersville when, in the early part of 1940, Pat simply disappeared. He had been given to brief absences of a week or two, but this one was final. He tried to get his wife to go with him to West Texas, where he heard things were better. A man could get a job in the oil fields, he figured. Or work in cotton: they were beginning to raise a lot of cotton in West Texas. But his wife wouldn't leave the Hunt and Collin County area; she had aged parents nearby. Audie was sixteen when, as he later recalled, his father "simply walked out of our lives and we didn't hear from him again." The older children were bitter about their father's desertion, the younger children puzzled. Audie said years later, "I suppose I hated him because I hate anyone who quits." Kindly neighbors said Pat Murphy was "sick," meaning mentally off-balance; others said his leaving was right in character, the logical and predictable act of a man who'd always been better at propagating kids than supporting them.

Over the years Pat Murphy surfaced now and then. One son ran across him working in a café in Marble Falls in 1942. When Audie became famous, reporters sought him out. In 1951 he was working as a caretaker at Echo Lake, in Fort Worth. He was proud of his son. In 1962 he turned up in Abilene. He had worked at a drive-in theater until it went out of business. It was a good job because he could watch Audie Murphy westerns when they played at the drive-in. In 1968 father and son were briefly reunited on a sad occasion, the funeral of the youngest son, Joe, who was killed in a car wreck in Collin County. Audie put his arms around the man who years ago had walked out of the family's life.

The old man outlived Audie, too. In 1971 when Audie died, newspapermen again visited Pat Murphy, looking for a story. The way Pat remembered it, he had left the Greenville area *after* his wife died, not before, and he threatened to get his shotgun after the people who were saying lies about him. "I'm a fighter . . . just like Audie was," he said. In 1973 when Audie Murphy Day was held in Greenville and scores of dignitaries, including the governor, came to pay their respects to the war hero, Emmett Murphy came too. Quite senile now, he couldn't remember anything about the hazy past. He could still play a couple of tunes on a harmonica, though, and dance an Irish jig. He outlived his famous son by five years, dying in a rest home in McKinney in 1976.

His father's leaving was one blow; his mother's death was another. She had three little children and was unable to make a go of things on her own. Audie helped out, but it wasn't enough. Soon she moved in with Corinne, who still lived in Farmersville and who now had two children of her own. Things had always been grim for the Murphys; now they were grimmer.

Josie began to sink fast. Poor, depressed over her husband's departure, defeated by life, she succumbed to a disease of the heart, endocarditis, complicated by pneumonia. Informed of her condition, Audie came over from Greenville to stay near her the whole time. He was hoeing in his sister's garden in the backyard when the final moment came. On May 23, 1941, five days shy of her fiftieth birthday, his mother died. At her bedside, he broke into tears. He felt helpless, as he said years later, "The first thing I can remember was wanting to do something for her. I still feel guilty that I never could." After the funeral, he visited Mrs. Cawthon. Out on some errand, she returned to find Audie on the back porch, crying.

In later years his memories of his mother's sad lot remained strong. In an article in 1956, he wrote: "Continued poverty and enforced self-neglect wore her down until she had no resistance to disease. She ailed steadily. In a home where food was hard to come by, medicine and treatment were unattainable luxuries, not necessities. She died when she was in what should have been her vigorous years." He made it clear where his sympathies lay: "Her story, including her early death, is not unusual in the history of a sharecropper's family, particularly when the sharecropper himself runs off, leaving his wife to take care of their children—in Mother's case, nine of us."

In a little over a year Audie had lost his father by default and his mother by death. He borrowed the money to pay for his mother's funeral and still owed the funeral home when he was in basic training in 1942. He sent back $25 and the funeral home wrote off the remainder.

The three youngest children, two girls and a boy, were placed in the Boles Home, a Methodist orphanage south of Greenville that was dedicated to the principles of work, Christianity, and self-improvement. There simply wasn't anything else to do with them. Audie was too young to raise three children by himself; Corinne had her own family to look after. It was also what their mother had thought best.

From the time he left school until he joined the Army in June 1942, Audie worked at a number of different jobs. Nothing paid very much. Farm work paid $1.00 or $1.50 a day, a man's wages. Several times during this period Audie worked for Mr. Haney Lee, whom Audie called General Lee after the most famous southerner of all, Robert E. The Lees owned a farm near Floyd. The first time Mrs. Lee saw Audie, she later recalled, she was struck by his neat appearance. He came to their door in 1937 selling subscriptions to the *Ladies' Home Journal*. Later, as their farmhand, he conveyed an even stronger impression. He seemed to be a fanatic about keeping clean. Consciously or not, and it was probably conscious, Audie aimed to separate himself from his father.

Like the Cawthons, the Lees were another set of surrogate parents for the boy. Audie liked General Lee and showed it by teasing him. One day he tied the farmer's long johns in knots, and Mr. Lee repaid the joke by dumping a cake of ice into Audie's warm bath water. Mr. Lee taught Audie to drive, and he occasionally borrowed their car. Treated like a member of the family, Audie washed the dishes and politely, though very timidly, played a congenial role in the Lee household. The Lees liked him. He worked like a Trojan, they said, and had a lot of pride. He wanted to be somebody. The Lees thought he got this from his mother; they said he worshipped her.

By 1940 Audie was living in Greenville, the biggest town in Hunt County. He got a job at a combination grocery store and filling station where he earned $12 a week. The wife of the owner remembered him as a "sad type person," who was "very sensitive" and capable of being "hurt very easily." Nobody who knew Audie well at this time would disagree.

His second job in Greenville was at a radio repair shop. He and another boy who worked there did not make a regular salary; they got paid if the owner made anything that week. Audie lived in town in a garage apartment. He made model airplanes and hung them all around the ceiling.

He went to the movies whenever he could. He saw one twice because it was about a favorite subject, war, and it starred his favorite actor, Gary Cooper. The movie was *Sergeant York*, Howard Hawks's superb folk ballad about the World War I hero Alvin York. It made vibrant the stories Audie never tired of hearing from his uncles who had been Over There. This film, which proved to be one of the best recruiting films of the era, touched him deeply, and why not? Its true-life story of a poor Southern farmer who loved his mother and rose from rural obscurity through feats in battle to become the most decorated soldier of World War I was virtually a prophecy of Audie's fate. The biggest difference between the film's hero and Audie was religion; Sergeant York was a Christian, and Audie wasn't.

Audie's future looked bleak. With a fifth-grade education he could only expect jobs of the kind he had been getting: pumping gas, being a general flunky at a radio repair shop, picking and chopping cotton. Long before manhood Audie saw the severe limitations of such work. Later he told a Hollywood friend that he stayed in acting because he had done enough hard work as a boy to last him a lifetime. He also said once, "The humanitarian award of the century should go to the man who invented the cotton-picking machine."

How, from such beginnings, could Audie have gone on to accomplish what he did? Certainly he had much to overcome. The figure of his failed father was a constant source of embarrassment; his mother, lost in an early death, was the image of unattainable maternal love. Audie's psychic condition as he stood poised on the brink of adulthood bears a striking resemblance to Ronald Reagan's. Reagan's childhood in the heartland was punctuated by embarrassment, lack of status, and a deep desire to overcome and erase the sins of his father. Reagan's father too was a drunk, a poor provider, and on the dole.

Both of these young men wound up in Hollywood where the possibility for creating new selves was rich with promise. Ambitious, photogenic, and ingratiating, Reagan found a niche in Hollywood in the late thirties and became a competent B+/A− actor. When the war came along, he fought it the only way he knew how: in films. He made training, morale, and reenlistment films for soldiers, defense workers, and the general public. He commuted to the war from Burbank, and fan magazines showed him returning to his wife Jane Wyman as though he were overseas somewhere fighting the war. It was all illusion, but he began believing it. When he later ran for governor of California, he told audiences that he had served as an adjutant at an Air Force base. That was true, but the base was in the film community, and the bombing runs he made were purely imaginary. When he said "Bombs away," it was on film, not over Tokyo.

Audie's war was quite different from Reagan's, but they wound up in the same place in the postwar world, both geographically and politically. Audie's passage from poor white to hero to Hollywood star was a bloody transit totally different from Reagan's bloodless celluloid war, and in the end Audie's was incomplete—the stylistic/cosmetic changes never took, never quite reached the depths of his being, never, as in the case of Reagan, replaced the darkness with the permanent sunniness of radiant self-confidence and optimism. But the same psychic need to overcome the sins and embarrassment of the father fueled them both, driving them through the Depression, the war, and Hollywood.

Imagine Audie Murphy in 1940–41. Feisty, cocky, sad, poised in his mid-teenage years waiting for something to happen, the way all teenagers wait. Then something happened. The whole world plunged into war.

For Audie Murphy and his generation, history intervened in the most extraordinary way. Events in far-off Europe and Asia, reported glancingly in the local newspaper, competed for attention with accounts of local arrests, baseball scores, and birth and death announcements. In 1935–36, Mussolini's Fascist regime waged relentless air war against helpless tribesmen on the plains of Ethiopia; the dictator's son, Vittorio, waxed poetic about how "one group of horsemen gave me the impression of a budding rose unfolding as the bomb fell in their midst and blew them up." In 1938, Hitler annexed Austria; in September 1939, his armies invaded Poland; in 1940, he made *Blitzkrieg* into a household word. It took the Axis powers just five days to conquer the Netherlands; nineteen days for Belgium; forty-two days for France. In less than two years Hitler had redrawn the map of Europe. Only the British held out, surviving both Dunkirk and relentless German Luftwaffe raids on London.

All through this period an intense debate in the United States became more intense—isolationists on one side and the Roosevelt administration on the other. The isolationist view had prevailed since the twenties. One result was an incredibly puny standing army. One historian has calculated that when the Dutch Army surrendered to the Germans in May 1940, "the United States moved up to nineteenth place on the scale of world military powers." The U.S. Army had less than a quarter million badly underequipped soldiers and looked, said *Time*, "like a few nice boys with BB guns." Nor had events in Europe yet swung the country into a fighting mood. Even though by late 1941 the United States had already committed vast sums of economic aid to Britain through Roosevelt's Lend-Lease Program, the nation remained firmly indecisive as to what to do militarily. Such uncertainty was reflected most tellingly in 1941 in a razor-thin vote, 203–202, in the House of Representatives to extend the draft for another eighteen months.

December 7, 1941, changed all that. FDR, considered a warmonger by many opponents, was thoroughly vindicated on that infamous Sunday morning when the Japanese climaxed two decades of expansionist aggression by attacking, at dawn, the U.S. Fleet anchored in Hawaii, destroying five battleships and killing two thousand four hundred men. After such an act, there could be no forgiveness. The United States could no longer remain isolated from the currents of epochmaking events. The next day, December 8, the United States declared war on Japan; three days later, on Germany and Italy.

Of that pivotal day, December 7, Audie later said, "I ran into the mail carrier on the way back from squirrel hunting and he told me about it. I thought, 'They can't do that'— and 'Where's Pearl Harbor?' " That was the mythic version, the hunter soon to be warrior. In fact, Audie and his pal Monroe Hackney were on a double date in Greenville. They heard the news in the afternoon, and Audie said he wanted to join up right away. But he was only seventeen. Underage and undersized, he looked much younger than his seventeen years. His height and weight—5′ 5½″, 112 pounds—fit almost exactly the statistical average of an American girl in 1941: 5′5″, 120 pounds. He thought he could overcome the size problem by extra eating. He even ate vegetables he didn't like in order to grow faster. He couldn't do anything about his age, though. The Marines turned him down, then the paratroopers. The Army said come back when you're old enough.

There was nothing to do but wait. Overseas, the war went badly at first. Wake Island, an American territory, and Hong Kong, a British colony, fell to the Japanese in December; the next month Manila fell, and in March 1942 General MacArthur was forced to leave the Philippines; in April came the fall of Bataan. But there were also some American gains: Dolittle's bombing raids on Japanese cities in April were a big morale booster; and a major naval air force victory at the Battle of Coral Sea, off southern New Guinea, in May, followed by the decisive naval battle at Midway in June, marked the beginning of the end of Japanese naval supremacy in the South Pacific.

The war had an immediacy on the home front during this period, too. In February 1942, a Japanese submarine shelled an oil refinery in Santa Barbara, California; in June, eight Germans landed from submarines off the coasts of three Eastern states and were arrested; and that same month the Oregon coast was fired upon by a Japanese submarine. To meet such threats, the Office of Civil Defense, established in January, provided civilians with silhouette guides to help them spot Jap Zeros and German Messerschmitts streaking down from the sky overhead.

As the nation mobilized for total war, social and economic changes occurred swiftly. Hysteria about the Japanese led to a government internment program, initiated in March, which eventually removed 100,000 Japanese-Americans from their homes. The newly formed War Production Board ordered the cancellation of all nonessential construction projects; price ceilings were set for retail products; massive drives to utilize scrap rubber were launched. High school enrollments dropped as more and more youths entered the work force. Women and bobby-soxers took jobs previously confined to males: they worked on fighter-plane engines and operated drills and poured steel in foundries. The wheels of government and industry were set spinning toward the greatest outpouring of industrial production ever accomplished by any nation.

Audie, impatient to join up, was one of 18 million men who would be processed by the armed forces from 1941 to 1945, one of a vast array of prospective soldiers upon whom minute as well as monumental forces would shape their individual and collective destinies. On June 19, for example, the day before Audie's eighteenth birthday, Winston Churchill met with President Roosevelt in Washington, D.C., to plan the invasion of North Africa. The next day Audie, now old enough, tried again at the Army Recruitment Office in the basement of the Greenville Post Office. He got his sister Corinne and the old doctor who had delivered him to prepare the proper documents, and the Army at last agreed to accept the determined but unpromising-looking youth. Early on June 30 he hitchhiked into Greenville from Corinne's house in Farmersville and boarded the bus for the Federal Building in Dallas, where later that day he took a physical and swore the oath to defend his country against all enemies foreign and domestic.

"Had it not been for World War II," reflects an Army officer who knew him in the 1950s and admired him greatly, "Murphy would have been a zero, a cipher. If you saw him on the street, before he got all the decorations and publicity, you'd never give him another look; he was just another snot-nosed kid from Texas." Perhaps so, but it is very hard to imagine Audie settling down and living the usual kind of life in Hunt County. Marrying, raising kids, farming until something better came along. Maybe working at a Dallas tool and die shop or managing the parts department at the new Chevy dealership in Greenville. Hunting and fishing in season and watching the years roll by, the kids go to school, the quiet, normal kind of Hunt County life. It seems highly improbable that Audie would have ever settled into such an existence. The childhood scars, the losses, the fierce burning compensatory pride masked by shyness and soft-spoken politeness—such passions would never allow him to live the white picket fence life that normal citizens expected to live and did. Or maybe, as with any hero, anybody who exceeds above the usual range of human experience, we can only see his early life as prelude to his later—a child destined to stand silhouetted against the flames of a burning tank destroyer in the snows of the Colmar Pocket, or to ride across the screens of a thousand small-town movie theaters in the 1950s.

2.
THE PURE PRODUCTS
OF AMERICA

"Poverty, privation, and misery are the school of the good soldier."
—Napoleon

So Audie became a GI—government issue. In doing so he took part in the greatest mobilization of manpower in the history of this continent. The size of the U.S. Army was an infinitesimal 267,000 in June of 1940, so small and ill-prepared that Hitler misread the United States as a country "whose conceptions of life are inspired by the most grasping commercialism" and therefore of no consequence to his grand designs. Five years later, in June of 1945, the U.S. Army had catapulted to 8,113,000 personnel, over ten times the size of AT&T, the largest private employer in the nation. Amid such numbers it seems incredible that one soldier could emerge as the nation's best known.

Many facts suggest how Audie Murphy both did and did not fit the norm. He came from the region with the highest rejection rate in the draft: the South (the West and Far West produced the highest percentage of healthy men). He also came from the single occupation group that accounted for a disproportionate number of ineffective soldiers: farmers. And from a large group of agricultural occupations that ranged from agronomist to cowpuncher, Audie's particular agricultural occupation—unskilled farmhand—was not even listed. He came from absolutely the bottom rung of American society; the only rung lower was a non-white agricultural field hand. Studies showed that farmers had a 37.9 percent rate of ineffectiveness, compared with 13.7 percent for men with white-collar pre-military careers. *Ineffectiveness*, as defined by economist Eli Ginzberg and his staff in their three-volume, postwar study commissioned by General Eisenhower, *The Ineffective Soldier: Lessons for Management and the Nation*, is quite a comprehensive term; it means both rejection for military service and removal from service because of mental or emotional defects.

In education, too, Audie came from the most unpromising background. He sprang from the group—grammar school or less—that produced the highest rate of ineffectiveness in the armed services—32 percent—and he came from one of the two regions that had the highest rejection rate because of poor educational systems: the Southeast and Southwest.

In age, Audie also belonged to a statistically distinctive group. Records through July 31, 1942 (a month after his enlistment) show that only 2.9 of the enlistments fell in the eighteen-year-old class; the dominant age groups were twenty-two (12.8) and twenty-three (11.7). By 1944, when Audie was twenty, the average age in the Army was almost twenty-six. The performance of younger soldiers, however, was superior to that of older soldiers, and after age twenty-eight the rate of ineffectiveness increased sharply.

Besides his youthfulness, there was another compensating factor in Audie's regional background. The South was the most bellicose region in the nation. White Anglo-Saxon Protestant southerners were six times more eager to fight Nazis than were the rest of their countrymen. Dean Acheson thought it was because southerners had always revered military heroes. And Texas was a place especially steeped in a long tradition of bellicosity. In World War I Texans had contributed disproportionately to the U.S. effort. Over five thousand Texans died in that conflict, which amounted to 10 percent of all combat casualties suffered by U.S. troops, a statistically impressive figure that far exceeded the Texan share by population percentage.

Nor had that belligerence waned. In a 1939 poll conducted by *Fortune* and Gallup, Texans showed themselves to be the most nationalistic and belligerent people in the United States toward Germany and Japan. And when war came, Texans enlisted in the Marines in disproportionate numbers, surpassing enlistments from Eastern Seaboard states. By June 30, 1942, the date Audie left Greenville for boot camp, Texas had already supplied the third-highest number of draftees, second only to the much more densely populated states of New York and Pennsylvania. But the most telling figures of all lie in these facts: with 5 percent of the U.S. population, Texas contributed 7 percent of the total armed forces, and its war dead amounted to over 7 percent of the total killed in action.

By joining the infantry, Audie showed a decided departure from the kind of berth most men sought. Because the United States exalted the specialist over the foot soldier, an unusual percentage of men was allowed to enter preferred units such as the Air Force and technical branches. Only 5 percent of the 1942 volunteers, for example, chose the infantry or armor. Rifle companies, reports historian Max Hastings, were turned into "a wastebin for men considered unsuitable for any other occupation." The lack of quality showed in such things as height; men in the infantry averaged approximately an inch shorter than the Army's average height.

The basic class structure of the Army bore out the ideology implicit in these statistics. Support personnel—non-combatants behind the lines—amounted to a 3 to 1 ratio over combat troops, and the U.S. Army was top heavy with officers: 7 percent of the total strength, contrasted with 2.86 for the Germans. Historian Robert Leckie has concluded that the United States set out to fight the "most professional and skillful armed force in the history of modern warfare with the least impressive men America had called to its colors."

On the battlefields of Europe, the infantry fulfilled their proletariat mission. They were disposable workers in the arsenal of democracy. In March 1944, for example, the infantry composed only 6 percent of the Army, but provided 53 percent of the total battle casualties. From June 6, 1944—D-Day—to May 8, 1945—VE-Day—12,000 to 18,000 GIs died every month; 40,000 to 60,000 were wounded.

Studies of motivation and performance conducted after the war and confirmed in recent work by such historians as Max Hastings, shed further, if indirect, light on Audie Murphy's performance. Many American soldiers were reluctant or unwilling to fight. Studies conducted by the Army in 1942, the year Audie enlisted, showed that 25 to 50 percent of the men "lacked strong motivation to fight and preferred to avoid combat service." The enlistment and draft process revealed various deficiencies in the nation's youth. Of some 18 million men who were screened for military service, 2.5 million were rejected then or later because of mental or emotional defects. Because of so many men who were "so poorly educated, so emotionally disturbed, or so without motivation," one postwar study calculated that the United States lost the equivalent of fifty-five divisions.

Nothing reflected by these statistics is meant to denigrate the performance of American ground troops in Europe, because in the end Americans fought, and fought well. To those Americans up front, it was no "crusade in Europe" as Ike's best-selling 1948 memoir called it; the war was a nasty job. Though their home ground was not under attack, though they were sent to strange places thousands of miles away and required to fight for they knew not how many years, though they did so because they were sent, not because of any compelling patriotic slogans, the fact that Americans traveled so far to fight "at so little provocation," as Robert Leckie puts it, is a testimony of a true fidelity to country.

Was it men or materiel that won the war? Stalin thought it was the latter: "Without American production the United Nations could never have won the war." Hermann Göring pronounced America's capacity to produce airplanes "unbelievable!" By 1944 the United States was producing munitions and ships at an astonishing rate, 50 percent more munitions than the combined enemy and 45 percent of the arms of all forces, Allied and Axis. But the contribution of American troops could not be underestimated, either. General Rommel knew how to evaluate that dimension. What he said completes the picture of the U.S. role in the Allied effort: "What was really amazing was the speed with which the Americans adapted themselves to modern warfare. They were assisted in this by their tremendous practical and material sense and by their lack of all understanding for tradition and useless theories." Audie Murphy, that youthful, undersized, and improbable warrior, epitomized the contributions made by the U.S. infantry at its best.

On the afternoon of June 30, 1942, Audie, after passing his physical and being sworn into the Army in Dallas, boarded a bus headed for Camp Wolters, in hilly, scrubby country southwest of Fort Worth.

Just under a hundred miles from Hunt County, it looked like it might have been a thousand. This was cowboy country, closer to the mythic Texas than where Audie was raised—much like the terrain he'd ride through in his later western movies.

Camp Wolters was a sprawling training center that could handle 25,000 men. Here the Army tossed together civilians from all over the country, stirred them, and emerged with a melting pot hodgepodge of regional and ethnic stereotypes. Italians from New York, farm boys from Tennessee, Poles from the Midwest, sharecroppers, steelworkers, white-collar workers, all were there to be transformed into a homogeneous outfit to be shipped somewhere—the South Pacific, North Africa, Europe, wherever there was fighting to be done. The only exception was black soldiers. Like the nation, the Army pursued a policy of segregation in World War II, and Negro soldiers were placed in separate divisions and commanded by white officers.

In its experience with a vast wartime draft the Army learned, among other things, that the ideal soldier needed "youth, intelligence, and proper physique." Audie had the youth, the intelligence (notwithstanding his very limited educational background), and, despite his slightness of physique, the physical skills. And he was ready to be trained according to the Army's needs, which were the same as they'd been in the Great War: to meld the individual into a fighting unit by unburdening him of notions of civilian rights; to teach him how to operate small arms weapons—rifle, mortar, and machine gun; and to give him some sense of what it might be like to undergo the chaos and noise of combat. In this summer of 1942 the helmets were the same as those of World War I, signs of a small peacetime army playing catch-up. Audie was issued a tinny-looking headpiece that made him indistinguishable from a doughboy ready to go Over There to fight the Boche in the trenches of France.

Because Camp Wolters trained all kinds, it trained the boy who would become the most decorated soldier of the war, and it trained, or tried to, a boy named Eddie Slovik. The contrast is instructive. Slovik, in the words of his commanding officer, "was not aggressive," and he should have been given a hardship discharge (his wife was an epileptic) or sent into a non-combat unit. Instead he was sent to the front in France in 1944, and deserted twice. On January 31, 1945, five days after Audie Murphy fought in the action for which he received the Congressional Medal of Honor, Private Slovik was executed, the only American soldier to receive such punishment during the war.

So there stood scrawny Audie Murphy, ready to be forged into a soldier. As though scripted for a service comedy, he instantly acquired a nickname—"Baby"—a moniker he didn't like but one he couldn't shake because that's what his tough top sergeant dubbed him. A shrimp even among infantrymen, who averaged an inch shorter than the average height of the rest of the Army, he didn't look like much of a prospect for a soldier. He was hardly bigger than the weapons he was expected to learn to kill with.

To a fellow recruit, he looked "no bigger than a guinea [hen] and was skinny and pale, like he suffered from malnutrition." But looks were deceptive, because Audie was actually in superb physical condition, as he wrote home jauntily to his sister and her family: "Came through with flying colors, eyes checked 20-20, ears and teeth 100 percent. (body! Oh, wouldn't you like to know)."

Audie quickly fell in with a group of Texas boys with whom he felt comfortable. He began to impress his buddies as soon as training in the field got under way. One of them saw Audie's actions as efforts to compensate for his size—the little-guy syndrome. Audie was "meek, mild, and reserved, but was a different person with a rifle and bayonet in his hand, as if he had to prove himself a man among men." Another remembers that Audie "particularly looked forward to the bivouacks and the field exercises." It was "like playing cowboys and Indians. To stay out there [in the field] all day and to bring the field kitchens out there and cook was a picnic to him." Field conditions in Texas in July were brutal. Under a relentless sun and the weight of full gear, Audie was tested to the limit of his physical ability. Once, during bayonet drill, he passed out from heat exhaustion. He fainted partly because of the heat but mostly because he was running a 100° fever, the aftereffect of immunization shots taken earlier in the day.

He loved bayonet drill, and for his proficiency with this weapon won the highest rating, "Expert Badge." He loved the rifle range, too, but his score was "Marksman," the third tier among qualification categories. Shooting from fixed position, he was good, but at spot shooting he was remarkable. Like the Sundance Kid, he was better when he moved. And under pressure, against a German sniper, he would be the best.

His buddies remember that Audie especially loved to fire a machine gun, volunteering for extra time on the firing range whenever possible. They also recall that he "loved his gun." He spent hours field-stripping it and continued to assemble it and disassemble it hours after other recruits had put their guns away for the day. He could field-strip his weapon blindfolded and with great speed. One day a buddy slipped an M-1 part in amongst Audie's Springfield '03 parts, and, blindfolded, Audie instantly recognized something was wrong when his hands touched the part.

Audie was unusually proficient in camouflage exercises, too. He had an uncanny ability, said one buddy, to "always see little things that were wrong that everyone else missed. He could pick a poor camouflage job apart in a minute."

Camp life kept him busy. Never much of a letter writer, he wrote home once during the thirteen weeks of basic training. Writing on cheap tablet paper of the Big Chief sort, he thanked his brother-in-law for a loan and told his sister to give his clothes to his younger brothers. His underwear, he joked, should be given to his brother-in-law, Poland, who was much larger than Audie. But giving away the underwear was not a joke; in the Depression every article of clothing was valuable as a hand-me-down. He also told a standard Army joke: "When I first got here I went to get a hair cut and the barber asked me if I wanted to save my sideburns. I said yes. He said okey [sic], you better catch them (the smart aleck)." Overall, he said, "I like the army fine so far, they let you sleep till 5:30. On the farm I had to get up at 4." Finally, he mentioned having taken out a $5,000 government insurance policy. He wondered whether he should take out any more (later he did): "I don't think thares any use of it tho because I don't intend to get killed any way and it costs pretty high."

Audie was a good soldier; it showed in training, in loyalty to his fellow soldiers, in discipline, in his relations with officers. When one of his Texas buddies had an infected finger, Audie insisted on taking his place in KP duties. When a Yankee officer started to dress down a southerner for slurring his "Here, Sir," to "Huh, Sur," Audie stepped forward to inform the officer that the soldier in question had been on KP and had not heard the officer's admonitions regarding proper pronunciation. Off duty, he palled around with guys at the camp beer garden, but he himself never drank or smoked. He kept quiet and listened.

Always quick-witted, he knew how to deal with Army regulations when they didn't make any sense. Once one of his Texas buddies pulled a joke on him by telling their sergeant that Audie hadn't shaved that morning. This was true; he hadn't. But the fact is he never shaved because there wasn't any reason to. When asked if he had shaved, he said no and was ordered to do so. He lathered up, applied a bladeless razor to his fuzzless cheeks, and returned to pass inspection.

In another standard scene from barracks life, Audie presided over a kangaroo court and ruled that the offending soldier, guilty of smelling bad, be given a GI bath, a painful and humiliating ritual in which the offender was stripped, taken to the shower room, and scrubbed with rough-bristled brushes until he got the point: Stay clean.

Despite Audie's fine showing in basic training, the company commander, as though scripted to do so, thought he was too small for a combat unit. Cook and Baker's School was where Audie needed to be sent. Audie wouldn't hear of it. He wanted to fight, and he managed to stay in an infantry combat unit. He had some romantic notions about what war was going to be like, notions that wouldn't be kicked out of his head until the fighting in Sicily. But that lay half a year away.

Oddly, he did decide to forgo one romantic bit of training. Originally, before he was old enough, Audie had tried to enlist in the paratroops, and at Camp Wolters Army airborne divisions put on a demonstration designed to recruit men from regular combat units. Audie and two of his buddies filed "tentative requests" to join up, but when they saw the paratroopers in action, saw the dangerous drop to the earth, they decided to withdraw their requests. They would remain earth-bound infantry.

After thirteen weeks, in October, basic training completed, Audie visited family and friends in Hunt County. They wouldn't see him again until June 1945. The citations he bore on his chest that summer, a Marksmanship Badge with the Rifle Bar and the Expert Badge with the Bayonet Bar, would be far overshadowed by the ribbons and decorations he would bring back from Europe. Already he looked different, his sister Corinne thought. "The crease in his trousers was so sharp that it looked like a person could cut their hand on it," she said. The Army had given him something he couldn't find following a mule in Hunt County or working at a radio shop. It had given him a high purpose, a mission, and three square meals a day. The Army saved many a boy from poverty; Audie was one of them. He spoke years later of what the Army meant to him in the beginning: "In the Army, I met men. I had good food and I had good clothes. Sure, they were Army clothes, and sometimes didn't fit me. But I knew enough about things to know that the wool in my uniform was real wool, and that my shoes were made of good leather, and it seemed to me that the men I met in the Army were men. More than anything else, I wanted to be one of them."

His short leave over, he boarded a troop train for the next stage of schooling, advanced infantry training at Fort Meade, Maryland. On the way, he got a taste of troop foraging when the train halted for three days to wait for the flood-swollen Potomac River to return to its banks. At Fort Meade he went through more training in marksmanship, field maneuvers, and obstacle and infiltration courses. The weather, often freezing cold, offered a hint of what Europe might be like. The training continued until January 1943. Weekend passes were easy to obtain, and Audie, the country boy, visited New York, Baltimore, and Washington. Photos from the New York trip reveal a jaunty, handsome young soldier in immaculate dress uniform.

At Fort Meade he was "Baby" still. He still didn't like it, but at least nobody called him Tex, he recalled later in a fan magazine: "I hate blabbermouth Texans, and besides, they wouldn't have believed it. I wasn't big enough to be from Texas." Two incidents from that period reveal the ability, determination, and steel of the young soldier. At a shooting gallery near the base, one of those carny jobs, Audie, using a .22 rifle, shot out five red dots on a playing card at thirty feet. Prize money was $25, but the man running the game refused to pay. Mad as hell, Audie reported the incident to the company commander, who visited the gallery and ordered the man to pay up or his operation would be placed off-limits. Audie got his $25, but the carny man wouldn't let him shoot there again.

The other incident involved an assignment Audie was given to escort two prisoners to the quartermaster to receive shoes. They were big men and mean; one was up for murder, the other for rape. Marching behind them, with a shotgun at the ready, he flipped the safety off when he saw them trying to split up. One of the prisoners looked back at Audie and asked, "What would you do if we tried to get away?"

"I'd shoot you—both of you," Murphy replied. He must have been convincing because they didn't get out of line after that.

When Audie told his commanding officer about the episode, he was asked what he would have done. He said, "I told you, I'd have killed em. I don't cotton to spending the rest of my life in jail for something other guys did."

At Fort Meade Audie had to stave off another attempt to assign him to a safe job. The company commander wanted to put him in the post exchange at Meade, where he'd have been nothing more than a clerk dispensing items to real soldiers headed for foreign lands. Nothing doing.

In 1942–43, the war in Europe was not being fought in Europe but in North Africa. To the British, the Middle East was second in importance only to their homeland. Oil was the reason. The Mediterranean and the vast oil reserves in North Africa were essential to British interests. The British favored a strategy that would at once protect their Middle East Command and weaken the German offensive against Russia on the Eastern Front. Britain had a powerful ally in Stalin. By taking on the Germans in North Africa, the Allies would force Hitler to withdraw crucial divisions from his Russian invasion to fight in the south. Roosevelt cautiously agreed with Churchill, and so Operation Torch, as it was called, was put into effect in the fall of 1942. It became the first true combined Allied effort, and it gave invaluable experience to both the Allied Command, now under the leadership of the Supreme Allied Commander, Dwight D. Eisenhower, and to green, unblooded American troops.

Not that the campaign in North Africa was flawless. Far from it. What the Allies had hoped would take six weeks took six months. The plan was to trap and destroy General Rommel's crack Afrika Korps, putting his army in a vise between the British on one side and the Americans on the other. Before Allied invasion forces came ashore on the Algerian and Moroccan coasts at Casablanca, Algiers, and Oran, on November 8, 1942, the British, led by the flamboyant Field Marshal Montgomery, had enjoyed some spectacular successes, winning two furious tank battles at El Alamein in Egypt between October 23 and November 4.

By November 11 Casablanca was secured by Allied forces, and there, early in the new year, January 14–23, 1943, Roosevelt, Churchill, and the Combined Chiefs of Staff held a decisive strategy conference. Churchill argued for attacking the "soft underbelly of the Axis." First North Africa, then Sicily, then France—such was the pattern of invasion and victory laid out by the wily and persuasive prime minister. The American Chiefs of Staff favored a cross-Channel invasion of France that year, 1943. They always had, but Churchill prevailed, and as soon as Torch was completed, the Allies would move on to Sicily. Overlord, the grand scheme to invade western France, lay nearly a year and half away. Had the Allies attempted an invasion of France in 1943, the results stood a good chance of being nothing short of disastrous.

Near the end of January, Audie and his Texas pals Avery Dowdy, Milton Robertson, and Corliss Rowe, still together, reported to Camp Kilmer, New Jersey, the jumping-off point for North Africa. Just before they shipped out, they went to the movies and saw Humphrey Bogart and Ingrid Bergman in *Casablanca*. Less than a month later, on February 20, almost exactly a month after the Allied summit, they steamed into the harbor at Casablanca.

Although the fighting was still fierce in the Tunisian desert, Audie himself never saw any combat in North Africa. On February 14, six days before he landed, untried American troops suffered a humiliating defeat at Kasserine Pass, forcing a withdrawal of some fifty miles before the Americans rallied and eventually, by March 3, drove Rommel back.

He was assigned to Company B (Baker Company), 1st Battalion, 15th Infantry Regiment, 3rd Division. The 3rd was a storied division, famous for its stand at the Marne River in July 1918. Its record in World War II included 531 days of combat duty and 39 Medals of Honor. It was the only American division to fight on all the Western fronts. The 15th Infantry Regiment had a long, proud history, too. It went all the way back to the War of 1812 and had been in continuous active duty since 1861. The 15th had served in China from 1912 to 1938, where it picked up its motto, "Can-Do," from Chinese pidgin English.

His first company assignment was platoon messenger, another safe berth that he doubtless resented. Twice he wrote home that he liked Africa fine and that he hoped "to see a little action soon." Although Audie saw no action in Africa, he did receive some intensive and invaluable combat training. At an Invasion Training Center at Arzew in Algeria, the 3rd Division underwent arduous thirty-mile marches that climaxed with the soldiers either crawling across a field under live machine-gun fire or making an amphibious landing. General Lucian K. Truscott, the 3rd Division commander, was famous for devising these long, grueling marches. "Truscott's Trot" was roundly hated by the men, but later they had to admit it had got them ready for what they'd face in mountainous Sicily and Italy.

During rest periods at bivouac, Audie liked to spend his spare time playing cards. For money. Corliss Rowe said that Audie "loved to gamble with cards and dice." His passion for gambling was a fixed part of his character. At times in his life it would serve him well, but too often in his later years it ruined him.

To new soldiers meeting Audie for the first time, he still "didn't look sixteen years old." He talked freely to one of these soldiers about his past and his hopes for the future. He said he had tried to enlist in the Marines and that he was an orphan who hoped to "make something out of the Army if he liked it." Audie's emerging self-portrait here is deeply within the American grain: an orphan with ambition.

Early in May, Audie's regiment, the 15th Infantry, rode in trucks to northeastern Algeria, close to Tunisia where the front was. Ready to move up to assault position, the 15th was pulled back when North Africa fell to Allied forces on May 8. The African campaign was over, and Audie had yet to face the ultimate test of battle. But he must have been doing a good job because the day before, he received his first promotion, to private (first class).

Much of the rest of May and June were taken up with still more training. The 15th Infantry took part in seizing inland objectives after the first beach assault divisions had achieved their mission. Audie, who was a great believer in training, felt that the training in Africa was far superior to that in the States. In Africa, he said, "they knew what to train for." He learned to hike at a rate of five miles an hour (Truscott's Trot) and go twenty-four hours in hot weather on one canteen of water. There was also a good deal of psychological conditioning necessary to get the men ready to do something which every ethical stricture in their previous background said not to: to take human life. General Truscott fired up the troops with a short speech on July 4, 1943. He told them: "You are going to meet the 'Boche'! Carve your name in his face!"

Audie's famous 1949 memoir, *To Hell and Back*, opens on a "hill just inland from the invasion beaches of Sicily." On the second page a soldier is killed from a shell landing nearby. By page four the narrator Audie is sweaty, hungry, and has blistered feet. "Where is the glamour . . . where is the expected adventure?" he asks. So begins an account of his experiences in the war upon which all subsequent accounts of his life must in part depend. Reviewers in 1949 found no reason to question the book's veracity; nor has any historian since. The book may not tell all the truth—does any book do that?—but it is as scrupulously honest as Audie's extraordinary recall could make it. In the pages that follow, *To Hell and Back* and many other accounts are woven together to provide a picture of Audie Murphy's war.

So it was Sicily where, for him, the shooting began. Sicily offered a kind of realistic extension of the training the men had received in Africa. The island was manned chiefly by Italian troops, not Germans; specifically, there were 315,000 Italian troops and only 90,000 Germans, most of whom were in western Sicily. The Allies chose to land in the south and southeast where the Italians were concentrated. By the summer of 1943 the Italians had lost heart, and they simply didn't put up much of a fight. On July 10, in southeast Sicily, the Allies made one of their most successful landings of the war. Everything was unraveling for the Italians' once cherished leader, too. On July 25 Il Duce was finished. Removed from power by King Victor Emmanuel, the deposed dictator was imprisoned, then, a month later, dramatically rescued by German commandos, after which time he established a sham fascist regime in northern Italy. Mussolini's story came to an end on April 28, 1945, when he and his mistress were executed and strung up like slaughtered hogs.

Audie came ashore with the 15th Infantry near dawn on July 10, at Licata, a port on the coast of southern Sicily. The U.S. troops met scattered resistance, and by the end of the day the beach was secured. In all it took only thirty-eight days to sweep the island. Ernie Pyle, who was with the 3rd Division that day, described the enemy defenses as "almost childish." "It was," he said, "like stepping into the ring to meet Joe Louis and finding Caspar Milquetoast waiting there." Still, Americans died, and Audie saw his first American casualty that day, a GI killed by an artillery burst.

Moving inland, the Americans didn't find much about southern Sicily to recommend it. Wrote war correspondent Ernie Pyle, "The south coast of Sicily seemed to us a drab, light-brown country, and there weren't many trees. The fields of grain had been harvested and they were dry and naked and dusty. The villages were pale gray and indistinguishable at a distance from the rest of the country."

In the first few days on Sicily Audie was assigned as a runner, but he constantly volunteered for patrols. On July 15 he received promotion to corporal and, finally, assignment to front-line duty. He was where he wanted to be, up front, where the fighting was. Now the task was to head to Palermo, 120 miles to the north. It took them twelve days of marching through rugged terrain, with hundreds of Italians surrendering along the way. Before they reached that objective, the 15th Infantry encountered close enemy fire for the first time. From the beginning Audie seemed headed for heroics or death.

His platoon commander remembered the first time he saw Audie under fire: "We got pinned down on a hillside in Sicily and when a tank finally came up and fired a couple of rounds at a house, Murphy jumped up, started firing from the hip and yelling for the rest of us to follow. He was that kind of soldier." He learned very quickly something about the so-called romance of war: "Ten seconds after the first shot was fired at me by an enemy soldier, combat was no longer glamorous. But it was important, because all of a sudden I wanted very much to stay alive." He also soon learned caution and the calculated gamble rather than the headlong romantic rush into the face of enemy fire.

Audie later explained his readiness to kill by the training he'd received in North Africa. "I can remember back in North Africa," he said, "when we were trained to a razor's edge. We were mean and raw. They told us to be ready to kill everyone in sight when we invaded Sicily—men, women and children. They thought that might be the only way we could take the island." In his classic postwar study *Men Against Fire*, the historian S. L. A. Marshall pondered the formidable barriers that stood between a man and the act of killing: "The fear of aggression has been expressed to him so strongly and absorbed by him so deeply and pervadingly—practically with his mother's milk—that it is part of the normal man's emotional make-up. This is his great handicap when he enters combat. It stays his trigger finger even though he is hardly conscious that it is a restraint upon him."

With Audie, aggression immediately overcame whatever checks might have been inculcated with his mother's milk. The Depression had a hand in that, too, in Audie's raw awareness of being a have-not in a world where others had more. Audie's first kill seems closer to murder than to any kind of heroic action, or at least that's how his account of what happened reads in *To Hell and Back*. It was on a patrol near Canicatti. Audie was ahead of Company B with a group of scouts when, in language that suggests bird hunting, "We flush a couple of Italian officers. They should have surrendered. Instead they mount two magnificent white horses and gallop madly away. My act is instinctive. Dropping to one knee, I fire twice. The men tumble from the horses, roll over and lie still."

Lest Audie be charged too easily with simple heartless murder, it's instructive to see what a British soldier and author, Raleigh Trevelyan, an eminently well-educated and civilized sensibility, felt the first time he killed a human being. He spotted a German close up, just a few dozen yards away. Then, writes Trevelyan, "My next actions were absolutely mechanical. Without hesitation I raised my rifle, aimed, fired. It was obvious that a bull had been scored by the way he sagged to his knees, then lay in a hunch without moving. It pleased me to have done this, and all the time I was aiming at him, I felt nothing but elation and a pounding excitement. In fact, my sensations were not unlike when I used to stalk roosting pigeons in the elms at the edge of the Hart Wood at home." Target shooting, bird hunting, and elation—such are the language and feeling of this passage.

Like it or not, analytical studies have found that men sometimes seem to experience moments of exultation and even pleasure in killing. Thus the great military historian John Keegan writes that "easy killing does seem to generate in human beings symptoms of pleasure, which the zoologist Hans Kruuk has tried to relate to the compulsive behavior of certain predatory animals when they come upon groups of their prey which are unable to escape from them."

In Audie's case he was challenged, he reports in *To Hell and Back*, by a lieutenant who asked him why he'd shot them. Audie's response: "That's our job, isn't it? They would have killed us if they'd had the chance." He mentions the training they'd gone through, how tough it was supposed to make them, tough enough to "shed the idea that human life is sacred." Audie, following training, shed it, accepting the imperative drilled into him by the Army, that "we have been put into the field to deal out death." He goes on to explain that the deaths of comrades have driven that lesson home to him, and he concludes, "Now I have shed my first blood. I feel no qualms; no pride; no remorse. There is only a weary indifference that will follow me throughout the war." Thus the note of the bored killer was struck the first time out.

Audie's quick readiness to return fire marked him already as an unusual soldier. According to S. L. A. Marshall, as few as 25 to 30 percent of the men carrying hand weapons in an infantry company ever fired them. That is, says Marshall, "the best showing that could be made by the most spirited and aggressive companies was that one man in four had made at least some use of his fire power." Marshall's controversial findings were based on extensive interviews of infantry companies in the Pacific and European theaters in 1944. He traced the poor showing in returning fire to two principal causes: the very nature of the combat experience and ineffective training procedures. The two were interrelated. On the training ground the novice soldier fired at visible targets and under the supervision of an officer. For many soldiers such firing was enjoyable, like a sporting exercise. The true condition of combat, however, was most unsettling. First, the battlefield seemed empty; there were no people there; more often than not one could not see the enemy. Second, the individual soldier felt alone, cut off from the density of troops bunched in parade or in close contiguity behind the lines. One was alone in an empty field. "We were fighting phantoms," thought many a soldier. When *Men Against Fire* appeared in 1947, the Army set out to improve its training procedures. More field exercises with live fire to simulate combat conditions and special emphases on close communication between a platoon leader and his men led to payoffs in the next war. In Korea, 1950, firing percentages in line companies increased to over 55 percent, nearly double that of World War II.

Audie Murphy was one of the small percentage of men in a company who counted the most, because he returned fire and because he was aggressive in taking and holding ground. And men who returned fire were also likely to perform other essential combat tasks as well. Said Marshall, "The hand that pulled the trigger was the same hand that was most likely to be found tossing a grenade, setting a satchel charge, or leading a sortie in the next round." Again and again in the months ahead Audie's aggressive behavior in combat would manifest itself in returning fire, directing artillery fire, and volunteering for dangerous sorties against the enemy. Clearly Audie understood from the beginning, again in Marshall's terms, that "essentially war is the business of killing."

Audie Murphy's war was classic infantry combat; it pitted armed men against armed men. Hence the great paradox of that great war: despite massive movements of men, equipment, and firepower unequaled in history up to that time, in the end the fate of armies and nations came down finally to thousands upon thousands of discrete moments of intense personal warfare by a man alone or in a small group. Historians of World War II are in agreement on this point. S. L. A. Marshall: "Fire wins wars, and it wins the skirmishes of which war is composed." Max Hastings: "All wars become a matter of small private battles to those who are fighting them." John Ellis: "In the last analysis, men and the weapons that they could carry with them were what counted. Artillery and tanks had an important part to play but they hardly ever sufficed in themselves to carry an important network of enemy strong points."

What counted was those the British called the "poor bloody infantry." They did most of the fighting and most of the dying. The figures bear this out. Ordinary riflemen constituted only 11 percent of a division's total, but they made up 38 percent of its casualties.

For the infantryman World War II was no Vietnam—a year in country, then rotation back. In Audie Murphy's war you stayed in country until either the war ended or you were killed or wounded badly enough not to be sent back to the front. It wasn't until 1944 that the Army instituted a point system for relieving combat veterans of front-line duty, and the war was over in Europe before most soldiers had a chance to earn enough points to come back home. Charles B. MacDonald has well summarized the infantryman's experience in the war: "For the infantryman it was a grim, colorless, almost hopeless existence. . . . That the airman got extra pay for 'hazardous duty,' while the infantryman, whose casualties were infinitely greater, got none, was particularly galling." John Ellis called his book about the infantry *The Sharp End,* meaning that the infantry always got the sharp end of the stick. Bill Mauldin, whose Willie and Joe cartoons represent some of the finest art to emerge from the war, held the opinion that "the infantry is the group in the Army which gives more and gets less than anybody else." That keen and sympathetic observer of combat, Ernie Pyle, called himself a "rabid one-man movement bent on tracking down and stamping out everybody in the world who doesn't fully appreciate the common front-line soldier."

In the bloody and depressing world of combat Audie became the embodiment of the good soldier, a well-trained, wary, savvy, alert, and fire-producing unit who could apply accurate small arms fire at the right place at the right time. He was an equal-opportunity soldier, killing snipers and machine gunners, knocking out tanks, capturing Germans on night patrols, directing artillery fire, doing everything the front-line combatant is required to do in order to take and hold ground, by inches, feet, yards, miles, through Sicily, Italy, France, and into Germany. Because that was what it was going to take to defeat the Germans. Or as John Ellis puts it, "In World War II, especially in western Europe and the Far East, it soon became apparent that every yard of ground would have to be torn from the enemy and only killing as many men as possible would enable one to do this. Combat was reduced to its absolute essentials, kill or be killed." Audie said the same thing in *To Hell and Back:* "Destroy and survive." A hard lesson, one of the hardest there is, and it seared his soul.

So Audie Murphy became by skill, training, intelligence, luck, and a dozen imponderables, an astounding soldier. General Keith Ware, a Medal of Honor winner who was killed in Vietnam, saw Audie in action at Anzio and was the commanding officer of the 15th Infantry during the Colmar Pocket action, Murphy's finest hour. Ware remembered him many years later as "the finest soldier I have ever seen in my entire military career."

His battalion reached Palermo, the capital of Sicily, on July 20. More Italians surrendered, and Baker Company drew for assignment guard duty and the job of rounding up any Axis soldiers they encountered. But then Audie came down with a nose and throat inflammation and was out of action for five days.

Returning to action for the push northward to Messina, he rode with his battalion through the streets of Palermo where he saw something far removed from Hunt County, Texas: "Lines of soldiers, with their weapons slung on their shoulders, stand before brothels, patiently awaiting their turn." British writer Norman Lewis saw similar acts of cheerless sex in Italy in 1943: "One soldier, a little tipsy, and egged on constantly by his friends, finally put down his tin of rations at a woman's side, unbuttoned and lowered himself on her. A perfunctory jogging of the haunches began and came quickly to an end. A moment later he was on his feet and buttoning up again. It had been something to get over as soon as possible. He might have been submitting to field punishment rather than the act of love."

The fighting in the north was the real thing; no pushover Italian troops this time. Audie and the 3rd Division ran into nearly fanatical German resistance. The Italians might be dispirited and easy targets, but the Germans were well-trained and dedicated soldiers. The German intention was to withdraw to Italy, and northeastern Sicily offered "ideal country for withdrawing," wrote Ernie Pyle. Here in these stony mountains the weather and ground were an ordeal. With temperatures of 110°. Sicily was hotter than Texas in August. On the route east to Messina, steep cliffs plummeted hundreds of feet down on the sea side, stony peaks towered up to 5,000 feet high on the land side, and in between was a narrow, winding, ribbonlike highway that the Germans defended to the death. Mules carried supplies to men huddled in the mountains, and a mule plunging down the mountainside made a sound you didn't want to hear, like a woman screaming, remembered one soldier. Water was in short supply, dust was a constant irritant, everybody was sopping wet from the muggy, cloudless heat. Welcome to World War II.

Sicily gave the 3rd Division its extremest version of bad summer weather, but the 3rd would get every kind of bad weather there was before the Germans were whipped. Being at war, for the foot soldier, meant fighting the weather as much as fighting the enemy. Ernie Pyle wrote of the conditions faced by the soldiers in Sicily: "The front-line soldier I knew lived for months like an animal, and was a veteran in the cruel, fierce world of death. Everything was abnormal and unstable in his life. He was filthy dirty, ate if and when, slept on hard ground without cover. His clothes were greasy and he lived in a constant haze of dust, pestered by flies and heat, moving constantly, deprived of all the things that once meant stability."

It was here too, in northern Sicily, that Audie learned to respect the German enemy. He watched the Battle of San Fratello from a safe perch on a hill above the Furiano River, where his company was ordered to protect a machine-gun emplacement. He lolled in the sunshine, eating grapes from a vineyard, seeing the battle rage below. He watched the Germans expertly lay down a pattern of fire that contained an American company and killed the company commander. After this, he knew there was going to be enough war for everyone. In *To Hell and Back* Audie summed up what he learned that day: "I contributed little to the battle; gained much. I acquired a healthy respect for the Germans as fighters; an insight into the fury of mass combat; and a bad case of diarrhea. I had eaten too many grapes." Audie's respect for German soldiers never lessened. After the war he once wrote how he loathed Hollywood movies that "poked fun at the enemy," that "made him out to be a stupid beast."

Sometimes, he said, the Germans "seemed to be better than we were." And even in defeat at Sicily, the two German divisions that took part in the fighting there, under Field Marshal Kesselring's command, managed a strategic withdrawal. Audie and the 3rd Division would go up against Kesselring's crack troops again and again.

Audie's respect for the German soldier has been borne out by many historians. T. N. Dupuy has concluded: "On a man for man basis, the German ground soldier consistently inflicted casualties at about a 50% higher rate than they incurred from the opposing British and American troops *under all circumstances*." Max Hastings similarly argues for the superiority of the German soldier in his study of the fighting during and after the Normandy invasion. But military historian Roger J. Spiller's skepticism should be kept in mind. After all, he points out, "One cannot help thinking that many writers are enamored of the stylishness of the German way of war, a way that has not produced military victory since 1871." By August 17, Messina had fallen and Sicily was pacified. It was from here that Audie sent his only letter home from Sicily. Like most of his letters, it said little about his actual experiences. Most soldiers' letters were the same way—and for understandable reasons: lack of time, lack of skill or patience, the threat of censorship, and perhaps above all the soldier's instinctive recognition that the civilian audience, the folks back home, wanted to hear only that he was okay, that things weren't so bad, that the war was going well. He wrote in August 1943, "I am still all together. Guess I'm just lucky?" There were five thousand soldiers of the 3rd Division who, dead or wounded, could not have said the same. The letter also mentioned his having sent his sister a hundred bucks and an offer to pay for his brother Richard's glasses if need be. Like his pride, quick temper, and determination, Audie's generosity was a permanent part of his character, evident throughout his life.

In *To Hell and Back* Audie spoke succinctly of what Sicily had meant by way of the education of a combat soldier: "The Sicilian campaign has taken the vinegar out of my spirits. I have seen war as it actually is, and I do not like it. . . . Experience has seasoned us, made us battlewise and intensely practical. But we still have much to learn."

Following the surrender in Sicily, Audie's 15th Infantry Regiment marched back from Messina to Palermo, retracing peacefully the bloody steps of its original drive to Messina. Now followed a three-week period of rest and renewed drilling. They were getting ready for another offensive. The next theater of operations, in Italy, would offer further training in the art of war.

The Italian campaign wasn't inevitable. At the Casablanca Conference, back in January 1943, plans for landings at Italy had been agreed upon, but events since then had changed rather drastically. By the late summer and fall of 1943 the big picture looked like this: The Italians were soundly whipped in Sicily, a defeat that spelled the end of Mussolini's regime. When the dictator was deposed on July 25, the Italian Army was deactivated, and Italy—Rome—no longer held imperative military significance. Such was the American view. The Americans favored and had always favored a direct assault on Germany, on "Fortress Europe."

But not the British; they saw things differently, especially Churchill. The British prime minister wanted Italy and he wanted Rome. Both were integral to the Southern Front or Eastern theory, part of Churchill's "soft underbelly" strategy to defeat the German Reich. He wanted to come at Germany indirectly, through the Balkans, through the east. He wanted to join up with the Russians on the Eastern Front. The reasons for such thinking were both cultural and personal. The British still had the imperialist view; they saw the Russian threat to Turkey; they hoped to contain Russia at the same time they defeated Germany.

At the personal level, the roots of the theory lay in Churchill's past, in the stinging defeat the British had suffered on the Gallipoli Peninsula in Turkey in 1915. Churchill, at that time First Lord of the Admiralty, conceived a plan to land troops at Gallipoli, capture Constantinople, drive Turkey out of the war, and join forces with the Russians in the Crimea. After a massive landing in April 1915, the Allied forces ran into surprisingly stubborn Turkish resistance. Stalled at Gallipoli, they failed to accomplish any of their goals, and in the end, in January 1916, were forced to withdraw from a military disaster that cost 55,000 troops dead, wounded, and captured. Now, a world war later, Churchill wanted to redeem the negative verdict of history. Taking Italy would open the way into the Balkans, ensure that British interests in the east would be protected, and vindicate Churchill's reputation as a grand military strategist.

But now, with Italy prostrate, Churchill's argument would seem to lose its force. Exactly the opposite occurred. One condition of

Italy's surrender reinforced his view. Allied troops would have to be stationed in Italy anyway to maintain Italian sovereignty and to keep it from becoming a German satellite. And whether the Allies took all of Italy or not, they needed the supply ports of Naples and Baria and the airfields around Foggia. These centers would remain crucial in future plans for attacking Fortress Europe and in maintaining open sea lanes in the Mediterranean. A further point in Churchill's favor was that if Hitler had to move German divisions from the Eastern Front to the Southern, there would be fewer German troops available to throw against the Allies in the cross-Channel invasion of western France. In short, Churchill argued, the Italian campaign would soften up Hitler for the knockout punch to be delivered in France during the final thrust into the German homeland.

Like Olympian gods, powerful men pointed to places on a map and said, "Here is where we will go next," and, like ants, the tiny men at the infantry company level, the dog-faced GIs, were sent pell-mell into the fray. Nobody at the front had any sense of the big picture.

In mid-September Audie's 15th Regiment boarded LSTs to make the short, choppy, stomach-churning trip to southern Italy. They landed at Battipaglia, just south of Salerno. From that September until June 1944, nine months later, the 3rd Infantry Division took part in what one of its officers called the "bitterest, most heart-breaking, most cursed battlefield of the longest fought campaign in Europe in World War II."

During September Audie and the 15th Infantry Regiment slogged their way along the Volturno River. In *To Hell and Back* he recorded several incidents that occurred during that march. Contact with the enemy was intermittent and apt to take place at any time. One night on a reconnaissance mission Audie and his patrol found a haystack where they decided to spend the night, only to discover that some Germans were planning the same thing. Startled, both sides withdrew without a fire fight.

Another time, in a three-man operation, "like a grim game of checkers," Audie and his best friend Lattie Tipton (called Brandon in the book after his postwar Texas friend Everett Brandon) were crossing a dry stream bed near a bridge when they saw the third member of their advance team go down under a hail of machine-gun bullets. Using a tommy gun, Audie covered Brandon while his

friend, unwisely Audie thought, scrambled close enough to lob grenades at the Germans. Between bursts from Audie's tommy gun and
Brandon's grenades, five Germans were slain, and the way across
the bridge cleared.

At another bridge they ran into the usual German-concealed
machine-gun nest guarding the approach. Only it didn't look that
way at first; everything looked quiet and innocent. Then Audie
spotted something awry, a shrub that seemed to have its leaves
pointing in the wrong direction. He raked the thicket with Garand
rifle fire, and snipers fired back. His extraordinary ability to read
natural terrain, evident in boot camp, served him well now. He
traced it back to his days on the farm: "As a farm youngster, the
land meant either hunger or bread to me. Now its shape is the
difference between life and death. Every roll, depression, rock, or
tree is significant." Audie used his childhood hunting experiences
to explain his actions in combat: "I got to where I could think like
a squirrel and in the war I learned to figure as a German soldier
would. Where would I hide if I were a German? I had an aversion
to getting shot and I would take the hard way to get there, with a chance
of not getting shot." Audie thus instinctively understood one of
S. L. A. Marshall's theorems of warfare: "The ground itself is the
great teacher; one must be ever ready to apply its lessons with a
fresh mind."

In mid-October the 3rd Division was ordered to cross the Volturno River, a vital natural barrier that the Germans were relying
on to stop the GIs. Using a variety of rubber boats, pontoons, and
home-made rafts jerry-rigged from anything that would float, the
3rd executed the difficult crossing in two days. One of Audie's friends
from Camp Wolters nearly lost his legs from German machine-gun
fire on that crossing.

In mountainous terrain in the Mount Lungo area—a "nightmare
for offensive troops," Audie called it—he and the 15th found themselves again watching mules pitch off the trails to their deaths, and
the men had to assume the burden of carrying supplies when the
footing was too difficult even for mules. Audie was particularly generous in helping fellow soldiers who were on the verge of exhaustion.

One morning at dawn a German patrol of seven men came
hunting the Americans, looking for a chance to "blow us into
mincemeat." Although suspicious of the open ground, the Germans
came on anyway, right into withering fire from Audie's company.

Three Germans fell with belly wounds; four surrendered. The wounded suffered for the next day or so, then died. From Hill 193 they could see the soon-to-be-famous monastery at Cassino. Hill 193 taken, B Company and the 15th pulled back. One of the soldiers says, in *To Hell and Back*, "I wouldn't give one turnip patch in Tennessee fer the whole damned country, and Sicily throwed in fer good measure." Nobody in B Company would have argued with him.

The fighting in the mountains around Naples seemed like that in northern Sicily: both terrains required maximum physical exertion of men and mules. In a very brief letter to his sister, Audie said, "I am in Italy and it [is] simalor to Sicily." Only now the test of weather wasn't heat, but almost ceaseless rain and increasing cold. In southern Italy in the winter, rain is the normal state of things, and the rain began in earnest that year on October 1, the day Naples fell; November was nothing but an interminable drizzle punctuated by occasional downpours.

In mid-November, after nearly two months of hard fighting, the 3rd was pulled out of the line and convoyed by trucks to a bivouac area twenty miles east of Naples. The casualty list for the 3rd in southern Italy read 683 killed, 2,412 wounded, and 170 missing in action. So far Audie remained unscathed.

Combat veterans now, they had little use for Army routine when it made no sense. The first thing they had to endure was a short-arm inspection for venereal diseases, an ignominy they found ludicrous because there had been a notable shortage of women at the front. But Army routine was "immutable," and they submitted. The rest of November and most of December, Audie and the 3rd enjoyed all the comforts of bivouac life: tents, cots, hot food twice a day. Drills in basic combat procedures kept the men busy, and new replacements were worked into the various units.

And there was Naples. A British soldier and writer, John Guest, found the city disappointing, another place hopelessly disfigured by war: "What I expected was broad boulevards, white buildings, glimpses at the end of the streets of a brilliant sea. What I found was a dirty, crowded, poverty-stricken town with outskirts, particularly the dock area, blasted to nightmare desolation." The devastation and suffering were part of the general demoralization wrought by war. Another British writer, Norman Lewis, never forgot something he saw in Naples, the sight of blind little orphaned girls coming into a café weeping. The experience, he said, "changed my outlook. Until now I had clung to the comforting belief that human beings eventually come to terms with pain and sorrow. Now I understood I was wrong, and like Paul I suffered a conversion—but to pessimism." The blind children, he knew, "were condemned to everlasting darkness, hunger and loss, they would weep on incessantly. They would never recover from their pain, and I would never recover from the memory of it."

In the meantime, events made the southern strategy seem inevitable. The Germans played into Churchill's hands by pouring divisions into the area around Rome in a massive buildup. Increasingly his vision of the Italian campaign acquired more and more logical force, and the wily old man prevailed against American doubts and won out completely. The key to Churchill's plan was Anzio, an ancient seaport on the Tyrrhenian Sea, the birth site of the corrupt emperor Nero and in Mussolini's era the site of showcase public works projects whose newly built canal was called the Mussolini Canal and whose new farmhouses bore the inscription *Anno Mussolini* and the year of his reign. Labeled "Operation Shingle" by Army stategists, Anzio was the navel of the soft underbelly theory. An amphibious landing there, followed by a swift thrust to Rome, a mere thirty-seven miles to the north, would do the job. Anzio, Churchill said, "will astonish the world."

In late December, Truscott and his men learned of their next assignment: an amphibious landing at Anzio scheduled for around January 20, 1944. Getting ready for the beaches required more specialized training, and the 3rd was moved to a swampy terrain near Naples. The extra time behind the lines was welcome, but the training for the landing was no picnic. Operation Webfoot, a practice landing, took place near Salerno on January 16–18, and it was a complete fiasco. Truscott argued strongly for more time to train, but the invasion schedule was firmly set for January 22. During this same period, on January 13, Audie received another promotion, to staff sergeant.

Audie missed the landing on the 22nd because, the night before, he came down with a severe case of flu. The last impression he wanted to leave was that he was a shirker, but his buddies, realizing how sick he was, reported him to the company commander, who ordered him to the infirmary. He was in bed during the landing and didn't rejoin his company until a week later. As it turned out, the landing at Anzio was very successful. The Germans were caught by surprise, and the 3rd suffered only eighty-four casualties.

Returning to his unit on January 29, a week after the landing, Audie saw grim reminders of the cost already incurred in what was going to be a long and painful stay at Anzio. As he hiked inland, he saw "trailerloads of corpses . . . the bodies, stacked like wood . . . covered with shelter-halves. But arms and legs bobble grotesquely over the sides of the vehicles." Returning to the front was always unsettling because, after being out of action, there would always be men, comrades, who'd been hit while one was away. This time it was someone he particularly liked, Joe Sieja, a Pole who'd only lived in America for five years. Sieja was the company comic, known for his attachment to a small gasoline stove that he carried everywhere with him. On one occasion it imperiled his life when it got caught in some brush and the Germans began firing at him. On the day of the landing, Sieja and another soldier, Jim Fife, an Indian, were "drinking some coffee behind a house when an 88-millimeter shell dropped on them, blowing Sieja to bits and seriously wounding Fife." Sieja is one of the two men to whom Audie dedicated *To Hell and Back*. The other was Lattie Tipton.

What began so well quickly went smash, however. Major General John P. Lucas, commander of the Anzio operation, was a prudent and pessimistic man who, most historians agree, failed to seize the opportunity afforded by the easy landing. He delayed, fatally so, and the Allies, waiting for reinforcements, lost the chance to break out of the beachhead and capture Rome before the Germans could reorganize. Said one Anzio wag of the failure in command: "They came, they saw, they concurred."

Once the Allies delayed, they were in a very tough position. Hitler ordered more German troops to the area in order, he hoped, to take care of what he termed the "abscess south of Rome." Soon the Germans had 125,000 troops holding the hills and mountains that encircled, horseshoe-wise, the coastal plain around Anzio. When the Allies finally attempted their break-out, it was too late. The Germans had command of the situation.

To forge the break-out, the Allies had to take Cisterna, a village several miles inland from the beach. Here they hoped to cut both a railroad and, more importantly, Rt. 7, the highway to Rome. Two battalions of Rangers, attached to the 3rd Division, were assigned the task. On January 30 they were suckered into a slaughter. The Germans yielded at the center, near Cisterna, drawing the Americans into a trap, then hit them hard from both sides with tanks and infantry and armored cars. More 3rd Division battalions were brought up to help, and the battle raged on for several days. This was the most sustained and murderous fire that Audie had faced. He felt fear on this occasion as he always did, he says, at the beginning of battle. "Fear is moving up with us. It always does. . . . But when you are moving into combat, why try fooling yourself. Fear is right there beside you." He continues, trying to describe the visceral quality of fear: "It strikes first in the stomach, coming like the disemboweling hand that is thrust into the carcass of a chicken. I feel now as though icy fingers have reached into my mid-parts and twisted the intestines into knots." Years later, long after the war was over, he talked again about fear: "Sometimes it takes more courage to get up and run than to stay. You either just do it or you don't. I got so scared the first day in combat I just decided to go along with it."

Audie's emphasis on fear should never be overlooked in any celebration of his combat exploits. Nor in any account of combat. According to S. L. A. Marshall, fear has the force of a universal law: "Wherever one surveys the forces of the battlefield, it is to see that fear is general among men." For Marshall, there were also the concomitant restraining emotions of shame and bonding that kept most men from acting like cowards. "The battlefield is cold," wrote Marshall. "It is the lonesomest place which men may share together."

Fear was a natural part of the soldier's environment. Like mud, he lived in it. One writer, Neil McCallum, tried to capture the particular essence of fear in relation to the wide-scale slaughter that the war demanded: "I do not believe it is entirely personal either, the fear of personal death. It lies in the fact that this killing is quite impartial; it has the cold indifference of a great organisation, it is an impersonal routine, a job. . . . The state of mind that action induces primarily and superficially is fear, with peaks of almost hysterical tension."

What is more, he continues, fear became "commonplace—like death, an accepted every-day, ever-present condition. War is no longer entirely freakish and uniquely barbaric. It becomes normal and real with the deep reality of a nightmare." To Audie, fear was a given; what counted was how one dealt with it. If not controlled, fear could endanger others: "What you hate is the selfishness in a man who won't try to conquer his fear, and instead uses the lives of his buddies to shield his own." One of Audie's buddies from Camp Wolters days remembers, "Audie was scared and so was I. And everybody else." James Jones, arguably the greatest of the World War II novelists, perhaps said it best: "I went where I was told to go, and did what I was told to do, but no more. I was scared shitless just about all the time."

During the heaving fighting near Cisterna, the Germans used 20-mm. antiaircraft armor against ground troops, guns with "deadly small shells that explode upon impact" and that, according to the international rules of warfare, were designed to be used against armor and planes, not men. It made Audie and the other troops furious. The concussion of exploding shells killed a soldier right beside Audie and blew Audie into a brief loss of consciousness, followed by nose bleeding. Effects from such explosions would bother him for many years to come.

In one instance, he and his platoon wiped out a group of Germans who panicked under tank assault and ran. When a new replacement shot his first German, one of Audie's company said, "You are now a full-fledged member of the Brotherhood of International Killers." *To Hell and Back* is full of such grim battlefield, graveyard humor. Laughing bitterly at their fate was one of the ways to survive. Because by now Audie felt that the war was "without beginning, without end. It goes on forever."

Audie's performance in this battle was noticed by his senior officer, Lieutenant Colonel Michael Paulick. Said Paulick many years later, "It was [at Cisterna] that I came upon Audie's company with the company commander wounded, and only two inexperienced lieutenants left. I took command of the company, and we continued the attack for three days; fewer than 30 men survived. Audie was the only non-commissioned officer left, and there were no officers except myself. If I had never seen Audie Murphy again, I would remember him from that action. He was a soldier, a born leader, potentially a fine officer." After Cisterna, Audie's ability was recognized by an unusual assignment. He was made platoon sergeant commanding the 3rd Platoon of Company B, an assignment usually held by second lieutenants.

With the First Battle of Cisterna lost and the attempted break-out a bust, the 3rd had to pull back to Anzio, where they would remain for interminable months. Now that the Allies had failed to push forward as planned, they were in deep peril. Stalemated, they were forced to dig in and slug it out with the Germans. Major General Lucas himself noted the World War I analogy in his diary: "The whole affair has a strong odor of Gallipoli." Churchill, as usual, found a memorable way to describe what had happened: "We hoped to land a wild cat that would tear out the bowels of the Boche. Instead we have stranded a vast whale with its tail flopping about in the water."

So they dug in; there was nothing else to do. Sandbags, grim reminders of the trench fighting of the Great War, were again required. Raleigh Trevelyan, in his wonderful book *The Fortress: A Diary of Anzio and After,* describes many direct parallels between Anzio and the Great War:

> In many ways this place is the classical setting for a battlefield of the 1917 vintage: shattered farmhouses, bared to their plaster walls, marked with vaccination scars; those crazy imitations of the Christian symbol, over the graves of men who most likely have never heard of Jesus except as a swear-word in American gangster novels; the gnarled trees, white as if some monster hand had peeled them; scrolls of rusted dannert wire; abandoned weapons of all sorts, from primed grenades to anti-tank guns; the brooding dark shapes of burnt-out lorries—all in a wasteland of churned-up earth and craters.

A journalist who was there drew similar parallels: "As the months passed this front line took on all the character of the Somme or Ypres in 1916. For the first and the only time in World War II the soldiers had to think in terms of communicating trenches, barbed wire in no-man's land and the rest of the grim paraphernalia of *All Quiet on the Western Front*." And John Ellis wrote, "At Anzio, after the Germans had begun to counter-attack, the beachhead turned into a maze of trenches and dugouts that looked no different from the wasteland of Passchendaele."

There was no safe place at Anzio—that "constant hellish nightmare that lasted for five months," as Bill Mauldin put it. Even the field hospitals could be reached by German artillery fire, because in effect there was only the front, the coastal prairie, fifteen miles wide and ten miles deep, and no behind-the-lines. At Anzio anybody could be killed from artillery fire at any moment. Ernie Pyle put it best: "People whose jobs through all the wars of history have been safe ones were as vulnerable as the fighting man. Bakers and typewriter repairmen and clerks were not immune from shells and bombs. Table waiters were in the same boat. There was no rear area that was immune." Hospital units were hit several times, and in the end ninety-two medical personnel were killed, including six female nurses. Seventy percent of the casualties at Anzio were caused by artillery fire. Bill Mauldin said the German .88 was the "terror of every dogface. It can do everything but throw shells around corners, and sometimes we think it has even done that." Then there was "Anzio Annie," a gigantic railway cannon, that lobbed shells onto the beach from over thirty miles away. Mauldin called it "that huge gun which made guys in rest areas play softball near slit trenches." One of the garrulous characters in *To Hell and Back* described the big gun in legendary, tall-tale style: "You wouldn't call it an air rifle. Rumor says its barrel's not over a quarter of a mile long. Krauts use old railroad cars for shells and a pile driver for a ramrod."

Soon a "doomlike quality" hung over Anzio, and the weather, like stage lighting, contributed its part: low-hanging gray clouds, rain, wind, and cold. Living conditions were simply awful. Raleigh Trevelyan said he'd "learned to accept the fact that Anzio makes you look ten years older." Another soldier at Anzio described what happened after one lived in such conditions. Wrote Paul Woodruff in his Anzio memoir-novel, *Vessel of Sadness,* "He concluded that the bunch of boys he'd known bursting with life had never existed. He'd dreamt it. They certainly weren't the same men lying on the earth around him now. These men lying in the mud were a species apart. They didn't belong to that other world. They'd always lived in the mud and filth with their wits scared out of them and that's how they'd end up. It was their lot."

The rain at Anzio turned the beachhead into a "sea of mud," and the sides of foxholes would collapse, leeching mud and water into the bottom. Albert Pyle (a soldier in Audie's company and no relation to Ernie, the war correspondent) remembered staying in the same foxhole, a machine-gun nest, for twenty-two days and twenty-three nights with only C-rations for sustenance. Audie described a typical dugout in *To Hell and Back:* "It is a deep hole. The bottom is sticky with ooze; water seeps in from the sides. Poles, grass, and sod form the roof." Sometimes when foxholes and dugouts collapsed, men smothered to death. Fourteen soldiers died in that manner in February and March. Or, pinned down by artillery fire, they had to huddle ankle-deep in water for hours. The effects on health were disastrous. Trench foot, a condition in which the foot, softened and infected by the pestiferous standing water, turned blue, ballooned to the size of a football, and started to rot, was rampant among the GIs. Trench foot at Anzio put soldier after soldier into the hospital: 525 cases alone in February. Yet Audie never got trench foot. He always made sure to remove his socks and squeeze them dry. There is no better indication of his ability to adapt to the nearly unbearable conditions of life at the front than this fact.

Time dragged by, punctuated by patrols and artillery bombardments. One night the Germans who were opposite Audie's platoon's position began to shout across the lines, "Roosevelt is a Jew and full of shit." A member of Audie's platoon yelled back in German (it was probably John J. Fredericks, who spoke German fluently), "Hitler is a bastard!" Albert Pyle, who'd heard stories about this kind of verbal warfare from the Great War, found it amazing to be reliving the same thing now. Because of the stalemate, there was also plenty of opportunity for the Germans to engage in propaganda aimed at undermining morale. Radio broadcasts from Rome featured a sexy-voiced female named "Sall-y" who taunted American and British troops by promising good food and kisses, and sweetened her message by playing scratchy versions of "In the Mood," "Chattanooga-Choo-Choo," and her personal favorite for the soldiers with their backs to the ocean, "Between the Devil and the Deep Blue Sea." Axis Sally also told lots of lies, and the GIs laughed at her absurdities while enjoying the nightly renditions of "Lili Marlene," the great German song that became the anthem for the Americans as well.

All through February and March 1944, the fighting was fierce. In February, for example, the 157th Battalion of the 2nd Regiment lost six hundred of eight hundred men in a week, and half of the two hundred left were themselves casualties.

Audie's 15th Infantry fought off German attacks and conducted patrols throughout this period. As a platoon leader Audie was at the center of things in Company B, and his narrative of this period is full of grim stories of anger, death, and survival. An inexperienced replacement argued with Audie about an order to help dig holes in which to bury dead cows. They had to be buried or the stench would be intolerable. The recruit continued to argue until Audie drove his fist into his stomach, clipped him on the jaw, and jumped astride him, battering his head against the floor. The recruit said he'd report Audie, but Audie shot back, "We left regulations in the rear. They were too goddamned heavy to carry." In this instance Audie had the complete support of all the old-timers. Another time, spurred by rage at the intolerable conditions, Audie chewed out a medical officer for sending men back to the front who were still crippled with trench foot.

Audie's local fame as an exceptional combat soldier was already well enough established that a new replacement who joined Company B at Anzio vividly remembered his first impressions many years later. Albert Pyle, who was eventually promoted to technical sergeant, was in Company B (though not in Audie's platoon) from February 1944 to January 25, 1945, the day before the action for which Audie won the Congressional Medal of Honor. Pyle recalls that Audie "looked much younger than the age of nineteen. He was quiet, in fact, almost shy, but a very responsible and aggressive soldier." Pyle was especially struck by Audie's carriage. He had "a particular and peculiar walk. It was a rather slow, stooped posture, and this movement reminded me of one who is prepared to stalk his prey. He was generally equipped with a carbine, which seemed to be his favorite weapon and many, many times I have seen him leading his men in the attacks and the bitter combat that carried us through the Italian fighting and on up into France." Another member of Company B remembered that Audie usually carried three weapons: a .45 revolver in his belt, a rifle slung over his shoulder, and the carbine in his hand. He always wanted as much firepower at hand as he could carry.

Combat placed a great premium on practical sense, knocked theory into a cocked hat, made abstractions pointless, taught that what worked was what counted, and only that. Bill Mauldin described its "ethics" well in *Up Front:* "You don't fight a kraut by Marquess of Queensberry rules. You shoot him in the back, you blow him apart with mines, you kill or maim him the quickest and most effective way you can with the least danger to yourself. He does the same to you. He tricks you and cheats you, and if you don't beat him at his own game you don't live to appreciate you own nobleness." In S. Berlin's memoir *I Am Lazarus*, there is a memorable formulation of the ethics of killing: "The question of killing does not present itself as a moral problem any more—or as a problem at all—for in such total war death and life are so dovetailed into each other that they don't seem separate or distinct as states of being and non-being." But the crucial thing, one hoped, was that afterwards you did not remain a killer. Mauldin felt sure that the killing he saw in the war was a temporary suspension of the rules governing civilized human beings. "But you don't become a killer," he assured his American audience in 1945. Harold Bond, who served in Italy, feared what might happen, though, to those inured to the hard life of the combat soldier: "He and men like him would have to give and give and give; perhaps they would have to give so much that never again would they be good for anything, even if they did live through the war." Audie expressed similar fears in his book and in many interview statements long after the war was over.

The immense acceptance of the quotidian facts of combat life—and death—is one of the great strengths Audie possessed. It would also cost him much in later life—he called it a weary cynicism—but at the front cynicism was about the only philosophy that made any sense at all. There is an excellent and sad example in the accidental killing of a fellow soldier by one of Audie's company. The soldier who was killed was returning to his lines after a patrol and forgot the password, or forgot to utter it, and paid the ultimate price for his mistake: he was machine-gunned down by a buddy. Audie, as platoon leader, could not afford to be sentimental about what had happened. The slain soldier had been a favorite, everybody liked him; but now he was dead, a report would have to be made, the whole thing would be forgotten as an unfortunate accident, and there was no point in spending a lot of time feeling guilty about what had happened. The war wouldn't stop for guilt; the Germans were as implacable as the weather.

Audie and his men found occasional relief from the cold misery of the trenches by occupying abandoned farmhouses in the area. Under relatively dry conditions, it was possible to make a small, smokeless fire from paraffin stripped from C-rations. The farmhouses were also invaluable for observing enemy troop and tank movements. It was from one of these houses that Audie, on the morning of March 2, heard a sound that made his hands start trembling, the rumbling of tanks. With his binoculars he counted twenty of them. Ordering artillery fire, he adjusted the aim until a tank was knocked out. He and his men gunned down the Germans as they scrambled for cover. Still, he realized, the crippled tank could be restored to service the next day. It was only one tank, of course, but it was of such discrete moments that the war could be comprehended by the infantry. "Infinite small threats make up the whole. Eliminate the little problems, and the big ones will take care of themselves," concluded Audie in *To Hell and Back*.

Audie then asked for permission for a patrol to knock out the tank that night. The officer in charge of the 1st Battalion, 15th Infantry, recalled, "Audie was selected as the patrol leader for I knew that he could do it." On the actual patrol, Audie was the one who knocked out the tank. He left his men to cover him and crawled up close enough to hurl two Molotov cocktails against the tank, but neither ignited. Then he blasted the treads off with rifle grenades. Racing back using a ditch for cover, he managed to return to his men in a hail of machine-gun fire, untouched. The tank was ruined, never to be recovered by the Germans. Audie's account of this action in *To Hell and Back*, like the account of all his combat experiences, is sparse and effective, and like other such moments, it makes no mention of the fact that for this action he received a decoration—the Bronze Star Medal. It was his first decoration for valor.

Such actions proved to Audie the importance of audacity in combat. As he said many years later, "If I discovered one valuable thing during my early combat days, it was audacity, which is often mistaken for courage or foolishness. It is neither. Audacity is a tactical weapon. Nine times out of ten it will throw the enemy off-balance and confuse him. However much one sees of audacious deeds, nobody really expects them." The other point was never to retreat. It was demoralizing, dangerous, and worst of all, it meant you had to retake ground already taken.

Life at Anzio was also one vast tedium of muddy existence during those periods of "utter boredom of static warfare," as Audie described them in *To Hell and Back*. Ever restless and aggressive, he found relief in the most dangerous way possible, by going on patrols to gather information regarding German whereabouts. Albert Pyle remembers that Audie and John J. Fredericks, the German-speaking soldier, "were forever going on forays trying to capture or shoot up the Krauts." They made a deadly team. Another member of Company B, Bob Millar, remembers how Audie and Fredericks worked it. "He had a boy who spoke German very well and sounded just like Kraut soldiers. When they got near a German outpost and were halted, the German boy would speak in the Kraut language and Murph would go up and poke a tommy gun in their ribs and bring them back to the Company C.P. This they did many times." These missions were so dangerous that most platoon members were very reluctant to go with Audie and Fredericks. But those who did go had a good chance of surviving. According to one soldier from Company B, "One thing about him, if he ever took you out on patrol, you always came back. He had the right instincts."

A taut episode in *To Hell and Back* shows exactly how dangerous these patrols to capture prisoners could be. As usual, Audie and his men located the Germans by the smell of their tobacco smoke. They sneaked up on the hut, and Fredericks went into his German routine, calling out to the Germans inside. When they didn't reply, Audie and the others in the four-man patrol hurled grenades into the hut, then went in to assess the damage. They found two dead Germans and one alive but terrified. After a brief fire fight in the misty dark, Audie's team raced back to their own lines, dragging the German with them. In the hurried rush Audie turned his ankle and had to hobble the final distance. The mission, though successful in one sense—they got a prisoner and nobody got killed or wounded—was a complete bust as far as intelligence went, for the "German" turned out to be a Pole who, besides being drunk, knew absolutely nothing of military value.

On March 13 Audie was hospitalized for the second time that winter and spring, influenza again. On his way to check their machine guns for the night, he passed out in the mud and had to be carried back to a hospital tent.

He stayed in hospital for a week. What he remembered most was a pretty nurse named Helen, which may have been a fictionalization of a later stay in hospital, at Aix-en-Provence in October 1944, and another nurse, Carolyn Price, who is not mentioned in *To Hell and Back*. The banter between Audie and Helen, as recorded in the book, was a warm mixture of toughness and affection. She shocked him by mentioning a "whore's bath" (sponging off in a washbasin), and through her kindness she broke down the shell of his tough-guy forties rhetoric ("They'll never make me cry; I'm not the crying kind."). He responded with heart-on-the-sleeve accounts of his mother and his impoverished childhood. Later, he wondered whether she was among the nurses killed by artillery fire.

Spring lifted everybody's spirit: flowers, new leaves, birds singing. The British soldier Raleigh Trevelyan grew quite ecstatic about that spring at Anzio, pronouncing Italy "perfect Keats country; Pan was everywhere, hamadryads lurked in the shade, here were naiads, there were the haunts of Syrinx." The new season also saw a buildup of Allied strength to forge the break-out and a renewed determination on the part of the soldiers to end the war before having to survive another winter.

A couple of letters of Audie's survive from the Anzio beachhead. In one he asked his brother-in-law Poland Burns to see about buying a "good used car (ford or cheve)" for him, "as I think it will be hard to get any kind of a car right after the war is over and I don't intend to do any walking after this mess, no sir." In the other, to the Cawthons, he mentioned the weather: "It rains most of the time here, sure is miserably [sic] weather." So spring at Anzio wasn't all singing birds and sunshine.

At the beginning of April the 3rd Division was pulled back for service as corps reserve, which meant renewed training and a chance to rest from patrols and fire fights. Audie placed rest at the top of his list, and for this reason he refused to order his men to perform close-order drill, a training requirement. For his insubordination he lost a promotion to technical sergeant. Promotions were not something, though, that he especially wanted, because, as he wrote in *To Hell and Back*, "It is strange to see a man bucking for promotion at the front, where an advance in rank only puts him closer to death."

At this time, back home, news about Audie appeared for the first time in the local newspaper. On April 21, 1944, the Greenville *Morning Herald* carried a story headlined GREENVILLE BOY ENJOYS REPRIEVE FROM STAY IN WET SLIT TRENCH. It was a publicity story for the Army, a kind of reassurance to the folks at home that their sons, having suffered discomfort in the trenches, were now resting, eating hot food, and attending religious services. The story made no mention of Audie's having recently received a Bronze Star.

In May he received two more awards. The Combat Infantryman Badge, which he would have been eligible for much earlier, after Sicily, was apparently awarded belatedly because of some book-keeping snafu. Instituted in 1943, this medal meant much to him and to all soldiers: it separated those who'd been under fire from those who hadn't. He also received the 1st Oak Leaf Cluster to the Bronze Star Medal, "for exemplary conduct in ground combat against an armed enemy." In other words, all those patrols and fire fights at Anzio.

In late May the break-out offensive against the Germans began. Allied artillery fire, day after day of it, softened up the German positions, and on May 23, at dawn, the 3rd Division fought the Second Battle of Cisterna, one of the bloodiest single-day battles of the war. Nearly a thousand men of the 3rd Division fell that day. Audie's 15th Infantry was ordered to cut a railroad and highway southeast of Cisterna. Audie nearly bit it on the steep grade of the railway track when the handle of his trench shovel got caught between two rocks as he tried to slide down the embankment. There he hung "like a pigeon . . . with lead spattering all about me." Breaking free, he slid to safety.

It was during this battle that Audie and his platoon watched, fascinated, as a sergeant from another platoon in B Company charged directly into enemy fire, received three separate wounds, including a shattered right arm, and continued to charge straight into the enemy position. In the official history of the 3rd Division (1947), author Don Taggart quoted Audie's account of the action: "The 200-yard interval was narrowing; the Germans were firing their machine gun, their 'spit' pistols, and rifles about as fast as they could squeeze the triggers. They must have sensed that Sergeant Antolak was sparking the charge and that he was the man they had to knock out." Then, against the urgings of his men, the sergeant charged a second enemy position. This time the sergeant was killed, but his actions inspired his men to storm the German emplacement. The sergeant, Sylvester Antolak, was posthumously awarded the Congressional Medal of Honor in October 1945, at which time Audie gave an interview in which he described in detail the heroic actions of the dead sergeant, one Medal of Honor winner paying tribute to another. The incident as later described in *To Hell and Back* ends with a remark that seemed to reflect Audie's postwar cynicism: "This was how Lutsky, the sergeant, helped buy the freedom that we cherish and abuse."

Later, on another day, as the 15th Infantry pursued the retreating Germans, five planes dived at the highway, strafing the Americans who scrambled frantically for cover. But the planes were American, and the casualties from this ghastly mistake numbered over a hundred.

On the final march to Rome the soldiers saw a country completely ravaged by war. In his volume of war memoirs, *Broken Images: A Journal,* John Guest said of the Italy of 1944:

> You do not know, though I expect you can imagine, what a country which has been fought over looks like. Everywhere the signs are unmistakable—one *knows* without thinking about the evidence. It is rather like those abandoned industrial areas at home; but here they are not abandoned; people are still living in them. Even if the houses are not in ruins, everywhere has a tired, disused look. Gates and hedges are broken. Rusting skeletons of vehicles lie in the ditches. Windows are broken. Roads in bad repair. The files untended. Ground under trees or by the roadside all chewed up and rutted. Empty food tins. Trees cut down or splintered. Charred remains of fires. Human excreta. Broken drains, pools and floods—all the million and one things which should be mended, tidied, tended, buried or otherwise seen to, are left undone.

Bill Mauldin said that Italy looked "as if a giant rake had gone over it from end to end, and when you have been going along with the rake you wonder that there is anything left at all." John Ellis agreed: "In terms of false expectations, Italy was undoubtedly the most unpleasant surprise to troops who served there."

Nor did Rome itself fulfill most soldiers' expectations. It was not the grand triumph that Churchill had imagined, at least not for soldiers like Audie. Nor, apparently, to soldiers better equipped to appreciate the glory that was Rome. Harold Bond, an American who later became a professor at Dartmouth, wrote of his eager anticipation: "All of my life I had wanted to see Rome, but when as a boy I read Caesar and struggled through the orations of Cicero I had never dreamed that I would see Rome for the first time from the back of a jeep, the city waiting in empty silence, expectantly watching as the victors moved through."

The city certainly failed to impress John Guest, who described what he saw there:

> Rome is most disappointing to approach by road. One gets no view of the city before entering it. The country just becomes flat, dull and neglected. Telegraph wires and power pylons spring up everywhere. The buildings are tawdry and modern—

concrete and peeling stucco. Everyone seems to have deserted the countryside for the city, and the desolation is increased by miles of army vehicles, petrol dumps, stores and encampments. Suddenly there are tramlines down the centre of the road with broken, swinging wires above, and one knows that one has arrived. Every now and then the road is torn up, with piles of rubble on either side—some pocket of resistance has been wiped out or some factory neatly destroyed.

What would Audie have expected? With a fifth-grade education he, like most American troops, had little basis for appreciating anything in Italy. The favorite books of American soldiers were dictionaries, *Nana* (Zola's nineteenth-century novel about a Paris prostitute, still a "dirty" book to ill-lettered American proletariats), comic books (which Audie read), and Marion Hargrove's best-seller about boot camp, *See Here, Private Hargrove.*

To Audie, Rome was "but another objective on an endless road called war." Promises of "wholesale drinking and fornication" turned, he says, into a "vast indifference." They pitched their tents in a public park and slept. Later, they had plenty of time to see the city. He wasn't impressed. He wrote to a wounded buddy from Camp Wolters days: "I have had two passes to Rome but was disgusted with the place, its nothing like I expected." For Audie, Rome must have seemed just an old ruined city with lots of beggars, whores, and homeless children. He and the other GIs were American innocents abroad. In *To Hell and Back* one of the replacements is a schoolteacher, that standard figure of comic opprobrium in American popular mythology. He waxes eloquent about the Eternal City and is roundly mocked by the GIs who prefer Cicero, Illinois, to Cicero the Roman orator. One tells the schoolteacher to "keep on roamin', pal."

Rome, like Naples, offered women, and according to Spec McClure, Audie's postwar friend who did nearly all of the writing in *To Hell and Back,* Audie enjoyed the successive pleasures of two sisters and then went after their mother. The editor at Henry Holt & Company balked at including this scene in *To Hell and Back,* but Spec, who was well acquainted with Audie's postwar capacity for non-stop amours, had no reason to disbelieve his story.

Audie was in or near Rome for several weeks. He was there on June 6, an excellent place to be on that day in 1944. Thus he missed the largest and most storied amphibious landing in world history.

From Italy in June and July he wrote several letters to Texas. Not much news in them, but a deep longing for home. Also he kept mentioning how much he liked to hear from his sister and "little mom," Mrs. Cawthon, and in one letter he asked his sister to send him some toothbrushes, Pepsodent, a knife, and some sweets. Training in Italy was boring, the war "is going very well, don't you think," and several "i can't think of anything else to write" closings.

3.
"A FUGITIVE FROM THE LAW OF AVERAGES"

"They wrote in the old days that it is sweet and fitting to die for one's country. But in modern war there is nothing sweet nor fitting in your dying. You will die like a dog for no good reason."
—Ernest Hemingway
"Notes on the Next War: A Serious Topical Letter," 1935

Operation Anvil, an amphibious landing in southern France, had been on the table for discussion among the Allies since August 1943. The Americans—Marshall, Eisenhower, Roosevelt—felt that opening a front in southern France would help protect the long-anticipated invasion of Normandy and give the Allies an invaluable supply port at Marseilles. The British were opposed because of the demands of the Italian campaign; but now that Italy had been taken, the American view prevailed. The code name was changed to Dragoon, and the date was moved back to August 1944. The after-the-fact explanation of the strategy, in *To Hell and Back,* is a model of simplicity. The Germans were like a man trapped in a stolen house. Justice was hammering on his front and back doors (the sweep from Normandy on one side, and on the Eastern Front, the Russians), and now a third party was coming through a trapdoor from the cellar: "We were that party," said Audie.

The training in Italy completed, the 3rd Infantry Division once again boarded landing boats and chugged toward southern France. Fearful before action as always, Audie looked around him at the other men, some seasick, some with nervous bowels, and saw, as many writers have seen in such moments, "the comedy of little men, myself included, who are pitted against a riddle that is as vast and indifferent as the blue sky above us." On August 15, at eight in the morning, they landed on the beautiful beaches near St. Tropez and Cavalaire. Strong air and naval support and limited German defenses made it technically a "perfect landing." Bill Mauldin said it was the "best invasion" he ever "attended." In a mere forty minutes Audie's regiment was headed inland where the fighting would be much heavier.

Recounting Audie's actions in France tests the powers of credibility. Poet Louis Simpson has said that the foot soldier's experience reaches if not surpasses the borders of language: "To a foot soldier war is almost entirely physical. That is why some men, when they think about war, fall silent. Language seems to falsify physical experience and betray those who have experienced it absolutely—the dead."

Audie Murphy was a hero of ultimate reality, and what he did in France is simply incredible. His personal crusade—it almost seems that—to rid the world of German soldiers (or was it simply to get the war over and return home?) took on extraordinary proportions that day of the landing. He was never able to explain his exploits, but over the years, in conversations with Spec McClure, he offered several theories. He said he grew tired of seeing men die who had something to come back home to, so he fought all the harder to get the war over as quickly as possible. He said he couldn't see the point of risking thirty men when one could do the job. He said he got bored. He said he had a mean streak in him a mile long. He said, "People think I brood about those Germans I killed. I don't. If my own brother had been on the other side, I would have tried to kill him too."

The day of the landing in France the legend began. A mile inland, on a steep cliff rising above forested and bouldered land, the Germans had built a large pillbox and installed a coastal gun. The hill would have to be taken if the 15th Infantry were going to advance.

Coming under fire, Audie saw two of his men go down; both dead. Alone now, he began to traverse a gully, heading up the hill, when he happened upon two Germans. Startled, they hesitated with surprise, and "that [was] their mistake." He killed them both with his carbine. Nearing a farmhouse, Audie found a light machine-gun squad pinned down and unwilling to move. He borrowed their gun and set it up in a ditch from where he could fire uphill but lie concealed beneath the level of German fire. He set to work, firing at anything that moved. Climbing up the hill again to relocate the machine gun, he came upon a ghastly scene, a young German with his jaw shot away. Intending to finish him off, he said, "I brace myself against sentiment. I can do nothing for the boy except put him out of his misery." But he couldn't pull the trigger; the German's "staring eyes" were "already filling with the shadows of death."

Now a German machine gun began to rake Audie's position, and he returned the fire. Suddenly he jerked around to find his buddy Lattie Tipton at his side. Against Audie's wishes, Lattie stayed with him, and they were moving up the ditch when two Germans fired at them point-blank, knocking off a piece of Tipton's right ear. Tipton, who Audie swore was the best shot he ever saw and the "bravest man I ever knew," killed the Germans with two shots. Under heavy fire again, Audie and Tipton still moved forward up the hill. They caught two Germans unawares and easily killed them. Under fire next from a German machine gun, they returned it, and the Germans held up a white handkerchief to surrender. Audie thought it might be a trick. He told him, "Goddamnit! Lattie, keep down."

"They want to surrender," said Tipton. "I'm going to get them."

"Keep down," yelled Audie. "Don't trust them."

But Tipton stood up to accept the German surrender and tumbled back with a death-dealing wound in his chest. Now Audie was "all alone," in the fullest sense of the word. His best friend lay dead, and though Audie irrationally tried to get Tipton out of the hole where he could have fresh air, the act was touchingly futile. Hurling a grenade into a German machine-gun hole, Audie knocked it out; then, in an act that he could only describe as a "nightmare," he became possessed of a "demon" and his "whole being [was] concentrated on killing." He went berserk, much like the sergeant he'd watched at the Second Battle of Cisterna who madly charged the German emplacements. Now Audie grabbed the German machine gun and holding it like a BAR (Browning automatic rifle) started up the hill, firing from the hip. He threw all caution aside and sought revenge. He got it when he found the German machine-gun nest that betrayed and killed Tipton. He raked them again and again and did "not stop firing while there [was] a quiver left in them." The hill was pacified, the red madness passed, and Audie came to himself, shaken and weak. He returned downhill to where Tipton lay and bawled "like a baby."

Later, Audie said, he resumed his old impersonal hatred of the German Army, seeing the war as "an endless series of problems involving the blood and guts of men." Audie never could understand what made Lattie expose himself that way. "He was not a fool. He had too much combat experience not to study the entire terrain before him." Nor was he able to explain his own conduct entirely. His moment of insane rage was something he never forgot. Years later, he said, "That was a personal score to settle. I only went off the rail that once."

After Tipton's death, Audie said, the war might have become more personal, but he saw in himself no essential change in his war psychology: "Actual combat experience is the only teacher. You never come out of a skirmish without having picked up a couple of new tricks; without having learned more about your enemy. Perhaps I was a willing student. But total involvement with the war was the only thing that kept me alive and pushing. I also had plenty of luck."

For his rampage that day, he received the Distinguished Service Cross, the second-highest U.S. Army medal for valor. The highest, he would win in the cold snows of northern France early the following year. Between August 1944 and January 1945 there was much blood to be shed, some of it his. In that stretch he was wounded three times, promoted to second lieutenant, and won the three highest decorations a grateful nation has to give to its bravest men.

After Tipton's death, Audie's need to be involved in action, not to have time to think, became an even greater spur. He volunteered for dangerous assignments—though he did not exhibit the foolhardy vengeance motives of the DSC action—and wanted to "do anything that creates the feeling of progress and accomplishment." On a cross-country courier mission he and his two-man detail bluffed three Germans, led by a craven officer, into surrendering. Still, Audie's lust for action sometimes got him into trouble. On one nocturnal mission on a foggy night, he and his patrol heard a German patrol nearby. Hiding beside the road, he attached his bayonet. He meant to kill the leader with a sharp thrust, but the bayonet glanced off bone, the injured German cried out, and both sides started blazing away in the dark. Returning to his company, Audie reported the incident to a lieutenant colonel by explaining, "Sir, a German started screaming out there; and we had to shoot." But the lieutenant colonel knew the score. He said, "Yes, goddamnit, I know, Murphy. You could not stay out of a scrap at a Peace Convention."

Now the progress of the 3rd Division was beginning to accelerate. French towns were falling like dominoes into the hands of the advancing army. Though the Germans were in retreat, and though some surrendered in gratifying numbers, their resistance was also at times fanatical. It was clear that the Germans would never be an easy foe. One day Company B came upon a stone farmhouse where a zealous German colonel was holed up alone, pouring out fire with a pistol and shouting that he would never be taken alive. Audie found the tactical problem interesting to watch, and then he came up with a solution. He crept up to the building, kicked open a door, then held a tommy gun around the side of the door and fired away, letting the gun arc around the room. The German fell, wounded and still defiant, and Audie captured him.

By now Audie was the compleat combat soldier. Proficient with all manner of small arms weapons, possessed of superb physical skills—including fantastic eye-hand coordination, keen intelligence, and his readiness to kill—he was familiar with every ground combat situation a soldier might expect to confront. Ambushes, snipers, artillery fire from the enemy, short rounds from his own side, strafing by airplanes, tanks—all were deadly, and he knew them all, day after day. Audie later evaluated his own performance in the war: "There was a time during the war when I got to be a pretty good soldier. That is, I learned to play the percentages; I learned to stay under cover whenever I could find it. I tried to stay alive, which is what the Army teaches you. But there are times you have to stick your neck out, naturally." And he was still lucky, without which all the other skills and abilities could be rendered meaningless in one blinding flash of artillery fire or a sniper's pinpoint precision from cover or the other thousand deaths a soldier is heir to.

Headed north toward the ultimate goal, German soil, the 3rd came upon scenes of epic destruction. On one fifteen-mile stretch of highway they saw the burning, smoking remains of a large German convoy, two thousand strong, that had been blasted by artillery and bombers. They called it the Avenue of Stenches because of the smell of burning men, gasoline, and horseflesh. The suffering, dying horses affected Audie and others more than the sight of wounded men; they were used to that.

At Montélimar, as in every town that had to be liberated, the fighting was house to house, a particularly deadly game of search and destroy. Here it was that Audie *saw* himself, in a moment that becomes a rich metaphor for the duality of the combat soldier: the pre-combat self and the combat self; the civilian who has become an executioner. The scene is played for full literary effect in *To Hell and Back:* "As we stand in one house, the door of a room creaks open. Suddenly I find myself faced by a terrible looking creature with a tommy gun. His face is black; his eyes are red and glaring. I give him a burst and see the flash of his own gun, which is followed by the sound of shattering glass." One might choose this moment as the best disclosure, the best revelation, of Audie Murphy's existential dilemma: as killer, executioner, good soldier carrying out his country's will, he becomes a "terrible looking creature." Seeing the horrific self in the mirror, he mistakes it for the Other—the Enemy—and kills it; only it is a true projection of his own self. The glass shatters. It is as though the "terrible" self cannot be acknowledged; to do so would mean laying down one's arms, and where he is, if he does that, he will be dead or dishonored—the last, to a warrior, being as bad as the first. In the book, no such heavy symbolic reading is offered. The scene dissolves into comedy when Kerrigan breaks into laughter, saying, "That's the first time I ever saw a Texan beat himself to the draw." In our collective memory Audie remains forever frozen in that moment: seeing the double in the mirror and murdering it. He thus becomes, symbolically, the good boy soldier repressing, murdering, the deadly self that has had to become, through the requirements of war, a killer.

But there was no time for stocktaking of the self. The job was survival, and Audie continued to perform with expert efficiency. Sometimes the Germans fell into his hands. He and his men were on a ridge south of Besançon when, as Albert Pyle tells it, they heard "a small car coming up hill to the top of the ridge. Murphy takes a BAR, slips down the road a short distance and knocks out the civilian car with several bursts of fire. The two Krauts escaped, but within that car we found several interesting items." The car contained thousands of French francs and, best of all, two to three hundred packs of American cigarettes shipped by the Red Cross to American prisoners of war and intercepted, illegally, by the Germans.

Such incidents of leadership and initiative on Audie's part occurred time and time again, Pyle remembers. His reputation had reached the point, said another member of Company B, that "I don't suppose there was a real veteran in the whole division who was not aware of him. If Murphy was in the front lines, we in the rear area went to sleep. But if we got word that he was falling back, we prepared to get the hell out of there. When Murphy started retreating, it was time to clear out fast."

By now most of the men in Company B were new men, replacements. Of Audie's original gang, his circle of friends, only two remained. The rest were dead or wounded or hospitalized for illnesses. On September 15, near the village of Genèvreuville, Audie joined the ranks of the wounded. A mortar shell landed almost right on top of him, and he thought, "This is it"—then lost consciousness. The blast blew the heel off his right shoe, gashed his foot, and broke the stock of his favorite carbine. Two men he'd been talking to were dead, and three others were wounded. Had he been three feet further away, he reckoned, he'd have been killed.

It was only a slight wound, and after a few days in hospital Audie was back at the front. Albert Pyle noticed that Audie was different from many others returning to the front after a stay in hospital. Most men lost their combat edge, developed a case of nerves, and had to undergo a difficult reentry period. Not Audie. He came back, picked up his damaged carbine, wound some wire around the stock, and went on. The carbine had a hair trigger, and he'd been lucky with it so far.

Audie's luck was always underwritten by an instinct to survive and an expert store of combat knowledge that was added to every day under fire. Leading his men forward, for example, he heard the fluttering sound of a defective U.S. artillery round that was going to fall short, right on top of his company. He yelled for them to get down. To the new men it seemed a miracle that a shell hitting so close didn't kill them.

In September, Audie's growing reputation among the men of Company B—everybody knew who fought well and who didn't—earned him a battlefield commission to second lieutenant, except that he refused to let himself be promoted. The commanding officer of the 1st Battalion, Lieutenant Colonel Michael Paulick, wanted Audie promoted; but the young soldier with the fifth-grade education was "embarrassed by his lack of formal education." And there was another reason: "he did not choose to leave the men he had fought with so long." So reported his company commander. Within a short time, however, Audie could not stave off that promotion. He was simply too good a leader of men and there was a growing shortage of junior officers.

All the fighting now, in late September and early October, was part of a plan to drive the Germans out of a defensive stronghold called Cleurie Quarry. This became one of the bitterest pieces of ground the 15th Infantry ever had to take. Poised on the edge of the Vosges Mountains, where the Germans hoped to stall the Allies, the quarry was a virtual stone fortress situated on a heavily forested slope. Its huge boulders, steep cliffs, and natural passageways made it an ideal spot to defend with machine guns, snipers, and small arms. Plus, U.S. mortar fire was ineffectual because of the impregnable cover and danger to its own infantry. The Quarry would have to be taken by individual men on foot—infantry fighting at its most deadly. Short of men and officers, as always, Company B had to do a job that Lieutenant Colonel Paulick said could easily have required a complete battalion. Attacks and counterattacks went on for four days. There was also the constant danger of German patrols at night. Audie was ready: "I whet my bayonet until it is razor-sharp and keep it always handy."

To Albert Pyle and the rest of Company B, the terrain here reminded them of something they'd seen before. Boulders, small streams, steep cliff approaches, and an enemy occupying excellent defensive positions recalled all the difficulties of Italy. The landscape also recalled the Great War. Pyle saw the remains of old trenches and, digging new foxholes, unearthed a French Army bayonet and later, in a village, found a canteen cup that belonged to an American soldier from 1918. The fighting in eastern France was so brutal, so sustained, that today, nearly fifty years later, the forests in Alsace, Lorraine, and the Vosges are deadly dangerous to loggers because of the amount of machine-gun lead still being discovered embedded in the trees, grim reminder of two world wars.

In the vicinity of the Quarry, but lower down and sheltered by an intervening hill, there was a house where Company B set up a command post. One night, in another of the seemingly countless violent episodes that defined their life now, Audie proved again to his company commander how valuable a soldier he was. He and other platoon leaders were assembled at the command post receiving instructions for an attack the next morning when suddenly, as Robert Millar, a non-commissioned officer in Company B, tells it, "all hell broke loose and they were right at the C.P. Flack was coming though the building and tracer bullets. We hit the floor and Murphy says, 'Come on, Bob,' and he grabbed a case of hand grenades and told me to get on those mortars and have them ready to shower the entrance to the Quarry. After tossing a half case of grenades he stopped that attack. The next morning we found German caps, blood [sic] and equipment they left when they withdrew. He did a marvelous job all by himself."

"Coolness and calm fury," Audie said, were the two great attributes of a man in combat. Men who survived combat, wrote Ernie Pyle, did so "because the fates were kind to them, certainly—but also because they had become hard and immensely wise in animallike ways of self-preservation." If they lasted long enough, each became what Pyle called, in a striking phrase, a "senior partner in the institution of death."

Audie and the other seasoned veterans never quite got used to seeing the spick-and-span new replacements that joined Company B. Clean-shaven, loaded with gear they wouldn't need, their pants starched and creased, the replacements too were struck by the old-timers, perpetually muddy, unshaven, and "un-Army" looking. Many of these new men were ill-trained, having been rushed to the front in a desperate bid to provide replacements for an army that, from August 1944 on, at times suffered from a grave shortage of infantrymen. Some of the new troops lacked a working knowledge of weapons.

Having seen his friends go under one by one, disappearing from Company B, wounded or dying or dead, Audie adopted a necessary strategy now, familiar to all men with extensive combat experience: not to let himself get close to the new replacements. Feeling "burnt out, emotionally and physically exhausted," he didn't want to know anybody well enough because later he didn't want to have to "turn over the bodies and find the familiar face of a friend." At this point in the war and in his narrative, there are strong signs of the later postwar Audie Murphy, a man struggling to control his emotions and looking for action, thrills, and danger to keep from having to deal with the pain of loss, grief, love, all the human and unmanning feelings. Before one of his decorated valorous actions at the Quarry, he said, "And I am bored with the lack of activity, which breeds the thinking that I try to avoid."

What happened is that two officers who wanted a closer look at the Quarry unwisely selected only four men to accompany them and got themselves into big trouble. Bored, with nothing better to do, Audie trailed after them, but well back and unbeknownst to them. He said many years later, "I figured those gentlemen were going to run into trouble; so I tagged along, about twenty-five yards to their rear, to watch the stampede." Here and elsewhere in the action in the forests of France, Audie seemed a kind of latter-day Hawkeye, Fenimore Cooper's Leatherstocking hero who possessed unerring forest skills, was a crack shot, was always detecting unseen enemy presences from the crack of a twig, and was always turning up in the nick of time to save the day for beleaguered comrades and innocents. So Audie on that day caught the Germans right after they opened fire on the detail. They took out three men in the first blaze of gunfire and grenades, but the officers dived into a shallow hole. The Germans had them now; it was only a matter of moments till they finished them off. But they hadn't counted on a rear guard.

Colonel Paulick, one of the officers, later recounted what happened next: "Machine gun bullets ricocheted around us, and the sound of our guns kept our ears ringing. It was then that I heard a familiar voice over the noise of battle. One by one he called the names of every man in the patrol, waiting for an answer. It was Audie. I realized then that he must have some sort of plan in mind and that our positions had something to do with it. Perhaps half a minute later the first of a series of grenades shattered the outpost. After the last explosions we rushed the position to complete the elimination. We found a machine gun, four dead Germans, and three wounded. To me the important thing about what I had just seen was Murphy's immediate grasp of the situation, his precise thinking, and his uncanny coolness in action. . . ." In this version Audie sounds like a hero out of Greek mythology, or Roland at Roncesvalles, calling out the names of his fallen comrades.

In Audie's account he sounds like a frontier scout, Hawkeye again. He stepped out from a big rock, and the Germans, seeing him instantly, swung the machine gun around to get him; only the barrel caught on a limb before the arc was completed, and the bullets missed. That's all the time he needed. A grenade and two bursts from his carbine killed two Germans; two more grenades finished the sequence. Four Germans dead, three wounded, and the eighth, a fat man, tried to run away. He reminded Audie of a clown and he hesitated to shoot him, but the clown was still armed and dangerous. Audie shot him.

For this action Audie won the Silver Star, and the language of the citation used an arresting word—"miraculously"—to describe his narrow escape from machine-gun fire.

Audie's decorated actions were like italicized incidents in a string of such exploits. At times it seems as though Audie could have been decorated on an almost weekly basis, because in France now he was becoming quite simply a soldier of astonishing accomplishments. Following the Silver Star action, either that day or the next, a German sniper killed two men in a heavy weapons platoon. It "irritated" Audie, he reports in a characteristic bit of understatement in *To Hell and Back*. He proposed to go after the sniper alone, but his captain ordered him to take a small detachment. Audie reluctantly agreed; then, as they moved up the slope, he ordered his men to stay back while he hunted the sniper alone. Poised beside a boulder, Audie heard a sound and spotted the sniper, who saw him at the same instant: "His face is as black as a rotting corpse; and his cold eyes are filled with evil. As he frantically reaches for the safety on his rifle, I fire twice. He crashes backwards." The German is like a figure out of nightmare. Once the German was slain, Audie wilted and felt like vomiting. Years later he told his pal Spec McClure that this was the second time he'd felt personal anger against the Germans. He also told him, "I took my time on that one. That sniper sonofabitch was lethal."

In 1955 Audie recalled this same episode in a rather different way. According to this version, "They say I killed 241 men in World War II. I only really remember one. He was a sniper in Germany. He had accounted for a couple of my buddies and I didn't feel anything as I squeezed the trigger. When the bullet hit him, I saw the expression on his face in the rifle sights. He didn't speak, but I had a hunch I knew what he was thinking in that last moment. He probably said in his mind, 'Lord, I am dying and I don't know why.' Then he collapsed like a rag doll and fell to the ground. For a long time, I felt sorry for him. After that, I pitied myself. I didn't want to kill anybody." The differences are revealing. Speaking colloquially to a close friend, Audie sounded tough and deadly. Speaking for public consumption, in a movie magazine, he sounded a regretful note appropriate to a softened postwar image of a man in the public eye.

Perhaps this episode was the most memorable because of the eye-to-eye contact, but there were numerous instances of Audie stalking and killing snipers. Albert Pyle remembers an incident when Audie escorted two officers to the edge of the Cleurie Quarry on a reconnaissance patrol. What happened next, he said, was "I heard three carbine shots and after about the same amount of time Murphy and the other two officers came slipping back down the ridge. Murphy was grinning and carrying a rifle with a very powerful scope on it. It had blood all over the stock and I asked him what happened. He said, 'Well, Pyle, I caught a Kraut asleep in his hole and he was the biggest, ugliest Kraut I ever saw, so I shot him in the head three times.' "

Company B carried the rifle on the company kitchen trailer for several months afterwards.

Another time during the fighting around the Quarry, remembers Bob Millar, Audie and his company were pinned down when Audie "crawled to the edge of the Quarry, looked the situation over, and noticed a German on the other side with a beautiful sniper's rifle with scope. He quickly zeroed in on him and put him out of action. He looked things over and could see no more Germans so he told his platoon to keep him covered he was going across to see what he had done to that fellow. He did and he brought that sniper's rifle which was pictured at one time in *Life* magazine."

After the war Audie spoke of this game of one on a side: "This is the most lonely game on earth, two men stalking each other with powerful guns; two men trained to kill in split seconds; two men without an atom of mercy toward each other." In his study of combat behavior, S. L. A. Marshall found that most men on the battlefield drew strength from "the near presence or the presumed presence of a comrade." But he also acknowledged that there were "men who do not need to draw moral strength from other men, who are at their best when they go it alone, who love danger for its own sake, and who become restive when life becomes tranquil." He might have been talking about Audie Murphy.

The fighting in and around Cleurie Quarry continued to be as bitter and bloody as any action Company B had seen. In one of these fire fights, on October 5, Audie won another Silver Star. This time he did it with stealth, valor (of course), and the pinpoint direction of artillery fire. What happened was that the Germans surprised the GIs with a well-camouflaged machine-gun and sniper emplacement along a creek bed. The surprise was that the Germans usually employed such tactics on high ground, not low. In the first burst of fire, several of Audie's company were hit. Then Audie led a six-man patrol down the hill, four of whom were hit by German fire. In a characteristic maneuver, Audie left the remainder of his patrol in shallow holes in the hillside while he continued downhill to get close enough to locate the enemy and direct mortar fire. He was "cold, wet and scared," he told a newspaper reporter in 1945. Settling finally in a shallow hole about two hundred yards above the Germans, he shot two snipers and then, for almost an hour, directed withering chemical mortar fire down on top of the Germans. They knew where he was, but couldn't hit him with either rifle or machine-gun fire, though the bullets pinged as close as a foot as Audie hugged the earth. Eventually the mortar fire did the job, and the Germans were all killed. In the citation that accompanied the 1st Oak Leaf Cluster to the Silver Star, Audie's gallantry was credited with killing fifteen Germans and approximately thirty-five other casualties.

In October Lieutenant Colonel Paulick's intention to promote Audie prevailed. Much impressed by Audie's "alertness and coolness under fire," Paulick told him that he simply had to take the promotion. Audie offered the same reasons against it as before, and Paulick made two accommodations to permit the promotion to go through: Audie would have help with the paperwork and he would remain with Company B.

Called to regimental headquarters, Audie, on October 14, along with two other muddy front-line soldiers, was sworn in as an officer. "You are now *gentlemen* by act of Congress," said Colonel Hallett Edson. "Shave, take a bath, and get the hell back into the lines." So much for being an officer and a gentleman. Promotion to second lieutenant was a kind of death warrant. Second looeys were sitting ducks for German snipers, who always liked to take out an officer if they had the chance. In a fifty-day period in Italy, 3rd Division line units suffered a 152 percent loss in second lieutenants. They had the highest casualty rate among officers in World War II. Add to this the fact that infantry riflemen had the highest casualty rate among combat troops. The combination increased the odds exponentially. Both the other men commissioned with Audie that day were later killed in action.

The other factor, of course, was time in the line. The more often you went into combat, the more likely you were to buy the farm. The first ten days of combat were the worst, statistically; more men were killed or wounded then. If a soldier survived the initiation period, then, studies showed, he was effective until about the twenty-first day. Then things began to slip, and by the forty-fifth day combat exhaustion began to take over. Studies of "battle fatigue" revealed the steady toll taken by combat. One such study, for example, showed that "between June and November, 1944, a staggering 26 percent of all American soldiers in combat divisions were treated for some form of battle fatigue." Nearly a million cases were reported in the U.S. Army in World War II. Combat veterans knew this deep in their bones. Said one soldier of that knowledge: "There is a condition . . . which we call the two-thousand-year stare. This was the anaesthetised look, the wide, hollow eyes of a man who no longer cares. I wasn't to that state yet, but the numbness was total. I felt almost as if I hadn't actually been in a battle, as if I had just awakened but couldn't get my body to the bathroom to brush my goddamn teeth." Eighty-seven percent of veterans in the Italian campaign said they'd seen a close friend killed or wounded in action. A high percentage felt that their own wounding or death was inevitable. Fight long enough, often enough, and you were a goner. As an official report titled *Combat Exhaustion* stated: "There is no such thing as 'getting used to combat.' " It concluded that "the fighting of the Second World War, in short, led to an infantryman's breakdown in a little under a year."

There was also the American policy of lengthy continuous service in the line. In World War II only the Russians matched the Americans in this practice. The Russian Army "granted no home leave to its soldiers from beginning to end; men remained with their units until killed or disabled." So too the U.S. Army. American soldiers could "look forward to a release from danger only through death or wounds." Feelings of "endlessness" and "hopelessness" were the natural results of such a policy. General Omar Bradley understood the plight of the infantrymen well: "Those who are left to fight, fight on, evading death but knowing that with each day of evasion they have exhausted one more chance for survival. Sooner or later, unless victory comes, this chase must end on the litter or in the grave."

By now of course Audie had seen several buddies severely wounded or killed. Men he'd been talking to were dead moments later. He felt, it is clear, that his own chances for surviving were dwindling. German resistance remained strong and deadly, and the wise and the unwise died alike.

In early fall there was a lot of rain. Audie mentioned the miserable weather in a letter to his sister in October. Now it was beginning to turn cold and there was snow in the mountains. What lay ahead was the coldest winter in Europe for twenty-five years. Resolute Germans and bad weather: what else did Company B expect?

Early on October 26, in the pre-dawn cold, the Germans launched a heavy artillery attack. Lying in his foxhole, Audie felt again the nameless terror of bombardment. With good reason: more soldiers were killed from artillery fire than from any other kind of weapon in World War II. In *The Men of Company K: The Autobiography of a World War II Rifle Company*, Harold P. Leinbaugh and John D. Campbell speak for all infantry when they describe the fearsomeness of an artillery barrage: "The noise, the shock, the sensation of total helplessness and bewilderment, the loss of control, the sudden loss of every familiar assumption—nothing in civilian life or training offered an experience remotely comparable." The sheer noise and the utter randomness of destruction raining down from on high left one without any sense of personal control, no sniper to track down, no machine-gun nest to destroy. Harold Bond has well described the sensation of enduring such a barrage: "In such a shelling as this each man is isolated from everyone else. Death is immediately in front of him, his own death. He knows only that his legs and arms are still there and that he has not been hit yet; in the next instant he might be." The big guns, especially the dread .88s, sent shrieking missiles of death in rolling clouds of smoke, fire, and fragmentation. The .88s were feared from Africa on, and gave rise to a song, "Eighty-eights Are Breaking Up That Old Gang of Mine." Explosions drove men deep into the ground, prefiguring their ultimate union with the earth—unless there was a direct hit and the soldier was atomized, nothing left to bury except dog tags and a hank of hair or maybe fragments of bones.

Trees, a special danger in bombardments, acted as natural conduits of fragmentation. If a shell hit the top of a tree, the effect was devastating. Shrapnel showered the terrain below, and anybody caught in the open was mincemeat. Such bombardments in the Huertgen Forest reminded Ernest Hemingway of World War I: Passchendaele with tree-bursts.

The theological implications of bombardment are worth considering for a moment. Despite all the popular talk about there being no atheists in foxholes, artillery fire and combat made an excellent training school for atheism. In the face of imminent death, some men turned to prayer, but some turned to fatalism and pessimism. In Audie's case the idea of personal salvation as subscribed to by his fellow soldiers annoyed him, as he reports of an incident during an artillery barrage in France. Hearing other soldiers praying, he thought, "For some reason I would always be irritated when I would overhear the words, '. . . please God, save me . . .' Then one day, as we were out in pretty open country and being pounded by heavy shelling, I heard a GI mumble these same words again and an answer formed in my mind, 'Hey, why save just you?' I wanted to ask. 'There's a whole company of us out here!' " In the signed article for *Modern Screen*, 1956, from which this incident is taken, Audie explained the role religion played in his life before, during, and after the war. The answer is not much. When a chaplain kidded him about not attending chapel, Audie replied, "You do the prayin' and I'll do the shootin.' " Audie's earliest experiences with fire-and-brimstone fundamental Protestantism had left him "close to never having any religion at all." Nothing in the war led him any closer to conventional Christian faith. Historian John Ellis makes the same point: "For many men nothing so utterly and completely dissipated their residual religious beliefs as the randomness and pervasiveness of violent death." Audie was one of these.

In his foxhole that morning—the 26th—Audie survived a tree-burst of shrapnel. All he suffered, his luck still holding, was temporary deafness. Despite the intensity and frequency of attacks from artillery, Audie and other soldiers continued to pull themselves together and carry on the fight. (Max Hastings has concluded that "one of the great surprises of warfare in the twentieth century has been the power of soldiers to survive what would seem to be overwhelming concentrations of high explosives, and emerge to fight with skill and determination.")

When day broke and the thin sunlight slanted through the trees, Audie led his platoon forward, deeper into the forest. The objective was a town called Brouvelieures, but Lieutenant Murphy never saw Brouvelieures, not that that made much difference. It was just another little French town where, if the Germans dug in, there'd be the close-in, house-to-house fighting in which the tommy gun, prized for its rapid fire, would be his weapon of choice. Here in the forest he relied on his lucky carbine, the one with the busted stock he'd wired back together. It had a hair trigger, and in all combat situations Audie kept the safety off.

The forest was full of German snipers, and the trees afforded natural cover. Up front of his platoon, Audie, with his radio operator a step behind, scanned the terrain and moved forward. Suddenly a shot snapped from somewhere, and the radio operator fell, a mortal wound just above his left eye. Audie dived for cover, and another shot glanced off the tree and etched a nine-inch line through his right buttock. The sniper—Audie saw him now—tossed back his camouflage cape and fired again, at Audie's helmet. Only Audie's head wasn't in it, and as he describes the action in *To Hell and Back*, "I raise my carbine and with my right hand fire pistol-fashion. The bullet spatters between the German's eyes."

When the fire fight ended, Audie was loaded on a stretcher. Albert Pyle was struck by the scene—indeed, he said it was one of his most lasting memories of the war. Shortly before he was hit, Audie had captured a German non-com and his radioman. Now, lying on the stretcher, he grinned and, with his carbine across his middle, he directed the prisoners down the hill even as he was being carried down it. He simply never stopped being the good soldier.

Gunshot wounds traumatize, inducing shock or localized numbness. Sometimes this lasts for a while, sparing the wounded great pain for a time, but eventually if death doesn't come, the pain does. Audie started to hurt pretty quickly, but he hadn't forgotten to laugh, either. He remembered one of his buddies in Company B who, wounded himself earlier in the fighting and now in hospital, had always predicted that if Audie ever got a commission, he'd get shot in the ass.

Instead of being sent immediately to a hospital behind the lines, Audie had to wait three days because the weather had turned really nasty. Rain and mud made traveling impossible. Before he left the aid station, a sergeant from his platoon visited Audie and borrowed his lucky carbine. In a fire fight later that day the sergeant and most of the platoon were destroyed.

At the 3rd General Hospital in Aix-en-Provence, near Marseilles, Audie's self-diagnosis was gangrene, and the doctor, who preferred at first to call it an infection, finally admitted it was gangrene. The treatment—penicillin and cutting away the dead and poisoned flesh—took over two months in all, the longest spell he was away from the front during his service from Sicily to Germany. The time in hospital was very important to Audie, though you wouldn't know it from *To Hell and Back,* which jumps from the wound and the treatment in hospital right back to the front in January 1945. It leaves out the most important thing that happened to him at that time. During his stay in hospital Audie had time to get some hot food and some rest, to have his wound heal, and to become a favorite of hospital personnel. He also fell in love with a nurse.

He seemed like such a kid to everybody. Colista McCabe, a nurse, saw him for the first time late one night. She'd heard about his growing fame, but the boy she saw hardly seemed the type. Audie was in the hospital kitchen licking the spoon from a batch of fudge the guys had made. He looked just like a child, like any-body's kid brother—slightly freckle-faced, grinning, absolutely charming. Like many another woman, Colista took to Murph immediately. He was "somebody you wanted to hug and take home with you." He was such "an appealing person."

Because he couldn't sleep, Audie was always slipping out of his bed at night. One of the men he talked to a lot during those long nights was Private Perry Pitt, a soldier from Tennessee with a severe shrapnel wound to the spine. Written off as a terminal case, he pulled through, though he would be a paraplegic for life. Pitt remembers the first time he saw Audie: "He looked like a high school kid. I was amazed how small he was. It was impossible to keep him in bed. He came down, found I was a farm kid, too, and he'd hand me water so I could drink." Night after night Audie, summoned in a whisper to Pitt's bedside, passed the long hours talking with the maimed and depressed soldier. During that time Pitt never once heard Audie say anything about the medals he'd won. They became close friends, and that friendship lasted the rest of Audie's life.

Colista's best friend and fellow nurse, Carolyn Price, got to know Audie even better. "Pricey," as they called her, was a fine-looking brunette with a warm manner and a good sense of humor. Slightly older than Audie, she felt a lot older because he looked so damned young. Twenty, he could pass for fifteen easy. To Carolyn, Murph "had the fresh boyish freckled face of a high school sophomore." If she'd been asked to pick the Great American War Hero from the officers' ward, he'd have been at the bottom of her list.

Carolyn worked night duty on Audie's ward, and Murph (as everybody called him) never seemed to sleep. He pretended to follow the doctor's orders, but as soon as Major Ginsberg was out of sight, Murph was out of bed. Carolyn was somebody he could talk to. He told her about his brother and sisters in the orphanage and how he wanted to get them out of that place. He and Carolyn talked of many things but never about combat. She felt that this part of his life was something "he could share with no one." He did tell her one thing, though, that bothered her. He said that after the war he was thinking about becoming a mercenary. Soldiering was what he knew best, and above all, he did not want to "return to his previous life in Texas."

Carolyn mothered the young soldier; it seemed impossible to do otherwise. He became the "teacher's pet" just as he had been back in grade school. There were those, however, who knew the other Murphy. A fellow officer in the ward told Carolyn, with considerable pride, "Don't let that baby face fool you, Lieutenant, that's the toughest soldier in the Third Division."

Carolyn saw a glimpse of Murph's violent side one afternoon when they went to a small bistro in Aix. Murph liked to get into Aix whenever he could find transportation, and he liked being with Carolyn when she was off duty. They were sitting there talking and minding their own business when some soldiers drinking at the bar started making wisecracks about a ninety-day wonder having a date with a nurse. Never was taunting an officer more misplaced. Murph's promotion had been earned under fire, and now Carolyn could see that buildup for violent action settling into Audie's manner: "His face became grim and white, his eyes grew cold and narrow." Only her pleading kept Murph from taking on the loudmouths at the bar. He paid for the drinks and he and Carolyn left fast.

At some point during his stay in the hospital Audie asked Carolyn to marry him. Things went that far, on his side at least. She refused to take him seriously. She told him, "Oh, Audie, you're a child." Like her friend Colista, Carolyn felt Audie needed a mother, not a wife.

Though he never talked about combat, he talked constantly about returning to the front. Carolyn heard him on this subject many times; so did Colista. Neither sensed any motive on Audie's part except comradely concern for his platoon. Although Colista and the others teased him about being a "professional killer," he was actually, she insists, the "last person who would enjoy killing." Those who knew him in the hospital saw in him no desire to return to the front to kill the enemy; rather, he wanted to rejoin his buddies and not abandon them. Bill Mauldin observed this tendency so familiar among front-line veterans: "A lot of guys don't know the names of their regimental commanders. They went back because their companies were very short-handed, and they were sure that if somebody else in their own squad or section were in their own shoes, and the situation were reversed, those friends would come back to make the load lighter on *them*." Studies of combat behavior showed the same phenomenon. Men fought and returned to fight because of bonds established with other men; the flag and patriotic abstractions had nothing to do with why they felt compelled to return to the front when they were out of it and their buddies weren't. The unit of loyalty had nothing to do with large military organizations; the men thought of themselves "as equals within a very tiny group— perhaps no more than six or seven men." And, wounded, they returned to rejoin the group because, says John Ellis, "in the last analysis, the soldier fought for them and them alone, because they were his friends and because he defined himself only in the light of their respect and needs."

From his hospital bed at Aix-en-Provence Audie wrote, for once, a letter that actually disclosed something of what his real feelings were. He wrote Haney Lee, the farmer near Floyd on whose place he had worked and lived for a while after his own family began to disintegrate. He seems to have regarded the older man as a kind of father, and Lee felt a paternal affection for Audie. Addressing the older man as General Lee, a joke Audie never tired of, he wrote, "Say Gen. those Krauts are getting to be better shots then they used to be or else my lucks playing out on me and, I guess, someday they will tag me for keeps. Nice thought anyway." He asked about Mr. Lee's hunting, then returned to the dreadful subject at hand: "I've seen so much blood I don't think I ever want to shoot anything else except (Krauts and Japs) ha. ha., fooled you didn't I." In a postscript there sounds, beneath the attempt to get out of the letter, a note of desperation: "Meant to send you a couple of Kraut PW's to help you farm, but thought before I closed, sorry, can't, sorry."

A second letter to Lee, in December, mentioned how much he'd like to see him and Mrs. Lee, but went on, "But thares work to do yet (dirty work). . . ."

Dirty work indeed there was. It was killing Germans, and that never got easier. While Audie was in Aix-en-Provence recovering from his wound, the gods were busy as usual. Between the American divisions and the conquest of the German homeland, which lay temptingly close, there remained many grim battles yet to come. One of them became known to history as the Battle of the Bulge. On December 18 the Germans launched a major counteroffensive in the Ardennes in Belgium, a rolling, wooded terrain punctuated with river valleys and small villages. By December 27, the Germans had been turned back. Historians agree that in the Ardennes American GIs experienced their "finest hour." Audie, who had had many fine hours, had the greatest yet to come. It would take place in the Colmar Pocket, one of the least written about actions of the European theater.

On New Year's Day, 1945, Hitler set into motion another counteroffensive. He called it *Nordwind*. Its purpose was to smash through what Hitler felt was the thinnest part of the American line, a 130-mile periphery in Alsace, south of the Ardennes. This is where Audie's 15th Regiment came into the picture. Since the landing at St. Tropez on August 15, 1944, B Company of the 1st Battalion had fought its way almost due north up the eastern side of France, one tiny village after another, Donzère, Montélimar, Besançon, Remiremont, Cleurie, and on, finally, to Strasbourg in northern Alsace where, from November 28 to December 19, the 3rd Division had occupied it as a garrison city. Symbolically Strasbourg was very important to the French, who regarded it as the capital of Alsace-Lorraine, that much-fought-over territory that the Germans had twice taken from them, in the Great War, and in 1940. The French national anthem, "La Marseillaise," had been composed at Strasbourg. The city had to be held, and in order to do so an area to the south called the Colmar Pocket had to be cleared. The 15th Infantry Regiment moved into the Pocket on December 21, and they were still there on January 14, 1945, when Audie rejoined Company B.

One writer has described the Colmar Pocket as a "Battle of the Bulge in reverse. As the division had pushed eastward, it locked thousands of Germans in a large wooded area, presuming they would subsequently surrender. They didn't. They wanted to fight. The division returned to the Pocket to empty it." Audie called it "one of the toughest assignments" in the 3rd Division's history. Strategically, he wrote, "it is a huge and dangerous bridgehead thrusting west of the Rhine like an iron fist. Fed with men and materiel from across the river, it is a constant threat to our right flank; and potentially it is a perfect springboard from which the enemy could start a powerful counterattack."

When Audie returned to Company B, things were as grim as they could be. That old specter from Anzio days, trench foot, made a reappearance in the frozen snows of the coldest winter Europe had seen in twenty-five years. Because of optimism surrounding the Normandy invasion and the belief that the war would be over before winter set in, and because of bad planning, American ground troops did not have proper protective clothing against the cold. No thermal underwear, no mittens, no fur-lined parkas—nothing, as one soldier from that time has written, that any peacetime skier or hiker would expect. "Cold injury," which meant pneumonia and trench foot, took a terrible toll—64,008 casualties, a little over four divisions. Ninety percent of the cold casualties were, of course, riflemen.

The Germans had plenty of armor, including tanks, and although the American attack on January 20 began well, within a few days, fighting in freezing temperatures, the Germans were holding and counterattacking. Audie's battalion, held in reserve, moved up on January 24. Snow was knee-deep; the cold was unmerciful, unrelenting. During the days the temperature rarely rose above 14°, and it was so cold on the night of January 24–25 as the 1st Battalion lay trying to sleep, waiting to attack the next day, that Audie's hair froze to the ground. On the 25th they encountered extremely heavy fire in the Riedwihr Woods, a tract of heavily forested land between Riedwihr and Holtzwihr, two tiny villages. A round of mortars killed the two lieutenants with whom Audie had been commissioned. Another round knocked Audie down, lacerating both legs from the knees down with tiny steel fragments. He didn't require medical attention for this, his third wound, which resulted in a 2nd Oak Leaf Cluster on his Purple Heart ribbon. Some of the fragments remained in his legs for the rest of his life. Ten years after the war Audie would sometimes sit and pick bits of shrapnel out of his body. Said Spec McClure, who saw him do it, "Every now and then a chunk works its way to the surface. It's symbolic. Murphy never will get the war out of his system."

Wounded or no, there was nothing to do but continue fighting.

He saw anew the horrors of war when a crippled American tank, bearing a cargo of burning bodies, returned past his foxhole close enough so that he could see "the white bones drip like icicles from what is left of a man's foot." In the forest the fighting broke into a random pattern of isolated duels. In one of these, Audie and a soldier were pinned down by a sniper. Forced to expose himself fleetingly, the German fell from a shot in the side by Audie, who finished him off with a burst. The German lay "like a tired child at the end of a busy day."

The day ended inconclusively, with the 1st Battalion having driven six hundred yards into the forest. Six hundred yards in a day's fighting—that's how slow the progress was. Seemingly near its end, the war remained as deadly and nightmarish as ever for the men at the front.

In this kind of warfare there was hardly any distinction between night and day, and thus it was that at 3:00 A.M. on January 26, Audie was placed in command of Company B, the former commander, a first lieutenant, having been badly wounded. As second lieutenant, Audie was the only officer left of a company now reduced to just 18 men capable of front-line assignment from a full complement of 235. As at Anzio, trench foot had taken a heavy toll; in January alone 801 men in the 3rd Division were out of action from this malady. The depletion of front-line troops in Company B was typical of what was happening in many divisions as the war in Europe dragged on. There was a severe shortage of trained replacements. S. L. A. Marshall has noted the staggering fact that on August 5, 1944, two months after the Normandy invasion, "the entire re-enforcement pool for infantry forces in Europe—here I speak of infantrymen ashore in France and ready to go into battle—consisted of one lone rifleman." That was the lowest point, but things did not appreciably improve as the war neared its close.

January 26, 1945, is the day Audie Murphy joined the immortals of combat in the long history of warfare on this planet. If epics were still written, his stand that day would be worthy of a chapter in some new *Iliad* or *Song of Roland*. Before dawn Audie led his company into position at the farther edge of the forest, opening into flat open fields, the "butt-end of a rough U, whose sides are formed by fingerlike extensions of the woods stretching toward Holtzwihr." The ground was frozen so hard the men couldn't make a dent in it, but at least the effort to dig foxholes kept them warmer than just standing around would have done.

At dawn Audie checked his orders with battalion headquarters. They remained the same—to hold the position. That wasn't going to be easy. Undermanned and unaided on the right flank, where an American unit had failed to arrive on schedule (they never did show up), Audie's company had for support two tank destroyers that, in Audie's judgment, were dangerously exposed. Worst of all, the Germans outnumbered the Americans in both troops and firepower. Around two on that cold, foggy afternoon, the Germans began to organize for an attack. Two companies of German troops, about two hundred soldiers wearing snowcapes and supported by six tanks, hove into view. Audie immediately got on the phone to order artillery fire, but he thought his company was doomed. In the opening barrage the Germans knocked out the second TD (the first had slid into a ditch and had to be abandoned) and a tree-burst killed his machine-gun squad. "At that moment," he wrote, "I know that we are lost."

Although American artillery fire was accurate, the Germans kept coming. The situation looked hopeless as German tanks drew close enough to use their machine guns. Audie ordered everybody to withdraw into the forest. He aimed to stay till the last moment, directing artillery fire and using his carbine, then race back to his men. He emptied his carbine, and the Germans were about fifty yards away when he spotted the burning tank destroyer and a "perfectly good machine gun and several cases of ammunition." Taking his telephone with him, he mounted the TD, raking off the bloody body of an American lieutenant whose throat had been cut. On the phone, he cracked the first of several funny lines. Asked how close the Krauts were, he replied, "Just hold the phone and I'll let you talk to one of the bastards." Then he began to fire the machine gun, its chatter, he said, "like sweet music." Three Germans went down. Wham! Another shell hit the TD. Staying on the phone, Audie continued to direct artillery fire and keep up his own deadly fire with the machine gun. "I bore into any object that stirs," he wrote.

Though flames licked up the sides of the TD, he remained calm, his "numbed brain . . . intent only on destroying." The smoke provided natural cover, and the flames, he said, made his feet warm for the first time in three days. When the smoke lifted in a gust of wind, he saw twelve Germans in a ditch, in a row, like partridges he killed them all in a neat stack, traversing the lot a second time to be sure they were dead. He said years later, "I turned the machine gun on them and stacked them up like cordwood." On the phone again, he quipped when asked if he was all right, "I'm all right, sergeant. What are *your* postwar plans?" A deadly calm characterized Audie's performance in this action—the exact opposite of his enraged and crazed attack on the German machine guns following the death of his friend Lattie Tipton. Here he was the angel of death administering fire coolly and methodically. Once years later, riding in a cab in Tokyo, where *To Hell and Back* happened to be playing at the time, he told an actor friend, Frank Chase, something about how he reacted under fire. Says Chase, "You know, he never would bring up his war exploits, and I said, 'Audie, what was it like, when you were in action?' and he said something that I thought was very interesting. He said, 'You know, when I get in a situation where it's tense and everything, things seem to slow down for me. It doesn't seem a blur. Things become very clarified.' "

Continuing, Chase recalls what Audie said about that particular moment on the tank destroyer, that day in January 1945: "When he was up there, he could see each of the Germans; they just weren't a blur to him; in other words he could see their eyes. It was very clarified, the machine gun was like his finger, like pointing his finger."

Under Audie's withering fire, the German infantry support dissolved, forcing the tanks to withdraw. The heroic stand was over. Knocked from the destroyer by concussion from an enemy barrage, Audie came to and noticed that his pants leg was bloody, not a new wound, it turned out, but a reinjuring of the slight wound from the earlier barrage that had left the tiny shrapnel pieces in his legs. Now he walked in a daze back down the road through the forest, not caring if the Germans wanted to kill him, too weak and exhausted, he said, to care. From there he heard the tank destroyer explode, something that miraculously had not happened earlier.

For this extraordinary bit of battlefield heroics, Audie received, as every schoolboy once knew, the Congressional Medal of Honor. According to Army regulations, this highest of the nation's honors that can be bestowed for valorous action is awarded on the basis that "the deed performed must have been one of personal bravery or self-sacrifice so conspicuous as to clearly distinguish the individual above his comrades and must have involved risk of life." "Incontestable proof" is also required. In Audie's case there were at least three witnesses. The most complete account came from Lieutenant Walter W. Weispfenning, a forward artillery observer, who saw the whole action clearly. His account became the central document in the Medal of Honor citation. He wrote:

I saw hundreds of Germans swarming from the woods. They all had automatic weapons. He was all alone out there, except for a tree and a tank destroyer that was about ten yards to his right. The artillery fire he directed had a deadly effect. I saw Germans disappearing in clouds of dirt and snow. A direct hit from a German 88 smashed into the tank destroyer and I saw the men bail out and withdraw to the woods with the rest of the company. Smoke and flames spurted from the tank destroyer and the German tanks advanced, firing their machine guns and cannon at Lieutenant Murphy. The Kraut infantry line came on. The tanks gave the tank destroyer a wide berth because its gasoline and ammunition might have exploded at any moment.

Then, Weispfenning continued, Audie did "the bravest thing I've ever seen a man do in combat."

With the Germans 100 yards away, he climbed onto the tank destroyer turret and began firing its .50-caliber machine gun at the advancing Krauts. He was completely exposed to the enemy fire and there was a blaze under him that threatened to blow the destroyer to bits. Machine gun, machine pistol, and 88-shell fire was all around him.

Twice the tank destroyer was hit by direct shell fire and Lieutenant Murphy was engulfed in clouds of smoke and spurts of flame. His clothing was riddled by flying fragments of shells and bits of rocks. I saw that his trouser leg was soaked with blood. He swung the machine gun to where 12 Germans were sneaking up a ditch in an attempt to flank his position, and he killed all of them at 50 yards.

The action lasted, Weispfenning estimated, about an hour. Combat time, however, is notoriously difficult to calculate with precision, and other observers put the lapsed time at no more than half an hour. Years later, when asked about the accuracy of his report, Weispfenning replied, "When a man is expecting to get his ass shot off in the next minute, he doesn't pause to consider how the incident will look historically. Audie deserved the Medal of Honor long before he got it, and I was only too glad to help out when the opportunity finally came." What Weispfenning meant, of course, is that in the fury of the fire fight, he didn't have time to think about making a report later on. After all, there might not be a *later on*.

Two other observers confirmed the essential picture of the action. Private first class Anthony Abramski, a rifleman in Company B, described Audie on the burning tank destroyer in dramatic images: "The Krauts threw everything they had at Lieutenant Murphy. As the destroyer had been knocked out with its three inch gun facing the enemy, he had to swing the 50 caliber around 180 degrees to engage the Krauts and he had to fire over the open turret. That meant that he was standing on the TD chassis, exposed to enemy fire from his ankles to his head and silhouetted against the trees and the snow behind him." Abramski saw Audie kill about twenty-five Germans and expected, he said, "to see the whole damn tank destroyer blow up under him any minute." Sergeant Elmer Brawley confirmed the devastating firepower generated by Audie that day: "The German infantrymen got within ten yards of Lieutenant Murphy, who killed them in the draws, in the meadows, in the woods—wherever he saw them." The citation accompanying the medal gave a body count of fifty German soldiers killed or wounded and concluded, "Lieutenant Murphy's indomitable courage and his refusal to give an inch of ground saved his company from possible encirclement and destruction and enabled it to hold the woods which had been the enemy's objective."

Once the action was over—Audie, back now at the battalion command post, felt, he later wrote, "no exhilaration at being alive. . . . Existence has taken on the quality of a dream in which I am detached from all that is present." But gradually that dreamlike state passed, and he resumed the mantle of determined warrior and leader. He did not rest on his laurels or seek a much-deserved rest. First, he ventilated his anger at what he considered inadequate artillery support. Then he refused medical aid and set about organizing an immediate attack upon the Germans while they were still reeling. So he and his command returned to the woods and hunted Germans who'd remained behind in small pockets of resistance. The war continued, the great Medal of Honor action already receding into history, the danger of catching a bullet with one's name on it as imminent as ever.

By now the whole German line in the Colmar Pocket was crumbling. The village of Holtzwihr fell on January 27, and the Americans rushed forward to put maximum pressure on the now retreating Germans. Audie's much-depleted company received replacements, men returning pale and shaken from the hospitals and rookies who,

he wrote, were "more peevish and defiant." Instead of a pep talk—
he said he was "fresh out of pep"—he had some advice: "This
company specializes in killing; and we haven't got time to take care
of a bunch of wounded krauts. If they want to give up, take them.
If they don't, kill them. As far as I'm concerned, you're all able
men until you prove yourself otherwise."

As company commander, Audie had no time for the individual
now; each man was "only a fighting unit." Audie followed a hard,
practical code best described by a British officer, speaking of his
experience in northwest Europe: "There's only one way to fight it,
strength; you must be strong with yourself, with your men, with
everything; never weaken; never show that you're afraid. Everybody
cracks up in the end of course, but you hope something will have
happened by then." Audie had every kind of problem to deal with—
frozen feet, shattered nerves, wounded men—and he made his decisions practically, militarily. And there were banal problems that
had their comic sides, as when a replacement with a case of the crabs
presented himself to Audie and asked what he should do. Audie's
advice: find some gasoline to douse them with, or pull your pants
down and freeze them.

At the Colmar Canal, between the Rhine and the town of Colmar,
Audie's battalion, ordered to bypass the town and head south to seal
off German supply roads, moved out at night, eating cold, slimy
rations on their feet, a "phantom body of troops doing a forced
march through hell." Men complained, vomited, bitched, and endured. The canal crossing was surprisingly easy, and for the next
two days the 1st Battalion moved fast, speed being crucial, sleep a
luxury they couldn't afford. The temperature had warmed a bit,
causing the snow to melt into viscous mud, and the troops were
forever hopelessly muddy. There was no point in trying to keep out
of it; they lived in mud, they didn't even need camouflage now.
Only by their helmets could they be distinguished from the Germans.

Then, near the town of Urschenheim one night, as they settled
in for a rest, they received orders to capture a bridge on the Rhône-
Rhine Canal, at Kunheim. Audie protested. He was certain that the
Germans, having pulled out of Urschenheim, would shell the area
where his battalion was or the town when they drew near—the
Germans nearly always did that—but orders were orders, and they
had to be followed. As they began to regroup for the march, the
shells came all right, and eight men were knocked out. One of

Audie's regulars, a brave man, went to pieces; he could not take it any more. Sent back to the medics, he returned the next day only to fall to pieces again in the next artillery barrage. His war was over. Audie felt keen sympathy for this courageous man's plight. It could happen to anybody.

Audie's unit had another close call during the advance toward Kunheim. They captured a group of exhausted German soldiers and were resting on the ground together when suddenly three German tanks accompanied by foot soldiers rumbled into view, not thirty yards away. Covered with mud, Audie and the others quickly clapped German helmets on their heads and stood breathless as the enemy passed without ever realizing they were Americans. The ruse worked perfectly.

Racing to the bridge they had been ordered to blow up, they got there just in time to see the last German tank cross and to watch the bridge, blown by the Germans, collapse.

The danger now was in penetrating too far too fast, allowing the Germans to encircle a unit in a deadly ambush. This happened to some units of the 7th Infantry Regiment, and Audie worried about a similar fate befalling his company. He and the 15th Regiment crossed another canal, the Rhône-Rhine, on February 2, marched into Kunheim, and then onward to Biesheim. The towns seemed endless in number, but each one brought them closer to the final, ultimate town that lay somewhere in Germany. The only German resistance left in Biesheim was near a Jewish cemetery. The 15th slipped into the graveyard at night, laughed at the irony of the "graveyard company" finding a perfect place for billet and ambush, and, knocking chinks in the walls, put their machine guns in place. The next dawn gave them a gift, twenty German soldiers in a slit trench, right in their machine-gun sights and unaware of the Americans in the graveyard. When the machine gun opened up, six Germans fell and the rest surrendered. "Just like something from the books," said one of Audie's men.

There were other grim sights that actually cheered the American soldiers. Albert Pyle could never forget seeing three truckloads of dead Germans, "their bodies . . . frozen, entangled among each other like so many frozen, dead chickens in packing cases." The GIs were amused at the frozen lumps rising and settling back at each bump of the road. Every German in that state, remembered Pyle, meant one less soldier to have to defeat.

Colmar surrendered on February 7, by which time most of the German forces west of the Rhine were finished. Two letters of Audie's dated on that day indicated some leisure at last from the constant fighting. In a letter to Mom Cawthon, he mentioned that "we have been awful busy," as though a description of work conceived in civilian terms could begin to comprehend the fury and destruction of the Colmar Pocket action; and in another, to his sister, he said, "it sure has been rough going in the snow." He also told his sister about the last slight wound and that besides a Purple Heart and Cluster, there "might be another medal for you soon."

For several days, from February 10 to the 18th, the 3rd Division enjoyed a lull in the fighting. Training programs and a chance to rest were sweetened by visits to Paris, where Audie went at least twice during this period. He bought perfume for his sister Corinne there. He seemed to like Paris much better than he had Rome. Also during this period, on February 16, he was promoted to first lieutenant.

Following this respite, the 3rd Division was pulled back to rest areas near Nancy, in Lorraine. Here there were more opportunities for rest and recreation, but by the end of the month new training was begun, and it didn't take a genius to figure out what the new objectives would be. Training exercises stressed town fighting and river crossings, many of them conducted at night. They were getting ready for "the big jump-off into Germany itself," Audie knew.

Now that the end of the war was truly in sight and not just a vague hope, everybody began to think even more about home and a new optimism pervaded the soldiers. But there was also a new fear: to be so close and not survive. John Guest wrote eloquently of those closing months: "How I want the war to end—the danger now begins to frighten me. To die at this stage—with the door at the end of the passage, the door into the rose garden, already in sight, ajar— would be awful." Audie didn't dare look forward with too much hope. He said he had "seen too much to grow optimistic." He believed in luck and knew he'd had more than his share of it. His luck could run out any time, and the next bullet might have his name on it. He resolved to "go on living from day to day, making no postwar plans." His battalion commander during the Colmar action assessed Audie's nature in similar terms. Colonel Kenneth B. Potter remembers that Audie possessed "an almost fatalistic view of life and combat." The war made him a man, Potter believes, but a particular kind of man, moody, morose, given to brooding over lost friends, a man who often would say, "The only real heroes are the dead ones."

At Nancy, on March 5, Audie received two medals for past glories: the Distinguished Service Cross for action at Ramatuelle in August 1944 and the Silver Star for his exploits at Cleurie Quarry in September 1944. That same day he wrote his sister a jaunty letter. He mentioned three triumphs: one, he was sending Poland, his brother-in-law, a Kraut rifle he'd taken from a sniper; two, he mentioned the two medals just awarded and the one to come, the "Cong. medal of honor." "Boy if I get that I will soon be comeing home," he said, meaning that each medal amounted to five points toward achieving the number required to be sent home. He said once, years later, that "the only thing they [medals] ever meant to me during the war was another five points toward coming home." The third triumph was hinted at in a P.S.: "the women over here are wearing the same thing in Brassiers this year. Believe it or not."

Training finished, the 3rd Division headed for the Franco-German border to take part in a direct assault on the Siegfried Line, the West Wall of Germany's defense. Audie's 15th Infantry Regiment was positioned near the town of Bining on March 12–13, but Audie wasn't with them. He had been assigned as liaison officer with the 15th, an assignment designed to keep him out of combat. Audie, one of his officers has recalled, received this assignment "much to his disappointment." The Army's reasoning was simple: it didn't want a dead Congressional Medal of Honor winner on its hands. That had happened before, and awards of the nation's highest honor to live soldiers were much preferable to posthumous ones.

Audie's job as liaison officer seems to have left him with plenty of time for the kind of free-lance operations he liked. Assigned a Jeep, a driver, and an interpreter, and serving as "contact man between the units of the division," he was now exempted from the "constant peril of the front lines." But knowing how lines could shift suddenly, he characteristically armed himself to the teeth. Besides the mounted .50-caliber machine gun on the Jeep, Audie added "a few rifles, two German machine guns, and a case of grenades."

There is a marvelous example of Audie's soldierly mettle recorded in *To Hell and Back*. In mid-March, at headquarters, he spotted a message that troubled him greatly. His former captain of B Company, plus the senior lieutenant, had been killed and the company was pinned down and left in the command of a green second lieutenant. Violating regulations, Audie placed loyalty to his company above rules, and rushed to the spot on the map on the Siegfried Line where B Company was stalled. He left his driver behind and walked in plain sight, carrying only a carbine, to the place where the company lay exhausted and demoralized. Paralyzed, they had taken a severe "psychological beating" and believed that the pillboxes in front of them swarmed with Germans. Audie believed otherwise and, alternately cajoling and berating them, he got the company onto its feet and led them through the Siegfried Line without a shot being fired.

On another occasion in Germany, Audie did something that was not recorded in *To Hell and Back*. He told this story years later, long after the war was over: "Once, on a patrol in Germany, I was able to sneak up on a German unit without being noticed. A hand grenade could have wiped out the lot of them. But I crept away without doing them any harm. They looked too much like our side—gabbing, horsing around, eating their rations peacefully." Audie went on to ponder that action. He wondered if his "turning chicken" might have resulted in those soldiers later killing some of his own buddies. But he believed that that "kind of reneging" must have gone on on both sides during the closing days of the war.

By mid-March the 15th Infantry Regiment, along with other units of the 3rd Division, was storming through Germany. Audie joked about the Army's progress in a letter to his sister on March 20: "As you see in the paper we are thru the Siegfried line now, soon the only line the Germans will have left is the Line of S——T which they have been shooting the population with for some time now, ha. ha." "We are moving so fast lately that I don't hardly have time to stop for chow," he told her in a second letter on April 2. A kind of cocksure tone informed another letter he wrote during this period. He listed his medals, including the Medal of Honor which he was waiting to receive "so i can come home." He also mentioned the Legion of Merit, to be awarded by the French government, and joked, "since that is all the Medals they have to offer i'll take it easy for a while, ha, ha."

Home was home, but this was Germany and the Germans hadn't laid down their arms yet. Hardened by the war, the Americans took nothing for granted when it came to Germans. When a house failed to show signs of surrender, Audie wrote: "We do not knock on the door and say, 'Please.' We simply rip its windows with machine-gun fire to point out the oversight. The method is most effective.'' The towns fell like ripe fruit into the hands of the advancing Army, and Germans surrendered in mass lots. Audie seems to have savored the surrender of German towns. By chance a young military historian named Martin Blumenson, regarded today as one of the leading military historians in the nation, happened to spend a day in the company of Audie Murphy in April. Blumenson had been sent to find a lieutenant who had vanished. It turned out the lieutenant was with Audie, and Blumenson was asked to join them as they searched for an American airplane that had been shot down. Blumenson, of course, knew who Audie was; he was already famous. Together, the team liberated several German towns that day. White sheets flapped from the windows, and the burgermeisters collected all the weapons, many of them ancient muskets, and turned them over to Audie and the lieutenant. On one road, a German farmer warned them of a German machine-gun nest ahead, and without any panic or haste Audie simply ordered the Jeep turned around, and they went back without incident. Blumenson was impressed and in awe of "this very self-possessed young man," who was "never flustered" and always "very calm."

On one foray into a German town, Audie's Jeep had outrun the forward thrust of the 3rd Division, and he and his driver suddenly found themselves in a town square swarming with armed German soldiers taking a break. Instead of turning quickly and trying to race out of town as the driver wanted to do, Audie and another passenger, a captain, decided to bluff their way through. Keeping their hands close to their weapons, ready to blast away if discovered, they drove through the square, waving confidently and creating the impression they were part of an advance guard of a large Allied force nearby. They escaped without a shot being fired.

To the Germans, April and May were the cruelest months. Nürnberg, a Nazi stronghold, fell to elements of three American divisions, including the 15th Infantry, on April 20, Hitler's birthday. In seven weeks, from March 15 to May 4, the 15th Infantry captured ten thousand POWs in combat and approximately two hundred fifty German towns and villages.

The last town that the 3rd Division captured was Salzburg, on May 4, and it was there that Audie's last encounter with the Nazis occurred. He was walking along the street with a second lieutenant when the lieutenant spotted a German colonel who was still wearing a pistol. The lieutenant politely said, "Please, sir, may I have your side arms?"

Audie intervened. "Don't say *please* to this sonofabitch. Tell him to *give* you his goddamned gun."

Audie thought he recognized the officer as Lieutenant Colonel Otto Skorzeny, one of the most feared of Himmler's Waffen SS, Hitler's favorite Aryan, the man who'd pulled off the nearly impossible mission of rescuing Mussolini from imprisonment in September 1943. The U.S. Army had been alerted to be on the lookout for this extremely dangerous man. The German officer, who proved not to be Skorzeny, turned over his gun—a good thing for him because Audie was quite ready, he said later, to kill the SOB.

Between May 2 and May 9, all the Germans left in the field surrendered. The war in Europe was at last truly over. May 8 was declared VE-Day. According to his account in *To Hell and Back*, Audie heard the news on a train he was taking to the French Riviera. Years later, though, he recalled hearing the news in Lyons. That version contains a very moving account of his reaction: "Then one night in Lyons people were chanting and shouting that the war in Europe was over. I could feel the blood drain out. My blood pressure went way down and stayed there, and I've been tired ever since." In any event he did go to the French Riviera for R and R. After soaking in a hot bath, he went to sleep and when he awoke, he could hear an orchestra playing "Lili Marlene." Looking through his suitcase he came across his service revolver and found solace in its satisfying, tactile *there*ness: "It works with buttered smoothness. I weigh the weapon in my hand and admire the cold, blue glint of its steel. It is more beautiful than a flower; more faithful than most friends." This passage from *To Hell and Back* contains the essential postwar Audie Murphy, the hero for whom there might be, as Audie wrote, "VE-Day without, but no peace within." Guns were to remain a central prop in the internal theater of his psyche.

He relaxed on the Riviera, but "like a horror film run backwards, images of the war flicker through my brain," he wrote in *To Hell and Back*. Those images would not go away. Although damped down by time and other problems in the years to come, they never left him, not entirely and not for good.

Lonely, he called the hospital at Aix-en-Provence and asked Carolyn Price, the nurse he'd met in October of '44, to come down and visit him. He sounded "lonely, bored, and unhappy" over the phone, but it was impossible for her to get leave at that time. Then one day she was returning to her ward when somebody said there was a young officer with a chestful of medals waiting to see her. It was Audie. His fame was growing, and later at the officers' mess where he and Carolyn had dinner, doctors came by to congratulate him. He seemed both embarrassed and pleased. Carolyn wrote their mutual friend, Perry Pitt, now recuperating back home, filling him in on news about Audie. She told Pitt that Audie looked "great" but limped worse than he did after the first wound. She also said he had so many ribbons his chest resembled General Marshall's, but that he still refused to wear them all. Finally, she said how much she wished he'd accept a discharge: "He's dreadfully tired, but determined to see this thing through to the end—his or the war's. His luck has been remarkable but he can't hold out much longer." Dated May 21, well after VE-Day, Carolyn was referring to the war in the Pacific, which was still raging. This visit was the last she saw of him till they met stateside in November of that year. By then much had happened in Audie's life, and the celebrity that he'd first gotten a taste of at Aix-en-Provence would still be new, exhilarating, and troublesome.

On May 20, Audie resumed command of Company B, 1st Battalion, 15th Infantry Regiment, then bivouacked near Werfen, a small town south of Salzburg. On May 24 came the official announcement that he had won the Congressional Medal of Honor. Four hundred and thirty-three men received that honor in World War II, and thirty-nine of them were members of the 3rd Division, a remarkable 11.6 percent of the total. Audie's own regiment had fourteen medalists. Perhaps the explanation for the 3rd's record might lie in the words of German Field Marshal Albert Kesselring, who commanded crack German divisions against the 3rd in North Africa, Sicily, Italy, and southern France. According to Kesselring, the 3rd Division was "the best division we faced and never gave us a rest." Besides being the most highly decorated division of the war, the 3rd also paid a heavy price in the loss of combatants. Over 34,000 soldiers of the 3rd Division were casualties, more than in any other U.S. infantry division that faced the Germans and nearly two and a half times its authorized size. Of the original 235-man roster of Company B, by the end only two remained, Audie and a supply sergeant. All the rest had been wounded or killed; only a few had been transferred.

The award was made at an airfield near Salzburg on the sunny afternoon of June 2, less than a month shy of Audie's twenty-first birthday. Nine U.S. senators were on hand to witness the ceremony and shake the hands of the honored soldiers. There is a piece of grainy film that has survived from that day. In it an incredibly young-looking Audie Murphy stands with tears in his eyes, receiving the highest military honor his nation could bestow. Lieutenant General Alexander Patch, who presented the award, asked Audie if he was nervous. He said, "Yes, sir, I'm afraid I am." Audie received a second medal that day, the Legion of Merit, an honorific award intended to recognize "any member of the Armed Forces of the United States . . . who has distinguished himself by outstandingly meritorious conduct in the performance of outstanding services." It edged him ahead of the legendary Maurice Britt, an Army captain from the 3rd Division who had received a number of awards for valor, including the Medal of Honor, and who had garnered a lot of attention from the press. Now Audie became the most decorated soldier in American history. That day on June 2 he had received or was authorized to receive a total of twenty-nine medals. In the end, after the awarding of several postwar medals, the grand total stood at thirty-seven. Eleven of them were for valor.

There was never anything cheap or diluted about the combat medals Audie won, yet to many soldiers there was something unsettling about the awarding of medals. There were many reasons to be cynical about such awards. Harold Bond has explained one widely held view: "All of us knew what they were for. They encourage a man to risk his neck another time and make others want to do the same, and wars are won by men who risk their necks." A commander in North Africa stopped recommending his men for decorations because too often the wrong men got the medals while the real heroes did not. It was bad for morale. Further, the whole process could be very capricious. In the Normandy landings, a staff sergeant named Harrison Summers accounted for more than one hundred Germans and was almost singlehandedly responsible for the success at Utah Beach, yet because of a clerical error he did not receive the Congressional Medal of Honor. S. L. A. Marshall, who reported this incident, felt that in all wars, "Homeric happenings go unreported. Sometimes the bravest meet death with their deeds known only to heaven."

Audie always felt a certain ambivalence about his medals. With the grim humor typical of his war memoirs, everybody who died, he said, was awarded a Wooden Cross. To a historian to whom he wrote after the war, he said, "Certainly there have been cases where people received medals when they did not deserve them. However, like everything else in wartime, this situation has always seemed rather a mass of confusion anyway." Audie often insisted that his medals really belonged to his unit, not to him. He told an interviewer once: "I feel as if they handed their decorations to me and said: 'Here, Murph, hold these!' " And a few years later: "They [the medals] belong to the unit. I just own a part."

His best-known statement on how he felt about his medals appeared in a magazine article written for Memorial Day, 1955. Ten years after the war, he explained why he felt like giving away his medals right after the war. He said, among other things, "War is a nasty business, to be avoided if possible, and to be gotten over with as soon as possible. It's not the sort of job that deserves medals." But did he actually give away his medals? Apparently he did give some to children such as his nephew. But those close to him looked after his war record and his medals even if he did not. Spec McClure kept copies of the written citations. Pam, his second wife, had the medals mounted in a display case for their sons. In one sense Audie couldn't really give away the medals; they were his for life, part of the historical record. Audie Murphy, the most decorated hero, was a tag line he could never escape.

By war's end the personal death toll wrought by Audie mounted to approximately 240, an incredible count for a foot soldier slogging through mud, rain, and snow, surviving snipers, machine-gun nests, and artillery fire. By contrast, World War I's greatest American hero, Sergeant Alvin York, was credited with 25 dead and 132 captured in his legendary action against the Germans on the Western Front on October 8, 1918.

Like Audie, York, a Tennessee hillbilly, came from humble circumstances, learned to shoot well at an early age, and knew terrain and the psychology of hunting. Indeed, when York fired at the Germans from cover, he thought of them as turkeys, as sport: it was a way of distancing the act of killing other humans. And when he remembered their reactions to being shot, he said, "All the Boches who were hit squealed just like pigs." In becoming a great soldier York had to overcome scruples, though, that Audie never did. A deeply religious man at the time he was drafted, York first declared himself a conscientious objector, but gradually came to believe in the necessity of taking up arms against the Huns. His fundamentalist Christianity gave him a bedrock of certitude during and after the war, and, like many soldiers who held strong religious beliefs, he was able to put the war behind him quickly and go on with his life. It was probably easier for York than for Audie because York's war was so brief. He was only in combat for a few days and performed his heroic feats in a single day. Audie fought for over two years and his heroism was tested again and again.

Like Audie, too, Sergeant York received national adulation. Though there was no shortage of American military heroes on the Western Front, soldiers who had performed deeds as spectacular as those of York, it was York who best fit the national ideal. A story by George Pattullo in the *Saturday Evening Post*, April 26, 1919, painted him in the broad strokes of a national hero. Entitled "The Second Elder Gives Battle," it cast the shy, lanky, ill-educated Tennessee farm boy in the mold of a legendary frontiersman, a Western gunfighter paradoxically imbued with strong religious convictions, a mountaineer individualist who outdueled a German machine gun. The composite stereotype evoked a deep nostalgic image of rural Protestant America.

Returning to America in May 1919, York was given, much to his dismay, a ticker-tape parade through the streets of New York. Subsequent public appearances confirmed the symbolic role he was being asked to play out in the national psyche. Cheering crowds saw in him several mythic attributes: he stood for pioneer America in the midst of an industrialized twentieth century; he was a citizen-soldier, the latest such hero in a long-standing tradition suspicious of professional military men; and he was a symbol of the triumph of the individual over the machine (gun). Like Charles Lindbergh in the next decade, Sergeant York captured the national imagination because he seemed to represent certain cherished notions deeply embedded in America's self-conception.

So, too, did Audie Murphy.

4.
SOLDIER'S HOME

"Krebs acquired the nausea in regard to experience that
is the result of untruth or exaggeration. . . ."
—*Ernest Hemingway, "Soldier's Home"*

With four years of bloody European fighting at last concluded, Hitler dead, Germany crushed, and American troops beginning to come home, the country was eager to celebrate victory. Although war still raged in the South Pacific and on Okinawa, the killing went on at a rate that forecast a grim prospect for the still-to-come invasion of Japan; the United States was primed for peace, ready for returning victors to kiss the girls and start forgetting the days of slaughter and death. It was a time for heroes, and in Audie Murphy America found the hero it needed.

At the awards ceremony in Salzburg, Audie learned that he had the choice of remaining in Europe with garrison troops or returning to Texas. He chose to come home. He told the press he wanted to sneak in the back door "because I don't go for this hero stuff," but that was exactly what awaited him. He left Salzburg on June 10, flew to Paris, then to Presque Isle, Maine, then to Houston, and finally, on June 13, arrived in San Antonio, site of the Alamo and the military heart of the Southwest.

For some reason Audie wasn't even on the official passenger list of the C-54 Loadmasters. The center of attention was the brass, and there was plenty of that on hand: thirteen generals, including Lucian Truscott, who had commanded the Third Army in Sicily and Italy in which Audie had served. There were also forty-five other officers and enlisted men fresh from the battlefields of Europe. But it was Audie who emerged as the celebrity of the hour. Of them all, only Audie would seize the imagination of the crowds and the press. Nobody could resist his shy, boyish good looks. He simply "stole the show," wrote one reporter.

In the reception line at the airport Audie appeared to incredulous reporters like a mascot or an Eagle scout. He was so shy he didn't give his name to anybody in the line. Asked if he'd pose for a picture with General Ira Eaker, a fellow Texan, Audie replied, "I sure wouldn't want to ask the general to pose for any picture with me." The general jumped at the opportunity. Audie saluted him sharply, the general pumped his hand, and the picture appeared the next day in papers around the state.

After the military entourage left the airport, they were treated to a full day of pomp, parades, and public acclaim. Two hundred and fifty thousand people lined the streets as Audie and the others rode past in flower-laden open command cars. The street parade was followed by a gondola parade down the winding San Antonio River in the heart of the city, a press conference, a reception, and a banquet. Tired to the point of exhaustion, independent as ever, Audie ducked out on the rest of the festivities. He skipped the gondola ride and the banquet that night.

Missing the banquet created more drama than if he had attended, because that was the first time he was identified as the soldier who'd won "every medal in the book." The audience and press were naturally intrigued with the idea of a soldier who had won not just the Medal of Honor but all the medals. The toastmaster said he had a special surprise announcement to make, but when he made it, he looked around and there was no Audie Murphy present to receive the applause. The next day reporters tracked him to his hotel room at the St. Anthony. The official story was that he'd been exhausted and fallen asleep. What really happened, he later told Spec McClure, was that he invited an elevator operator to his room, seduced her, had a steak dinner, and went to sleep.

Audie's disappearing act beguiled the reporters. He was great copy. In his hotel room the next day Audie yielded to entreaties to tell something of his exploits. But he was reluctant to talk much about actual combat experiences. When a woman reporter asked him to recount "every detail about how you won the Congressional Medal of Honor," Audie drew a laugh when he said, "Oh, no, not that." He insisted, "There wasn't much to it."

Finally, after much persuasion, he produced copies of his citations for reporters to read. He also talked briefly about his war experiences, reducing the Medal of Honor action to the briefest of sketches, and concluding with a remark about how gratifying it was to see the Germans surrendering en masse, defeated and bedraggled.

He was scheduled to fly to Dallas, courtesy of the Dallas *Morning News*, but he made private arrangements with A.P. reporter William Barnard. They left early the next day, at six. The drive from San Antonio to North Texas gave Audie a chance to relax, and the landscape unrolling before his eyes prompted him to talk about war and peace.

Gazing at the tranquil Texas countryside, green and golden in the June sunlight, dotted with cattle and rows of young corn, Audie thought of peace now instead of combat: "This is what I came home to see. You can't realize how swell this is until you've been away. Here I am riding along a highway—but I'm not watching every bit of the way for mines. Up there is a bridge, but I'm not sticking my head out of the window to make sure it hasn't been blown—I'm sure it hasn't."

He went on: "All this makes me feel fine. Over there it was a helluva thing. I don't like to talk about it, but I'm telling you it was a helluva thing. It wasn't bad for me in Africa, but in Sicily and Italy and France it was bad." Because all good reporters of the time had cut their teeth on Hemingway, Barnard's version of Audie Murphy talking has an unmistakable Hemingwayesque sound to it.

Given Audie's customary unwillingness to talk about the war with the curious or even with close friends, this outpouring of thoughts on the highway to Dallas seems surprising. In any case the discourse reveals very clearly how Audie Murphy could be used to express symbolic functions in the social arena. Through Audie, Barnard was telling Texans and Americans what they wanted to hear:

the war was over, the soldiers were back, and they were ready to resume their civilian life. They were the same as before they had left for Europe. They, and we, could go on with the business of living; there wasn't a thing to worry about.

After San Antonio, wherever Audie went and whatever he did that summer, was news. The press had found, wrote reporter Bishop Clements, its "most unique and yet typical American youngster," and Audie Murphy, modest hero, poor boy made good, rags-to-glory soldier, was being transformed from an anonymity to an icon through word and photographic image, a familiar process in American popular culture.

The press in Dallas was interested in everything Audie did. As a returning veteran, he found the home front to have its own mystifications, and the press in turn found his reactions amusing and consoling. One headline read HOME FRONT IS TOUGHER THAN WAR. Such a notion was, of course, simply ludicrous. When Audie went shopping in Dallas, the press was there to report his reactions to the effects of the war on the home front—rationing, for one. He was unable to buy a new pair of shoes because he didn't have a shoe stamp; then he discovered that gasoline coupons were more valuable than money; then he wasn't able to buy a can of meat because he lacked something called "red points" and had to settle for a can of chicken à la king, the contents of which he proceeded to spill on his pants, causing him to blush and remark, "If it takes points for pants, I'm a gone goose." Such stories normalized the returning warrior by subjecting him to the requirements of a routinized, bureaucratic home front.

Since early in June Farmersville had been priming itself for Audie's visit. Transparent boosterism led the town to appropriate the burgeoning Audie Murphy legend. It was only by accident that Farmersville had been identified with Audie in the first place. On a service form he listed the address of his closest kin, Corinne Burns, his favorite older sister, as Farmersville, which is where she lived. But he had never lived there, and the town held some bitter memories. That was where his mother had died. Also, it wasn't even in Audie's home county. Kingston, the little community closest to the starve-out farm where Audie was born, wasn't big enough to hold a celebration. Celeste, where he had lived for several years and gone to grade school, didn't seize the day. Greenville, the county seat and perhaps the most logical choice, wasn't as aggressive as smaller

Farmersville, a town with a mayor appropriately named R. B. Beaver.

Mayor Beaver saw in Audie Murphy a chance to put Farmersville on the map. He vowed, "We'll nab him sooner or later and he'll get what's coming to him." His eagerness knew no bounds. Citing Audie's heroics and medals, the mayor said, "He'll just have to count on making a few sacrifices when he gets home." Audie himself resisted the notion. "Shucks," he asked reporters in San Antonio when they informed him about Farmersville's plans, "what do they want to do that for?" Then he added, "I'm scared to death of that reception at Farmersville." He said he didn't see any reason why there should be a parade for him; he just wanted to go home quietly. The press loved this, the idea of an American boy who'd killed hundreds of Krauts being scared of a ceremony in his honor.

In McKinney, the county seat of Collin County, sixteen miles west of Farmersville, a caravan of local dignitaries met Audie and escorted him to Farmersville. In town the first thing he did was go to his sister Corinne's house, termed a "white cottage" in the quaint imagery of the news stories, actually a small frame house on the edge of town with a little patch of Bermuda grass in the front yard.

Corinne, her husband Poland Burns, and their small son greeted Audie out front, in the yard. "Well, how's everything?" somebody asked. The usual diffident quality of the reunion of a rural Protestant family not given to much expression of emotions was intensified by the glare of publicity. Reporters were on hand to gather impressions of the homecoming. Audie, freckle-faced, lips already sunburning, face set in a kind of tense way, seemed exactly the same as ever to his sister.

"He hasn't changed a bit—not a bit. I was afraid he would change but he hasn't. All that has happened hasn't done a thing to him. I can see he's the same," said Corinne. In her determination to find Audie unchanged, she was no different from anybody else on the home front in 1945. One of Audie's aunts said the same thing, in anticipation of his return: "All this won't have changed him any. He won't feel that he's done much—that's because he's had a hard life—nothing has ever been handed that boy. He's had to work for what he got."

It was important for the aunt to believe this and for Corinne to confirm it when she saw Audie; it was important for everybody to feel this way. What Americans wanted to think about their returning soldiers was simple. It was what Audie Murphy was meant to represent in the public sphere: he was Huck Finn come home from the war, the barefoot boy with cheeks of tan, everybody's little brother who had been away to face the great death and returned unscathed.

There were of course a few ironies. In a true sense, in the nightmare sense of Mark Twain's greatest book, Audie *was* Huck Finn, a boy with a searing past, a derelict father adrift somewhere in Texas, a mother too early dead, a family splintered and scattered. There wasn't any family home for Audie to come back to. His three younger siblings, who arrived at Corinne's house within a short time while Audie and the others were still visiting outside in the yard, were brought over from the Boles Orphan Home, south of Greenville, to see their famous big brother. Joe Preston, ten, came, and two sisters, Nadine, thirteen, and Billie, eleven. Nadine, looking pretty in a flowered print dress, told Audie he had done "awfully well," and he was astonished at how she'd grown up so much in the past three years. She looked like a young woman now. Billie was proud of her brother, and Joe seemed to be in awe of the whole event; he didn't say a word.

Soon more relatives arrived and now there were too many people to crowd into the little house, so they all went downtown to the Coffee Shop Café where Audie ordered fried chicken. Asked about the upcoming celebration scheduled for the next day, Audie said, "I'm as shaky as Hirohito's dreams." The newspapers loved that kind of line. In fact they probably made it up.

The next afternoon, under a broiling sun, a packed audience of five thousand farm folk and local merchants stood on the roped-off square for an hour and a half to listen to speeches and see the boy who was putting Farmersville on the map. Many of the farmers were clad in overalls, their wives in simple cotton dresses. Children played underfoot and people leaned out of upstairs windows of two-story storefronts and some found perches on the baking roofs overlooking the spanking new grandstand. Everybody cheered for Audie Murphy. They couldn't resist his scared look, his freckles, his complete ordinariness. He was one of them.

The program began with a concert by the band from the Ashburn General Hospital in McKinney. After that there were prayers, a welcome by the mayor, a rendition of "America the Beautiful" by a local girl, a speech, a reading of Audie's battle citations, and another speech, this one by the local banker who presented Audie with $1,725 worth of war bonds raised by local citizens. Then Audie was called upon to speak. He knew he would be. He told a friend before the program started that he'd rather be slapped in the face than have to say something. But the mayor demanded it; the audience of well-wishers and citizens demanded it. He rose, nervously it seemed to onlooking reporters, and delivered a few brief remarks. They were perfectly appropriate and completely in character:

"About the best way I can express gratitude is not to say too much. I know you people don't want to stand in this hot sun any longer and just look at me. What I want to say is that you can all be proud of your sons and sweethearts who fought over there. I have seen them all and I know they're doing a wonderful job for you." The last thing Audie wanted to sound like was a long-winded politician. His style, brief, self-effacing, laconic, was the style of the common people of that time and place.

The program ended with the assembled throng singing "America" and everybody went home. But the day belonged to Audie. His triumph was complete, and a Dallas newspaper headlined its story with military imagery, FARMERSVILLE SURRENDERS UNCONDITIONALLY TO MURPHY.

Farmersville had its day in the sun, but the mayor's belief that the town would somehow permanently benefit from its association with the war hero is not apparent today. The dusty little square surrounded by one- and two-story buildings contains an Audie Murphy Memorial Stone with a poem he wrote engraved upon it and an American flag flying from a flagpole. The population, a little over two thousand, is basically the same as it was in 1945. The Audie Murphy celebration that blazing June day—it was 98° in the shade— is still the biggest thing that ever happened in Farmersville. There is no memorial to the second most famous young man from Farmersville, who really did come from there: Charles "Tex" Watson, deranged hippie and killer in the Sharon Tate murders.

Audie stayed with his sister in Farmersville, but his days were pretty busy. Always restless, he kept on the move. One day he dropped by the local drugstore and received a cordial greeting.

"Now make yourself at home in the store, Audie, whenever you have time to loaf," said the manager.

"Thank you, sir. The last time I tried that here I was run out." Audie's reply tapped a deep vein of resentment for the way things had been before he became a war hero, when he'd been just another poor country youth in overalls. Possessed of a fierce pride evident from his earliest contact with the world outside his family, Audie still had the raw edge of the dispossessed about him.

At his own request he paid a visit to wounded GIs recuperating at Ashburn General Hospital in McKinney. To reporters on hand, Audie seemed more relaxed among the GIs than at any time since he'd been in the spotlight. He walked among the bedridden soldiers, greeting them, lighting one soldier's cigarette in a photo opportunity for the press, and enjoying the camaraderie of men who'd been where he'd been and made sacrifices like he'd made. He drew the comparison in one remark: "I could talk to hundreds of soldiers all day long. But I just didn't know what to say to all those civilians." Nobody could understand combat except those who'd been there.

Audie told the wounded GIs he'd be back and he'd bring his girlfriend with him. The girlfriend was Mary Lee, a pretty brunette from Floyd, a tiny community between Farmersville and Greenville. Floyd had a schoolhouse where Audie had attended the fifth grade, the last year of his formal schooling. Mary Lee, a coed at East Texas State College, had figured in several remarks made by Audie since his arrival in Texas. The press was delighted because part of the all-American package that they saw in Audie was the obligatory girlfriend. There is one photograph of her that appeared in newspapers and in the famous article in *Life* the following month. She's wearing a very short skirt and high heels to show off some good gams in the best Betty Grable manner, and she's "chatting" with Audie as he pauses to lean on a lawn mower. In this photo Audie looks no older than twelve, and he's just barely bigger than the lawn mower. This photo and her status as his girlfriend both appear to have been completely phony. In any case Mary Lee quickly disappeared from Audie's life after the first media blitz.

He was in Dallas on his twenty-first birthday, June 20, and it was quite a day. He visited an aunt and his four nieces, one of whom, Elizabeth Lingo, would later go to Hollywood and become the personal secretary of his first wife, Wanda Hendrix. Everywhere he went his growing celebrityhood followed him. "People were crazy to touch him," remembers a friend. On Main Street five giggling girls spotted him.

"Aren't you Lieutenant Murphy?" one of them asked.

"I never heard of that character," said Audie as he signed his autograph.

Another girl was completely confused. She asked, "Are you Lieutenant Murray?" He said no, and she was still confused, "Well, I thought you might be. You know Gary [sic] Grant is here today."

A third girl asked him to put down what he was "commonly called." He wrote, "A fugitive from the law of averages." Here Audie was echoing a popular GI saying, taken from one of Bill Mauldin's Willie-and-Joe cartoons. Two GIs are crouched behind a pile of rubble while tracers crisscross the space just over their heads. One says to the other, "I feel like a fugitive from th' law of averages." Anybody who survived combat felt that way.

It wasn't Cary Grant who was in town, but Gary Cooper, who had come to Dallas to promote an amiable little western entitled *Along Came Jones*. Coop was Audie's favorite movie star, and Audie, who would one day be dubbed a "pint-sized Gary Cooper," got to meet him. The first thing Audie said to him was, "I should have on stilts to talk to you."

Coop, who'd won an Academy Award for his portrayal of Sergeant Alvin York in Howard Hawks's 1941 film, asked Audie if he'd like to hear how Sergeant York captured 132 Germans. To which Audie said, "No, but I'd like to know how you went like a gobbler." He was referring, of course, to the most memorable moment in the film, when Coop/York imitates a turkey gobble to get Germans to poke their heads up from their trenches.

Another reportable incident occurred when Audie went into a military shop to buy campaign ribbons. His old ones, issued before his commission to lieutenant, were worn out. The clerk, following protocol, required identification, and Audie didn't have any. When one of Audie's friends protested and the clerk finally understood that the slight youth before him was the "Farmersville hero," the ribbons were immediately produced.

In a Command Post Exchange store, where he went to buy a shirt, clerks, onlookers, and enlisted men made such a fuss over him that he couldn't shop. Audie quipped to the crowd, "In the next war I'm sure not going to do anything."

The Lingos threw a little birthday party for him that night, highlighted by fudge cake, a favorite dessert. The next day, Audie attended a Salesmanship Club luncheon where he made a hit with some of the local movers and shakers among the Dallas establishment. Arriving late, he told them the kind of stories that newspapers loved to retell. He'd gone into a barber shop that had women barbers, he said, to get a shave, and one of them had cracked, "Are you kiddin'?" When Audie said he'd been shaving for two years, the barber was waiting with the oldest line, "Yeah, and I'll bet you cut yourself both times."

Greenville, where Audie had worked before the war and where he'd signed up for the Army, threw its own celebration for the young soldier. On June 27, "Lieutenant Murphy Day" kicked off with a police escort bringing Audie into what the newspapers called a "city"—and maybe by Hunt County standards, it was. The cavalcade rode right under the famous banner that greeted visitors coming down Lee Street

The	GREENVILLE	The
Blackest	WELCOME	Whitest
Land		People

and on to the local hotel for a Rotary Club luncheon. There Audie was persuaded, most reluctantly, to make a few remarks. The Rotary News column in the local paper gives an inside view of his public manner, in reportorial detail usually missing from front-page coverage intended to hype the young hero. According to the Rotarian account, "His remarks were few and hardly audible to the members in the rear of the room. Among other things he said that the army taught them to fight and didn't teach them to speak; so he just wasn't a speaker. But he said that he was certainly glad to get back here where the people looked natural and spoke his language; that he appreciated all that was being done for him but it was entirely too much." Inaudible though they might have been to some, his remarks drew a standing ovation.

Following the Rotary luncheon there was a thirty-minute parade along Lee Street. A military band and the Greenville High School Band and Drill Team provided the music as ten thousand bystanders looked on. Some of them were teenage girls, and they mobbed the young hero, said a headline, like bobby-soxers mobbing Frank Sinatra. They clamored for his autograph, and one girl emerged from the pack, crying, "I got it, I got it." Audie had signed his name on the flyleaf of her copy of *Forever Amber*, that year's steamy bestseller.

After the parade a formal ceremony was held at the courthouse where several prominent citizens spoke and Audie was awarded a check for $1,000. Again he was required to speak. It was the longest speech he'd given since he had started making public appearances:

Gee, it's really great to be back among real and sincere people again and today I would like to take this opportunity to pay a tribute to the Mothers and Fathers who are here. For, it is they who perhaps suffer most in time of war. Too, I would like to express my gratitude for the swell job you have done on the home front. You have given us everything we asked for in the way of tools for modern warfare. With your son's spirit, courage and determination and the mighty weapons you have given them to fight with, he has made his enemies fear and respect him. Though I need not remind you that the war is but half won, there is now no doubt in anyone's mind what the final outcome will be. I would like today to say to each of you here at home, congratulations on a job well done.

The off-the-cuff remarks at the Rotarian luncheon came from Audie's heart; but the bandstand speech was political rhetoric intended to make the home front feel good about its role in helping America win the war. Some of this language suggests that Audie had the help of a speechwriter. Melvin T. Munn, on the staff at Dallas's KRLD radio station, said he wrote a number of speeches for Audie in the late forties. In any case President Truman could hardly have done better in praising the contributions of the home front.

That night the day's patriotic theme was capped with a military show-and-tell program held at the local athletic field. "Here's Your Infantry" featured decorated combat veterans performing a variety of acts designed to impress upon the home front the skills and expertise required of our fighting men. These included assembling and disassembling firearms of every type from rifles to bazookas; the use of booby traps, mines, and demolition materials; and a demonstration of the size and composition of squads and platoons. The climax, a mock attack on a Japanese pillbox, had particularly strong impact: "The sudden realization that these men crawling along to attack a Jap pillbox are the hometown brothers, fathers and friends they knew as civilians has hit the audiences more forcibly than anything except an actual view of battle could do." All of it must have seemed incredibly unreal to Audie and the other soldiers who had faced real bullets at the front. The home front was strictly show-biz.

Audie went through such ceremonies with good grace and appealing modesty, but he was wearing a public mask. There were disclosures of other, truer feelings. In Greenville, he stopped by a grocery store where he had once worked to see an old acquaintance, Eddie Ayers. Infirm with arthritis, Eddie told Audie how proud he was of him, and Audie said, "Eddie, the real heroes are dead."

Audie's local fame had its pleasant side, too. He didn't mind the adulation of teenage girls. His former neighbor, Mrs. Cawthon, recalls an incident from that summer that attests to Audie's popularity. She has been asked about Audie Murphy so many times that her stories have the feel of formulaic recitations. This one, narrated with disarming disingenuousness, tells of an afternoon he spent at her house resting. He was very tired. (Tiredness, exhaustion, is one of the dominant notes of that summer for Murphy.) He took a nap in the bedroom at the front of the house, next to the parlor. When he woke up, he could see into the living room where girls had gathered to see the handsome young war hero and newspaper celebrity. He said, Mrs. Cawthon remembers, "Well, I must of died and gone to heaven. Look at all these pretty angels."

Audie kept getting invited to public celebrations. McKinney held a rodeo over the Fourth of July, and Audie was there all three nights to lead the formal parade into the arena. This was the first of scores of rodeos that he would be invited to in the years ahead. On July 8, the VFW inducted him into its organization with a predictable flourish of flags and publicity.

Such public events provided intervals between the real business of living. People paused in their lives to see the young hero, then returned, as they must, to the task of earning a living. Audie would have to do that, too, but in the meantime the currents of popularity carried him toward a destiny impossible to imagine for a boy from his background. Media coverage, peaking in July, would help determine the course of Audie's future.

The first attempt to convert Audie's story into drama was a radio show in Dallas. Billed as the South's largest weekly network broadcast, "Showtime" emanated from the Palace Theater in Dallas and was sponsored by Interstate Theatre, the largest motion picture chain in the state. Its July 1 edition featured an "extra special guest, Lt. Audie Murphy" and a "special Radio Drama of the Heroic Events in the Colmar Pocket." This was the first attempt to dramatize the exploits that won Audie the Medal of Honor. The producers and director wanted Audie to portray himself, but when they heard him read, decided that the words didn't sound real. "Well, he may be a hero, but the Lord knows he'll never be an actor," they concluded.

They wouldn't have got an argument from Audie on this score.

"What a sweet little guy, so shy he can hardly talk," said the other actors.

A professional impersonated Audie in a script filled with the kind of rhetoric that Audie would have found exaggerated and embarrassing. The script focused on the Medal of Honor action: "It all started back in January of this year. . . . We were taking a pretty bad going-over . . . the Krauts—that's what we called the Germans—had broken through in the Colmar Pocket. . . ." (Was there any American in 1945 who didn't know what Krauts were?) Then the drama segued into a battle scene replete with all those sounds radio was so effective at recreating: small arms fire, artillery, the rattle of machine guns. Other moments in the radio script, though, were so patently phony that it's impossible to imagine Audie saying such words. Once the shooting is over, Audie says in the script, ". . . the Krauts were dead . . . two hundred of Hitler's Supermen—just as dead, just as still as the kids from Nebraska, and Maine, and California, and yeah, the kids from Texas." Then, for the home folks, a little conventional piety: "I was an awful lucky guy, and I knew then for sure that *God was on our side*!" The war scenes end with Audie saying now it's time to drive the Hun back across the Rhine into the "filth and blood and chaos" that was the Third Reich.

The show ended with a flight of cheesy populist rhetoric: "For this is a nation where a bunch of shoe clerks, and farmers, and insurance salesmen, and college boys . . . and, well, Americans . . . can get together in a fighting team that utterly crushes a nation whose men are trained warriors from infancy." The democratic myth, America's army of civilians, was perfectly embodied in the Murphy story. The patriotic orgy ended with a bit of transparent flag-waving: "I'm just a twenty-one-year-old country kid . . . but I've seen American boys . . . *your* boys . . . get their insides blown out to keep that flag wavin'. . . . Please, God . . . keep it wavin' an awful long time."

Following the Frank Capra–Norman Rockwell America envisioned by the script, the real Audie Murphy answered a few questions from the MC.

Since one of "Showtime"'s main purposes was to advertise movies for the theatrical chain that sponsored the radio program, it didn't hurt to have America's most decorated soldier putting in a pitch for a movie, a mixture of patriotism and advertising that was a constant theme in the many attempts that were made to capitalize on Audie's fame. The movie being touted couldn't have been more appropriate. *The Story of G.I. Joe*, the best war film of the era, offered a gritty, realistic, and yet poetic look at combat drawn from Ernie Pyle's Pulitzer Prize-winning war reportage. It starred Burgess Meredith as Pyle and Robert Mitchum as an Army officer, Captain Henry T. Waskow. The movie traced the campaign of American soldiers from Tunisia through Sicily and Italy, a recreation that Audie must have found chillingly familiar. Certainly the scene in which Captain Waskow is brought down by mule from a mountain, dead, would have seemed real enough. James Agee, the best American film critic of the era, called it "a great film."

"Showtime" had a regional audience, and the Murphy story had built-in appeal in the South. But it would also play on the national level, as other media were about to demonstrate. Besides the intensive newspaper coverage that Audie's presence continued to generate, there was also the first journalistic effort to tell Audie's story in narrative form. That month a series of first-person accounts entitled "A Hero Tells His Story" appeared in newspapers around the nation. Actually written by William Barnard, the A.P. reporter with whom Audie had driven to Dallas from San Antonio at the beginning of his Texas homecoming, these pieces, signed "Audie L. Murphy," recounted the principal actions Audie fought in, and told for the first time of such famous episodes as the incident in which he fired at his reflection in a mirror. They also mentioned in detail Audie's citations for valor, something that he later scrupulously avoided in his book-length memoir.

But it was a cover photograph in *Life* magazine for July 16, 1945, that lifted Audie to the level of national hero and set into motion events that would shape the rest of his days.

In the age of television it's difficult for today's video generation to imagine the impact *Life* had on American culture. *Life* created an iconographic America of great potency and imaginative power. In its day there was simply nothing that came close to matching the magazine's ability to define the national psyche. Just as Vietnam was fought on television, so World War II was fought in the pages of *Life*. The most famous pictures of the war appeared in *Life*: that's

how you knew they were famous. They were also great documentary
art: the raising of the flag at Iwo Jima (a staged photo, it turned out,
but a great one); the piles of heaped skeletal remains of Jews murdered in the concentration camps of Nazi Germany. These images,
and thousands more, filled the pages of *Life*. As the war wound
down in the summer of 1945, *Life* quite naturally turned to the
postwar era.

Heroes are usually sorted out once a war is over, and if the war
is unpopular, like Vietnam, no heroes emerge at all. Sergeant York's
valorous action occurred in October 1918, near the war's end, and
he came to the fore in the spring of 1919, after the war was over.
So, too, Audie's most famous action occurred near the end, and the
awarding of the Medal of Honor took place, of course, after the war
in Europe was over. It was perfect timing. Audie Murphy came
home to America at the exact and propitious moment for being
turned into a celebrity. The case of the second most decorated hero
in World War II illustrates an alternative scenario.

For a time in 1944–45, it looked as though the most celebrated
soldier of the war might be Maurice "Footsie" Britt of Arkansas.
Like Murphy, Britt won a pile of medals, including every significant
military honor the United States could award. Like Murphy too, he
was a Southern farm boy and belonged to the 3rd Infantry Division,
though not to the same battalion as Murphy. Britt, a big man at
6′ 3″, 205 pounds, performed heroically in North Africa, Sicily, and
Italy. Later, when Audie began to win medals, the 3rd Division
newspaper reported their successes like a sports story, as though
Audie were in a contest with Britt: MURPHY CROWDS BRITT'S RE-
CORD, and, later, MURPHY EQUALS BRITT'S RECORD OF EVERY
MEDAL. Previously wounded three times, Britt received his last
wound at Anzio, a wound that, he says today, "boogered me up
pretty bad." His right arm had to be amputated.

The wound ended his combat duty, and because he was on a
hospital ship headed back to America, he missed attending a joint
British-U.S. medal-awarding ceremony planned in England just
before D-Day, to build up troop morale. So Britt came back to the
United States a year before the war was over and received his Medal
of Honor at the University of Arkansas football stadium in Fayette-
ville, scene of his collegiate heroics in the late 1930s. His wound
also ended a promising career as a professional football player with
the Detroit Lions, where he had played his rookie year in 1941,
finishing the season just two days before Pearl Harbor.

Had the war ended earlier, had Audie Murphy been killed in action, had any number of things happened, Maurice Britt might have wound up with the honor and public recognition of being America's most decorated war hero. Instead, Britt returned to his home state and went about building for himself a very successful postwar life seemingly unaffected by the trauma of combat. He was too busy making a living and raising a family, he says, to have had time to think much about the war.

Looking back today from a distinguished career of public service in Arkansas—he was the state's first Republican attorney general since Reconstruction—a father of five and grandfather of ten children, Britt remembers that "a lot of young men had trouble adjusting." The mystery is why some did and some didn't. Heroes like Ira Hayes, the Indian Medal of Honor winner who became an alcoholic, experienced postwar difficulties while other heroes did not. Audie's fame helped Britt because after Audie returned and became the media's darling, "the media left me alone." Early on, Britt discovered the burden of being a Medal of Honor holder. He realized that people put him on a "pedestal" and that he had to "be careful about [his] behavior." On balance, he believes that the medal spurred him on. Audie, however, "probably received too much early adulation," although he "coped fairly well."

When Britt was elected to the post of attorney general, in 1966, he received a telegram of congratulations from Audie that asked, "Isn't there anything you can't do?"

It was a nice gesture, and Britt cabled back, "I ain't no movie star yet."

It is arguable, of course, that Maurice Britt could ever have made the cover of Life. Though Britt's background provided the stuff of a very marketable image—early poverty in the Depression South, college, a distinguished athletic career—it is hard to believe that Life would have wanted to portray a man permanently and visibly scarred by battle, a man with a missing right arm.

Life—and America—preferred a more benign image of the war hero. Audie Murphy, no matter what demons might lurk below the surface, was ad-man perfect. Publicly, the baby face was an ideal mask. The freckles and sunny smile could fool anybody if you saw him only in photographs, not up close where the face more often than not revealed a certain tautness, a flickering tension that expressed itself in every part of his being, a terrible restlessness and nervousness and, sometimes, an absent-spiritedness as though he weren't really there but somewhere else, in a darker, bloodier place where men were dying.

What *Life* did was to turn one fierce, complicated, and tormented ex-farm boy into a symbol of normality, visually consolidating the set of meanings that had begun to cluster around the young lieutenant in the stories churned out by both the wire press and local newspaper writers who had been covering his return home. To Lois Sager, who wrote several pieces about Audie, he was "the nicest boy you ever saw." Another reporter spoke for all: "So that is what Murphy is like—a swell kid, absolutely modest and sincere and genuine and unaltered by terrible experiences." That last phrase—*unaltered by terrible experiences*—was the key: that's what Audie Murphy was intended to represent in his incarnations as the nation's darling young soldier-hero.

This "Most Decorated Soldier," as the caption announced, stared straight into the camera, teeth even and white in a friendly smile, chest adorned with three bars of medals. He symbolized the American GI who had endured combat and returned home un-scathed by it all. The country needed to believe that our boys could be sent into violent encounters with death, dispatched from the safe haven of American homes and farms and small towns and cities into the bloody, war-ravaged, ancient cesspools of human iniquity in Europe, be trained and praised for the act of killing, and return unaffected by it all, remaining psychologically innocent. So it was terribly important that these returning veterans be perceived as still our boys, untouched, unchanged, the nightmare behind them. They could resume their lives just as the American people could resume theirs; though, in truth, to many returning soldiers the "Good War" hadn't exacted very much from the American public—a little ra-tioning, some inconveniences, but nothing remotely similar to what it had exacted from the boys who didn't come back and from those who did.

So there he was, Audie Murphy, the all-American boy. What a wholesome kid! So completely different from the other kid who became an American pop hero in the mid-forties, Frank Sinatra. By 1945, with his surly bad manners and celebrity disdain for everything outside the orbit of his own desires, Swoonatra had begun to stir up a lot of negative feelings. Sinatra troubled many adults because of how teenage girls went crazy when he sang to them, crying and carrying on like bacchanalian nymphs. ("Teenage," by the way, was a new term first used in 1945.) And his disdain for USO shows made him very unpopular with troops in Europe. Audie, on the other hand, was a legitimate hero, no pop star who threatened public morals.

The story of Audie's life—from son of a sharecropper to war hero—spoke not to some disturbing new present but to a past that possessed cherished values. He harked back both to America's agrarian tradition and to its recovery from the troubled dislocations of the 1930s. The success of Audie Murphy symbolically redeemed America from the Depression. The photograph of the anonymous Marines lifting in poetic unison the flag on Iwo Jima has been read as the final flowering of the collectivist vision of the New Deal, a group of anonymous men unified in a common purpose to restore the nation's glory, the arching flag. Audie Murphy's smiling farmboy visage restored the individual to the center of attention; it represented a movement away from the collectivism of the thirties and the highly organized military bureaucracy of the war years toward a new evocation of the Sergeant York icon: the single individual who, like Davy Crockett, keeps on a'comin' and who makes a fundamental difference in the course of a nation's destiny. *Life* was therefore visually authenticating what the reams of newsprint were saying about Audie: the Depression had prepared him for the war, made him lean, hungry, and determined, made him strong.

The *Life* cover also gave us the war hero as boy-next-door. The accompanying photographs and text place Audie Murphy in a familiar world of small-town Americana. In one he is leaning on a sign that says "Farmersville City Limit—Population 2206." Other photographs show him having a soda at the local drugstore, chatting with a lady to whom he used to deliver newspapers, blowing out the candles on a birthday cake with his sister and her family, and talking with Mary Lee, the "Girl Friend." The captions underline his shyness: he "usually blushes when he gets within ten feet of any girl." Two larger photographs are particularly striking. In one he displays to his oldest orphaned sister, Nadine, a rifle with a telescopic sight and bayonet that he took from a German sniper whom he "dropped . . . with one bullet between the eyes." Here the instrument of war, taken from the dreaded Kraut, becomes a souvenir and is domesticated within the boundaries of an ordinary American home.

The second photograph is a minor classic. Norman Rockwell

might have painted it. Audie is in a barber's chair getting his hair cut by a woman barber. He looks about twelve, as he often does in these homecoming photographs. Observing from outside, through the barber-shop window, is a crowd of men dressed in khaki work clothes, some wearing suspenders and hats and caps. In their solemn seriousness they might be mistaken for a chorus from some thirties agitprop play about the working classes. They stand gazing at the incredibly youthful boy-hero, formerly one of them, now elevated to national glory.

The Audie Murphy cover heralded the beginning of the new era. Though plans for the invasion of Japan were well developed, the mood in America, in *Life,* was one of expectancy and relief. *Life*'s editorial in the issue in which Audie's story appeared trumpeted the certainty that the country felt: Japan's "complete defeat is as absolutely inevitable as anything in human history." Early that morning of July 16, the confirmation of *Life*'s optimism was previewed: at dawn in the desert near Los Alamos a bright flash made a second dawn—the first atomic bomb exploding. In less than a month mushroom clouds would bloom over Hiroshima and Nagasaki.

Those close to Audie, family members and friends who saw him away from the flashbulbs and note-taking reporters, glimpsed another side of him that the public, enchanted by his seeming normality, did not. They saw signs of stress, tension, nervousness. In borrowed cars Audie burned up those country roads. He drove too fast. An older brother remembered Audie roaring eighty miles an hour down a white-rock road and dipping down into a ditch at one point to avoid a collision with an approaching car. Corinne remembered him firing a gun at a glass window in a gas station that was closed. He laughed and told her he didn't know it was loaded.

Visiting in Dallas at his cousins', Audie gave further hints of a psyche troubled by combat experiences. He had difficulty sleeping, and one night his cousin Elizabeth Lingo heard him "shouting out the names of the men in his company." Sometimes late at night he prowled the streets of Dallas, with Elizabeth following at a safe distance. She says, "Audie would probably have killed me if he had known that I was following him. But I was afraid he would fall and couldn't get up."

Corinne knew about his nightmares, too. One morning he told

her, "Sis, I didn't sleep a minute last night, I fought the damned war all night long." Another time, deep in sleep, she woke to find all the lights in the house on. Audie had turned them on to keep from falling asleep and having those bad dreams.

There were also instances of flashback behavior of the kind common among soldiers still jittery from combat. His old friends the Haney Lees thought he was extremely nervous and remembered that he "kept drinking 'green colored' medicine out of a small bottle." One time at their house when they were all listening to the Victrola, the needle made a high screechy sound and Audie jumped over the back of the divan in a swift, unconscious move—just like in a Willie-and-Joe cartoon where one of them zips up a zipper and the other dives for cover.

Corinne's husband, Poland Burns, remembered two telling incidents from this period.

Once at table, right in the middle of a meal, Audie was putting some black-eyed peas on his plate and as he went to get another spoonful he froze. He seemed like he was in a stupor, Poland remembered. Poland asked him if it had something to do with the war and Audie shrugged it off with a laugh. After some prodding, he told them what had happened. Once on patrol behind German lines Audie and a small band of soldiers ran straight into a German trap. Cut off from their company, he and his men managed to keep from being overrun for several days until they could break through the circle and return to Company B. Audie shot the head of one German nearly off, and in another instance—the crucial one that now triggered his memory—he shot a German in the head during a night fire fight. At daybreak the next morning he saw the German's brains spilled out on the ground. He told Poland, "When I saw that spoonful of black-eyed peas, it suddenly reminded me of that dead soldier's brains and I wanted none of them."

Another time Poland witnessed a flashback episode characteristic of what is now known as post-combat stress syndrome. One day Audie wanted to check out a new gun that Poland had acquired, so they drove over to a recently built tank (Texan for a small pond) near Floyd. Audie, carrying the rifle, was walking along the edge of the 10–12-foot-high dirt embankment when he slipped on a rock. Like a cat he caught his balance, left hand steadying his body, the right holding the gun in position to fire. Again he froze. Poland figured correctly that this was another war memory. Again Audie laughed to cover it up, but he went on to tell the story. One time, he remembered, he was walking along a creek bottom that was wet and slippery. He lost his footing and looked up to see a German soldier ramming a shell home. Audie swung his carbine up, one-handed, and shot the German between the eyes.

Public acclaim and private trauma—such were the days and nights of Audie Murphy that summer of '45. It was one thing to be called "Blood and Guts, Jr.," as his buddies in Company B dubbed him, but it was another to try to get over the war by himself. He was so tough, so seemingly well adjusted, so normal that the Army neglected to put him through any kind of routine psychological debriefing process. Years later he would criticize in public the way the Army dealt with the problem of releasing soldiers straight from the killing fields into the bloodstream of civilian life. Fifteen years after the war was over, he said: "They took Army dogs and reha-bilitated them for civilian life. But they turned soldiers into civilians immediately and let 'em sink or swim." He kept coming back to the high and permanent costs of war. "War robs you mentally and physically," he said in 1962. "It drains you. Things don't thrill you anymore. It's a struggle every day to find something interesting to do." Asked in 1970 if anybody ever gets over a war, Audie said, "I don't think they ever do."

5.
A BEACHHEAD IN
BEVERLY HILLS

"Last year it was kill Japs, and this year it's make money."
—*The Best Years of Our Lives*

hen the *Enola Gay* dropped its payload on Hiroshima on August 8, 1945, the war was truly over. Six days later the Japanese surrendered. The homecoming for Audie was over, too. Now it was time to decide what to do, how to construct a life in postwar America. If Audie was worried, he wasn't alone. The whole country was deeply concerned about the problem of returning veterans. Women's magazines displayed a keen anxiety. The *Ladies' Home Journal* asked the crucial question: "Has Your Husband Come Home to the Right Woman?" *Good Housekeeping* advised families to give a returning soldier two or three weeks to get over talking and "oppressive remembering," and then, if these symptoms persisted, send him to a psychiatrist. *Recreation* chirpily held that "Convalescing Can Be Fun." Hardly any potential problem was overlooked. In *Sex Problems of the Returned Veteran,* a popular book of 1946, Dr. Howard Kitching warned women, "It is impossible to tell men to go and kill an enemy and risk their lives in doing it, and expect them at the same time to be honest, chaste, kind and unselfish all the time." *House Beautiful* placed its faith in the "home . . . the greatest rehabilitation center of them all!"

Anxiety about the future seems to have been particularly acute among GIs who'd served in rifle companies. The problem, according to Harold P. Leinbaugh and John D. Campbell, was lack of training for the arts of peace: "A lot of men in the Army learned a trade, becoming pilots, skilled mechanics, medical orderlies, supply experts, and administrators; but when a rifleman left the service his skills were difficult to transfer to civilian life. We joked we were going to become hit men for the mob, but we actually considered the matter a serious handicap for the future." Or, as Audie once told a friend, "After being in the front lines, you're living like a wolf—kill or be killed—and pretty soon the sixth sense comes upon you, and the reality—this is all you know. All of a sudden they hand you a paper and say the war's over, now you're discharged; what do you do?"

Yet the fears of most Americans, both civilians and soldiers, turned out to be groundless. Home-front worries about veterans evaporated in the midst of nearly full postwar employment and the benefits provided by the GI Bill. Most soldiers, a 1949 study showed, were guided by "an individualistic motivation to get back on the same civilian paths from which the war was a detour." And most returned home with neither bitterness nor an agenda for social action. Statistics bear out the restorative power of normality. Most men put the war behind them and went on with their lives. By 1947, 85 percent of veterans had returned to live in their home state; and 72 percent of those between the ages of eighteen and twenty-four lived in their home county. The vast majority had roots, family and community ties, that helped anchor them. A study in 1951 showed that there was "remarkably little difference in the adjustment of veterans and nonveterans four years after the close of the war." Historian William L. O'Neill concluded that "of all the surprising developments in the postwar years, the easy accommodation of this mass of men was perhaps the most astonishing."

Again, Audie Murphy was different. After the war he never again lived in his home county or state. And nobody who knew him felt that he ever became fully adjusted.

Audie spent much of the summer pondering his immediate future. In San Antonio in June he had told the press, "I want to finish my education. I want to take up mathematics and history. I want to go into the radio business." Finishing his education sounds like the idea of a high school graduate or someone whose college career was interrupted by the war. But Audie's "education" consisted of five grades (usually reported as eight in press releases) and school had been interrupted by the exigencies of survival long before the war. The remark about the radio business sounds like a response to a back-page ad in a magazine: "Learn radio repair in thirty days and pave the way to a life-long career." He also entertained the idea of attending Texas A&M and studying veterinary medicine or attending a business college. The one thing he never considered doing was resuming his prewar occupation of farmhand. Cotton fields and tenant farming held no allure for him.

Continuing in the Army in some capacity appears to have had its appeal. He seems to have seriously considered trying to enter West Point in order to secure the training he would need to achieve a distinguished postwar career in the military. Senior officers still in Europe were encouraging, but as General Hallett D. Edson wrote him from Germany in August, he'd have to "study like [he'd] never studied before." In the end he chose not to try for West Point. Those who knew him well felt that he would never have been able to focus his restive attention and energies enough to meet the demanding academic standards.

He knew what he didn't want to do—he didn't want to be a public hero and live off of fame generated by his exploits in the war. In a market economy the only thing Audie had of value was his fame, and he was very worried about that; he didn't want to betray all the soldiers living or dead who'd fought beside him in Europe. But there were those who saw in Audie exactly such opportunities. He later spoke bitterly of efforts to exploit his fame during this period: "At home, some wanted to hire me because I was a famous killer, others wouldn't for the same reason. I couldn't get a job that left me any self-respect."

Where he went, most improbably, was to Hollywood, land of manufactured illusions. From that time on, California became his home, deny it as much as he might to himself or to friends in Texas who felt he really belonged back there among people he knew. Like many other Depression-tossed and war-buffeted Americans, Audie found work, marriage(s), and success in California. He also found darkness, danger, and nightmare, qualities he carried within himself and would have had to face wherever he laid his troubled head.

The story of how he made his way to Hollywood is a complicated one. Chiefly it was through the combined efforts of new friends in Texas and a soon-to-be friend on the West Coast, James Cagney. Audie's appearance on the radio program "Showtime" brought him into contact with local newspaper people and with executives of the Interstate Theatre chain, an organization that managed 170 movie houses in Texas. Felix McKnight, an editorial writer for the Dallas *Morning News,* introduced Audie to James "Skipper" Cherry, an executive for Interstate, who immediately took the hero under his wing. Said Cherry, "We all fell in love with him. He was such a wonderful kid we thought he'd be a natural in Hollywood." Cherry became Audie's mentor and remained thereafter his counselor and adviser—Audie named his second son after him. It was Cherry who introduced Audie to Paul Short, former manager of the Majestic Theater in Dallas turned independent producer and an invaluable link in Audie's eventual rise to leading-man status.

According to McKnight, the boy the Interstate executives adopted was a "very reticent, freckled, skinny, shy sort of a kid" with no polish at all, a country boy with a thick Texas drawl. He was "genuine" and "real" but utterly lacking in any degree of sophistication.

The Interstate Theatre executives weren't the only ones who saw something in Audie that they believed could be translated into a film career. The *Life* cover was working its magic. Several talent scouts approached Audie with offers of screen tests. Another group wanted to make a biopic of Audie's life. He ignored all of these feelers. But the Interstate people were more persuasive; they had good contacts in the film industry in California. R. J. "Bob" O'Donnell, co-owner of the theater chain, knew James Cagney. So did Raymond Willie, Cherry's boss.

According to Audie, not long after *Life* hit the stands, Cagney wired him an invitation to come to Hollywood. "At that time, I wasn't interested at all. In fact, I was on a fishing trip and ignored his wire, I'm afraid. He kept wiring and calling and finally called Mr. O'Donnell and asked him to send me out." James Cagney had formed an independent production company with his brother William, and they were on the lookout for new talent. From his photographs and his fame Audie seemed a real prospect for the struggling company. Also there was obviously some sympathy of one short Irishman for another. Audie talked the matter over with O'Donnell and Willie. Finally he decided to accept Cagney's offer to visit.

He had still to be discharged from the Army, and on August

17, the day before his official leave was up, he began the necessary paperwork. On August 22 he received a terminal thirty-day leave, and on September 21 he went on inactive reserve.

But the decision to go to California was not made without misgivings. On September 18, at an "Audie Murphy Day" celebration in Corsicana, a little town south of Dallas, Audie gave a rather dark interview to a local newspaper reporter. According to the reporter, Audie said he was considering reentering the Army about Christmastime if he wasn't "better able to better adjust himself to civilian life by then." He also said about his impending trip to California, which was scheduled for just two days later, "And I'm not very happy about going to Hollywood, either."

So why did he go? Money was why he went and why he stayed. He said so many times—"I did like the idea of maybe making some money in movies." He also went because it sounded interesting; there might be a kick or two out there on the coast: "People don't realize that after you've come out of a war nothing gives you much of a thrill. I wasn't especially excited about coming to Hollywood; I was simply interested in seeing it."

The young hero who met James Cagney at the L.A. Airport was hardly anything like what the home folks or the American public saw in the newspaper and *Life* photos. Cagney was very surprised: "When I met him at the plane, I got the shock of my life. Audie was very thin. His complexion was a bluish-gray. He walked with a 'hayshaker' stride" (i.e., like a farmhand, a rube, swinging from side to side). Although Cagney had reserved a hotel room for Audie, now, upon seeing him, he felt he was in "such a nervous condition that I was afraid he might jump out of a window. I took him home and gave him my bed."

Cagney's shocked awareness of Audie's true condition was sharply at odds with all the glowing reports coming out of the press back in Texas and the assurances from his sister and Hunt County neighbors that Audie was totally unaffected by the war. Perhaps his physical condition had something to do with his family's perception. He now weighed 138 pounds, 26 more than when he'd gone into the Army, and he was around 5' 7", two inches taller. But an observant stranger like Cagney was closer to the mark. What he saw was a young man strung wire-tight. Exhausted after more than two years of combat, pursued by the demons of battle and the newer ones of publicity, Audie needed rest more than anything else.

He stayed in a small guesthouse at Cagney's rural retreat on

Coldwater Canyon in Beverly Hills, a tree-covered hillside estate with an oval racetrack, a New England–style home, and a feeling of remote farmland. At that time Beverly Hills was one of the loveliest places in America, and Cagney's estate offered a truly idyllic site to rest.

On this first visit Audie took it easy for about three weeks and got to know the Cagneys. They weren't the only ones in the film capital who were interested in his potential. He had several offers, all of which he turned down, he said in a 1948 interview: "I had all kinds of offers. Someone wanted to work with me on my book and to give him a percentage. I had offers for bit parts and walk-ons in pictures, but they were mostly publicity gimmicks and I didn't take them." He delayed making a decision until he returned to Texas; then he made it fast and telegrammed Cagney his acceptance. He would earn $150 a week and take acting lessons. The Cagneys in turn would try to secure roles for him in their own productions or farm him out to other film projects.

When Audie returned to Hollywood, Cagney held a press conference in his knotty-pine den. Audie was there dressed in civvies— a white shirt, gray plaid trousers, and an expensive red tie. He was nervous and when the reporters asked how he would like a career in the movies, he began, "Aww . . ."

Cagney did most of the talking while Audie drummed his fingers nervously. Cagney explained why he had brought the young war hero to Hollywood: "I saw Audie's picture on the cover of *Life* magazine and said to myself, 'There is the typical American soldier.' " He turned Audie's shyness into a plus: "Anybody who has Audie's kind of reticence is lucky. God knows there's all too little of it. It's so much more valuable than that positiveness in young people that only gets in their way in trying to learn something." Cagney also said he saw a special quality in Audie that the motion picture business had need of: "There is assurance and poise without aggressiveness—a good, healthy point of view. Call it a spiritual overtone. There is something that could be used in our business; there is acting ability." In another, later interview, Cagney cited a further quality absolutely necessary to even begin to think about a career in motion pictures: "I saw that Audie could be photographed well from any angle, and I figured that a guy with drive enough to take him that far in the war had drive enough to become a star."

The most striking observation in all of Cagney's remarks is surely the one about Audie's "spiritual overtone." Others would see in his screen image similar qualities. But if that was the case, why was he to be cast in so many films that brought out the opposite quality—quiet deadliness? Because both qualities were there, making Audie Murphy on screen both an image of innocence and its opposite, the capacity to kill. The mystery of Audie Murphy, on screen and off, was how such seeming innocence could be at the same time so deadly.

Audie always appreciated the older star's generous support. In a 1946 interview he said that what convinced him to have a go at acting, more than anything else, was "Jimmy. He's so darn sincere and nice. It made sort of good sense, the way he put it up to me. He said if it didn't work out, he wanted to send me to agricultural college."

Audie returned to Texas for the Thanksgiving holidays that year, 1945, and one of the people he saw was Carolyn Price, the nurse from Aix-en-Provence days. He'd kept in touch with her, and now she was in San Antonio for processing and reassignment. Carolyn thought he seemed a bit ill at ease in civilian clothes, and he certainly hadn't yet adjusted to his fame. He called the airport to make reservations, she remembers, and the plane was booked solid. But when the agent learned his name, things changed: "Of course, a seat will be made available, Mr. Murphy." Carolyn found him the same "humorous, charming, unpretentious, rather tense, extremely likable Murph of pre-fame days." They talked about his future, and he explained the one reason he'd accepted the invitation to go to Hollywood. "I need the money."

So Audie and Carolyn once again went their separate ways, she to Fort Knox, Kentucky, to continue her tour as an Army nurse, he to romantic Hollywood where, she imagined, he was living an exciting, glamorous life. Then one midnight he called her, lonely and depressed, and asked her to come to California. But she was still in the service and couldn't leave. Eventually they lost contact altogether.

In 1946, the year Audie set out in earnest to become an actor, Hollywood reached the zenith of its power and popularity. Although momentous changes lay in store, things could not have looked better for the motion picture industry that year. Attendance was the highest in the history of the movies: the average weekly audience hit 90 million, and the take was $1.692 billion in movie admissions.

But 1946, as it turned out, was no harbinger of better things to come. On the contrary, the industry faced many problems in the late forties. A Supreme Court anti-trust ruling forced studios to relinquish their theater chains, a source of great profit and stability for two decades. New films from postwar Europe like *Open City* challenged studio hegemony. Industrywide hysteria generated by anti-Communist hearings conducted by both state and federal congressional committees cut into the industry's artistic talent and confidence. And of course there was television—the severest threat of all.

Just a year after the record-setting pace of 1946, the studio oligarchy was beginning to show signs of decline. In 1947 Louis B. Mayer reduced his MGM studio staff by 25 percent. The craft unions saw employment fall from 22,100 in 1946 to 13,500 in 1949. Profits in 1948 were down to $55 million compared with $120 million in 1946. By 1950 audience attendance had dropped an alarming 25 percent. Every area of the industry was affected, but actors were hit hardest of all. There were 742 under contract in 1947; by 1956, that number had fallen to 229.

So in this roller-coasterish, volatile world of filmmaking, during a period of transition and decline that marked the end of the classic Hollywood studio era, Audie Murphy, an indisputable hero in reality, set out to make a living for himself in a profession where illusion was the natural order of things. No wonder he had problems. Far greater actors such as Montgomery Clift, who came on the scene the same year Audie did, in 1948, had plenty of difficulty coping with Hollywood. Said a press agent who knew Clift well: "The minute you refuse to play the game in Hollywood exactly as they want it, and that means totally giving up your body and your soul and your guts to becoming a *star,* you become an outsider. The minute you have integrity, which is what Monty had—you are an outsider."

But Audie was different from most actors. He had already *done* something notable, and he had never imagined being an actor. Unlike, say, another figure of the 1940s, Ronald Reagan. In a compelling analysis of Reagan's persona, Robert Dallek labels Reagan an idol of consumption as contrasted with an idol of production. An idol of production is a hero who has accomplished something. Inner-directed, aggressive, and driven, such a figure lives *in* the world, *in* history, and carries out great projects—whether winning a war, building a financial empire, or writing a great book. Audie Murphy was an idol of production, the instrument of American will in the war against the Germans; his production was the taking of ground, the killing of Germans.

The idol of consumption is different: he doesn't *do* anything; he is a celebrity. His status as idol derives from fantasy, not reality. In short, Ronald Reagan.

In Audie Murphy's case the transformation from idol of production to idol of consumption was costly, if not deadly. The process begun by the *Life* cover and perpetuated in his film career created, over the years, the only Audie Murphy that was left: an idol of consumption who, toward the end, had limited market value at minor racetracks, golf tournaments, and civic parades. In modern America everybody who is famous becomes an idol of consumption; in Audie Murphy's life we see the process starkly revealed.

The contract with the Cagneys depended upon Audie taking acting lessons. He received some instruction from the great Cagney himself. Working on an outdoor wooden platform on Cagney's estate, they concentrated on dancing, voice projection, and judo. The instruction in judo was intended to teach him how to carry himself better. Audie needed to improve his carriage and learn how to "handle his meat," Cagney's theater jargon for an actor's limbs. Cagney's own dance teacher, Johnny Boyle, the guy who'd helped him with the spectacular dance scenes in *Yankee Doodle Dandy*, also gave Audie some lessons in dancing. Cagney recalled how those lessons went: "We tried to work with Audie. Tried to teach him how to dance. I showed him the waltz clog, and you should have seen him. You wouldn't believe it. He had a real hayshaker walk, you know, so when I showed him the waltz clog his feet went flying. It was really something."

Audie's tutelage with Cagney continued into the spring of 1946. Cagney gave him two pieces of advice he never forgot: "When you say something, mean it!" and, "Don't ever know where the camera is." In a letter to the Cawthons, Audie spoke with pride of his work and his friendship with Cagney: "I am fine and working everyday: the work is easy it consists mostly of reading and learning to speak lines correctly. I go almost everywhere with Jimmy and we have a lot of fun. I like him fine."

At some point Cagney urged Audie to enroll in the Actors Lab, which he eventually did in May of 1946. A notable force in Los

Angeles, the Actors Lab was founded in 1941 as part professional training school and part theater. Over the years many famous actors attended its classes and directed or acted in plays, among them Lloyd Bridges, Dorothy Dandridge, Marilyn Monroe, Shelley Winters, and Anthony Quinn.

The Lab held its classes in a long low wooden building behind Schwab's, the legendary drugstore on Sunset Boulevard. It had a very serious theatrical agenda. It introduced the Stanislavsky method to Hollywood and fostered theater of a high quality. The Lab's sense of social commitment, always strong, may have been intensified that year by the large number of veterans among its new enrollees. Seventy-one of the one hundred twenty students enrolled that spring were veterans. GIs attending on the GI Bill provided one of the main sources of income for the Lab immediately after the war. Tuition was only $50 for the six-month course.

The Actors Lab had leftist political leanings, nothing very startling except that in Hollywood, in that period, anything that smacked of liberalism was suspect. Petitions for this and that were circulated, and everybody talked the liberal line. Not surprisingly, the Lab came under attack from the mid-forties on. In 1945, a trade magazine carried an article claiming that the Lab was "dominated by people who are red as a burlesque queen's garters." Then, in 1948, it came under severe attack from the right. California State Senator Jack Tenney took as his inspiration the sensational success of J. Parnell Thomas's chairmanship of the Committee on Un-American Activities of the House of Representatives. HUAC, it will be recalled, subpoenaed representatives of the motion picture industry in October 1947, interrogated them, and eventually cited ten of nineteen "unfriendly witnesses" for contempt. The "Hollywood Ten," as they came to be known, were subsequently sent to prison.

Spurred on by such hysteria, Tenney's California Senate Fact Finding Committee on Un-American Activities interrogated four members of the Lab's executive board. The committee report, issued in 1948, defined the Lab's purpose as being to "draw ambitious young actors and actresses into the orbit of Communist front organizations." There was no evidence to support such claims, only the usual techniques of loose inferences and innuendos. Typical was Tenney's stupid discovery that the Lab had "produced two plays by a Russian named Anton Chekhov." Though no convictions resulted, Tenney's attack hurt the Lab badly. By late 1948 attendance had fallen off, private students had begun to drop courses, and Lab personnel who had testified before the committee were blacklisted.

Although his letters show that Audie attended Lab classes at least from May through August, he later told friend and gossip columnist Hedda Hopper that he only went to acting school for two weeks and decided to quit because he didn't want to attend their Thursday night meetings to talk politics. He told her that "even though the school was subsidized by the Government, there were a lot of leftists and Commie lovers in it." He said, "the school seemed to be more interested in my political convictions than in my prospects of becoming an actor." He also told his friend Spec McClure, "I went there to try to learn to act and not to sign petitions."

He was also critical of the dramatists revered by the Lab. "They'd praise Clifford Odets and run down Eugene O'Neill as a writer. When I asked how they could get Government funds to run a school like this—I was told the Boss in the Veterans Administration was a Commie." Many years later, in 1962, he summed up his cold warrior view of the Lab experience: "At the acting school I was an ignorant country boy but even I could see they were teaching Communism and not acting. They did all Russian plays, for example, but they were finally exposed." In point of fact, the Lab's "Russian" plays during the summer of '46 when Audie was enrolled were home-grown American plays: Clifford Odets's *Awake and Sing* (June 24) and Arthur Laurents's *Home of the Brave* (August 13). Both were timely: the Odets play featured John Garfield as an embittered ex-war hero and the Laurents play dramatized the plight of a traumatized combat soldier.

Audie seems to have been a complete naif in the complex alignments that defined an increasingly politicized and paranoid Hollywood in the pre-Joseph McCarthy forties. How else to explain his sometimes contradictory public stances? In August 1946, for example, he defended Ronald Reagan from an attack made upon him for his membership in the American Veterans Committee. Ronald Reagan himself did an about-face in this period, too, shifting from liberal Democrat to conservative Republican in the space of a year. In his autobiography, *Where's The Rest of Me?*, Reagan gives a wide-eyed account of how he'd been "awakened" to Communist infiltration of certain organizations that he belonged to in 1946–47, including the American Veterans Committee and the Hollywood Independent Citizens Committee of Arts, Sciences, and Professions

(HICCASP). After he began to speak out against reds and after he resigned from both organizations, his studio (Warner's) and the police were worried about threats to his safety. As a result Reagan started packing heat, things were so scary: "I mounted the holstered gun religiously every morning and took it off the last thing at night." It was against such a background that Audie signed a letter that was published in a trade magazine, along with such Hollywood heavyweights as Melvyn Douglas, William Holden, and Douglas Fairbanks, Jr. It said in part: "The attack on Ronald Reagan is an attack on all in our community who served during the war in work for which their valuable motion picture training fitted them, work which had to be done at home."

The next year, 1947, however, he sided with the liberals. On October 28, he signed an advertisement called "Hollywood Fights Back!" which appeared in the *Hollywood Reporter*, a trade paper. This document, sponsored by an organization called the Committee on the First Amendment and signed by four senators and over three hundred people from the motion picture industry, condemned the HUAC hearings as an attempt to smear the motion picture industry. HUAC, of course, considered the Committee on the First Amendment a Communist front organization. The next month, on November 26, Audie attended a large rally on behalf of screenwriters being attacked by HUAC for their leftist sympathies. Many big-time stars spoke, including Judy Garland, Edward G. Robinson, and Margaret Sullavan. Judy Garland asked a potent question: "I ask you when they put words in concentration camps, how long will it be before they put men there too?" Audie spoke briefly, and the gist of what he had to say was reported in the American Communist periodical, the *Daily Worker*. According to an article entitled "Stars Urge People to Rap Snoopers," Audie Murphy, the most decorated soldier of World War II, said that "the methods of the committee are a challenge to those liberties for which servicemen fought." These public political acts found their way into an FBI file on Audie that was maintained the rest of his life.

Sometime during the next year, Audie did a turnaround and spoke out on behalf of the very side he had been signing petitions against. At a rally of a group called the Progressive Citizens of America, his friend Hedda Hopper attacked the "communist 'cry babies' of the Screen Writers Guild" who were raising money for a defense fund on behalf of indicted film writers. Miss Hopper introduced Audie, who "commented on the attempts being made by the Communists to infiltrate veterans organizations." This item too was clipped and placed in his FBI file. As Audie said later, "I had a continual battle to stay out of the movements."

During this period the Hollywood community was far more interested in him as a symbol than an actor. Dore Schary, the number-two man at MGM and a well-known liberal, tried to recruit Audie to run for Congress. At a meeting at Schary's home he assured Audie that he could be elected. Audie looked around the room at the people and said, "Hell, I can't even make a living. Why would I want to run for Congress?" That ended the discussion. He left after five minutes.

From 1948 on, when he endorsed conservative hero General Douglas MacArthur for President, Audie remained a conservative cold warrior, and his somewhat inaccurate statements about the Actors Lab reflect the kind of political certitude that comes with hindsight.

Politics aside, the Lab had much to teach Audie, and it taught him some of the skills he needed by helping along his transformation from awkward farm boy to potential professional actor. He showed considerable savvy at the beginning by signing up under the name of "Bill" Murphy to avoid any recognition of his war record. As Bill Murphy he took lessons in speech, voice, acting, singing, walking, and fencing. So here was the most decorated soldier, a seasoned executioner skilled in the most up to date methods of twentieth century mayhem, learning to slash about with that ancient, honorable weapon, the sword. Jan Gulick, an expert in swordsmanship, was his fencing instructor, and Margaret P. MacLean taught him how to improve his diction. The textbook in the course was *Good American Speech*, and MacLean's job must have been challenging. She said that Audie's "precious Texas accent will be good to draw upon for character parts in the future, but it is not standard speech for stage and screen."

He showed considerable improvement in his speaking style. Although many listeners felt Audie never lost the soft hint of a Texas inflection, others thought he eventually erased the Texas sound in his speech. A Hollywood writer in 1951 pronounced him "highly articulate," with "no trace of the sharecropping farmer in his speech." People back in Texas were astonished at the change they heard. Felix McKnight, the newspaperman who remembered Audie as a pure country kid in 1945, found him in the mid-1950s a "shockingly sophisticated" man, whose speech, once twangy and countrified, was now a "more sharpened, honed voice, almost a stagy voice." The Lab didn't accomplish all that, but it started Audie on the way to improved diction, and there would be more training in the years ahead. Too, Audie was very observant, and what he didn't know he often learned from watching and listening. He told Mrs. Ray Woods, wife of his car dealer friend and benefactor in Dallas, that he learned proper table etiquette by hanging back and imitating how those in the know ate. Self-educated in the true sense, Audie became, by the end of his life, "damn near cultured," said his friend and director, Budd Boetticher. He did it through acting school, acting in films, observing, and reading. What did he read? He read tons of scripts, and the novels on which scripts were based, and he read a lot about the Old West, and he read Shakespeare and novels such as *Look Homeward, Angel,* which he told an interviewer in 1948 was his favorite book.

Besides improved speech, he worked also on carriage and movement. Still, partly because of his hip wound and partly from some unique early rhythm developed, perhaps, from walking on the sod furrows of Hunt County, Audie never lost a kind of fast, forward-lurching hitch movement in his stride. Friends like stuntman Bobby Hoy could do the Murphy hitch-stride perfectly—he still can—and in some of the films, of course, you can see Audie doing it.

Teaching methods at the Lab varied widely, but in all classes the training went beyond simply learning to say lines. In Phoebe Brand's class, for example, the student had to enact everything he had done that morning when he got out of bed. He had to create the illusion of brushing his teeth and make the audience believe it. Or he had to drink an imaginary cup of coffee and convince the audience the cup was empty when the last drop had been savored. Once Audie was asked to sew up an imaginary pair of gloves.

In the classes filled with returning GIs the soldiers presented a potential problem. Lab teachers were particularly aware of the possible dangers in the use of affective memory, a key technique in the Stanislavsky method. This technique asked the actor to draw upon a similar event from his own life. The strangulation scene in *Othello,* for example, would require the actor playing Othello to reach back into his own past and recreate an instance when he felt a rage murderous enough to strangle someone to death. Teachers, well aware of yellow journalism news stories about soldiers running amok, were loath to place soldiers and themselves in psychologically dangerous terrain. So Audie was not going to receive any psychoanalytical exorcism of the past in that setting.

It is intriguing to imagine how the Lab might have changed Audie in other ways. The case of another veteran is instructive. Russell Johnson entered the Lab straight from military duty. After flying forty-five missions as bombadier-navigator in a B-25 in the South Pacific and being awarded a Purple Heart, he enrolled in the Lab in August 1945. Like Audie, he came from a poor family and experienced early disruptions, at age eight being placed along with two brothers in an orphanage when his father died. Like Audie, he came from a background, in Ashley, Pennsylvania, of nativist prejudice and working-class culture. He grew up in a world characterized, he said, by "anti-semitism, anti-negro, anti-everything but white Protestant." The Lab transformed him. He began to understand the Jewish point of view; he began to see that Negroes were human beings; he began to understand how a person, an actor, might be involved in positive ways in his society. The Lab broadened his perspective, and he came to feel that his life was permanently enriched by that training. In 1952 Johnson became the second war hero—after Audie Murphy—to sign a contract with Universal-International, and he appeared in many films thereafter, especially westerns in which he played a craven sheriff or heavy. Such expanded social and ethical perspectives as those experienced by Johnson, however, seem to have had little effect on Audie.

One of the best things that happened to Audie at the Lab was meeting a young aspiring actress by the name of Jean Peters. Bright, high-spirited, and possessed of a fine, trim figure, she was the first classy girl that Audie dated in Hollywood—or the first that he fell in love with. Jean was a college girl from Canton, Ohio, and in 1945, before coming to Hollywood, she was Miss Ohio State. Louella Parsons described her in 1947 as not "a beauty at all . . . a greenish-gray-eyed girl of 21, much like an average co-ed in appearance," and "so intelligent." Louella was wrong; Jean Peters was beautiful. Under contract to 20th Century Fox, she was being groomed for stardom. Eventually she would star in such films as *Viva Zapata,* *Apache,* and *Three Coins in the Fountain,* but she would achieve more enduring fame for her strange real-life role as the wife of Howard Hughes.

Audie and Jean, or "Pete," had a torrid affair. Audie told a close friend that he "laid" Jean nine times one night. They had a grand time of it that summer, but it all went smash when another Texan invited the couple, along with some other young people, to fly on his private plane to Catalina Island for a party. The Texan was Howard Hughes. True to form, he became infatuated with Jean Peters. He stole her away from Audie, and he did it on the one basis on which Audie could not compete: money. Big money. In 1946 Howard Hughes was one of the most glamorous and sought-after figures in Hollywood, and one of the richest. Who could resist such promises of glitter and luxury? Jean couldn't, but she liked Audie a lot and it wasn't easy to give up somebody with such driving physical hunger. She thought it would be a great idea if she remained Audie's girl, too, but he couldn't accept that condition. He liked her, but he wasn't about to share her with Hughes. Later, he said that Jean was a fine girl except for two faults: greed and ambition. Audie was very angry about the turn of events. He once told a friend just how angry, saying he'd tried to get to Howard Hughes to kill him and got past all the bodyguards save one. As with many of Audie's proclivities, his known dislike of Hughes couldn't have helped his career, either. He would never be able to work for Hughes's RKO, for example.

All through the summer and fall of 1946 Audie continued to live in the guesthouse at Cagney's estate. He had a room and a bath and the run of the kitchen. He remembered that period as a time of waiting. Cagney remembered something else. Because Audie didn't like to stay by himself, Cagney put his publicity agent and friend Charlie Leonard in the house with Audie. Leonard was a nervous guy himself, and when Audie would wake up in the night screaming, Leonard would spring up with a gun in hand. One time Audie came awake just in time to prevent Leonard from shooting him.

Audie rode horses and fished and took it easy. In November it was announced that he would appear in *The Stray Lamb*, an offbeat fantasy film about a girl, a guy, and a horse, starring Cagney and Robert Montgomery. That same month he visited New York to take part in a round of promotional activities, which included a visit to a Veterans Hospital, induction into the 3rd Division post of the American Legion, and an Audie Murphy Day at Ebbets Field. There was some irony in that last event because Audie hadn't even had the opportunity to learn to play baseball when he was a kid.

In a wide-ranging interview conducted at his hotel, Audie reflected on his past year in Hollywood and his personal situation. He explained once more his doubts about going into the acting business because of what his war buddies might think. "Look at that jerk cashing in on his war record," he imagined them saying. But their letters of encouragement had made him go ahead. He also said, when asked about girls, "I hate women." Then he laughed at how that sounded. What he meant was he was tired of insincere girls. But he also expressed a deeply skeptical view that, in the light of the rest of his life, sounds striking: "Sometimes I have very little faith in most men, and none at all in women." And he spoke of being tired of fame, tired of everything really—"One thing, when you come back from overseas, you get hardly a kick out of anything. Nothing gets me excited now. You get that way after a while in combat, taking everything that comes along. You have to." Now, in peacetime America, with everything in an uproar—he didn't specify what, but 1946 was a year of labor unrest and growing alarm about the Russian threat—he wondered "what you did all those things for."

As for the movie business, Audie found it "sort of a challenge. If I do accomplish anything with it, it would be quite a victory for me." Challenge was right. Just getting a part was a challenge. His expected first role fell through when *The Stray Lamb* was shelved because of a carpenters' strike. Labor disruptions and the opposition of Warner Brothers, Cagney's former studio, made the Cagney brothers' bold attempt to forge an independent production company tough going, as they were only able to mount three productions between 1943 and 1948. Audie also tested for another Cagney production, probably *The Time of Your Life*, an adaptation of William Saroyan's play. Although he lost the part to Richard Erdman, Cagney, who saw the two tests, "believed that Audie was the better of the two. But, being so close to him, I was in no position to argue." In any event Audie didn't feel much confidence in his future in Hollywood, if he had one. He wrote to his old friend from the hospital in Aix-en-Provence, Perry Pitt, "They're trying to teach me, but I'm afraid they don't have much to work with."

While Audie waited for something to happen in the movie business, he continued to be on the lookout for girlfriends. He wasn't able to impress every starlet, though. Some found him too shy and lacking in savoir-faire. One girl complained in a fan magazine, "Doesn't drink or smoke, you know, and won't even allow you to talk about the war." Another snickered at his social backwardness: "He doesn't even know the difference between Ciro's and Mocambo. He's a country bumpkin, a farmer."

But it wasn't long before another serious love affair developed. It began in a classic Hollywood way. Audie saw a photo of an attractive girl on the cover of a back issue of *Coronet* magazine (February 1946). Said Audie, in fan magazine lingo, "I took one look at that sweet little puss and said, 'Brother Murphy, that's it.' Then I hotfooted it over to the office of my publicity friend to ask how a guy like me could possibly meet a girl like her." Charles Leonard, the "publicity friend," arranged a small dinner party at Cagney's home late that autumn.

The girl, seventeen, was a starlet. She was a Southern girl with a Southern name: Dixie Wanda Hendrix. Born in Florida in circumstances less than elegant—her father Mack was a carpenter by trade—Dixie Wanda had played in theatrical productions in Jacksonville, where she and her family lived. When her drama coach got in touch with a Hollywood talent scout who expressed interest in her prospects, Wanda, at sixteen, moved to Hollywood with her parents and quickly began to put together a promising career in the movies. She dropped her first name and eliminated an accent so thick with Southern syrup that a movie magazine parodied her this way: "Ah know ah hev a dreadful accent, but ah'll get rid of it. Ah'm a verry detuhmined puhson." She signed first with Warners and then Paramount, finished her high school studies on the Paramount lot, and appeared in her first film, *Confidential Agent*, in 1945. Barely 5' tall, weighing not quite 90 pounds, she had dark hair, green eyes, and a porcelainlike complexion. Dressing her was "like making clothes for a doll," said a wardrobe designer. Naturally the fan mags called her a "pixie from Dixie."

When Wanda arrived for dinner, Grace Fischler, editor of *Movie Stars Parade*, introduced them. The whole thing, from magazine cover to arrangement to meeting to courtship to the end, was inextricably bound up with Hollywood culture.

A true romantic, Wanda remembered everything about that night, including what Audie wore—a blue pin-striped suit—and what they ate, roadhouse fare of hamburger steak, green beans, a mixed salad, and ice cream for dessert. Dressed in a yellow peasant skirt, a black blouse, and sandals, she was met at the door by a young man far different from what she had expected. Knowing his reputation as a war hero, she couldn't get over the sharp contrast.

She expected, she said, a "cross between Victor McLaglen and General Eisenhower." "Naturally," she said, "I had heard about Audie Murphy, the most decorated soldier of the war. The whole world heard about him! However, I couldn't believe the diffident, sensitive, fine-featured boy who opened the Cagney door that night could be the Goliath who single-handed had wrecked a good part of the enemy army!" (Perhaps Wanda meant David, but she said Goliath.) Many years later, after Audie was dead, she recalled again the impact of that first meeting: "I'll never forget my feeling when the door opened to the guesthouse and Audie was standing there. He wasn't very tall, and he was slight, but he had the greenest eyes and beautiful auburn hair, with a sprinkling of freckles over his tan.

"He said 'hello,' and it was the most potent 'hello' I had ever heard. He was like a charge of dynamite. He kept staring at me all through dinner, but he didn't talk very much."

Wanda made a striking impression on Audie, too. He said later, "I had never met anyone like Wanda. But in the back of my mind I had carried a vision of her for years. I had never really had a girl. Not even during the war did I know of one to whom I cared to write. While other fellows read their love letters, I usually cleaned my rifle. The girl I loved existed only in my imagination; and believe it or not, she looked amazingly like Wanda."

He spent the evening watching Wanda. At ten he drove her home, shook hands, and told her he'd call her. The next week when he called for a date, she was too busy with her work at Paramount and turned him down. After she turned him down several weeks in succession, he got mad. Later he told her, "I decided you were just being high-hat, and no actress was going to push me around."

In December 1946, Audie was back in Texas for a visit where he made headlines again. It was the first publicized instance of that tendency toward violent encounters that would punctuate his life after the war, although he appears to have been blameless. Driving north of Dallas, near the little town of Vickery, known in those days as a place where tough guys hung out because Vickery was a "wet" oasis in a desert of dry, liquor-free towns, Audie picked up a hitchhiker. It was raining and the guy, who was wearing a field jacket with chevrons, looked like an ex-GI. He was also big, 6' 2", 190 pounds. After a short distance he jammed what he said was a .45 into Audie's ribs and told him he wanted the car and all of Audie's money.

This was a serious mistake, and Audie told him so. Then, said

Audie, "he backhanded me across the face with his left hand, mean-while keeping the pressure on my ribs, and that got me a little mad. I think he'd been seeing too many B productions, or something. He wanted to be tough, you know. I think he thought I was just some school kid coming home for Christmas or something like that." When the hitchhiker ordered Audie to stop the car and get out, Audie discovered that there was no gun (it was the guy's knuckles), and "so we started fighting and I got the door open and knocked him out of the car and I jumped him in the middle of the stomach with both feet and I was so doggone scared I didn't hardly know what I was doing, and we fought for about 10 minutes and finally he didn't get up anymore."

Then Audie drove to a filling station and called his old Highway Patrol friend Everett Brandon. Audie didn't press charges, but the story leaked out anyway, and a photo story hit the newspapers. LITTLE AUDIE MURPHY WINS ANOTHER BATTLE AS HE WHIPS "GIANT," read a typical headline. Back in Hollywood the whole thing looked like a publicity stunt, which miffed Audie pretty badly.

Some time passed before Audie saw Wanda again. After a while he got over being mad at her for not finding time to go out with him. Then one day in the spring he went to her home to see her and this time things clicked: they started going together; they became an item.

The national press loved the idea of their being in love. *Life,* which was why he was in Hollywood in the first place, did a story on their love affair because it was "unlike so many in moviedom . . . the real thing." Fan magazines were crazy about their romance, too. They ran photo spreads on their dates. One magazine shot them having fun at Knott's Berry Farm, visiting the Ghost Town, posing beside a house made of bottles. Another magazine layout showed them deep-sea fishing and mooning around on a boat. Another showed how it was possible to have a date on just $7.00. The piece is a classic bit of Americana. Audie picks up Wanda in a snazzy convertible. Gas: $1.20. They dine at an Italian place in Hollywood, the Ristorante Chianti, at a cost of $3.40. Then they go window-shopping for .00. Next they go to the movies for $1.60, then stop by a Westwood Village Driving Range where Audie drives a bucket of balls while Wanda watches. They cap the evening with a couple of Cokes at a drugstore just around the corner from Wanda's house. Cost: 20 cents. At her door Audie plants "two smackers" on her lips and goes home. Total cost: $7.00. They could have been Jimmy Stewart and Donna Reed in *It's A Wonderful Life*.

Audie and Wanda were perfect fan magazine fodder in those innocent bygone days when the interests of the fan magazines and the studios fit seamlessly together in the interlocking mutuality of publicity. Things were so cozy between the magazines and the studios that, for example, in 1951 *Photoplay* paid for Tony Curtis and Janet Leigh's honeymoon in return for an exclusive. The number of Audie-Wanda love fests in the magazines suggests that Audie cooperated with the system more than some of his later hard-boiled remarks would suggest.

Audie's health was still a problem. What he called his "trick stomach" would sometimes double him up with pain when he was eating. He had trouble sleeping, had trouble like that for years. The bad dreams wouldn't go away either. In a letter to the Cawthons in April 1947, he mentioned his health: "I have not been doing so well lately, have had a time with my stomach, thought for awhile I would have to go to the hosp, but it is some better now." A physical examination conducted in June that year by the Veterans Administration revealed that he suffered from week-long headaches and vomiting spells in the morning. During such episodes he was plagued by nightmares, almost all of which dealt with combat. He had to take sleeping pills to keep the nightmares at bay.

In Hollywood, as in most social networks, the personal and the professional are often intertwined, and so it is not surprising that Audie's courtship of Wanda led to his first part in a movie. That summer her agent landed him a small role in a Paramount film about West Point called *Beyond Glory*. It starred Alan Ladd as a West Point cadet, and Audie played Cadet Thomas, one of Ladd's buddies. Ladd, he said later, gave him some helpful tips. "I was rather sensitive then," he said, "and inclined to fly off the handle. Alan Ladd took me aside and told me that I shouldn't let little things worry me. He just suggested I keep my eyes and ears open and do my job. That is what I've tried to do. My big problem then was— and still is—that I'm impatient. I wanted to do everything yesterday. I have since learned that it doesn't pay to get four ulcers on a two ulcer picture."

Audie was also sensitive about his status as the most decorated hero. When a Pentagon colonel visited the set and started talking about Audie's exploits and asked for an autographed picture, Audie blew up. "Let's cut out the bull. I'm no longer a soldier. If you want a picture of me as a movie character—though damned if I'd know why—then fine and dandy."

Beyond Glory was directed by John Farrow (Mia Farrow's father), an underrated journeyman whose credits include *The Big Clock* and *Hondo*. Although *Beyond Glory* wasn't much of a movie, in the light of the postwar era and Audie's personal problems it bears, as do many of his films, an uncanny relationship with his off-screen life. *Beyond Glory* set out to tell a different kind of war story to a "public perhaps tired of deeds of derring-do." The film explored the problems of a decorated and traumatized soldier (Alan Ladd) who returns to military service by enrolling at the Army Academy at West Point. While there, he is falsely accused of harassing a junior cadet, and in a series of flashbacks and trial scenes his war experience, trauma, and postwar cure are set forth.

Ladd's role would have been an excellent one for Audie himself. The parallels are striking. Like Ladd's Rocky Gilman, Audie suffered post-combat trauma; like Rocky, he felt guilt for those who had died when he had lived; like Rocky, he hoped to find stability and happiness by marrying a pretty, demure brunette. Finally, there was the tantalizing reminder that Audie himself had considered West Point as a career after returning from Europe. He looked great in West Point gray.

Audie himself certainly saw parallels with his own life. Intensely interested in the problem of returning veterans, he felt that this film failed to treat their plight believably. But then Audie didn't think much of any of the recent war films he'd seen. He was especially critical of *The Best Years of Our Lives*, objecting particularly to the "part with the kid with no hands." This critically acclaimed and popular 1946 film made the handicapped veteran into a kind of circus act, Audie thought; the whole thing left him feeling squeamish. In point of fact, *The Best Years of Our Lives* might have hit too close to home. Not all the problems in that film were ones of physical handicaps. One returning flier (Dana Andrews) was haunted by nightmares much as Audie was.

Director Farrow had kind things to say of Audie's first outing: "Audie has as much natural acting talent as any newcomer I've ever worked with." Audie characteristically disparaged his performance, "I had eight words to say, seven more than I could handle." Actually his part was bigger than he admitted. He appeared in three scenes, performing creditably in each. Although most reviews made no mention of him, the *Hollywood Reporter* listed his as among the "pleasing performances" turned in by actors in minor roles. Another reviewer said, "You'll recognize him, he's the one with the Southern drawl, and he does right well for himself."

For this role the Cagneys loaned him to Paramount, where he received $3,000 for ten weeks' work. According to their contract with Audie, they were entitled to a percentage, but they let him keep all the money. At the end of the ten weeks, however, the contract was terminated. Audie and Jimmy were never on bad terms. Cagney said of him many years later, "It turned out we had no use for him really. He couldn't act." Audie was always grateful to Cagney for his help: "Cagney was always wonderful to me. He simply had nothing for me to do, and you can't take money for doing nothing."

But Audie's relations with Bill Cagney, Jimmy's brother, were a different matter. As Jimmy put it many years later, Audie was a "decidedly egocentric young fellow," who "did not get along too well with the help around the Studio." Audie and Bill Cagney had a run-in. At a party Audie was mixing and serving drinks, a service he performed for the Cagneys on such occasions, and Bill started kidding Audie about his judo skills. Audie got mad, there was a scuffle, he flipped the much heavier Cagney on his back, and Cagney had to be helped upstairs. (It was never a good idea to challenge Audie in a social setting.) Later Audie spoke of how Bill Cagney hadn't believed in him: "Bill Cagney told me I'd get lost in this town. MGM made a test of me, and they said I'd never get anywhere. Well, that sort of made me mad. I was about as low as I could get in the picture business, but I never like to quit anything when I am down."

In the months following the end of his relationship with the Cagneys, Audie was more adrift than ever. He moved out of his quarters at Jimmy Cagney's estate around August 1947, and lived for a time at a gym, a health emporium run by Terry Hunt, on La Cienega Boulevard. At the gym there were massage tables and Army cots to sleep on. The period at Terry Hunt's gym, where he stayed until early 1948, was a time when, Audie said later, he "almost became bitter . . . toward the complicated circumstances of life. To me, it seemed disorganized. There were no chow lines, no commanding officers, no bulletin boards directing your activities for the day. I was up to my ears in energy with no place to spend it."

The gym wasn't a bad place to be. The stacked cots reminded him of Army barracks, and he liked the company of the men who hung around. The physical regimen was good for Audie, too. He worked out and put on muscle and weight and developed a good welterweight build at around 140 pounds.

Even where Audie chose to live had political implications in the Hollywood of that era. There was a lot of concern over the rent-gouging of returning veterans, and comedian Henry Morgan expressed public indignation about America's most decorated soldier having to live at a gym. (At one time there were eight veterans living at Terry Hunt's.)

L.A. was full of veterans looking for work, ex-soldiers who'd fallen in love with Southern California when the service had brought them there during the war. Hollywood liberals took up the worthy cause, and one of them, a young screenwriter named Sy Gomberg, came up with an idea for dramatizing the plight of America's homeless ex-soldiers. He organized an all-night camp-out at McArthur Park, and he called it "the Big Sleep." Gomberg, who knew that Audie Murphy was in town, went to see the most decorated GI to try to enlist him for the event. Says Gomberg, "He wouldn't do it, and he told me why. He wanted to. His heart was in the right place, but at that point Audie had been so battered about the use of his name and had had a terrible experience recently with James Cagney's brother Bill."

Gomberg continues, "He was almost in tears when he said to me, 'I can't do it.' I said 'Okay' and I started to leave, and he called me back. He told me he had been used in Texas very badly and he had been used when he first came to Hollywood, very badly." And so for all those reasons, he couldn't take part in the Big Sleep. This episode suggests how ardently Audie resisted being turned into a symbol, but it was never easy.

During the filming of *Beyond Glory* Audie met David McClure, a legman for Hedda Hopper and, like Audie, a veteran of the European theater. "Spec" (a nickname derived from the fact that he wore spectacles) was, according to well-known publicity flack Jaik Rosenstein, a "guy with a long, scrawny frame and a lot of freckles and rimless glasses and hair that shoots out in all directions and who still speaks with the slur of the small town in the Deep South whence he came."

Spec had first learned of the war hero, like most people, from the *Life* magazine cover. Years later Spec recalled his reaction when, in July 1945, with the occupation forces in France, he saw the famous picture of a soldier "so young, so fresh and untouched by war." Spec said to a buddy, "I wonder what the hell he did." Now he wanted to meet him, and so he arranged with Paramount Studio to have lunch with him. Wanda Hendrix would be there, too, the studio said. Spec and Audie were on time, but Wanda was delayed by a conference with her costume designer. Audie was angry and sullen until Wanda arrived. After chewing her out, he cheered up, and he and Spec talked. It was the beginning of a long and intimate friendship. They had several things in common: Irish heritage, poor backgrounds on Southern tenant farms, a grim sense of humor, and a tendency to brood.

There were differences, too. Spec, fourteen years older than Audie, was a well-educated and intellectual sort—he had graduated Phi Beta Kappa from the University of North Carolina in 1932. He described himself as a "voluble, hard-drinking reporter in whom cynicism and idealism are forever fighting for control." Spec fit almost perfectly the developing folklore of the Hollywood publicity writer: "Cynicism is the leg-man's occupational disease. He doesn't believe in Santa Claus—or in movie stars."

Like Audie, Spec had also been profoundly affected by the war. Though he'd been in the Signal Corps and not in combat, he nonetheless suffered from ailments he would later identify as post-stress symptoms. At one time or another Spec suffered from depression, a temporary speech block, attacks of hallucination, and insomnia, which he never entirely got rid of. He also drank a lot. His postwar depression, he believed, was a delayed reaction to the scenes of ruin and desolation among which he had lived in war-torn Europe. In his own self-characterization Spec said that during this period he was "usually drunk, leaden with hangovers, or fighting off a nervous breakdown." Following the war, Spec went on a "ten-years' drunk." As late as 1957 he still suffered enough from war-related stress that psychiatric care was recommended for him.

As the years passed, Spec began to see that Audie had perhaps more problems than he himself did. Finally he seems to have become obsessed with Audie Murphy. During Audie's lifetime Spec was his pal, his ghostwriter, his unofficial publicist, his Boswell. Following Audie's death, he remained the guardian of the Murphy legend, a dedicated friend of Audie's widow, simultaneously protective of Audie's reputation and devoted to collecting all the facts that could be known about the real Audie Murphy. Spec McClure probably knew more about Audie Murphy than did any other person, and his death in October 1986 marked the end of almost forty years of intense involvement in the life of an enigmatic American hero.

In the beginning, Audie was very difficult to be friends with. A "moody, brooding, incommunicative individual, trusting nobody and suspicious of all," wrote Spec later, Audie would invite him to dinner and then say nothing the whole time. He would withdraw within himself and quietly curse everything in sight. He was so tense that a waitress setting a glass of water down too hard would cause him to explode. He was touchy about the littlest thing. But Audie also had many qualities that made Spec like him. One was his generosity. Once, Spec remembered, Audie had a hundred dollars and he had nothing. So Audie said to him, "You take fifty—you can't be broke." Then Audie spent his fifty, and he was broke.

In Spec's view, Audie had a lot going for him as a potential actor. He'd already lost his Texas accent when Spec first met him, and spoke perfect grammatical English. He'd also lost the farm-boy stride that Cagney had sought to eliminate. Spec felt that Audie had "more to offer the film industry" than any young actor in Hollywood. Not many other people felt that way, though. One who did was the great director Ernst Lubitsch. He told Terry Hunt, Audie's pal who ran the gym, that Audie possessed the face and the personality to become a star in the manner of Gary Cooper, a pliable screen persona awaiting only the right director. Lubitsch's death in 1947 ended any possibility of a film connection in that direction, however.

After his work in *Beyond Glory,* Audie went through another long spell of waiting. He later said of this period, "Then, my name just about became a public football. I was announced for a series of films about which I knew nothing. And at that time I was not even eating regularly."

Thrown once again into the jobless limbo of a would-be actor, Audie, in the jargon of the trade, couldn't get arrested. Living now on his Army pension ($113 a month) he knew lean times again. He said later of this period, "I had a shower for breakfast and a steam bath for dinner." He was so poor he had to borrow $5 to attend a Purple Heart dinner at which he was the honored guest. "But it was no novelty to me to be poor," he said, "so I waited until things got better." He lived largely on promises, and though mentioned for a dozen pictures, as yet he had played in only one.

Christmas 1947 was a lonely time. A movie magazine writer converted Audie's Christmas Day into the stuff of Dickensian pulp. The way the writer told it, he saw a young man walking by the intersection of Wilshire and La Brea, on Christmas Day, picked him up, and gave him a ride. The young man with the sad smile related a story of his family's poverty, then disclosed his identity as Audie Murphy. He said, "To be absolutely honest I'm living on a cot in the back of Terry Hunt's gym while I'm trying to write a book about my war experiences." When the writer offered him $20, Audie refused it. He had $11, he said, that Terry Hunt had given him. It had to last the week.

Audie asked the writer to drop him off at Earl McKissick's filling station on Santa Monica. This was another favorite hangout of Audie's, then and for years later. Here a little vignette took place. Earl's children were playing with their new toys when a kid darted up and nabbed a toy airplane. Audie chased him down, listened to the boy's story, and gave him a ten-dollar bill. That left Audie with a buck. The fan magazine headlined this little piece of sentiment as "Hollywood's Loveliest Christmas Story." Some of it may have been true.

In the meantime Spec kept trying to help Audie get a foothold in the film industry. He believed in Audie's prospects when almost nobody else did and tried to use his considerable contacts to find parts for Audie. The going was hard, partly because of Audie himself. On his own he rarely returned phone calls or opened his mail. On occasion Spec found himself having to defend Audie against rather ludicrous arguments. At his boss's house once, he listened to Esther Williams tell Hedda Hopper about how hard it was for some actors to find work in Hollywood. Spec said he agreed and told of how much difficulty Audie Murphy was having.

"But can he *act?*" asked Esther Williams.

"For Christ's sake, you should be the last person in the world to pop that question. Can *you* act? Audie can fight, and you can swim. If you couldn't swim, where the hell would *you* be?" exploded Spec.

In February 1948 Spec wangled him a bit part in what turned out to be a dreadful little film, *Texas, Brooklyn and Heaven*. It starred

Guy Madison and Diana Lynn and was one of those films that seems to have originated from a title concept and little more. A poll taken during the early forties revealed that the three places with the most box-office appeal were Texas, Brooklyn, and Heaven. That was enough for a movie to be concocted around the premise of a hero who leaves Texas, travels to New York City, and falls in love with a young woman, also from Texas, who has always wanted to live in Brooklyn. One reviewer tagged it perfectly when he called it "easily one of the most abortively heavy-handed items we've run across this year." Audie, who plays a newspaper boy for the Dallas *News*, is on screen for about two and a half minutes. Dressed in slacks, white shirt, and a tie undone at the collar, he strides through the office, delivering bits of mail and exchanging a few lines of dialogue with the lead, Guy Madison, no great shakes of an actor himself. The film has an accidental documentary value in the light of subsequent history. An establishing shot of downtown Dallas features the School Book Depository Building, which fifteen years later would be emblazoned on the consciousness of the nation.

Audie picked up $500 for his appearance in this film and also got to keep four shirts that he wore to pose for an advertisement. He gave two of them to Spec, saying, "The shirts are almost as bad as the picture."

After this trivial role in a terrible picture, Audie's attitude toward his career prospects hardened. One conventional means of building a career was to take any part you could get. Audie had good reasons for not doing that: "When I was down and out, people tried to tie me in on commercial things—a few shirt ads, whiskies, cigarets and other things like that, for the name value, I guess. I don't drink or smoke and at that time I couldn't afford a shirt. I turned those down. You see, the thing I have to watch out for, if I do something bad, it's not only going to reflect on me . . . but it reflects on my old outfit and all the guys around me."

The other tactic was to hold out for starring roles. Having played two small parts in two routine films, he decided that from now on he'd accept a starring role or nothing. When Pine and Thomas Productions got in touch with Spec for a bit part for Audie, $500 for three days' work, Spec was elated. A piece of cake. Audie was broke, so was Spec, and they were making plans to write what would become *To Hell and Back*. They needed the money. Audie was sunning himself on the roof at Spec's apartment when the call came.

He didn't even bother to come down from the roof to talk about it.

"I'll never do another picture unless I can star in it."

"And what makes you think you can act?"

"And what makes you think that any of these other characters working in pictures can act either?"

6.
BREAKTHROUGH

"I aim to learn everything I can about this business. I don't want to be caught with my dukes down, see."
—*Audie Murphy*

In 1948 things began to go Audie's way. First he got a book contract, and then he got the lead in a film. The book had been on his mind off and on since his return from Europe. Now, with Spec, he was going to do it. A newspaper report in December 1947 announced that a book with a dandy title was in the offing: *To Hell and Back*.

In February of the new year Spec took a leave of absence from Hedda Hopper to devote himself full-time to the project. He drew upon several sources: a scrapbook made by Audie's cousin, Elizabeth Lingo; the accounts contained in the citations for Audie's various medals; and Don Taggart's recently published *History of the Third Infantry Division in World War II*, a valuable work replete with statistics and maps. But the main source was Audie himself. Although Audie wrote less than 10 percent of the book, it was essentially his story as he wanted it told, and he and Spec worked on the book together, in a true collaboration and under at times almost claustrophobic conditions.

Most of it was written in an apartment Audie had moved into after leaving Terry Hunt's gym. For a time he had a roommate, Harry Reginald, an ex-flier and small-time promoter whom Audie had gotten to know at the gym. Now Reginald had moved on. The ramshackle apartment was a real dump. Situated on the corner of Melrose and Gardner, it was on the ground floor across from a bus station. It was as noisy as a machine shop, and the decor was bachelor-grim. There was a picture of Wanda, a row of cowboy boots, some lurid paintings left by Reginald, and the German sniper's rifle that Audie had brought back from Europe. Though Audie himself was always impeccably groomed, the apartment was usually littered with old newspapers, unopened mail, clothes, and discarded tin cans. Here, Audie and Spec refought World War II. Audie would lie on his bed on his back, hands cupped behind his head, staring at the ceiling. He gave thumbnail sketches of some of the men in Company B. He dictated pieces of action, with Spec taking notes. A surviving scrap of this material reveals how the method worked: "German grabs for safety—Murph drops to one knee to avoid presenting full lenth [sic] target—shot twice—threw handgrenades—men come up— . . ." From such notes Spec fleshed out the narrative.

Spec would show him a battle map with dates and specific locations of Company B, and Audie would swiftly narrate what had happened. Spec would then write it up and Audie would read it, make corrections, or throw it away. Often Spec rewrote pages four or five times before going on. Sometimes Audie would say, "This is not right."

"For Chrissake! What *is* right?" Spec would ask.

Then Audie would either tell him or not. Sometimes he simply refused to explain or say anything more about the scene until he was in the mood.

Sometimes Audie wrote portions himself, in longhand. Spec thought—correctly—that Audie had a talent for immediacy and apt imagery, but lacked the patience to write sustained pieces. (In one 1948 interview, Audie gave a different account of the composition of the book. In this instance he implied that he wrote a lot of it himself, in longhand, and that Spec would type up the material and make changes and provide continuity. But Audie also said he "needed a lot of help.") According to Spec, Audie wrote ten pages of longhand; that was all. Surviving manuscript materials confirm Spec's account of the book's composition.

A few surviving pages in Audie's hand do indeed reveal a real talent for narration. One section begins: "its funny how things never seem just right to a dogface, but maby it isnt supposed to be, however this night had seemed unusually long & the snow colder than I ever dreamed it could be & the sound of pick on frozen ground beat against my eardrum like [illegible word]." Audie also wrote part of the famous Colmar Pocket action sequence. It begins: "a slight breeze rustle the frozen limbs about me, & you half expected someone to give out with White xmas, although xmas was a mon[th] pass, a hell of a thing to think of anyway."

He continues:

I direct the artillery, & the first big Barage came in on the nose god, I loved that artillary. I could see Kraut soldiers disspear in clouds of smoke & snow, hear them scream & shout & yet they come on & on as tho nothing would stop them. I gave the arty. orders to fire on my own position. The Gs were no more than fifty yds away now, & the It. at the CP kept inquiring as to the whereabouts of the Germans. So I asked to hold the phone a min & I would let him talk to them it was here that I had to abandon the phone & start shooting funny but I had not stopped to think how I would get out there & back to the rest of the Comp after spending all my carbine ammo. I spotted a fifty Cal. on the burning tank, with several boxes of ammunition in the rack.

The directness, immediacy, and syntactical fluidity of these passages suggest a natural ability to write narrative prose, and it appears that Audie's narrative sense influenced Spec for the better. Audie wanted the book to be written in the first person, to express the grim humor of men in combat, and to avoid at all costs any bombastic or lofty, heroic tone. Spec felt comfortable with the present tense, too, because at times he was uncertain about the facts and felt it permitted speculation when there was a paucity of verifiable facts.

By contrast, Spec's original version of the opening pages was overheated, Audie told him. Spec's discarded opening began: "Often yet, when asleep in the heart of a great American city, I dream of battle. . . ." Then the dreamer imagines himself reliving an episode of combat: only now he has foreknowledge, he knows where the sniper is, and he can correct errors made in the past. The eyes of the German sniper are filled with "frost and evil," and the sleeper-dreamer awakens in a "cold sweat of fear and alertness," seeing the cross hairs of the sniper's rifle trained on a buddy's stomach. He is powerless to prevent what will happen. Now the awakened dreamer begins to relax, soothed by the quiet noises of the city, but such comfort is short-lived. The sequence ends, "I switch on a light, reach for a sedative; and the long procession of the phantom dead begins again in the brain."

Audie thought this material was too "emotional," and he didn't want the public to know he was having nightmares. His penchant for a spare, understated factual presentation acted as a curb on Spec's tendency to write a kind of overwrought metaphorical prose. The results are obvious. The published version of *To Hell and Back* begins quietly, without any heavy emotional buildup: "On a hill just inland from the invasion beaches of Sicily, a soldier sits on a rock. His helmet is off; and the hot sunshine glints through his coppery hair. With the sleeve of his shirt he wipes the sweat from his face; then with chin in palm he leans forward in thought." Audie later told an interviewer in 1949 that he found writing a way of expressing himself without "being overbearing," an interesting statement. He also said he was working on a novel-length piece of fiction about a returning veteran. This may have been the germ of what would eventually become an idea for a sequel to *To Hell and Back*.

In the middle of summer 1948, Audie and Spec interrupted work on the book to take what turned out to be a kind of gonzo trip to France. Audie received an invitation from the French government to visit Paris and receive the Legion of Honor and another Croix de Guerre, with Palm. He was to be the official guest of President Vincent Auriol and General Jean de Lattre de Tassigny, French Army chief of staff. There would also be a tour of the battlefields where Audie and Company B had fought. The trip to France made it impossible for him to attend another war-related event, a reunion of the 3rd Division to be held that summer. In a letter declining the invitation, Audie wrote Colonel Kenneth B. Potter about what the trip to France would mean to him: "I requested the tour of the battlefields to refresh my memory, as I've been struggling to complete a book about the experiences all of us shared. It's about two-thirds finished, and tentatively titled 'For a Young Man's Heart.'

. . . If I can tell the story as we all saw and lived it, it will mean more to me than anything I will ever do in the movie business."

He took Spec with him as a "publicity specialist," but Spec, by his own account, was a "specialist only in getting drunk," so Audie had to handle public relations himself. Audie borrowed $1,000 and in New York, just before they left for Europe on July 4, he bet $100 on a horse race.

In Paris the press met Audie at the airport and took a lot of photographs. In many of them there was a pretty brunette who stood smiling beside Audie. He didn't know who she was; neither did Spec; but as it turned out, she was trying to garner publicity from close association with Audie. Harry Reginald was behind the whole thing. The girl was a chanteuse named Genevieve to whom Reginald had attached himself. The whole trip and the invitation from the French government were in fact concoctions of Reginald's elaborate promotional scheme. It was he who had nudged the French to celebrate Audie's wartime exploits. Audie was supposed to tell everyone that he had heard Genevieve sing on the radio during the war and had been searching for her ever since.

What happened next took on the quality of farce. The French papers carried photographs of Audie and the singer he didn't know under the headline, AUDIE MURPHY AND HIS FIANCEE. This teed Audie off and it got him into plenty of trouble with Wanda back home. There was a long transatlantic telephone call that Audie stuck Spec with.

On the official side Audie took part in Bastille Day celebrations in Paris. There, at the Invalides, in a formal ceremony presided over by General de Tassigny, Audie was awarded the Legion of Honor and the Croix de Guerre.

In Paris Audie had some fun at Spec's expense. Spec got blind drunk, which made Audie unhappy. So he put him to bed, went out into the streets of Paris, and found a poor deformed guy who had had his eye shot out. Audie gave him ten bucks to sit next to Spec and be there to freak him out when he woke up.

In all Audie and Spec traveled some 1,500 miles across the French countryside where the Third Army had fought its way toward Germany in late 1944 and the winter and spring of 1945. Audie had expected, he wrote Major Potter, to "find some of the same old foxholes we were run out of in Riedwihr." He was right. Three years after the war he could find the exact places where Company

B had engaged in fire fights. The search began at "Yellow Beach," near Ramatuelle, where the landing had taken place. With his phenomenal feel for terrain Audie was able to locate most of the landmarks, including the rocky bluff where the dummy cannon had been installed. Near Ramatuelle he identified the exact spot where Lattie Tipton had fallen. Spec was amazed: "On the battlefields he would go straight to unmarked spots where pals had died. If we were alone, he would give me graphic descriptions of the men and the battle. But if others were present, he would simply keep quiet. He seemed simply not to want to disturb the memory of these dead men around strangers." Another time, near Riedwihr in the Alsace, he pushed aside some bushes and there was the burned tank destroyer where he had made the stand that won him the Congressional Medal of Honor. Spec examined it, noting three punctures from .88s, the charred insides, and the missing turret that had been blown completely off. Such field experience was doubtless useful to Spec as a writer. It helped him see the war through Audie's eyes, from the ground level.

At Strasbourg Audie pulled another trick provoked by Spec's drinking. Spec and a photographer named Dick Dial, commissioned by the Tourist Bureau to photograph the tour, drank all night on the train ride from Paris to Strasbourg. Audie warned them several times to slow down, but they didn't, and the next morning they both had brutal hangovers. A tour of the city was planned by Strasbourg officials, and when Audie learned of this, he feigned sickness. He wanted to teach his pals a lesson. By default Spec and Dial were feted as guests of honor, and they suffered mightily. In the meantime Audie was put up at the mayor's home, where he promptly tried to seduce the mayor's daughter. At the luncheon when he rejoined Spec and Dial, he asked them, "Well, how did you two drunks like being celebrities?"

At Riedwihr Audie was honored as the liberator of the village. Although the villagers were in error—he had fought near there, in the Medal of Honor action, but had not liberated the place—the simple ceremony touched him deeply. He listened as French schoolchildren, "arranged in wobbly little rows," sang "La Marseillaise."

Audie was moved by what he saw in France. He later wrote: "It was still a war-ravaged country, with building walls still teetering uncertainly, trying to decide whether to stand or fall. Debris was everywhere. The Nazis had thrown a horrible party in a house that wasn't theirs." The trip gave him a better understanding of why the war was fought: "Then, I had only one desire, and that was for the war to be over. I wanted to go home. I didn't like France. I didn't like Italy. I was in a strange country. I had no feeling for the oppressed French and Italians." Now he felt that the "spirit of freedom was hovering over . . . France."

The trip also showed both Audie and Spec how far the war had already receded in the minds of many Americans. *Life* expressed an interest in doing a photo story on the trip, and a number of photographs of Audie in France are contained in the files at the magazine's home office in New York. But the story was canceled in favor of a story about an extravagant party thrown by Elsa Maxwell on the Riviera.

When Audie and Spec returned to New York, Audie made headlines with some typically direct remarks. He called U.S. diplomatic representatives in France "fat-headed" and accused some of them of "laying down on their jobs." This minor fracas quickly disappeared from the newspapers. More productively, he signed a contract with Henry Holt & Company for *To Hell and Back*, on the basis of about 160 completed pages. He received an advance of $1,500, with Spec guaranteed 40 percent of the royalties.

Back in L.A. he and Spec continued to work on the book. They missed their October deadline by a month, sending in the completed manuscript in November. The book was published in February 1949, and received excellent advance word in the influential book trade magazine *Publishers Weekly* where Alice Hackett noted its "Ernie Pyle flavor" and called it "one of the better factual descriptions of life and death, cold nerve and battle fatigue, patrols, and endless replacements of dead buddies by green soldiers."

Other reviewers concurred. The *New York Herald Tribune* described it as a "complete case history of a combat man," a judgment that summed up the overwhelmingly favorable response the book received. Gladwin Hill, a former war correspondent, in the *New York Times Book Review* praised it as a "vivid, gripping, mature picture of combat" that was "rather notable" because, unlike such classics as *The Red Badge of Courage* or Ernie Pyle's journalism, this was a book that was not "vicarious." Hill, one of the few reviewers to detect the hand of a "writing man who has obviously given the soldier's recollections a polish job," found the book filled with "exceptional sensitivity and balance." (David McClure's name, incidentally, did not appear on the book.) He also praised Audie's "forbearance in . . . eschewing reference to his own ironic postwar experiences." In the column "Books of the Times" in the *New York Times*, Charles Poorer called it a "remarkably interesting new book" that would refute the opinion expressed in some quarters that Americans "have no ideas of realities of war." Poorer found Audie's portrait of GIs the best since Bill Mauldin's cartoons, saying, "it gives you Mauldin's characters in action." He also praised the style for its understatement, humor, and realism. The *Saturday Review of Literature* found it a "terrible, powerful book" in which "there is no civilian conscience." The Chicago *Sun* admired the book's "objectivity," and the *Library Journal* noted approvingly the absence of reference to Audie's many honors. The *Christian Science Monitor*, which pronounced it "one of the most arresting literary products of World War II," felt obliged to warn the inexperienced reader to expect a kind of narrative initiation into the "price the infantry soldier paid—paid in all ways—for the actions demanded of him."

Such laudatory reviews spurred sales of the book, and on March 27 it broke onto the *New York Times Book Review* Best-Seller List, at number 10. It stayed on the list through June 19, reaching as high as number 8 in both April and May. By mid-spring Eisenhower's *Crusade in Europe* began to drop down the list, after having been number 1 for the previous year. Other war-related books on the list at the time included Churchill's *Their Finest Hour* and, in fiction, Norman Mailer's *The Naked and the Dead*. Audie's book, however, did not make the year's top ten, but then the competition was pretty stiff; there were three hit books on canasta in 1949. *To Hell and Back* has since gone through many editions including, most recently, a paperback entry in the Bantam series "Classics of World War II." It stands as one of Audie's lasting accomplishments.

The great success of *To Hell and Back* doubtless accomplished part of Audie's intention to "remind a forgetful public of a lot of boys who never made it home," but it also revived his name and contributed to his visibility on the Hollywood scene. Once again Audie's fame as a warrior was his chief entry into the marketplace.

During the months when the book was being completed, Paul Short, a Texas-based producer and friend of Audie's Interstate Theatre circle, started pushing hard to put together a movie deal based on a script called *Bad Boy*. Short had in mind only one actor for the lead: he wanted Audie Murphy. *Bad Boy* had a built-in promotional advantage because the plot dealt with juvenile delinquency and the meritorious work of Variety Clubs, International, a charitable organization to which 8,500 theater men belonged, representing 17,000 theaters in the United States and abroad. In Texas, for example, the picture would be guaranteed preferential treatment by the Interstate Theatre chain.

It was a good role for a young actor: the hero Danny Lester was, as one reviewer described him, a "teen-age, trigger-happy, baby-faced thug." But getting Audie the part wasn't going to be easy. Steve Broidy, head of Allied Artists Studio, couldn't see Audie for the lead role. He wanted a big name and he told both Short and Spec that "the kid never would go over on the screen." But Short was stubborn. "No Murphy, no story," he told Broidy. So finally, just to get rid of the problem, Broidy agreed to test Audie for the part. Audie was confident, too; he told Spec, "Okay. Quit worrying. I'll go do there and knock the——off that part."

It was just a bluff, though. He was scared stiff and showed it. Scriptwriter Robert Hardy Andrews recalled vividly what happened: "He had been up all night, memorizing the screen-test script, but he stumbled over speeches and had to be calmed down and corrected, politely out of respect for his medals, firmly because $500,000 was riding on his name.

"Finally, we cut the lights, sent for black coffee in paper cups, and made dialogue cuts and changes aimed to lighten the load he carried. He thanked everybody and tried again. We got further along this time, to the point at which the action directions called for him to pick up a gun and aim it, ready to kill.

"Then Audie Murphy changed. The boyish face still looked 15, not 24; but his eyes were suddenly old, his slim body was a coiled spring, and we looked at each other and nodded, and the director said 'Cut. Print it.' "

Audie talked about his own reaction to that test: "I crawled down under the seat and had my coat up over my head and was shaking and everything. I'd never seen anything that looks so ghastly. It really frightened me." He also pledged to become a better actor or give it up. Audie was hopeful, as he told an interviewer in October 1948: "I didn't mind the waiting so much because I was getting good training. I had, I still have, a lot to learn."

The making of *Bad Boy* was an ordeal for Audie from beginning to end. He had reason to feel insecure and uncomfortable. The cast consisted of polished professionals, Lloyd Nolan, Jane Wyatt, James Lydon, and James Gleason. But James Lydon and the rest accepted Audie; they didn't resent his top billing. To Lydon he was a "frightened young fellow who happened to be very, very famous in some other line that we could not understand by just looking at him and being closely associated with him for the twenty-one days it took us to make this little potboiler."

Jane Wyatt, later famous for her role as Robert Young's wife in TV's "Father Knows Best" and today still working on TV in a soap opera, was an established actress at the time. She recalls, "I along with others regarded him as a kind of curiosity." He was the "cutest little boy" and "so very nice, but he was by no means a forceful figure on the set. A very nice kid—that's all."

Lydon got to know Audie a little better, being thrown into more contact with him. Though about Audie's age, Lydon was already a veteran actor. His credits included legitimate drama in New York and the title role in the Henry Aldridge movies of the forties. He recalls how every morning for a week he and Jimmie Gleason and Lloyd Nolan and Audie would ride out in the studio van to Thousand Oaks, north of the city, where they were shooting the film. Audie sat in the front seat with the driver and never said a word. When anybody asked him something, he would answer very quietly, but volunteer nothing.

The first morning, about twenty miles out of L.A., Audie very timidly asked the driver if he would mind stopping the car. The other actors watched, wondering, as Audie got out, walked round to the back of the car, and threw up his breakfast. Lydon and the others felt maybe it was a war injury or something. They told him they were sorry he was ill. He didn't say anything.

On the set, Audie was "very nervous, very upset as any beginner would be." At lunchtime, he'd invariably be missing and someone would ask, "Where's Audie?" Someone would get up, a propman or a grip or something, and start to look around. Audie was behind a bush out in the wilds, throwing up his lunch. He never did explain anything to Lydon or anybody else. To Lydon, Audie's remoteness spoke volumes: "He always looked like he was kind of deep in thought about something else, or that he really wasn't with you." But he apparently appreciated the cast's sympathy. After it was all over, he said that "they were wonderful."

Everything about the film was difficult, even the fight scenes.

Audie told the press, "Unless you have been in fights in which you're not supposed to hurt a guy, you have no idea what fighting for the screen is like. It's a tough job." His sense of humor didn't fail him, however. One day on the set he kept botching a scene until the director, Kurt Neumann, snapped, "What's wrong?"

"I'm working under a great handicap," replied Audie.

"What handicap?" asked Neumann.

"No talent."

This became one of the legendary stories about Audie's ineptitude as an actor. Over the years it was told of one Murphy film after another.

Rarely seen today, *Bad Boy* occasionally appears on early morning TV and is available for rental under the title *The Story of Danny Lester*. An undistinguished forerunner of films about adolescent antisocial behavior, *Bad Boy* begins by showing just how mean Danny Lester is: in the opening frames he beats up his supervisor at the hotel where he works and robs a roomful of Texas oilmen. A bystander calls him a modern-day Billy the Kid. Brought before the bar of justice, he is sullen, volatile, and unregenerate. Charged with sixty-two previous offenses, Danny already has the record of a hardened criminal. Against her better instincts, a female judge is persuaded to remand him to the custody of the Variety Club ranch at Copperas Cove, Texas, where there are 2,400 acres of "wide open Texas space."

Danny, however, severely challenges the Variety Club faith that there are no bad boys, only boys that have been treated badly. He alternately provokes the anger and resentment of the other boys while appearing to be the soul of courtesy and good manners in the presence of the wife of the head of the ranch. Finally Danny completely runs amok: he robs a jewelry store, steals a car, and flees from the ranch—a hunted fugitive. He does everything, Audie joked later, that the Johnston Office would allow. The plot is resolved and Danny headed on the road to redemption by a contrived psychological revelation that explains Danny's malevolence. Wrongly believing that he killed his mother, he has been bad ever since. When the head of the Variety Club (Lloyd Nolan) proves that her death was accidental, Danny knows peace for the first time. At the end of the film he is the Variety Club's latest success, a scholarship student marching in full-dress uniform in the U.S. Army Corps at Texas A&M.

As conceived by Short and Robert Hardy Andrews, the film

bore some fascinating biographical parallels with the real Audie Murphy. Audie pointed to the biographical parallel himself, "Being an orphan, just like the kid in the story, I know I could have done the same thing he did." In fact, one of Audie's brothers had been placed in the Variety Club ranch at Copperas Cove. Like Danny Lester, Audie was a youth without a father and one whose strongest parental attachment was to his deceased mother. Like Danny, Audie was quiet, polite, reserved, shy, and yet possessed of inner fires that could flame out with great intensity. Finally, Danny's attending Texas A&M echoed Audie's own flirtation with that possibility when he returned from Europe in 1945.

Reviewers were struck by several things about Audie's performance. One was his "boyish appeal," which, wrote one reviewer, "keeps the character of the boy from becoming completely unsympathetic, for a more oily and unregenerate young felon never existed." In L.A. the critical reception was particularly favorable. *Cue* called attention to his "surprisingly effective performance," and the *Los Angeles Times* praised his "remarkable performance for a newcomer." The two most influential trade magazines gave him good marks, too. The *Hollywood Reporter* spoke of his "professional authority" and the certainty of future assignments. *Variety,* while noting some of his "thesping deficiencies," nonetheless pronounced him a "likely contender in the bobbysox idol league."

Not everybody liked him, of course. One reviewer thought he was "ill at ease," and another said he needed to develop skills beyond "that baby-face deadpan" if he were going to make "a bad boy really come to life." The most disparaging review came from Bosley Crowther of the *New York Times:* "Precisely why Mr. Murphy should play a juvenile crook is neither apparent nor reasonable in other than exploitation terms, for he is not overable to act. His gaudy displays of insolence are like a kid's in a cops-and-robbers game."

Only one reviewer spotted a darker connection between Audie and Danny Lester, and he hoped that what he saw wasn't the case. In a remarkably prescient analysis of Audie's persona, Robert Hatch of the *New Republic* wrote, "I hope he is an actor, and a good one, for if he is not he is an extremely dangerous citizen. Murphy conveys the dead and deadly blandness of a boy who has tried to make himself invulnerable. He shows a specious charm, and an alert plausibility that go far beyond toughness. He is maddening and sickening, and he is worst when he is being most helpful." Hatch blamed these qualities on the script, but Audie's attempt, perhaps unconscious, to appear invulnerable in his role as Danny Lester was a true self-revelation that only Hatch seems to have caught. Off screen, in real life, many observers would see in Audie Murphy a lonely and painful determination to be just that: invulnerable. A few men and quite a few women saw another side: the deeply vulnerable self that the soldier-hero and civilian tough guy tried to keep hidden.

On balance the critical reception of Audie in his first starring role was encouragingly strong. His screen debut placed him among a new generation of youthful postwar male stars. In 1948–49 Montgomery Clift, Farley Granger, and John Derek all made their first films. One reviewer summed up the new crowd: "They are all so different—Clift, the best actor, Derek the most devastating in appearance and now, Audie, the most warmly appealing."

Bad Boy was just the beginning, as Paul Short saw it. He kept up a flurry of publicity about future projects. He had several script ideas in mind, and Audie would star in all of them. He tried to peddle *To Hell and Back* even before it was published. He let it be known that a Dallas millionaire, D.D. "Tex" Feldman, was going to back a Broadway production based on Audie's book. At the same time he promoted the idea of a film version with Audie playing himself, Barbara Stanwyck as the female lead, and George Stevens as director. They were all pipe dreams, nothing more.

Short also had plans for four "action pics," as the trade magazines called them. These included three westerns—"The Pride of Texas," "The Woods Colt," and "Buckskin"—and a contemporary urban cop picture, "The Police Story." None of these ever went into production, however.

Audie's twin projects in that busy year didn't mean that his perpetual discontent was not present. It most assuredly was and it surfaced in predictable and unpredictable ways. During the first half of the year he spent a lot of time at Spec's apartment on Cahuenga Boulevard where he brooded and killed time by writing poetry. Spec said Audie would write all night, working on one poem, then destroy it in the morning. Or sometimes Spec would find scraps of paper and envelopes with poems written on them scattered on the floor. To his later regret he threw most of them away, and only a few survived.

Audie's poetry seems to have come out of some folk source deep in his background. Famed outlaw Bonnie Parker, from similar roots, also wrote poems, ballads that told in simple, direct language the story of her notorious life with Clyde Barrow. Audie's poetry has the same sort of ballad feel to it. The refrain from one of these poems, quoted in full in *To Hell and Back* but attributed to another soldier, not Audie, goes like this: "The crosses grow on Anzio, and Hell is six feet deep." Poetry offered one way to express his feelings about the war and to pass the long nights.

Audie spent his days hanging out at his own apartment, at Wanda's, at Spec's, at Terry Hunt's gym, at Earl McKissick's filling station on Santa Monica. Earl, an ex-cop disabled by a criminal's bullet, liked to tell preposterous stories about the Hollywood starlets who'd seduced him. They'd come driving up in their little sports cars ready for action, and Earl was only too glad to be of service. Al Foster, a Cherokee Indian mechanic who worked for Earl, was another good friend. He made guns for Audie and kept his car in repair for free. Another friend in this period was Volney Peaveyhouse, a former bomber pilot whose nerves had been wrecked by dangerous night missions over France during the war. Peaveyhouse lived with his wife in a trailer in Pasadena.

Audie was always intensely loyal to such friends. When Earl McKissick's son Roddy got a bit part in a Clifton Webb film, *Sitting Pretty* (1948), the proud father sought to purchase fifty tickets for the premiere at Grauman's Chinese Theater, to give away to friends. Dressed in greasy workingman's clothes, he was snubbed by the theater people. When Audie found out about it, he raised hell. He straightened out the theater management, and McKissick received an apology and fifty complimentary tickets. Audie was that way his whole life; he made the cliché about giving the shirt off his back a literal fact.

These were his friends outside the industry, and he didn't have many inside. A few writers, Spec McClure; among the actors, the only ones he knew, he said in a 1948 interview, were Cagney, Bob Montgomery, Alan Ladd, and Ronald Reagan.

Work on the book and the film often connected in direct ways with the other big event of 1948, his successful courtship of Wanda Hendrix. Like nearly everything in Audie's life, this romance ran hot and cold. Wanda was an ambitious young actress from a protected family background. Her mother was as ambitious for her daughter as Wanda herself was. Audie Murphy didn't look like a prize catch, an ex-war hero whose acting career until late in the year seemed stalled if not finished. Still he and Wanda continued to see each other. He could be very thoughtful. Each day she was on the set making *Abigail, Dear Heart,* at Paramount in April 1948, he sent her a red apple every morning to ward off that year's dread Virus X, a species of flu. His attachment to her was a strong factor in his not giving up on Hollywood and returning to Texas. He said, "If it hadn't been for Wanda, I would never have stayed in this town."

In the public arena Audie and Wanda remained the darlings of the press. They were cute and wholesome and youthful. As early as June 1947, their romance was reported at the "going steady" stage, with prospects of an engagement announcement rumored to follow. A year later, speculation contended that money was the reason they hadn't yet married. The press urged Audie not to let "money throw Cupid!" The press was right; money and romance were intimately connected. Audie, who held traditional ideas about the roles of man and wife, was unwilling to marry Wanda unless he could support her. Where he came from, the man's job was to support his wife and the children that flowed from their union. The fact that his own father hadn't was something he never forgot. The woman's job was to back up her husband in a sheltered, suburban, white picket fence kind of home. Audie wanted exactly what the American government wanted after the war: for women to give up the jobs they'd held during wartime and return to hearth and home. Wanda of course had been a teenager during the war, but she was most decidedly a career woman now, in her late teens, and she was beginning to make big money. That was a problem for Audie, as he told Sheilah Graham: "I can't marry until I have a job. I want to be able to support my wife. I couldn't live on her earnings." For her part, Wanda was ready to marry much earlier, but, she said, "he would not let our marriage come about until he could pay all the bills."

Neither Wanda's studio, Paramount, nor her mother was keen on the idea of Audie and Wanda getting married. According to Audie, the studio thought "it'd have been okay if I was one of those well-known playboys. Or a millionaire. But they were afraid she'd lose her box-office appeal if she married me." Wanda's parents objected on several grounds. The kids were too young, Audie didn't have solid prospects, and above all, Wanda's career was soaring. In 1947 she appeared in four films: *Ride the Pink Horse, Nora Prentiss, Variety Girl,* and *Welcome Stranger.* In 1948 she starred in *Miss Tat-*

lock's Millions and *My Own True Love,* and in the fall she was off to Italy to star opposite Tyrone Power in *Prince of Foxes,* a Renaissance costume drama. At age twenty, stardom seemed to be within Wanda's reach.

She and her parents couldn't have known, but 1949 would be the zenith of Wanda's motion picture career. Her marriage to Audie probably had nothing to do with the downturn. In any case the curve of her career was one of decline. By 1951 she was reduced to making such films as *The Highwayman,* another romance costume drama, and after that the only roles she could get were in B westerns like *The Last Posse* (1953). In the mid-fifties she married James Stack, actor Robert Stack's brother, and when that marriage ended some years later, she tried a comeback in another nondescript western, *Stage to Thunder Rock* (1964). In 1969 she married businessman Steve La Monte, and that one too ended in divorce. In the mid-1970s she was said to be writing a book about her romance with Audie. There were those who felt that she never got over her first love and marriage to Audie. She died in 1981, a sad, premature ending.

Their relationship was always up and down, stormy and volatile. Audie had strong opinions, Wanda knew that. She changed her style of dress to fit his tastes. She liked frilly things, but he thought she looked better in simple, classic lines (he was right). Spec, who knew them best, said they fought constantly. He described the typical dynamics of their relationship in this way: "They accuse, deny, admit, discuss, and finally end up with their arms around one another."

One episode that Spec remembered took place one night when he and his fiancée, Treva Davidson, another member of Hedda Hopper's staff, went out to dine with Audie and Wanda at an expensive Italian restaurant. It was Wanda's idea, and when the check came, nobody had enough money to cover the bill. Audie was furious and made Wanda write a check. She didn't want to, but she did, and then Audie ripped it to shreds. She wrote another check. Then they returned to Audie's apartment where, before leaving, she left a ten-dollar bill where Audie could see it. He tore it to shreds, too. Less than an hour later, he and Wanda were perfectly calm and the rest of the evening went smoothly.

Audie's interest in other women continued unchecked during his courtship of Wanda. One time when he borrowed Spec's apart-

ment for a liaison, Wanda tracked him there and overheard a female
voice. The next day when she called him about it, he said he had
been reading.

"With the lights out?" she asked.

"I was using the Braille system," he replied.

He took a military attitude toward such adventures. He used
the code name "Strategic" to alert Spec to what was going on.

Audie, who always felt closer to working-class people than he
did to Beverly Hills types, ran head-on into Wanda's quite different
view of society life. She liked the rituals of social intercourse and
accommodation that paved the way to career success. She appreciated the importance of playing the game. Audie didn't. Wanda knew
that talent alone wasn't enough, but Audie refused to play by the
rules: "I dislike the back-slapping and throat-cutting that usually
go on at these social affairs. I don't drink. I don't particularly care
about dancing. I hate to waste an evening prattling nonsense. So
I'm bored stiff at these events." To Audie, Wanda was "conscious
of her career—all the time." He wasn't. He said, "I think living is
more important." There was another reason he had no use for the
Hollywood social scene, as he told Spec once: "I have seen too many
good men die to humble myself before people whom I do not respect." Such an attitude was of course bound to be noticed inside
the closed, hothouse world of the motion picture business, a world
that thrived on rumor, illusion, and sociability.

But more than that, Audie seemed incapable of concealing his
dislike of those he considered phonies. In interviews he was not
reticent about saying what annoyed him about industry people. He
objected to the casual familiarity, even to "good morning's" and
"how do you do's." But he objected most to the more flamboyant
styles: "They slap each other on the back and then big hugs and
kisses and then 'Ooooh, darling'—everyone says it—and I think
they overdo it to the point of being sickening," he said in a 1948
interview. According to his pal Budd Boetticher, Audie "never bothered about what he said to somebody if he thought they deserved
it. You cannot tell somebody he's an asshole in front of people and
have that fellow want to take you to dinner. He was very outspoken
and he was tough."

At one splashy Beverly Hills party that Wanda and Audie attended, there was an incident that underlined his basic toughness
and aloofness. He had a run-in with Lawrence Tierney, an actor of

such huge height and width and imposing demeanor that he re-minded Shelley Winters of a gangster. James Lydon tells the story best:

"At that time there was a very large drunken Irishman and mean, who had just become a star. Name of Larry Tierney. He had just done Dillinger. And Audie was going at the time with Wanda Hendrix, who was another terror. The pair of them looked like they should have a halo on them. They were tiny and demure and sweet.

"Anyway, Audie and Wanda were going together at the time and they were at a very lovely party in Beverly Hills, Bel Air. Lots of guests. And Tierney was loaded, and using all the foul language, and making a total ass of himself. And Audie very quietly went up and tapped him on the shoulder and said, 'Mr. Tierney, you don't know me, my name is Murphy and I'm here with my girl, and please, don't do that anymore.'

"And Tierney looked at this little waiflike child and said, 'Get away from me.'

"And so Audie left and about ten minutes later, he came back and said, 'Mr. Tierney, this is very disturbing, please don't do that anymore.'

"Tierney shrugged him off, and Audie went away again. And the third time—Audie always spoke very quietly, you could just barely hear him with a microphone—the third time he came up to him and tapped him on the shoulder again. Tierney turned around and he looked him right in the eye and he said, 'Mr. Tierney, I've told you twice and I'm not going to tell you again. Get your hat and coat and leave right now.'

"And Tierney looked at those eyes and got his hat and coat and left."

Audie's eyes were the thing that everybody remembered. Lydon remembers them to this day: "Audie had steel gray eyes. They were cold, almost deadly, in this very angel-like countenance and this very, very slight, certainly unthreatening stature."

Audie himself referred to this incident years later: "I remember one night at a party when I got in a beef with Larry Tierney. If somebody hadn't stopped me, I would have very happily killed him."

Audie was sort of stampeded into asking Wanda to marry him. It happened this way. When Audie and Spec were returning from the tour of the French battlefields in July 1948, the American press in New York were far more interested in whether Audie was going to marry Wanda Hendrix than they were in recalling the reasons for the trip in the first place—his exploits on the battlefields of France. At Idlewild (now Kennedy) Airport they asked him about the relationship, and Audie said he'd marry Wanda "when I can afford it." According to Spec, he'd meant to say the opposite, "when she can afford it," as a wisecrack. Tired, he'd slipped up on the pronoun. The press flashed the news across the continent, and in California Wanda's mother, much opposed to her daughter's marrying the out-of-work actor, said the kids were too young to marry and that Wanda was departing soon for Italy to star in *Prince of Foxes* with Tyrone Power. Wanda's mother intimated that working with Tyrone Power might make her daughter forget Audie Murphy.

Audie was furious when he saw that story. From his hotel room, with Spec present, he called Wanda and got everything settled. "Hello, Skipper, are you going to marry me? Okay, darling, I'll see you in a few days."

"What did she say?" Spec asked.

"She said she's ready."

"Brother, you're engaged."

When Audie returned to L.A. in late July, Wanda met him at the airport, and after hugs and kisses they told the press they planned to marry "any day now." Then he bought a simple gold engagement ring set with a diamond and in early August he slipped it on her finger. Audie, Wanda, his cousin Elizabeth Lingo, who was Wanda's secretary, and Mack and Mary Hendrix all celebrated at the Ristorante Chianti, the same place the couple had gone that night of the $7 date. The wedding would take place at Christ Memorial Unity Church in North Hollywood in December, the exact date depending on when Wanda returned from making *Prince of Foxes* in Italy.

While Wanda was in Italy, Audie rented an apartment from the mother of his old pal Harry Reginald and began to buy furnishings. The press relished such a role reversal and chirped about Audie's being up to his knees in upholstery materials and pots and pans. It was funny, the press said, to hear the most decorated soldier discussing "watermelon pink" as a color motif. "Maisonette Murphy," one writer called the little two-bedroom apartment in West Hollywood.

Wanda's being so far away seems to have made him nervous and even more determined to marry. He was wary about "wolves" trying to date Wanda. "That's another thing that scares me," he said. "These Hollywood jerks who yell 'darling!' when they see a girl and then make a grab for her." He vowed he'd "bash" anybody's face in who made a move in Wanda's direction. A month later, in December, he felt better. Poised to launch the new year with a book, his first starring film, and marriage, he told an interviewer, "Things look very good now."

The press was 100 percent in favor of the marriage. In the jaded world of Hollywood gossip columns their romance was a welcome change from the usual studio-manufactured pairings. "It's very refreshing to meet two young people as wholesome and real as Audie Murphy and Wanda Hendrix," chattered a typical gossip column item. To members of the Hollywood community like James Lydon, they were "the cutest couple you ever saw. They looked like two kids in a choir." They were marketable, too. The Lane Cedar Hope Chest ran ads in magazines and newspapers that showed a smiling Wanda receiving her "own true love gift," a cedar chest, from a smiling young groom-to-be clad in his Army dress uniform. These two "real-life sweethearts" were "starting their dream home," purred the ad.

Movie Play called it the "Love Story of the Year." Both the principals knew better. In a treacly article in *Photoplay* that appeared the month they were married, Audie, even amid the hype of a ghost-written piece, sounded very tentative: "Anyhow, I'm pretty positive now that it is the only marriage for me." He went on to talk about how he and Skipper or Charlie or Slug, his pet names for Wanda, were going to have a boy named Danny and a girl named Kathleen and several other kids to boot. Skipper, he said, had changed him for the better, had made him a "kinder person." He also spoke about the metaphysics of romance from the male perspective. Despite the trashy rhetoric, the statement is a kind of index of gender thinking in that era: "The way it is with a guy is that he starts with an idea of his dream girl. Then, if he finds her and she lives up to the dream, the mood of marriage just sort of drifts over him. He's trapped for life and scared about it and glad about it, all at the same time."

After almost two years of a troubled courtship, Audie and Wanda brought that period of their lives to a conclusion, they hoped, through the time-honored tradition of holy matrimony. Audie believed that there was "nothing wrong between us that marriage wouldn't fix up." He couldn't have been more wrong.

They married on January 8, 1949, an event marked by both comic anxiety and dark forebodings. Audie forgot the wedding license and had to race back to his bride's house to retrieve it. Among those left waiting at the church were Paul Short, Audie's best man; pals Harry Reginald and Terry Hunt, who were ushers; Wanda's maid-of-honor Elizabeth Lingo; Wanda's family; a hundred guests; and Wanda. To make matters worse, Wanda was still suffering from a bad case of the flu she'd caught in Italy and come down with shortly after returning to California. She'd been forced to go to bed with a temperature of 103°, and she was still shaky.

The photos in the fan magazines revealed nothing beyond the predictable images of marital bliss. Audie looked properly joyful as he took part in the familiar rituals of cake-cutting and posing for album shots. Wanda, after having her hair lightened for her last two films, had dyed it back to its natural nearly black shade because that's the way Audie liked it. She looked like a happy bride in her ivory slipper satin with full skirt and Basque bodice, an Edith Head design. Some luminaries from Hollywood were on hand to lend further glamour to the occasion. Edith Head herself was there, and Ann Blyth, a star at Universal at the time, and Mona Freeman, another brunette actress. To look at these stars is to realize how thoroughly *au monde* Wanda was. It was an era of demure brunettes. Donna Reed played the part beautifully, and in real life Jane Wyman played it for Ronald Reagan. Sexier, more assertive brunettes like Lauren Bacall worked the other side of the street.

The photos didn't come close to revealing the tensions that flickered beneath the sunny surface. According to Wanda, "From the beginning of our marriage, Audie changed suddenly. I thought I knew him well, but it was as if I had married a stranger." Nearly thirty years later she described the mortal chill she felt on her wedding day: "Everything was going fine while we went together. But the day we got married, standing at the altar, he rejected me. It was the moment when I lifted my veil for him to kiss me that I noticed the change. His eyes were those of a stranger."

Afterwards, in the limousine that whisked them away from the church, Audie moved to one side of the car, away from Wanda. At their "honeymoon apartment," Audie said something that Wanda never forgot: "If there's a God in heaven, I hope he forgives me for what I've done to you tonight." Years later, Audie told a reporter, "She had no more right around me than a lamb around a grizzly."

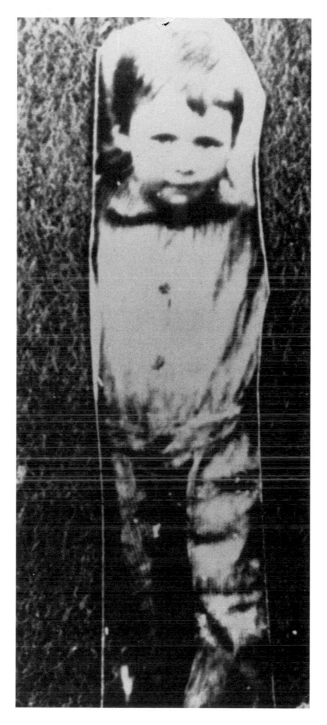

Audie at age two, 1926. (W. Walworth Harrison Library, Greenville, Texas).

Audie in Austria, June 2, 1945, wearing the Congressional Medal of Honor and the Legion of Merit, awarded that day. (Texas Collection, Baylor University).

Audie in basic training at Camp Wolters, July 1942, looking for all the world like a doughboy from the Great War. (Texas Collection, Baylor University).

The *Life* cover that catapulted him into national prominence and a trip to Hollywood. (James Laughead, *Life Magazine*, © 1945 Time Inc.).

Sister Nadine, Audie, and a rifle that he brought back from a slain German sniper. Part of the *Life* layout, July 1945. (James Laughead, *Life Magazine* © 1945 Time Inc.).

Audie gets a haircut: a bit of Norman Rockwelliana done in *Life*'s classic style. (James Laughead, *Life Magazine* © 1945 Time Inc.).

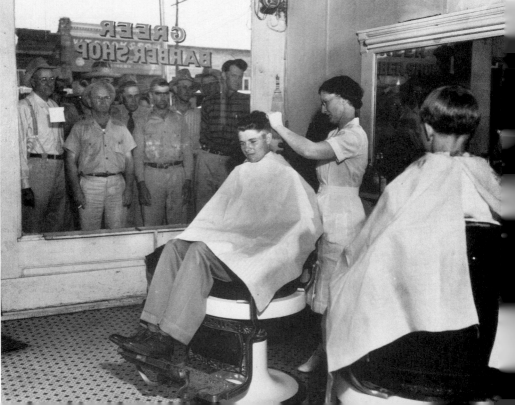

Sergeant York meets Audie Murphy, Dallas, July 1945. Audie wanted to know how Coop was able to gobble like a turkey. (W. Walworth Harrison Library, Greenville, Texas).

Audie looking innocent and disheveled after encounter with hitchhiker, near Dallas, December 1946. (Wide World Photos).

Tending garden at Jimmy Cagney's estate in Beverly Hills, ca. 1945–47. (W. Walworth Harrison Library, Greenville, Texas).

Three friends: David "Spec" McClure, Audie, and Wanda Hendrix, 1948. Spec and Audie were writing *To Hell and Back* at this time; Audie and Wanda were dating. (Texas Collection, Baylor University).

Audie in solemn moment at graveside of war dead, France, 1948. (Texas Collection, Baylor University).

Audie as West Point cadet in his first screen appearance, *Beyond Glory*, 1948. (MCA Publishing Rights).

Marketable Americana: Audie and Wanda pose for newspaper ad. (W. Walworth Harrison Library, Greenville, Texas).

First starring role, as young hoodlum in *Bad Boy* (1949). (Larry Edmonds).

Audie's first starring role for Universal, *The Kid from Texas*, 1950. (MCA Publishing Rights).

Audie as Stephen Crane's Henry Fleming in the *flop d'estime*, *The Red Badge of Courage*. (Turner Entertainment Company).

Audie and Pam, All-American couple. (Texas Collection, Baylor University).

In action still from his smash box-office hit, *To Hell and Back*. (MCA Publishing Rights).

Audie riding into a town full of hypocrites, in dark, pre-spaghetti-style Western, *No Name on the Bullet*. (MCA Publishing Rights).

Venetia Stevenson and Audie; their off-camera romance spiced up the making of *Seven Ways From Sundown*, a 1960 Universal shoot-em-up. (MCA Publishing Rights).

As an aging Jesse James in cameo in last film, *A Time for Dying*. (Budd Boetticher).

With Michael Redgrave on the volatile streets of Saigon, in *The Quiet American*, 1958. (© 1958 Figaro Incorporated. Renewal 1984 United Artists Corporation).

Audie at his desk, a couple of weeks before his death. (Budd Boetticher).

Beneath all of this highly charged, melodramatic language, it is hard to know what is really being said. Was Wanda a virgin? Or did the act of marriage make Audie suddenly treat her differently?

Audie caught the flu from Wanda, delaying their wedding trip. They spent the first week of their married life at the apartment in West Hollywood. Audie had gone all out to decorate it for her: wall-to-wall carpeting, French Provincial furniture, pale green walls, a fake fireplace, a bedroom furnished in maple, a dining nook, a remodeled kitchen.

The press mentioned several proposed sites for their honeymoon: Mexico, the desert, Texas, Oregon. Texas is where they went, finally, when Audie recovered enough to travel. They honeymooned on the ranch of Ray Woods, the Dallas automobile dealer who owned a spread north of the city. Like nearly everything in their lives, it was a photo opportunity.

"In Heaven, Texas" ran the title of an elaborate movie magazine piece. They were shown admiring a copy of Audie's brand-new book *To Hell and Back*, having a pillow fight like two kids at camp, and making biscuits in a flurry of checkered aprons. In one photo Wanda, decked out in western garb, looks uncomfortably like Dale Evans, while Audie, also in rugged western attire, presents her with a freshly slain rabbit ready for the pot. They went horseback riding, they hunted, and one day they drove over to Celeste, the little town where Audie had gone to grade school. They strolled about the streets and stopped in at Nix's store to visit with the locals and admire some newborn puppies. In McKinney they visited with Audie's highway patrolman friend Everett Brandon, who gave Wanda a shooting lesson with a pistol. To Audie's Texas friends, Wanda seemed both the "clinging vine type" and someone who was "always on stage."

The honeymoon lasted ten days, after which Wanda went back to Hollywood to begin work on a new film, *After Midnight,* and Audie plunged into promotional trips plugging *To Hell and Back* and *Bad Boy.* They would be apart much of that spring, indeed much of the year.

Audie, who hadn't had so much publicity since he had returned from the war, cooperated with both his publisher and the studio in extensive promotional activities. For the book he made radio appearances and attended autograph parties.

Publicity efforts for *Bad Boy* were even more extensive. In a swing through Texas climaxed by the film's premiere in Dallas on

February 16, 1949, Audie made appearances at both Texas A&M University and a joint meeting of the House and Senate in Austin. At A&M he donated twenty-five signed copies of *To Hell and Back* to the university, and in Austin he gave a full-scale twenty-five-minute speech before the assembled legislators. Although he had not yet mastered the art of public speaking, he knew how to play to the audience's awareness of his nervousness. He apologized for occasional stammering "and for that clacking noise, which is caused from my knees knocking together." In a speech compounded of standard social doctrine regarding the new problem called juvenile delinquency, he proposed that lawmakers make parents more legally responsible for their children's wrongdoing and that juveniles charged with misdemeanors not be placed in jails. In an interview he made the tie-in with the movie explicit: "Not enough people pay attention to youngsters. I hope *Bad Boy* can do something about that. It ought to wake up some delinquent parents, who are usually the ones at fault." The promotional angle made at least one legislator angry. Senator James E. Taylor of Kerens objected to recessing the Senate to hear the war hero speak. Said Taylor, "I've seen men buried who deserved more medals than Audie Murphy ever got." After Taylor's objections were roundly denounced, he publicly apologized to Audie, and the matter was closed when Audie sent a telegram saying there were no hard feelings. Ironically, Taylor's remarks were scarcely different from what Audie himself had been saying ever since he came back from the war—that the real heroes were dead. Audie was a big hit with the legislators, and he gave them and the governor signed copies of his book.

In Dallas the premiere of *Bad Boy* was a glittering affair, with a packed house and friends from Hunt County as well as Dallas in attendance. Before the screening of the film, there was a live variety show on stage followed by the appearance of Audie and his co-stars Jane Wyatt, Lloyd Nolan, and Jimmy Lydon. Audie acted as master of ceremonies and performed creditably, demonstrating a "refreshing lack of the often seen slick professionalism" that "instantly won his audience with his shy boyish charm," said Fairfax Nisbet, a Dallas *Morning News* reviewer.

Audie was on a non-stop schedule. The next day he attended a book autograph party and hit the road for openings of *Bad Boy* in Oklahoma City, Tulsa, Memphis, and New Orleans. The regional focus would become characteristic of the marketing of many of his subsequent films, and though he was not yet comfortable making public appearances, regional audiences loved him anyway. In time he would become a seasoned pro at this sort of thing. The publicity blitz was a complete success. *Newsweek* summed it up well: "Everywhere Murphy's geniality won friends, his book won readers, and his movie won fans."

It had taken Audie about four years to get a foothold in Hollywood. Now he had done it. On the strength of *Bad Boy*, one of the big studios was interested. Universal, which had been around since the pioneer era of early Hollywood, thought Audie had the stuff to be a cowboy hero and would fit in well with its multitiered plan to cope with the shifting vagaries of the film business in the late forties. TV had killed the classic B western, driving two famed sandlot studios, Republic and Monogram, out of existence. In and out of financial crises in 1946, 1950, and 1952, Universal counted on a two-level production line of well-made adventure films along with cheap, low-budget, but profitable series such as the Ma and Pa Kettle comedies and the Francis the Talking Mule films with Donald O'Connor. In the early fifties the studio scored triumphs with big westerns such as *Winchester '73* and *Bend of the River*.

Where Audie figured in studio plans was in medium-level Technicolor westerns that would outclass television's small screen black-and-white shoot-em-ups, supply small-town audiences with plenty of action and traditional plot lines, and satisfy the still steady appetite for B westerns. So Universal signed him to a seven-year contract. It looked like a pretty good deal: $2,500 per week for forty weeks a year. That added up to $100,000 a year, just under three quarters of a million for seven years, before taxes. All he had to do was learn to act passably, and he would be set.

7.
KID WITH A GUN

"I don't know what else the studio could have done but put me in horse pictures. They were sort of on-the-job training for me."
—*Audie Murphy*

Movie magazines called Audie Murphy the kid with a gun. They were right in more ways than they knew. He earned his niche in history with a gun, and it was with a gun that he built his career in movies. He made no fewer than ten westerns that had "Gun," "Bullet," or "Rifle" in the title. The identification of Audie and guns grew so fixed in the public mind that he felt the need to explain himself, saying, in 1953, "Maybe everybody thinks of me, even in a Western movie, as the baby-faced killer who shot all those krauts. What they don't know is that I stalked and watched maybe twice as many—and never took a crack at one."

Audie's first film for Universal set the tone for many to come. In May 1949, back from the exhaustive promotional tours for *Bad Boy,* he began work on *The Kid from Texas,* which told yet again the story of William Bonney, a.k.a. Billy the Kid. In a deliberate attempt to evoke Audie's well-known Texas roots, the screenwriters altered the historical record by changing William Bonney's actual birthplace, New York City, to El Paso. From a marketing standpoint the title could not have been better.

Yet there was some anxiety on the part of both producer Paul Short and the publicity staff at Universal regarding the casting of Audie Murphy in the role of a well-known outlaw and killer. Short spoke to the question in an interview: "I have been criticized for casting Audie first in *Bad Boy,* then in the role of Billy the Kid, the worst bad boy of the old West. . . . Why have we done this to Audie? Why have we made a heavy of the hero of heroes in World War II?" Short's answer: Audie was simply following in the footsteps of such great stars as Clark Gable and Spencer Tracy who had begun their careers as heavies. The other reason was more convincing: such roles did not require sophisticated acting skills, which Audie had yet to develop. As Short put it, "We have made it as easy for Audie as possible, by casting him as Billy the Kid, who did most of his talking with his gun."

The story of Billy the Kid, which had been filmed many times, had always made the Kid into a romantic figure, but the earlier actors, Johnny Mack Brown, Robert Taylor, even Jack Beutel of Howard Hughes's notorious *The Outlaw,* had all been men. *The Kid from Texas* helped define a new subgenre, the kid western. Audie played Billy as a juvenile delinquent, the first of a long line of youthful protagonists as the western searched for new ways to reach the large audience of increasingly affluent teenagers in postwar America. Audie, the first of the Billy the Kid kids later played by such actors as Paul Newman and Kris Kristofferson, made a career out of such parts, even joked about it once, saying he was kidding his way through the movies.

Audie saw Billy the Kid in the light of his own background. Billy was a childhood favorite, he said, "a kid caught in a web of circumstances," a boy "who might have gone straight under different circumstances." Audie felt an instinctive kinship with Billy: "When I was a youngster, I might have become another Billy the Kid if I hadn't had wonderful neighbors who pitched in and gave me jobs and helped in numerous ways." Audie also liked the idea of playing Billy "as a quiet guy, a real human being who made mistakes at times, instead of as a swaggering superman."

The studio carefully crafted its publicity campaign to take advantage of Audie's reputation with a gun and yet to avoid any negative identification with a flagrantly antisocial type. Universal saw Audie as a western action star, not a romantic one. Put bluntly, "a still of Audie Murphy looking at a girl certainly won't sell any tickets," advised a Universal executive. Audie Murphy with a gun in his hand was something else, but Universal had to be careful about pushing that image in the wrong direction. One memo stated: "We should be very careful in the handling of the 'Bad Boy' copy line in conjunction with Murphy's name so that the name definitely indicates that 'Bad Boy' was a title of a motion picture and that it is not a descriptive phrase for Audie Murphy." A later memo showed further sensitivity to the problem: "The feeling up front is that the 'Bad Boy' reference adds nothing to Murphy's stature and also that as a personality he is well enough known to get along without the line." So the "Bad Boy" reference was dropped from both print and radio ads.

Audie's war record was a constant temptation. Without his stubborn resistance, Universal publicity flacks would have relentlessly played upon the military angle. A typical memo reveals the staff's thinking along those lines in promos for *The Kid from Texas*. They envisioned an Armistice Day photo-layout showing Audie "in civilian clothes with American Flag and racked guns in background," "Audie hunting ducks—pointing up this is way he prefers to use guns," and "Audie at home in den with guns and keepsakes from Europe in background." His refusal to let his war record be exploited was well known within the studio. Frank McFadden, a publicity staffer who knew Audie well, advised management that "he is very touchy about being identified with veterans' organizations. We should stay completely away from any affair of this type, including making him an honorary member of any post or unit . . . he does not want in any way to trade on his war record."

In other respects, however, Audie was cooperative and worked especially hard on promotional tours, a major part of Universal's campaigns. *The Kid from Texas* tour featured him and six other Universal players, including Scott Brady, Peggie Castle, and Ann Blyth, in a six-day swing through Texas from February 26 to March 5, 1950. They premiered in Dallas, then went by train to San Antonio, Houston, and Fort Worth. Premiere activities in Dallas included press conferences, appearances at Sanger Brothers department store, appearances on several radio and television shows, a parade, and multiple live stage shows at the Majestic, where the film was being shown.

Audie's job was to emcee the stage show. The Dallas *Morning News* reviewer noted that Audie had "developed considerably" since his first appearance for *Bad Boy,* having "gained in poise" and yet retained "the boyish charm that is one of his greatest assets." The rest of the show consisted of songs and skits by Scott Brady, Leslye Banning, and Ann Blyth.

Audie was a smash hit everywhere he went in Texas. Frank McFadden, chief shepherd of these tours, telegrammed the studio about the Houston stopover: "Audie is idol of people here." McFadden added a note on their itinerary: "We travel nights, do interviews and four shows a day. Between times we try to eat." In San Antonio they broke records; long lines waited at the theater all day long. Audie's old friends at Interstate Theatre were delighted. R. J. O'Donnell sent Universal a triumphant cable about Audie's success. Audie himself later wrote of this tour: "Everyone was wonderful to me and said a lot of nice things about the picture. But I must admit that my Texas friends and neighbors are pretty well prejudiced in my favor, and even if the picture had been bad, they probably wouldn't have admitted it."

The film went over very well, too. Fans responded to Audie's screen persona. Dressed in black, handsome, pouty, and deadly, he looked very good in *The Kid from Texas.* He handled the action scenes with assurance, especially the fast-draw shootouts, and he was effective in those scenes in the subplot where he stood apart, the lonely outsider, looking with longing and a kind of Dreiserian hopelessness upon the rich life of the well-placed girl with upper-class advantages. The first hint of potential popularity came at a sneak preview screening in L.A. in August 1949. Sneak preview cards show that Audie was the audience favorite by a landslide, with 103 first place votes compared to 35 for co-star Gale Storm. Comments reflected both predictable success for the film when it opened and a promising future for Audie as a western star. One viewer saw him as a "John Derek type," and a second accepted him as the "Kid" but found him not in the same league as another star of the era: "Audie is good as the 'Kid'—but no one can surpass John Wayne as 'the man.' Audie is here to stay but he should have snatched a kiss somewhere." Another comment must have been especially heartening: "Audie Murphy is a great potential actor. At first I thought the movies were only cashing in on his fame as a war hero but he's OK for my dough." There was also one comment that made a kind of subliminal connection between Audie and his warrior image: "I thought Audie Murphy's ability to handle guns was extremely fascinating and thus I liked those scenes."

For the most part the reviewers liked the Kid from Texas, too. The *New York Times* appreciated his good looks and ability to sit a horse well. *Variety* said Audie handled the Kid assignment "in commendable fashion." *Film Daily, Independent Film Journal,* and *Box Office* all approved of his performance. The *Hollywood Reporter,* however, felt that his "charm and real personality" were not yet sufficient to overcome his limited talents. *Fortnight* took a much dimmer view: "He plays the part with characteristic wooden-faced lack of emotion. Let's face it—Rome wasn't built in a day, and merely saying Audie is an actor doesn't make him one." To scriptwriter Robert Hardy Andrews, negative reviewers missed the point: "What they missed was that he wasn't characterizing: he was being Audie Murphy. William Bonney started shooting and couldn't stop. Audie Murphy came alive when he was Billy the Kid. Waiting on the set, he was ready not to act, but for action."

If *The Kid from Texas* was a big step forward on the road to a career, the other film Audie made that year wasn't. Shot in 1949 and released in 1950, *Sierra* was ill-conceived from the beginning. It had only one thing going for it, spectacular scenery filmed in gorgeous Technicolor, but that wasn't enough to carry an otherwise gabby, improbable, and depressing little western. The story line required Audie to play the sullen, antisocial son of a reclusive father (Dean Jagger) falsely accused of a crime and forced to live in the mountains. For the third film in a row, Audie was playing a bad boy, and even the movie magazines were struck by the irony: "It's strange that Audie, a war hero in real life, should be typed on the screen as a lad who runs afoul of the law." Audie looked uncomfortable most of the time in this film, and his costuming didn't help. He was dressed in buckskin, in a kind of forerunner of the fringed suit Alan Ladd wore a few years later in *Shane.* In publicity releases director Al Green said Audie had "natural acting ability" and predicted that "if Audie was correctly handled the compelling charm of his soft voice and rugged personality might take him as far as Gary Cooper's smile took Gary." But there was nothing in the film that warranted such confidence.

For the first time some reviewers pulled out all the stops in denouncing Audie's performance. Bosley Crowther in the *New York Times* dismissed it as "one of those pictures that would humiliate a

10-year-old child." *Fortnight* made the film a pretext for evaluating the whole question of Audie's bid for stardom: "Probably not since Guy Madison has the screen presented the public with such a riddle as the rise of Audie Murphy to stardom. This boyish war-hero-turned film actor has recently been turned out on Universal-International's range to roam the nation's screens as a cowpoke hero. That he is miscast and unequal to the actor-sized job at hand may be the fault of the producer, but it certainly doesn't make exhibits like *Sierra* any easier to sit through." Such charges were never entirely laid to rest.

In that first spring, 1949, Wanda tried hard to accommodate the needs of career and marriage. She knew that Audie was very demanding, very difficult. An event in March made her feel good about her ability to help him. Audie was the subject of Ralph Edwards's radio show "This Is Your Life" on March 7, 1949. The show brought together several people from Audie's past, one of whom was the daughter of Lattie Tipton, his close Army friend whose death had so devastated him. Audie, Wanda said, was "greatly shaken, almost beyond being able to speak." She comforted him, one of the few times in their marriage when she felt able to reach him: "It made me feel wonderful to think that I could be soothing to him. It made me feel I was needed." Most of the time she felt the opposite, but there was no lack of opportunities when he clearly needed comforting. Once they went to a movie and saw a newsreel of German children, and Audie began to cry. He told her, "I may have killed their fathers."

By the time he began work on *The Kid from Texas,* though, things had already deteriorated badly. When Wanda visited Audie for a week on the set at Idyllwild, California, in June, it was news because already, a bare five months into their marriage, they were separated. In a movie magazine the obligatory picture story, "Second Honeymoon," mentioned rumors about troubles in the marriage, called Audie and Wanda the "mascots" of the movie company, and detailed their moonlit walks and horse rides, all of which proved to be futile efforts to restore things to a dreamy romantic state. One photo showed Audie being cradled by a caring Wanda; another, unintentionally more revealing, showed Audie in his Billy the Kid costume taking aim with a telescopic rifle while Wanda looked on, holding her ears to cushion the sound. Audie's propensity for gunplay was evident. The Production Notes mention that he "treated members of the cast and crew to almost incredible feats of marksmanship with rifle and pistol, clearing the location site of snakes and other pests." He also dazzled cast members with his fast-draw ability. Co-star Gale Storm's son, just a child then, still treasures a photograph of himself, duded up in cowboy gear, cap guns blazing, standing menacingly beside Audie.

Like their romance, wedding, and honeymoon, Audie and Wanda's marriage was conducted under the full glare of public curiosity stimulated by newspapers and fan magazines. In the summer, reports of further trouble began to percolate through the pages of newsprint. The "made for each other couple" was on the ropes. In August, Wanda told a columnist that Audie "fights the war in his sleep constantly." She said he hadn't been well for a long time and mentioned his two ulcers. His poor health and irascibility were taking their toll on her, too. She was underweight. The only thing to do, it seemed, was to separate for a while. Audie was going on a business trip to Texas, and she was going to try to join him there.

Right in the midst of their difficulties they were brought together as co-stars in *Sierra*. Wanda hoped that working together in the spectacularly beautiful Cedar Mountains, near Kanab, Utah, would provide an ideal romantic backdrop for rekindling their marriage. She arrived on the set still limping from a broken foot from which the cast had been removed too soon, but the first day of shooting, she said, was one of the happiest of her life. "All I had to do was relax and be carried around the set in my husband's arms."

That was about the only nice thing that happened in Utah. Audie had painful fever blisters and a severe case of cracked lips from sunburn and literally could not smile because of the pain. He wasn't in much shape for kissing on screen or off. Some scenes had to be reshot later because of his condition.

There was a lot of tension between them, and press reports of difficulties didn't make matters easier. One day after seeing some newspaper articles about their marriage, Wanda started sobbing. Audie, in front of cast and crew, picked her up, hugged her, and whispered in her ear, "Take it easy, baby."

For Wanda, things kept getting worse. The altitude caused nose bleeds and shortness of breath, and in one take she was stung by yellow jackets.

She was either accident-prone on this film or the studio publicity flacks were working overtime. There is evidence they were working overtime. In one scene, when she has been bitten by a poisonous snake, the script called for Audie to administer first aid by firing his pistol in a way that would just graze the wound, after which he would suck out the poison. This wacky variation on the old standby of the hero sucking the poison out à la Montgomery Clift and Joanne Dru in *Red River* prompted a studio memo proposing to cook up a news story out of it: "We can get a wire break from the location site if we want to make an accident of it."

Another time Wanda was "lost" when the mule she was riding wandered off. Audie and a "hastily formed Sheriff's posse" dashed off to find her.

Another headline from late September read: AUDIE MURPHY SAVES BRIDE FROM FLASH FLOOD IN UTAH. What supposedly happened was that a quick rush of water down a narrow draw of Kanab Creek imperiled Wanda and Audie, and with regular western hero derring-do, he swept her off the ground onto his horse and they raced out of the canyon to safety. Like the other rescue stories, this one seems to have been greatly exaggerated.

The "ice-cream-soda romance" melted fast. Even as the film was being made, by early September things had deteriorated to the point where Audie was quoted as saying that a divorce might be the best solution.

Finally, shooting on *Sierra* came to an end, and the real blow fell, back at the Universal lot where Audie announced to the press he was going to Texas for a while. He said, "It's all my fault. She's done the best she could, but I think if we live under separate roofs for a little while, maybe we can work out our troubles."

Wanda, caught by surprise, was too stunned to do anything but acquiesce: "If that's what you want, that's the way it will be." Then she wept in her dressing room and later left fast in her car.

So they split up, hoping to find a way to patch things together. Movie magazines had a field day dissecting the foundering marriage. Maxine LaFarge, in an article entitled "Love Takes a Beating," was not optimistic about the chances of recovery. She stressed differences in career goals and sided with Audie's values: "He does not believe in using people, in contacts, in being seen with the right personalities at the right restaurants." Wanda, on the other hand, wanted fame, money, and glamour, and enjoyed playing "the Hollywood game." LaFarge also suggested that Wanda and Audie's romance was doomed by the very nature of its origin in fantasies created by magazine cover glamour. When reality dawned, she felt, romance was finished.

One of the most thorough public inspections of the marriage appeared in *Screen Stories*. Author Cynthia Miller visited the couple during a photo session intended to celebrate their first year of marriage. In this ironic setting Wanda looked "cool and crisp," but Audie was "wan and melancholy." All during the session "there was an impatience about Audie, a restlessness to get the picture-taking finished, to stop living this photographic lie." In her extensive analysis Miller wound up taking Audie's side, directing attention away from his much-talked-about failings and proposing instead that perhaps the fault lay not altogether in Audie but in Wanda. The case against Audie was pretty strong, Miller conceded. One studio executive traced the problems to Audie's military background: "Veterans in the throes of readjustment aren't easy to get along with. They don't make such great husbands, either." A press agent at Warner Brothers had another theory—money. Wanda was making a lot more money, which was bound to bother a man like Audie: "There he is, one of the great heroes of the War, and he's playing second fiddle to a little girl who doesn't even weigh a hundred pounds. It undoubtedly hurts his ego, and that's why they fight." Another opinion, ventured by a friend of Wanda's, stressed a fundamental difference in temperament: "Audie is as stubborn as a compass. He wants his own way about things. He's also basically anti-social, and Wanda is not, and that's all it amounts to."

Miller turned the tables by looking at the faltering marriage from another angle. In her experience, she wrote, "The truth is that actresses, not war veterans, are the most difficult human beings to live with. Millions of women have married and stayed married to returning war heroes. But how many men have stayed married to film actresses? Very few."

To Miller, the main problem was Wanda's ambition versus Audie's traditional ideas about male/female roles. Wanda wanted to pursue stardom in all the familiar ways: attending the right parties, posing for pictures, bathing herself in the glow of publicity. Audie had only scorn for such career moves. When they quarreled about such matters, he told her, "Now, look. If you want to go to these parties, please go. There are dozens of guys to take you. I just don't like them."

Miller also denied all the negative things said against Audie. He wasn't neurotic; he wasn't cynical and disillusioned; and he didn't live off of his wife's earnings. Miller let Audie speak for himself:

"Hollywood's been good to me and it's been good to Wanda. There've been a lot of stories out to the effect that I'm a psycho, that I'm a bit off my nut, that I'm hard to get on with, that I'm still adjusting myself to civilian life. That's bunk."

In the end Miller was not optimistic about the marriage enduring. Nor was Audie. "If people aren't happy together before children start arriving will they be happier afterwards? These are questions that Wanda and I will have to work out."

Wanda was not silent about their difficulties; it seems no one was. In a signed article in *Photoplay* she spoke of the problems and hopes that surrounded her relationship with this "high-strung sensitive boy." She spoke of his private anguish stemming from the war: "In his dreams, Audie still fights the war." She compared his condition of "war-jangled nerves" to someone's running a fever.

But the biggest problem, she felt, was Audie's pessimism. She traced its roots to his unsettled early family life and, of course, to the war. Even his recent success provided no solace: "Sometimes he gets to wondering, 'What is it all about? Why has all this come my way?' He thinks about the other boys who were in the war, particularly the boys who didn't come back. They haunt him."

While Wanda was in Florida, Audie got in touch with her. He was staying at the ranch of his old friend Ray Woods, the Dallas automobile dealer, where he and Wanda had honeymooned. He invited her to join him, and Wanda agreed. "Audie had made the first move so I felt the next was up to me." She met him there in November, and they enjoyed a kind of second honeymoon. They went squirrel hunting, and Audie claimed that Wanda was a pretty good shot. Mostly they luxuriated in a Texas November, the best month of the year in that hot land, and tried to get things back on an even keel.

In November and December there was a flurry of news reports announcing their plans for reconciliation. Both, of course, made statements quoted in the press. In L.A. where she had returned to begin shooting a new film, *After Midnight*, Wanda said, "We decided to give our marriage another try. If after a few months things don't work out, that will be that. But at least, we will have tried." Audie remained in Texas to finish a hunting trip. In December, a week before Christmas, he was back in L.A. ready to start over. He said, "Everything is still okay. We are going to give our marriage another whirl to find out whether the trouble has been due to Hollywood or ourselves." There it was again—the Hollywood thesis. In Texas they had felt they fared better because they weren't in Hollywood. In Texas things were simpler, and they had talked again about moving there, buying a ranch, living quietly out of the glare of L.A.'s klieg lights. This was a constant litany of Audie's. He may have meant it, but he never did anything about it. Some of the statements sound like farm-boy sentimentality. On that publicity swing through Texas earlier in the year, Audie told *Newsweek*, "Farmers are happier." Trying to imagine Audie and Wanda on a Texas farm is not easy. Audie had seen the bright lights of L.A. where there were racetracks, fast money, beautiful women. Texas made a good reference point for nostalgic ideas of pastoral rectitude, but Texas would never become Audie Murphy's home. Not now, not in the future. Years later, he'd take trips back to Texas to remind himself of what a cotton farm looked like, and every time he'd return to L.A. with renewed energy to make another film, make some more dough.

Wanda had set about finding a new apartment where they could kick their marriage into gear again. She discovered just the right spot: a secluded apartment on a hilltop with a grand view of L.A. below. It had a swimming pool, eucalyptus trees, yucca plants, and plenty of sunlight. She decorated it like a picture from a Hallmark Father's Day card: soft draperies, a bright red sofa with hunting scenes woven into the pattern, a green chair for contrast. Apartment beautiful—fireplace, television, the works.

Audie came bearing gifts: a brace of quail packed in ice and, a bit more romantically, a pair of expensive maroon and powder blue lounging pajamas. Wanda gave him a pair of gold cufflinks shaped like the map of Texas with a diamond marking Dallas, site of their most recent nuptial joy. There, in the new apartment, they planned, as one of the fan magazines put it, to plod "steadily through the dark woods toward the bright plain of marital happiness."

They struggled through January and into February of the new year, but by February 17 things had reached such a pass that Wanda, a little over a year after their marriage, filed for divorce, citing "extreme cruelty" as the reason. Although this charge was required by California law, in this instance it seems to have had some basis in fact. At the hearing in April when the plea for divorce was granted,

Wanda mentioned Audie's constant criticism as a source of discord. She told the press, "From the beginning of our marriage, for some unknown reason, he was constantly criticizing me both privately and in the presence of others. He criticized the way I dressed, the way I moved, the way I talked, the food I prepared, the expressions on my face—anything whatsoever—until I was at the point of tears." Another time she detailed such criticism. If she tried to fix a romantic candlelit dinner, Audie complained that he couldn't see his plate. If she wore colors that he said he liked, he complained that they looked terrible on her. She couldn't please him. It is not hard to imagine similar charges being brought in dozens of divorce cases that year. But there were some unique elements in the case of Audie and Wanda.

Many years later, after Audie was killed in the plane crash in 1971, Wanda talked about their relationship and filled in some of the details that hadn't appeared in print before. The picture she painted of their marriage was dark and tinged with the threat of disaster. Audie, she said, "had the most beautiful smile, but unfortunately he never smiled very much. The war had taken its toll upon him. He was an ancient young man." Audie said the same thing of himself. When he was twenty-five he told a reporter, "Actually, I suppose, I'm about fifty."

His unpredictable rages kept Wanda's nerves on edge. She never knew when he was going to blow up over something. She said, "The only thing I did know was that if I didn't wind up in the nut house, I'd wind up in the grave."

Audie could be very cold to Wanda. According to Spec, "Audie was so cold and brutal toward her that I quit going to see them."

Once Audie came back from a trip to find her on her knees in the bedroom, crutches nearby. She had broken her ankle in the months just before shooting *Sierra* and needed the crutches to get around with. He stared at her and asked, "What in the hell are you doing?"

"Praying."

"Get up. And get rid of those sympathy sticks."

Wanda was something of a firebrand herself. She wept, she threw things, and she threatened to kill herself. Her dramatics made Audie taunt her the more. He'd say, "Okay. Bring up the emotion a little. More anger in the eyes. Now look hurt. Turn on the tears."

Things got so bad Wanda urged Audie to see a psychiatrist.

The doctor "said that if he didn't come for treatments, as he got older he would become progressively worse, and that's what he did." Audie's version of how the session went was grim. Afterwards, said Audie, the psychiatrist "went to see *his* psychiatrist."

The worst thing, though, was the guns. Audie was gun-crazy. He kept the apartment full of them. Close friends like Spec knew all about his obsession: "He never seemed to feel secure unless he was close to a gun. On three occasions he awoke from a troubled sleep, grabbed the pistol, and began firing. He shot a mirror to bits. He shot an electric clock off a wall. He shot out a light switch."

Wanda learned more than she wanted to about this side of her husband's character. "The big thing in his life was his guns," she said. "He cleaned them every day and caressed them for hours." Such behavior scared the hell out of her. "There were times he held me at gunpoint for no reason at all. Then he would turn around and put the gun in his own mouth. I finally told him one night to go ahead and shoot. He put the gun away and turned all white."

Always there was the threat of violence. Director and friend Budd Boetticher remembers an incident from that time.

"She locked him out of their apartment when they were getting a divorce, so Audie went home and brooded about it. You know, he always carried that .45, he was very accurate with that thing, and he came back to the door and said, 'Wanda, get out of the way.'

" 'What do you mean?'

" 'I'm not coming in, but move over to one side of the door.' And he went blam, blam, blam, and blew the lock off, and kicked the door open with his fist, and said, 'I just wanted you to know I can get in there any time I want to.' "

On April 14, 1950, the plea for divorce was granted. A tearful Wanda told Superior Judge Edward R. Brand, "Physically and mentally I was ill. I was very nervous and lost weight, and was under the care of a physician constantly." Her friend Eloise Hamlin confirmed that Audie treated his wife rudely in front of dinner guests. Her lawyer Oscar Cummins reported that in order to try to keep together a pair that everybody agreed were "made for each other," he had arranged numerous reconciliation meetings, all to no avail. There was nothing for Judge Brand to do but accept the petition. He said, "Mr. Murphy's war record is well known, and I am sure it contributed a great deal to his attitude."

Wanda left the courtroom weeping. She was hurt, and she stayed hurt for a long time.

Audie mostly kept quiet about the divorce. He had lunch with Spec on the day Wanda appeared in court; he was in high spirits. Gossip columnists reported that he appeared to be more relaxed, more outgoing. Some movie mags, however, painted him as a "Lonely Joe," a sad sack who couldn't adjust to life on the fast track. The truth lies somewhere in between. Certainly he was glad to be rid of the pressure of the troubled marriage. He said he'd fought more in eight months of that marriage than he had during the whole of the war. So it was a relief to be out from under that kind of emotional barrage. When he did talk publicly about the divorce a few months later, he thought he understood what had happened:

"I suppose ours was doomed from the outset. Wanda Hendrix is a sweet, gentle-spirited girl and I want her to have all the good things in life she's worked so hard to get. But we were a lifetime apart in our mental attitudes if not in years. I grew up during the war and I suppose I was intolerant of the things that Wanda, like most other women, valued—maybe I was unduly cynical."

Years later, when he was at the height of his success, he spoke again of that first marriage. This account stressed more fully his own problems and tallied closely with what Wanda and Spec said. "I was in no shape to get married. I had nightmares about the war— men running and shooting and hollering and then my gun would fall apart when I tried to pull the trigger."

Every war produces its own nightmares. Vietnam vets, in a recent study of combatants' nightmares conducted at the Audie Murphy Veterans Hospital in San Antonio, dreamed of killing their buddies, of killing children and women and committing other atrocities. Their least stressful nightmares were "the killing of enemy soldiers." The nightmares of World War II combatants, on the other hand, showed that most men dreamed about the terror of artillery fire. Since more casualties occurred from armored weapons than from any other source, the collective dreaming experience made sense. Fear and helplessness were dominant in such dreams; men cowered in holes, clutching the ground, terrified by the prospect of impersonal annihilation.

Audie's nightmares were different; they bore the stamp of personal trauma. In his dreams the personal dimension was uppermost: Germans came toward him and his gun fell apart. Embedded in a Freudian context, the gun, as every parlor psychologist knows, is a phallus, and the gun-phallus disintegrating in one's hands is a fear of both impotence and death. Impotence on the field of battle causes death; on the field of love, near-death. Although Freud shied away from interpreting war dreams, he wouldn't have had much trouble with Audie's. Nor would Jung. For Jung, Audie's German soldiers would have represented the Shadow, the dark part of the psyche that, if left unacknowledged, can lead to a dangerous suppression of our capacity for evil, can lead to our projecting what's within us onto the Other—other people, other races, other ideas. Instead of coming to terms with the Shadow, we act in accordance with its darkest impulses. We remain in its thrall, leaving us paralyzed to change, to be made whole again.

8.
WAR AND PEACE

"In Korea guys are dying—the real McCoy.
And here I am *playing* at it."
—*Audie Murphy*

In 1950 war was once again much on Audie's mind as the United States was drawn into armed conflict in a distant country on the other side of the world. In late June, North Korea crossed the 38th Parallel in a full-scale invasion of South Korea. To meet the threat, the United States, acting under UN auspices, put two American divisions into the field. Expecting a quick end, the United States just as quickly bogged down. Green troops, outmoded weapons, and fierce North Korean fighting resulted in a prolonged, ugly war that President Truman preferred to call a "police action." Hopes soared after a brilliant U.S. victory at Inchon, but when the Chinese entered the war in November and the North Koreans recaptured Seoul in early January 1951, Americans had their first taste of a limited war. By the time of the cease-fire in July 1953, the war with no real victors had cost America 58,000 lives.

The outbreak of hostilities reminded Audie, as if he needed a reminder, of a larger world beyond that of the film industry's make-believe culture. Still ambivalent about his chosen profession, he felt he had to do something that mattered, and he seriously considered leaving Hollywood altogether for a while. What he did do was nothing so drastic, however. In July he joined the National Guard in Texas, the 36th Division. At the state headquarters in Austin he gave a dramatic explanation: "I think that World War III has already started, and I want to get all the training I can." His importance to the Guard was apparent. Accompanied by three generals, he appeared before the Railroad Commission to make a pitch for oil: "I don't know anything about oil, but I hope you'll save some for the Thirty-sixth Division. It looks like we're going to need it." Holding the rank of captain, he took part in field exercises at Fort Hood, slept in officers' field quarters, gave instruction and drill, and marched with the troops in their final parade. He felt comfortable with such men because they "didn't make any fuss over him and treated him like just another damn soldier," says a retired lieutenant colonel who knew him at that time.

He also made two films in 1950, one just before the invasion of South Korea and one just after it. The first was a routine western and the other was one of the most famous films of his career. *Kansas Raiders*, shot in late May and June and directed by Ray Enright, gave Audie another turn as a youthful, legendary outlaw—in this instance, Jesse James. *Movie Life* pointed out what was becoming obvious: Audie was in danger of being typed as a bad boy. But *Kansas Raiders* was something more; it was, as one reviewer noted, a "war movie" that bore particular relevance to the postwar era.

In *Kansas Raiders* Audie brings a band of young men into the camp of the famed Civil War guerrilla leader, William Quantrill, and pledges their services to fight Yankees. The issue is clear to Jesse. "Some men need killing," he says, especially the kind who maimed his mother, destroyed his family's home, and murdered his father. Quantrill offers revenge and glorious victories, but what Jesse soon learns is that Quantrill makes war against outnumbered and outgunned civilians, not soldiers. In the name of military glory and the "Black Flag," his banner (and the film's original title), he slaughters civilian populations; his "battles" are really massacres. Sickened by the slaying of innocent people, Jesse refuses to ride with Quantrill. Still, he is powerless to leave. We never quite know why, but his attachment to Quantrill has the quality of neurosis. It's as though the orphaned boy cannot detach himself from the sick violence of the father.

While Jesse sees war in traditional terms, armed men facing each other on the field of battle, Quantrill carries out a policy of total warfare, redefining war, making it absolute and waging it indiscriminately against civilian populations, like the bombing of cities by German and Allied forces in World War II.

Reviews of *Kansas Raiders* in general found Audie's performance better than the part he was assigned to play. Several were struck by the "strangely indecisive" nature of "one who later became a notorious desperado." That tension between "killing for revenge and horror of killing," however, is exactly where the interest of the characterization resides. Another reviewer felt that Audie's performance was "okay," and one even went so far as to call it "brilliant and convincing." Of course not everybody agreed. The Los Angeles *Times* stated that although he was not a "skilled actor," his performance would satisfy action fans; the *Motion Picture Herald* declared that Audie "seems to have still a way to go before reaching star caliber"; and the *New York Times* wished he could have added a little more expression to the single note of "grim determination." With *Kansas Raiders* Audie was beginning to develop a trademark style: a soft-spoken, tight-lipped manner beneath which flickered the promise of swift and deadly violence.

Besides making contract westerns with Universal, Audie was interested in doing prestige, non-western films with other studios. One that came his way was another war movie, but he didn't get the part, chiefly because he still refused to play the Hollywood game the way it was supposed to be played. Spec McClure in particular found Audie's attitude both endearing and frustrating. One day in April 1950, producer Jerry Wald told Spec that he was looking for somebody to star in a World War II story, *Force of Arms*.

"What I want is an Audie Murphy type," he said.

"Why not Audie himself? He's available and could use the job," replied Spec.

Wald thought it over and agreed to meet Audie for lunch at Warner Brothers, but the meeting proved fruitless. Audie refused to try to sell himself or ingratiate himself in any way. According to Spec, Audie clammed up and wouldn't talk, and Wald later settled on William Holden for the part. Wald, however, left a record of that luncheon which showed that a real conversation had taken place. In a studio memo he related what Audie had said: ". . . during the war killing became a matter of something that was run of the mill. After the war was over, he found himself gradually losing his desire to kill, and became irritated when he was aroused by reading a headline or talking about somebody having been killed in civilian life. He told me that the reason he goes hunting so much is because he gets an emotional outlet for any desire he might have for killing. . . ."

Then, mainly as the result of friends' efforts and the vision and tenacity of a great director, he landed the lead in a war movie that promised to be everything he needed—a great role in a film based on a classic American novel, with script and direction by none other than John Huston. How Audie came to play the Young Soldier in MGM's *The Red Badge of Courage* is a complex story.

Studio politics, always byzantine, were never more so than during the making of this film. At MGM an undeclared war had broken out between two powerful men, vice presidents Louis B. Mayer and Dore Schary. They had very different ideas about what American cinema should be. Schary, the romantic idealist, lusted after the kind of film that was always hardest for Hollywood to pull off: he and producer Gottfried Reinhardt wanted an artistic *and* a commercial success. They were sold on the idea, on the script by John Huston, and on Huston as director. Mayer, the schmaltzy entertainer, was opposed to the project from the first. His famed instinct for what would sell told him that the American public would not go see a film without a hero, a love interest, or an exciting story. Americans would pay to see Ma and Pa Kettle movies, but they wouldn't pay to see an artistic film, even a war film, done in the European manner.

Mayer hated everything about the project. He hated Huston's most recent film, *The Asphalt Jungle,* a picture full of "nasty, ugly people doing nasty, ugly things." He considered Huston's work too intellectualized, a brand of "stark realism" in the new postwar style imported from Europe. Now his studio was going to make another unpleasant film about "blood and killing," a picture he wouldn't make, he said, "with Sam Goldwyn's money." Said Mayer, "I would rather shoot Huston than shoot the picture. We could then put the money into a defense in court. No jury would convict me."

In the end the decision belonged to Nicholas M. Schenk, MGM's president. He gave Schary the go-ahead either because he wanted to teach the younger man a lesson or because he wanted to force Mayer to resign. He accomplished both purposes.

Once the decision to make the film had been settled, there still remained the problem of casting, and Huston's choice of Audie Murphy was bold and controversial. Again it was Spec McClure who played an instrumental role in getting Audie what promised to be his biggest break yet. When Spec heard that MGM was making *Red Badge*, he called Huston and told him Audie was a natural for the part. Huston agreed but said that his producer wanted a star. This was true; Reinhardt and Schary both wanted someone like Montgomery Clift or Van Johnson, who had starred in Schary's earlier war film, *Battleground*. According to Spec, it was his powerful boss Hedda Hopper who kept the pressure on and got Audie the part. Hedda Hopper had been a friend and champion of Audie ever since she'd first met him, in 1947. A staunch patriot, she admired his war record. Audie often used her staff as a kind of office to take telephone messages for him, that sort of thing. Hedda responded enthusiastically to Spec's suggestion and called both Huston and Schary. Hopper herself explained what she told the MGM executive: "I called Dore and said it would be nice seeing a real soldier playing the part of a screen soldier for a change. With so many of our young men going to Korea, putting Audie in the picture would aid in boosting their morale. Audie got the part."

Spec said that Hopper's influence showed how things worked in Hollywood: "She—in a way—was responsible for casting a part in a book she never read."

Paul Short, Audie's producer for his first two starring pictures, knew the signal importance of this role, too. He wrote Huston a note of thanks: "I regard this . . . as Audie's one really great opportunity in his career." Audie felt the same way, that with such a film he might be able to "continue in the movies long enough to make . . . people think that I wasn't just using pictures as a soft touch." He especially appreciated the chance to work with Huston: "I'd never have tried it if Huston hadn't been making it. I've always been interested in Crane's study of man under fire, and jumped at the chance when he took it over." It was at Spec's urging that Audie had first read Crane's story of Henry Fleming, the Youth who "had been to touch the great death and found that, after all, it was but the great death." Said Spec, "Murphy loved the classic story. He pointed out many subtle facts that I had missed in the book." Told that Crane wrote the book without ever having been in a battle, Audie said, "But he knew that you're all alone in a battle."

Huston, at forty-three already a legend in Hollywood, was totally committed to Audie. "I championed Audie Murphy," he said proudly. He explained why: "He was in the necessary age bracket, he is a good actor and can be a better one, and he has had the combat experience which helps give his role as a soldier complete credulity." An eloquent man, Huston was drawn to what he calls Audie's "rare spirit": "They just don't see Audie the way I do. This little, gentle-eyed creature. Why, in the war he'd literally go out of his way to find Germans to kill. He's a gentle little killer." To Huston, Audie possessed a quality that transcended ability. There was a "greatness" in Audie, he said. "You sense it every time you're near it. You see it in Audie Murphy's eyes. It's like a great horse. You go past his stall and you can feel the vibration in there. You can feel it." Huston stuck by Audie all the way.

Huston had to stand up to Reinhardt because the producer had grave misgivings about not casting a star. According to one observer, Reinhardt was bitterly opposed to casting Audie. But Huston was a strong and cunning champion, and by the time James Lydon and others tested for the role, they knew Audie had it locked up and their tests were just formalities.

Audie wasn't the only bit of risky casting in the film. Huston selected John Dierkes, a man with no previous acting experience, for the role of the Tall Soldier. Huston had met Dierkes in London during the war and liked him. Huston also signed Bill Mauldin, famed World War II cartoonist, for his first acting role as Henry Fleming's buddy, the Loud Soldier. Huston had met Mauldin in Italy in 1943 when he was shooting his great documentary *San Pietro*. The rest of the cast included pros such as Royal Dano, Arthur Hunnicutt, and Douglas Dick. As usual, Huston looked for local people with great faces to fill in the crowd scenes. He sent his men into the pool halls of Chico, California, where they shot much of the film, to search for "grizzled sonsofbitches." There would be nothing Hollywoodish about his film, nothing that would please Louis B. Mayer.

Like Huston, Audie felt that if the film could capture the honesty of the book, it would be a fine piece of work. Most war films failed miserably, he thought, because they were either "glamorized too darn much or they put swish 4F's in them." With his usual bluntness, he included Dore Schary's own recent hit *Battleground* in his indictment. "I didn't like it worth a darn," he told an interviewer in 1948. He thought the humor was "phony." Humor at the front was much saltier, much rawer. But *The Red Badge of Courage,* he felt, could be different. It could tell the essential truth that all wars were alike. The story of the Youth was "something I knew and felt," said Audie. "There's a thin line between being a hero and a coward. That's something the book tries to show and something I learned, too." He wanted to capture on film the novel's permanent sense of truth: "Physically and from the equipment standpoint, the Civil War was different from the last one, but the psychology of this could be any war. Psychologically, wars don't change."

Huston got some of the best work of Audie's career out of him, but it was never easy. He had constantly to maintain an air of confidence and manly cheer around Audie; at times he almost seems to have had to blow the breath of life into the forlorn young soldier. Lillian Ross, a writer for the *New Yorker* who covered the filming of the *Red Badge,* was on hand to observe all she could. She was an "inquisitive little lady," remembers Huston's agent Paul Kohner, and "everybody was afraid of her." In *Picture,* her celebrated book that resulted from the making of the film, she depicted Audie as someone who often appeared "to be lost in a distant dream." She witnessed one little vignette when Huston used his irrepressible spirits to try to lift those of the melancholy young hero. Huston addressed Audie as though he were a "frightened child." Dressed in western-style clothes and boots, Audie "gave him a wan smile and said nothing." Huston boomed along, laughing, carrying the conversational ball, while Audie said almost nothing. Finally Audie said from nowhere, "I've got a sore lip," and briefly related how earlier that morning he had gone riding and sunburned his lip rather badly. Afterwards, over a late breakfast, Huston was still trying to inject some spark into Audie. He asked him, "Excited, kid?" Audie's reply, startling for a young man of twenty-six, was consistent with things he said his whole life: "Seems as though nothing can get me excited any more—you know, enthused? Before the war, I'd get excited and enthused about a lot of things, but not any more."

All of Huston's powers of confidence and charm were required to help Audie bring out what Huston was certain was there. The relationship was paternal, and at times Audie could act like a mischievous boy. In the first showing of some rehearsal footage, Audie spoke up from the darkened theater, saying twice, "I was biting my cheek so hard trying to keep from laughing." Each time Huston said patiently, "Yes, Audie." Audie's habit of mocking his efforts as an actor was a familiar method of covering up for anxiety and insecurity. There were still times when his anxiety took physical forms. One day before shooting began, he told fellow actor John Dierkes that he was suffering from an attack of malaria and a bad case of nausea.

When Audie spoke of his work in the *Red Badge* he typically gave all the credit to Huston: "Anything I do in this picture is because of Huston. I'm not an actor. Huston gets what he wants out of me." Another time he was, for Audie, downright ebullient: "This sort of acting is the life for me. Mr. Huston is one of the greatest directors and grandest guys I've ever met. He gives me the feeling that I'm doing something fine and worthwhile."

Douglas Dick, who played the pompous Lieutenant, remembers how hard the going was at times. Now a psychologist in L.A., Dick says Huston "thought he could probably make an actor out of anybody, but he was not able to make an actor out of Bill Mauldin and Audie wasn't too good an actor. And there was a very important scene with a watch under a tree . . . and they took it and they took it and they took it! They had to take it again in the studio as I remember . . . it just wouldn't come off." Audie, though, "turned out all right," Dick believes. Huston got what he wanted out of him.

Huston couldn't afford to let Audie improvise. The increasingly nervous producer, Gottfried Reinhardt, made sure of that. On the day that shooting began, Reinhardt wrote Huston a memo advising him, first and foremost, to look after Audie. "He needs your constant attention, all your ingenuity (photographically and directorially), all the inspiration you can give him. He shouldn't be left alone for a single second. Nothing should be taken for granted." As shooting progressed, Huston continued to champion Audie's work, and at times Reinhardt agreed that Audie looked very good in the rushes. Once when Huston was going on about Audie, how he was superb, marvelous, sensitive, alive, Reinhardt interrupted to ask just one favor. "Get Audie to smile in the picture. Just once."

Paul Kohner, Huston's agent—and Audie's for a number of years—often visited the set and remembers an incident from that time. Revered in old Hollywood, Kohner goes back to the early days of the industry. He was brought over to this country from Germany in 1920 by Carl Laemmle, the man who founded Universal Studio. Kohner has his office still on Sunset Boulevard, where he has been for the past fifty years.

During one of his visits to Huston's ranch where filming was under way—he says in English with a distinctive German accent—

he saw that "this was a day when there was a battle scene. Huston was sitting on a parapet high up, and next to him was an assistant director, and on one occasion this man yelled at the top of his voice, to the soldiers who were lined up for action, 'Audie! Don't move around all the time!' And suddenly it became very quiet, and out of that tremendous crowd of people one solitary figure walked toward that parapet—it was Audie—and he came up and he grabbed this man on the shirt front and he said, 'Don't you ever talk to me like that again!' This big Irish fellow, he was shivering, he said, 'Yes, sir.' Something hit Audie the wrong way; it was the way he was yelled at."

Huston remembered that the assistant director "was just in the habit of yelling at people and he yelled at Audie. Audie wasn't in the habit of being yelled at. He turned wrathfully on this man, who immediately apologized and shrunk into himself." Douglas Dick remembers this incident, too: "I don't think I've ever seen anybody as angry as he got at the assistant director one day. This fellow was flying off the earth. I could picture him [Audie] killing eighty-three Germans or whatever it was."

The flare-up of anger that Kohner and the others saw was certainly a part of Audie's makeup that Huston knew all about. He was drawn to Audie's capacity for violent action. Huston always loved such men; he had the same tendencies in his own character. His gentle handling of his young war hero/actor carried over into the private arena as well. At the venerable age of eighty, still working, still directing, Huston, one day in March 1987, was in his suite at the Grenville Hotel on Crescent Heights, just off Sunset, right in the center of storied Hollywood. Only a week earlier he had completed a typical John Huston project, filming James Joyce's *The Dead*, an interior story much like *Red Badge* in that both literary classics deal in subtle internal psychological nuances difficult to objectify on the screen.

He sat in the middle of a sunny room from whose windows one could look down on the rooftop of where Schwab's used to be, now a nostalgia shop called Junk for Joy. He appeared exceedingly frail. Dressed in white pants and a white cotton T-shirt, he presided over a room that looked as though someone were just moving in or just moving out. There were unframed paintings, mostly French Impressionist, placed around the room, leaning against the walls as though they might be hung up later or were about to be packed away.

At this point in his life there might have been a thousand other ways to spend his time, but this day he was remembering an old friend. Hooked up to an oxygen tank to offset difficulties in breathing brought on by emphysema, Huston recalled in his charming archaic rhythms that Audie Murphy "had a host of admirers, of course, among whom I would certainly be numbered." Then he began, slowly, laboriously, to recall an incident that happened some thirty-seven years ago when they were shooting *Red Badge*. One day on the set Audie called him aside to tell him something that might become a problem. The off-screen incident, one of many such episodes in Audie's life in Hollywood, takes a while for Huston, with labored breathing, to describe. He tells it this way:

"During the *Red Badge*, one Monday Audie came to me—we were shooting out in Calabasas—Calabasas was a rather barren area at that time; no houses anyway, not at all like it is today. I have seventy-five acres there, and we were using it as the location for most of the shots of the Civil War, the battles.

"Anyway, Audie came to me and said he wanted to speak to me privately, and so we drew aside and he said, 'I think you should know something, John, that happened to me yesterday. There may be repercussions about what happened.'

"He was driving along Ventura Boulevard in his car, and alone, and another car with two men in it was ahead of him, was making passes with their car at some kids on motor scooters, and it was dangerous, what they were doing, and Audie pulled up beside them and said, 'You're damn fools to be doing that; somebody might get hurt.'

"And the kids turned off then, and Audie went on, and the next thing, he came to a stop light, and the next thing, these guys had pulled up beside him and invited him to get out of the car. He had been riding, that was what he was doing out there in the valley, and he had his riding crop in the car. One of the men came forward, and he just leaned out and slashed him across the face with his riding whip. Then the other guy came, then Audie got out of the car. Now I heard the description of what happened by somebody who, after the fracas, recognized Audie and said come with me, and took him to a house that was a little way off Ventura, on a side street, and let Audie wash up although he had no wounds to bathe.

"What had happened was, these two guys came at him, and Audie would knock one down and then the other one, and one would get up while the other was being knocked down until he had them both down and kicked the living shit out of them, and according to this bystander, they were twice his size, which made no difference to Audie of course.

"And the next day, this was very funny, there was an account in the paper how two men had had to go to the hospital and they had been attacked by someone in a car with a Texas license. The newspaper didn't know who it was. Now Audie thought they might trace him and have some lawsuit against the company or against him or arrest him, and he was putting us on warning."

Nothing further came of the incident, but a Valley newspaper reported that the two men in the hospital felt they'd been yanked savagely back to the days of horse and buggy when a man with a riding whip was a formidable foe, or in their words, a maniac. The Texas license plates convinced them they'd run up against a frontier vigilante.

In such moments Audie truly came alive, leapt out of that languorous passivity that so struck Lillian Ross. When danger threatened or when the chance for adventure or a fight occurred, Audie sprang into action and knew once more the intensity of armed conflict. Then—and when he was pursuing a girl, or when he was gambling. In those times the spiritual lethargy lifted, and he felt alive, not burned out.

Bill Mauldin heard the story from Audie, too. On the set he got a firm impression of Audie's intensity. Huston remembers that Audie "kind of bore down on Bill a little bit. Kidding." The kidding had a serious edge, though. In one scene Mauldin's character, the Loud Soldier, was supposed to accuse the Youth of cowardice. Mauldin felt the incongruity, and Audie viscerally recoiled at the notion. Wrote Mauldin, "There's something mighty incongruous about saying, 'Whatsa matter, ya *skeered*?' to a scrappy character who had in real life clobbered a fair-sized portion of the German Army. The script was even harder on poor Murph. Every time I sneered the awful taunt at him, the back of his neck turned dull red and his hands began to curl into fists. After several unsuccessful retakes, he whirled on me and said, 'Listen, you rear-echelon ink-slinger, I know we're only play-acting, but you don't have to say that like you *meant* it!' "

So, Mauldin says, they rewrote Stephen Crane. The script was changed to accommodate Audie's gut-level reaction. Mauldin confesses first to fear, then Audie admits that he too was scared, "but only for a minute, mind you."

Reinhardt's fears about Audie were somewhat allayed as the film began to be assembled. Dore Schary said, "Audie is swell. Much better than I thought he would be." Audie attended the first screening of the film to an outside audience and was surprised at what he saw. "Seems I didn't do all that," he mused, and John Dierkes said, "You sure looked good." Huston thought it was the best picture he had ever directed, and coming from the man who had made *The Maltese Falcon* and *Treasure of the Sierra Madre*, that was something. Hedda Hopper loved it, said it was the greatest war film ever made.

Such euphoria quickly evaporated, though. Schary had earlier been very supportive. He wrote Huston as the rushes came in: "It looks, kid, like we all are gonna do what we said we were gonna do" and, a week later, "The stuff continues just great on *The Red Badge of Courage*." Now, upon seeing the assembled footage, he felt the film needed some changes. Preview screenings before general audiences scared the hell out of him. They proved that though the film might be great art, it was headed for box-office disaster. The first public preview was in Schary's judgment "disastrous." People either loved it or hated it. Too many hated it; there were a lot of walkouts, always a bad sign. Even worse, some very serious scenes, such as the death of the Tattered Man, drew laughs instead of sympathy. To Huston, "the reaction of that audience was the most disheartening experience I have ever been through in a theatre with one of my works."

Now began the process of trying to salvage the film commercially. Schary had always maintained he supported the film as both an artistic undertaking and a commercial enterprise; now all the emphasis fell on the second half of that difficult balancing act. Schary wanted to add narration to explain to confused audiences what it was they were seeing. To many in the audience, the title of Crane's great novel meant nothing; they'd never heard of *The Red Badge of Courage*. In fact, there were some negative McCarthyesque reactions to the word "red," and Hedda Hopper, a true-blue patriot if there ever was one, announced in her column that the film carried "absolutely no Commie implications." Anybody who'd say that "should hang his head in shame."

Before the next preview Schary made several changes in the film. He wrote a prologue that told the audience who Stephen Crane was and that his novel had been "accepted by critics and public alike as a classic story of war." Actor James Whitmore, recently hired by Schary, read the narration off camera. This version drew better reactions than the first, but the audience still laughed at the Tattered Man's death scene. Schary and the other MGM executives knew it would never be a box-office picture. In his autobiography *Heyday*, Schary said the story was too simple for the average audience and asked, "How could America's greatest war hero be a coward?"

Louis B. Mayer and his taste for proletarian kitsch were vindicated by the *Red Badge*'s eventual failure. "All that violence? No story? . . . I know what the audience wants. Andy Hardy. Sentimentality!" he explained. From the studio viewpoint, the best you could say about this film was to call it art and cut back on the advertising budget. That's precisely what MGM did. But not before Schary had further tinkered with the film. He cut the Tattered Man scene; ditched several lingering shots of despondent soldiers; reduced the running time of shots that had been intended to run long, such as the closing one of the Youth's regiment marching away from the battlefield; and otherwise performed surgery that in one instance left the Youth wearing a bandana one moment, without it the next, then wearing it again.

Huston, in the meantime, had departed for tropical Africa to film *The African Queen*, leaving Reinhardt and Schary, they felt, in the lurch. Said Schary, "I guessed he had found a usable raft but that we were to go down with the ship." But from Huston's point of view, the film was in the form that he wanted when he left. As he said years later, "It was while I was gone that the studio proceeded to change it, which they would have probably done whether I had gone or not."

Huston was not the only one who felt that *Red Badge* had been ruined. In 1955, following the success of *To Hell and Back*, Audie, with the backing of friends in Texas, tried to buy *The Red Badge of Courage* from MGM. He wanted to shoot some additional scenes and rerelease it, feeling that MGM hadn't done right by the film either in its editing or promotion. MGM refused. Huston and Reinhardt fared no better. In 1957, Huston asked Reinhardt to try to obtain from MGM a copy of the original negative print. Reinhardt learned that it had been destroyed, and he wrote Huston, in a kind of final comment on the film's fate: "So, I am afraid, *The Red Badge of Courage* is perpetuated according to Dore Schary's taste and the only consolation is that the picture survives him on the lot."

What Huston wanted to achieve in *The Red Badge of Courage* could probably never have been a successful commercial undertaking at that time. The theme of the novel, which he was trying to get down on film, was simply too disturbing, too ambiguous to be understood by the masses looking merely for entertainment. According to Huston's intentions, which were closely in line with the novel's, the war in the movie "must not appear to be a North vs. South war but a war showing the pointlessness of the Youth's courage in helping to capture, near the end of the picture, a fragment of wall." Said Huston, "Now we're at war, but this picture is very basic. It takes no stand. It doesn't say war is good or war is bad. It's just a very careful examination of youth in crisis."

In his statements to the press Reinhardt tried to connect the Civil War with World War II, thinking in this way to point up the connection between Audie's off-screen fame and the role he plays in the film. Said Reinhardt, "The story, actually, is about a GI, with the clock rolled back nearly a hundred years. Audie plays an ordinary guy that ordinary audiences can appreciate."

Fine arguments all, but Americans in 1951, victorious in World War II, now mired in another, far more ambiguous undeclared war in which there would be no victor, were not ready to ponder the thin line between cowardice and bravery. The very theme that intrigued Huston and his young soldier-star was precisely what did not interest general audiences in the least. The irony, humor, and pathos of Huston's war movie were lost on viewers who wanted a rousing, dramatic story in which Audie Murphy won the Civil War. Viewers were simply not sophisticated enough to approach the film with the kind of intellectual detachment that it required. In retrospect Huston himself thought he understood why people so emphatically disliked the film's realism: "It was at the time of the Korean War and I remember myself turning the pages of *Life* magazine and skipping over those pages that had pictures of the Korean War."

Reviewers liked the film better than audiences did, though, in fairness, once the studio decided it would not make money, their withdrawal of support virtually ensured its failure at the box office. The *Red Badge* played in smaller theaters and, saddest of all, found itself on the second half of a double bill featuring an Esther Williams musical. One review, calling it a "war picture that's different," summed up the commercial prospects: "No glamour. No cuteness. Whether it will be box office is something else again."

Audie himself received the best notices of his career to date.

Certainly there were some outstanding reviews in places that counted. *The New Yorker* said Audie "behaves with the soldierly competence that might be expected"; *Newsweek* called his acting "boyishly eloquent"; and *Time* said presciently, "He is brilliantly shown to be the same man: equally confused and irrational, whether as a hero or as a coward." The *Saturday Review of Literature*, a prestige middle-brow publication, made an astute assessment of Audie's performance: "Audie Murphy as the Youth is sensitive, almost womanish, in his responses, wonderfully conveying in the end the dead, somnambulistic feel of a man in combat."

Even *New York Times* reviewer Bosley Crowther, no fan of Audie's work, found good things to say about his performance this time out:

> Audie Murphy, who plays the Young Soldier, does as well as anyone could expect as a virtual photographer's model upon whom the camera is mostly turned. And his stupefied facial expression and erratic attitudes when grim experiences crowd upon him suggest what goes on in his mind. These, coupled with the visual evidence of all that surrounds him and all he sees, plus the help of an occasional narration that sketchily tells us what he feels, do all that can be expected to give us the inner sight of Mr. Crane's book.

One of the most positive reviews, in *Commonweal*, commented on the on- and off-screen personas of Murphy:

> Audie Murphy plays the youth as if he were living every moment of the role, suffering every step as he advances against the enemy, wondering if he will stay to fight like a man or if he will run in cowardice. (I met Mr. Murphy recently and I was surprised to find that he has in real life the same boyish face and fresh, polite attitude that he displays in the movies. It is almost incredible that this youthful, untroubled face belongs to the man who won so many medals in World War II.)

But some national publications offered negative assessments. Robert Hatch in the *New Republic* identified many faults in the film, including an "inexperienced and impassive Audie Murphy." Manny Farber in the *Nation*, pointing also to Audie's real-life war record, said he was "hardly the type to project so much hot, florid perplexity and despair at what the world is doing to him."

Perhaps Huston should be given the last word on Audie's performance. When the film was completed, he said he was satisfied with what the young soldier had accomplished: "For a kid who's had no dramatic training, he's developed into a fine and sensitive actor." Another time he defined Audie's special appeal: "He's got the ability to win audiences. He arouses the maternal instinct in women and the fraternal spirit in men. Not many actors can do that." Huston never wavered in his high opinion of Audie's performance, saying unequivocally in 1987, in one of his last interviews, that it was a "splendid, beautiful performance, everything I had anticipated."

Audie and the *Red Badge* provoked, from beginning to end, a stimulating amount of commentary about art versus commercial entertainment, acting versus directing, and real wars versus representations of wars. What the reviewers and the public saw, however, was not the film that Huston made. That film, before it was altered, may or may not have been one of his greatest. He believes it was. In his autobiography *An Open Book,* Huston wrote that the *Red Badge* proved the truism that audiences' tastes change. Thirty years later, he points out, the film is hailed by many as an American film classic.

Because he was powerful, smart, and a survivor, Schary emerged unscathed from this *flop d'estime,* as one studio insider labeled it; his reputation as a supporter of serious artistic films was intact. This was a picture the studio could be proud of. But neither Reinhardt, Huston, nor Audie realized from it what they had hoped. Reinhardt put *Red Badge* behind him by landing a job as a director of a film with stars and a story; Huston made a pile of money from *The African Queen;* and Audie returned to Universal where he would be on horseback for the foreseeable future.

Ripples from the past, from that momentous *Life* cover, continued to touch Audie. Back in 1945 a pretty raven-haired young Braniff stewardess named Pamela Archer fell half in love with the young soldier's picture on the cover of *Life.* She followed all the news stories about him. "I'd read just about every line that had been printed about him, and you can well imagine that the Dallas papers covered the subject of Audie Murphy pretty thoroughly. My crush on Audie got to be pretty much of a standard joke among the gang at the airport."

Later, in 1947, Pamela heard from a Braniff pilot that Audie was going to attend a big square dance to be held at the annual rodeo at Ray Woods's ranch near Dallas. To honor his pal, Woods had in fact named it the Audie Murphy Rodeo. There, Pamela hoped to meet her romantic hero, but things went awry. As Pam told it, "There were lots of people square-dancing, and I got lost in the shuffle. The next thing I knew there was Audie, Audie Murphy himself, and he was walking right towards me. And you know what? He didn't even look at me! Not for a minute. He just walked right by. Audie Murphy walked right out of my life without ever having walked in."

When Audie married Wanda Hendrix, Pam's fantasy was put on hold. Then, after the divorce, she read terrible things about Audie, "how he was moody, neurotic, and shell-shocked. But I just couldn't believe those stories." She also read stories mentioning his romances, chiefly with starlets who made good copy in newspapers and movie magazines.

There were certainly stories to be told. Recovering from his failed marriage, Audie resolved to play the field—which, in a sense, was no different from what he'd done during his marriage. "I still see Wanda once in a while," he said, "but the divorce still goes. I'm not going to marry again for some time." Without Wanda, there were naturally some lonely times, but Audie never went long without finding female companionship. He said, "Look, I've got a right to have a roving eye." Many of the girls were from outside the circle of Hollywood starlets, brief affairs conducted with whirlwind intensity, then dropped. During his years in Hollywood there were always anonymous women whom he pursued or who pursued him. Spec, who knew a great deal about this side of Audie's life, described the pattern: "Few women could resist him. They seemed to all want to mother him. Audie preferred to be mothered in bed. With each new girl he seemed to develop a flaming passion for a few days or few weeks. Then he would find some way to get rid of the women and at the same time make them feel guilty. I knew about many of these girls as Audie would give them my telephone number. He didn't want them calling him at home. So they would call me and cry on my shoulder." Some women wised up fast. Said one girl, "When I first met Audie, he looked so young and helpless, I wanted to mother him. That passed. I never knew a guy who could take such good care of himself.''

Among the starlets that he dated and that Pam read about, it was Peggie Castle, another brunette, who got the most play in the fan magazines. Audie used his contacts at Universal to land Peggie her first acting role. She went on the promo trips for both *The Kid from Texas* and *Sierra,* but their relationship seems never to have been anything very serious. Besides, Peggie married U-I exec Bob Rains in February 1951. Another girl Audie dated was Princess Sita B. Singh, of Kashmir, India. During a prolonged visit to Hollywood, she spent the better part of a month in Audie's company. This "oriental charmer sent his blood pressure up a few points," said one gossip writer, and she invited Audie to India for a hunting trip. He accepted but never made the trip. In the end she threw him over for another actor, Louis Hayward. It was Hayward, not Audie, who saw her off at the boat when she left to return to India.

Audie might date starlets, but he didn't intend to marry another one. He didn't intend to marry anybody for a while, he insisted. He said, "From now on I'll be a poor man's Howard Hughes." In a more complete sense than he might have meant, he did become a kind of Howard Hughes—insomniac, secretive, suspicious, paranoid, a tireless pursuer of women, a man in touch with the dark underside of America.

Pam, who knew only what she read in the fan magazines, tried once again in the summer of 1950 to meet her romantic fantasy hero, the handsome boy of her dreams. She and her friend Gloria Knight decided to take a vacation in Hollywood. Just before they left Dallas, a pilot friend told them, "Hey, you two. I saw Audie Murphy when he was in town last week. When I told him you were going to the coast, he said to be sure and call him. Always likes to see a couple of gals from Texas, I guess." The girls developed a plan: Pam would meet Audie Murphy, and Gloria would meet Farley Granger. Pam was successful; Gloria wasn't. Pam called Audie, left her number with Mrs. Reginald, Audie's landlord, and he got back in touch with her. He invited the two girls to have lunch with him at Universal. The next night he took them out to dinner at the Malibu Inn, and again the next night. According to Audie later, he was smitten by Pam: "The first time I saw her," he said, "I was a goner. It was at the Miramar Hotel in Santa Monica. She'd come out on a vacation with another airline hostess. I took them both to dinner.

I'd just walked away from an unsuccessful marriage to Wanda, and I wasn't in the market for another wife, or for love. I took them out because they knew friends of mine in Texas. But that Pam. Every time I looked at her, I felt wonderful."

Finally Audie and Pam managed to have dinner alone. "The day before I was to go back to Dallas, he took me to a restaurant near Newport. It was a wonderful drive along the ocean highway, and I guess I fell in love with Audie that night, or maybe I'd been secretly in love with him a long time before that." At dinner she told him about having just missed meeting him three years before, and he told her, "You might have changed my whole life." On her return flight back to Dallas Pam read a copy of *To Hell and Back*, a gift from Audie. From that first genuine contact in July 1950, the lives of Audie and Pam were inextricably connected. There would be marriage, children, happinesses, unhappinesses, separations, betrayals, pain, love, and sorrow.

Pamela Archer, a dark, quiet girl, was born in Kansas, in 1924. A member of a large family (six children in all), she was placed in an orphanage after her father died in an oilfield accident. For nine years she lived at the Wyandotte Indian School, in Wyandotte, Oklahoma. Then she attended Bacone Junior College, in Muskogee, a predominantly Indian school, and later, she spent one semester at the University of Kansas. In 1944 she moved to Dallas and became a Braniff airline hostess, later being promoted to hostess supervisor.

Shy, reserved, she struck everybody as a sweet girl. She was also a career woman with lots of drive. In the days when pretty stewardesses were part of the emerging folklore of airborne America, Pam had a first-rate position with Braniff. As hostess supervisor, she received choice assignments to exotic locales like South America. Pam's apartment roommates from that period liked her, considered her mature and easy to get along with. She was not wild. She was in fact everything Audie was looking for, if what he wanted was a stable marriage, a quiet home life, a family, all the ties that bind. She did not have an actress's temperament and did not like the limelight. She was not a volatile personality ready to explode at a moment's notice. She was capable of anger, of course, but it built slowly and after the fact. She didn't know she was angry until later. Audie's flash-point anger was right there on the surface; hers was slower.

Their courtship was conducted by telephone at first. He promised he would call her when she returned to Dallas, and he did, just two days later. He continued to call. Pam relished her long-distance romance, kept quiet about it except with her housemates, and kept reading in the movie magazines about Audie romancing starlets.

One gossip column squib that might have intrigued her, had she seen it, linked Audie with a Sharon Teggle of Chico, California, where the *Red Badge* company was on location for several weeks. The news item said that Sharon worked at Oser's, the town's leading department store, trimming windows—this was true—and that Audie spotted her one day when she was arranging a showcase and went in and began dating her. In fact, her name was Sharon Quiggle, not Teggle, and she met Audie under entirely different circumstances.

One day on her lunch hour she walked out to the nearby park where the movie company was shooting. It was a natural thing to do; many of her classmates at Chico State College were soldiers in the mock battles. A 5′ 4½″ brunette with dark eyes and olive skin, dressed in stylish pale yellow pants, she was a real beauty, and she wasn't on the set two minutes before a man walked up to her— Audie's stand-in—and said Murphy would like to take her out, was she interested? She was. She bought a new pink and gray dress for the occasion. Audie wore a gray suit, boots, no tie; it was an expensive Western look. He seemed "very very young," about twenty-one, and "looked handsome." Because he'd had to grow long sideburns for the historical period depicted in the film, he looked like a hood, Sharon felt, but he was so nice and so charming that she soon forgot about appearances. "He wasn't really shy when you got to know him," she says. He had a gun in the glove compartment, she noticed.

Audie spent as much time with Sharon as he could. One day he introduced her to John Huston and his new bride, Ricky Soma, in the Hotel Oaks coffee shop. Audie told Sharon that Huston was a "great guy" and "very helpful" to him; he said he admired Huston a lot. The famous director seemed to Sharon a "very likable man." He said Sharon was pretty enough to be in pictures.

When the filming was over and Audie returned to L.A., he invited Sharon and her folks to visit him in the city. They stayed at the Ambassador Hotel, and the first night in town, Audie took them to Chasen's, *the* place to dine. After dinner Audie took her for a drive, and she noticed something odd about his handling of money.

There was a wad of folding money stuck casually in the visor on the driver's side. It struck Sharon as careless. They drove up to the Griffith Park Observatory, the most famous lovers' parking spot in the city. Audie was very affectionate. To Sharon, he was "very macho on a date" and "irresistible." He was "very attentive, a lover."

One night he took Sharon to his apartment to pick up a copy of *To Hell and Back* to present to her. There were stacks of books there, Sharon noticed, and she later wondered if he took all his girlfriends to his apartment under the same ruse. She and Audie became "intimate." Looking back, Sharon says, "I was naive and he was overwhelming."

When Sharon returned to Chico, she completely lost touch with Audie, never even spoke to him again. It wasn't either one's fault. She got married. Audie called her home frequently, but Sharon wasn't there now, and her mother wouldn't tell him anything until finally, when he insisted, she told him Sharon was married and that was that. Years later, Sharon considered seeking him out. Once, she heard, he asked a friend about her. She still has the copy of *To Hell and Back* that he signed for her. She still has the dress she wore on their first date.

In the meantime the long-distance romance with Pam was still going on. Although he told Sharon that Pam "wasn't all that interesting," the story that appeared in the fan magazines was quite different. The way Audie explained it, "The first time I met her I didn't get to spend much time with her. I went away on location for *Red Badge of Courage* and I missed her like blazes." As for her appeal, he said, "There were many things I liked about her when we met. She had so much natural poise and dignity. She was a quiet person—and not in the least inclined to yay-yah-yah all the time. Above all, she was someone who made me feel at ease, someone who was restful and yet very interesting."

Audie didn't intend to get remarried so soon, but he did. After *Red Badge* he spent a good part of the fall and winter in Texas and saw a lot of Pam. They went horseback riding, shooting, hiking, even dancing, something that surprised Audie's friends. Pam had qualities that he believed he needed. They were qualities not so very different from those he had loved in his mother and that he had sought in vain in the rather high-strung and ambitious Wanda. In her post-marriage reflections recorded in signed movie magazine articles, Wanda blamed the failure of her marriage to Audie on their youth. They were too young, too immature, she said, to make it work. She too recognized Audie's search for his mother in his matrimonial decisions. Pam even looked like Audie's mother, thought Wanda. The raven hair, the quietness that approached taciturnity, the Indian blood—these were qualities held in common.

From the beginning Pam's domesticity appealed to Audie. At the house she shared with the other Braniff hostesses, as often as not she'd be ironing when Audie came to see her, and she liked to fix meals there instead of going out to a restaurant every night. Audie had complained about Wanda's ineptitude in the kitchen from day one. Pam looked like she had the temperament and desire to be a first-rate mother, and Audie loved children; he wanted a big family. Pam was also good-looking. Audie said she wasn't a "beauty, but she's lovely. And so *quiet*." All in all, Pam seemed to embody what most men thought they wanted in the fifties, a stay-at-home wife and homemaker.

Telephone calls and whirlwind visits—Audie and Pam were very much part of the new airplane culture of postwar America—intensified the relationship, and the better Audie got to know Pam, the more he was struck by similarities in their background. She too had had to learn to work when still a child. She had seen distant parts of the world but didn't seem worldly or sophisticated; she seemed normal and unpretentious.

Soon Audie began to speak of the future in a way that included Pam: *we'll* do a lot of horseback riding next summer, that kind of talk. Or he'd say teasingly, as if borrowing lines from a B movie: "Pamela Archer sounds too stagey—like one of the tea-drinkin' set. Maybe we'd better change it. You're cute, anyway. Think I'll marry up with you one of these days." Still there were those stories in the fan magazines. Said Pam, "I'd pick up a paper and I'd read about Audie and Peggie Castle, or Audie and someone else, and well, I just didn't know what to believe. I knew that I loved him and I felt that he loved me, but I also knew that his divorce from Wanda wasn't final until April 18, and that anything might happen before then." At one point rumors about other romantic interests prompted Audie to call *Movie Life* to object to a story that said Pam was running second to Peggie Castle. Rumors were fueled by pictures of Peggie visiting Audie on the set of *Kansas Raiders*. Audie pronounced the story "ridiculous." He added, "Pam's a wonderful girl . . . but I won't talk about my marriage plans until my divorce is final."

In February 1951, at Audie's urging, Pam flew out to the coast. She stayed with Audie's friends, the Perry Pitts, in the Valley. Perry and his family had moved to Van Nuys in 1950, and Audie and Perry had resumed their close friendship. To Perry, Audie was much the same: "same walk, same grin, same fellow, giving everything." Perry "couldn't see any change in him other than he was a little more cynical about life." Audie especially enjoyed playing with Perry's kids, helping them take Tinker Toys apart, that kind of thing.

Audie took Pam around and showed her the city, including the little bungalow on Fountain and La Cienega where he lived. Most surprisingly, he arranged for her to meet Wanda Hendrix. He explained, "I thought it might be a good idea just in case Wanda wanted to warn her." It was a curious thing to say, but very accurate. Wanda could have warned her of many things. There is no evidence that she did, however. The other message in Audie's remark is that, in a sense, by making such a statement, he was warning Pam: I am not what I seem. Later, he said explicitly in otherwise innocent fan mag articles brimming with domestic bliss: I am not what I seem. Kidding, he said after they were married, "Wait until she knows me better. She'll find out when she's used to me how mean I really am."

Two months later, on April 2, nine days before his divorce became final, he flew into Dallas early, at 7:00 a.m., and Pam, who'd worked until midnight the night before, was there to meet him. He was wearing his new gray gabardine suit and looked great, and Pam was wearing a two-piece cotton dress.

Back at her house she fixed breakfast, but Audie interrupted her while they were having coffee to present her with a gift, a diamond solitaire, announcing his intention to marry her. She exclaimed, "But it's so expensive!"

"Expensive? It's downright economy. With all this transcontinental commuting I've been doing between California and Texas, it's cheaper to get married. A wedding license only costs two dollars," he said.

She asked what about her job, and he said she could give two weeks notice to Braniff. Pam was delighted. She laughed and said now she'd have to pay her friend Gloria, the one who hadn't met Farley Granger, that ten dollars they had wagered on the outcome of Pam's star-struck romance.

A few days before their wedding, Audie went to Austin to be

honored by the Texas legislature. The occasion was the hanging of an oil portrait of Texas's favorite soldier in full military regalia in the Capitol—it hangs there still—and Audie made a predictable but popular joke about it: "My mother always said I'd be hung someday, but I wish they could have waited until after my wedding."

On April 23 Audie and Pam were married in Dallas, at the Cox Chapel of the Highland Park Methodist Church. You couldn't get more Dallas-respectable than that. S. H. Lynch, a Dallas business-man and friend of Audie's, gave the couple a dinner at the Cipango Club. Skipper Cherry, Audie's friend and theater circuit executive, was his best man; Annabel Schiesher, Pam's close friend and fellow hostess, was her attendant. Pam wore an off-white raw silk suit with sequin-dotted collar and cuffs of pale rose. Audie wore a dark, tai-lored suit. The only sour note was a missive Pam received the day of the ceremony warning her not to marry Audie. The letters clipped out from a magazine to avoid telltale handwriting, it said: "Pamela: If you marry Audie, you will live in fear. I love him." It was signed "Tigress." Pam said it was a "bit of a shock but I wasn't dismayed for I had dreamed of Audie for six years. But the identity of 'Tigress' remains unsolved." She might well have asked, in fear of whom? Tigress or Audie? The letter didn't say.

On their wedding night maybe Pamela thought it was Audie she had to fear, or maybe not. But there was a little episode that pointed to troubled nights in the future. After they were both asleep at the "77" Ranch Motel in Dallas, there was a scraping at the window. Audie, always a hair-trigger light sleeper, sprang awake and reached under his pillow for his gun. He cautioned Pam to be quiet. Outside they could see the shadow of a man as he bent to raise the window. Audie took aim, but Pam cried out, "Audie, don't shoot, please," and the burglar fled. Pam joked about it in press reports, wondering if that was what "they mean by a shotgun wedding."

From the motel they moved to familiar quarters for the rest of their honeymoon. They stayed at a guesthouse at Ray Woods's ranch, the same place Audie had honeymooned with Wanda. Like the first marriage, this one was another photo opportunity for the fan mag-azines. Pictures showed Audie and Pam lounging on the same floppy sofa where he and Wanda had projected such bliss. Shots of domestic harmony, conversation over coffee, selecting records for the phono-graph—such were the joys of "Mr. and Mrs. Texas." There was also a photo of Pam firing a .45 revolver, under Audie's careful tutelage.

In Hollywood they took up their married life in a small four-room bungalow right in the center of things, on the corner of LaCienega and Fountain, in a Spanish-style apartment building. The apartment was homey and cool and quiet, but both hoped to be able to move to a larger place, a house of their own, soon. Pam plunged into creating an orderly, well-run household. She made him breakfasts, which he never used to eat; she kept their apartment sparkling; she was a good "partner." Under her warm care, Audie, said a typical fan magazine, "dares to dream again." The dream was simple: Big house, big garden, big dog.

Pam did the June Allyson bit; she gave herself utterly to the creation of a happy home. Said one fan magazine, "Her sole interest in life thus far is Audie. She cooks for him, cleans for him, takes his phone messages, washes his clothes. She subordinates all her plans to his." Pam said she was "content to be a homebody." Concluded one magazine, "The only career she wants is to be Audie's wife."

Marriage, which sometimes fixes a man's purposes, clarifies his career objectives, didn't entirely do that for Audie. In the summer of '51 the old restlessness and uncertainty were still there. All through this period, he was riven with doubts about his chosen career. The National Guard gave him a way to do something for the Army and for his country. During maneuvers at Camp Polk, Louisiana, Audie returned for two weeks to the professional pleasures of Army life. He gave instruction in the use of the bayonet, and, according to an officer in the guard, his "kids were walking on air, he made tigers out of them." In a searching interview with Tommy Turner, a Dallas *Morning News* reporter, Audie expressed again his deep ambivalence about what was becoming his life's work, acting. Hollywood, Audie said, was not a place he was too impressed with, "and it may be mutual. The studios think I'm difficult. They would come up with a screwy idea of having me photographed sipping a straw in a milkshake with some girl. It was silly and I balked at it." He might have balked, but he did it. Throughout Audie's career he did more Hollywood things and played ball with the studios more than his remarks outside the industry would ever indicate. In this interview he also spoke feelingly of the difficulty of being a celebrity, of people suspecting the motives of whatever he might do. He liked to do things for other people, he said, but somebody would always question his motives. So it was hard being a Hollywood hero.

The reporter formed his own impressions of Audie that he didn't record in the interview. Years later, he remembered how Audie seemed to him at that time in 1951: "Audie was really a sad person who felt he was drifting somewhat aimlessly, after having been robbed [by battle] of his innocent youth and very suspicious of being 'used' by people or organizations. I got the definite impression that it was a crucial transition time for Audie, when he felt he was standing at a big crossroads, and didn't quite know which way to turn. It was in between his war career, the postwar adulation, the knowledge that he never was going to really be a big success as a play-actor." Turner's sketch of Audie as someone "sort of withdrawn, basically shy and in sort of a skeptical, suspicious mood" was a very accurate portrait of a man who was never going to achieve peace within.

Audie of course returned to Hollywood and to Universal. He dismissed previous speculation about quitting the business. "Oh, I know, it's been reported that I'm through with pictures," but that just wasn't so, he insisted. He wanted to succeed as an actor, to show everybody that he'd made it on ability and not capitalized on his military fame. He was philosophical about his future: "I expect they will be casting me in Technicolor Westerns again. Come to think of it, I don't much mind. I'd rather do something the kids go for than be in another artistic success." He wanted to prove once and for all that he'd shaken the troubled veteran image, that he wasn't "a mixed-up guy." And finally, he said: "I want to be happy."

9.
QUICK-DRAW
AUDIE

"Sure the exhibitors love me; I'm a two-bag man. By the
time I'm through shooting up the villain, the audience has
gone through two bags of popcorn each."
—*Audie Murphy*

Following his marriage and the dashed hopes of *Red Badge*, Audie settled into his allotted role at Universal. Along with Francis the Talking Mule and Ma and Pa Kettle, Audie became a standardized Universal product, a small but vital part of the movie landscape in the early fifties. In a string of westerns made in those years he continued to show steady improvement in his acting. The growth didn't happen by accident. By 1951–52 he had begun to work on all phases of his acting, and in the films to follow, climaxing with *Destry* in 1955, he was to hit the peak of his craft and popularity in the western.

One area of expertise that he acquired easily was the fast draw, the *ne plus ultra* of any self-respecting movie cowboy. In the late forties and fifties, when every actor had to prove his manhood by making a western, there was a kind of fast-draw culture that pitted earnest would-be Hollywood gunslingers against each other. Audie naturally wanted to be the fastest draw in tinsel town. Since he had an instinctive affinity for guns, he sharpened his skill so that nobody was better at it.

Audie handled a gun so well, said Michael Dante, who made two westerns with him in the sixties, that "I loved watching him fondle it when he worked with a gun. He was very, very smooth. He fondled it and treated it like it was something very precious. Very smooth. No panic. Very cool, very quiet. I'd never seen anybody handle a six-shooter like him."

Photographic evidence proved his skills. Once a picture editor at Universal set up a fast-draw contest between Audie and three professional sharpshooters. The editor intended to make a series of photographs of the action, but Audie, who beat all three pros, was too fast; the pictures just came out blurs.

Another fast-draw expert who appreciated Audie's speed but never faced him in a contest was Ben Cooper, a baby-faced actor who played in many B westerns, including two with Audie. Cooper operated in the 0.5-second league with Audie, the split-second speed required to clear the holster and fire that was the ultimate test of one's claim to be a fast gun. Today, many years later, Cooper can whirl a .45 from his holster and place it between your hands before you can clap them. Just like in the movies.

He remembers how the competition stacked up in the old days: "At one time people said there were four of us who were the fastest in town, and that was Audie, Dale Robertson, Rory Calhoun, and myself." But it was Hugh O'Brian who thought he was the fastest. O'Brian issued a money challenge to prove it, and Ben Cooper remembers what happened.

"Hugh used to come on strong. At that time he was very enamored of his ability with a gun. And then he started coming on to Audie, and Audie said, 'I'll tell you what. You get real bullets in your gun and I'll get real bullets in mine, and we'll have a go at it. What'ya say?' " O'Brian backed down in a hurry. Friends in Texas could have confirmed the wisdom of O'Brian's decision. They had seen Audie demonstrate his fast-draw skills with live ammunition by blasting okra pods in the garden.

Another Universal star, Tony Curtis, knew how fast Audie was, but he misread the deeper seriousness. For some reason Curtis and Audie didn't get along at all. Curtis had first incurred Audie's dislike when he dated Wanda Hendrix after she and Audie broke up. He later claimed that in a fight scene in one of their films, Audie, jealous and angry, forgot to pull a few punches. But the decisive incident came over a fast-draw encounter. Curtis told a fan magazine what happened: "We used to meet on the set and play a game called 'drop the handkerchief.' Audie would hold one end of a big handkerchief and I would hold the other. We both had guns on our hips. The first one to let go of the kerchief could go for his piece. Audie never lost. Man, he was fast! He would have that gun planted in your stomach before you knew it."

A stuntman told what happened next. "He hid a gun loaded with blanks behind his back and when Curtis lost, he whipped it in front of him and yanked the trigger—and shot Tony. Now this is a dangerous thing. You can get terribly burned from close-up blank-fire, but I guess Audie figured Tony was well padded, what with his heavy leather belt and flannel shirt and leather vest.

"Anyway, he yanked the trigger and Tony's face turned pure white! He began to keel over! I thought the guy was gonna die of a heart attack! When he recovered, he walked away from Murphy and never spoke to him again!"

Tony Curtis's old pal Kirk Douglas, in his recent autobiography *The Rag Man's Son*, recounts similar tricks by Audie and pronounces him a "vicious guy."

Riding well was another requisite skill, and Audie became one of the best riders in Hollywood. His friend Casey Tibbs rated him near the top, and Casey ought to know. A legendary rodeo performer, he won nine championships in a ten-year period, 1949–59, and was twice World's Champion All-Around Cowboy. Like Audie, Casey made the cover of *Life*, in 1951. Casey met Audie on the Universal lot in 1951, when both were working on pictures. One day after shooting, he and Audie worked out a while on the punching bags. When they finished, says Casey, "we went into the steam room to take a steam and so naturally we stripped down and everything and so I knew Audie, and knew of him, and read of him, and I said, 'Mr. Murphy, if you're so brave, how come half of your ass is missing?'

"And he thought it was the funniest damn thing because he had the cheek of his ass shot off. Everybody else just cringed when I said it; everybody else said nobody else in the world could have got away with it. He thought it was funny and we became really close friends."

Looking back on those days many years later, Casey rated all the stars he'd ever ridden with. "Ben Johnson is the best. I'd have to rate Joel McCrea second, followed by Audie Murphy, Dale Robertson, and James Caan."

Audie could draw and fire a gun and he could ride, but could he act? He himself never really felt he could, and those in the industry are divided as to whether he got by on his personality or on his improving skills. Audie's insecurity about his abilities as an actor never disappeared, but many others saw marked improvement over the years. Huston, of course, saw something great early on, in *The Red Badge of Courage*, and the number of reviewers who rated him favorably in his westerns steadily increased. Audie himself remained skeptical: "Sure I like making Westerns. I'm one actor who isn't hankering to play Hamlet—unless I could be Hamlet on horseback."

In any case he worked on his acting, perhaps harder than is generally known. He didn't want to publicize such efforts because of fear of failure. It was safer to take an I-don't-give-a-damn approach, to dismiss acting as a serious vocation, while secretly attempting to improve himself in front of the camera. The fact is, he attended acting school at Universal during this period. In the forties Universal set up classes for its stable of players, the first studio to do so. The school developed twenty-five competent actors and actresses during the early fifties. In the mid-fifties, when the school changed its curriculum, it was a time to celebrate successes of the past. Said a *New York Times* article, "It has paid dividends through such personalities as Rock Hudson, Tony Curtis, Jeff Chandler and Audie Murphy, among others, who now are established box-office attractions."

Estelle Harman ran the school when Audie was enrolled. Over thirty years later, she is still in the business of training actors at her Actors Workshop on North La Brea in Hollywood.

The school gave instruction in voice and speech, dancing and singing, horseback riding, and gymnastic exercises. Audie worked most on diction. Harman wanted him to "clean up the diction" and "to develop other alternatives." Shakespeare was the ticket. Audie studied Shakespeare with Harman. She says that his "honesty and sensitivity humanized Shakespeare." The other Universal actors appreciated what Audie brought to the Bard. Somewhere in her files Harman has tapes of Audie reciting Shakespeare.

Each year at the conclusion of the school term the actors put on a review for producers. *Inside U-I* was a "glorified and exclusive review" to show off its actors and to encourage loan-outs to other studios. For one show Audie worked up scenes from William Saroyan's play *Hello, Out There,* but Saroyan at the last minute refused to grant permission for the work to be performed. A fan magazine ran a photo of Audie, saying he "suffers for his art in big scene from *A Lonely Guy.*"

Audie attended sessions in the school for a year and a half, and later he took private lessons with Harman. This was exactly the kind of thing he would do. A perfectionist, he wouldn't have wanted anybody to know that he was working behind the scenes to improve his acting; he would have been embarrassed.

She found him "very bright" and possessed of a "hungry mind." There was in Audie, she felt, a need to express himself. He talked about writing a book about his early years in Texas. He was an outstanding student because he was hungry to know more and learn more. Although he worked hard to improve his acting, he was always self-conscious about being an actor. He wanted better roles and told Harman when Universal assigned him to a new film, "But I've made this movie before." He was "standoffish and shy" with other actors, and there was something in his "manner that kept them at arm's length."

Audie, Harman, and her husband, a psychologist, became life-long friends. She remembers him as "mischievous, humorous, delightful company." Politically very conservative, Audie read a great deal, she noticed, and was able to hold his own in a discussion. He was generous to a fault. One day in the Universal commissary, she scolded him for tipping the waitress $5 for a cup of coffee. Audie felt the waitress needed the money. One time Audie invited Harman to the races, and she was struck by how cool he was, considering he put down a lot of money. She was not exempt from Audie's penchant for practical jokes. Once on the Universal lot another actor made passes at Harman, and Audie defended her honor. The two men began to fight, much to Harman's dismay, when suddenly both dissolved into gales of laughter. It was a setup; she was one more victim of Audie's humor.

Audie's first western for Universal after his return from *The Red Badge of Courage* was an all-too-typical actioner called *The Cimarron Kid,* which began shooting in May 1951. Audie played once again a misunderstood youthful outlaw, in this instance Bill Doolin, a member of the Dalton gang. The rest of the cast reads like a who's who of future television personalities: Hugh O'Brian ("Wyatt Earp"), James Best ("Dukes of Hazzard"), Noah Beery, Jr. ("Rockford Files"), and Leif Erickson ("High Chaparral"). Working with such professionals gave Audie time to grow and develop. The payoff would be slow but assured.

Like many of these westerns, *The Cimarron Kid* had enough gunplay to worry the Production Code Administration (PCA) which was responsible for overseeing scripts and movies to keep Hollywood films both moral and free from government censorship. "Excessive slaughter" was the problem in this instance. Joseph I. Breen, a well-known Catholic intellectual who headed up the PCA, objected particularly to the "unacceptable killing of a law-enforcement officer which is not essential to the plot" and to "featuring a religious medallion on a criminal." Both of these details "might prove offensive to certain portions of motion picture audiences," he argued, and changes were made accordingly.

Fan reaction brought about another change. Originally the script called for the Kid to bite it, but Universal changed the ending, explaining: "Audie, who receives more fan mail than does any other male U-I star, was killed in his first western for the studio and his fans have not forgotten it." Fan mail statistics, which the studio monitored with the care given by any stockholder to signs of upward market trends, showed just how popular Audie was. In February 1951, totals for the previous month pegged Abbott and Costello with 842, Ann Blyth with 2,766, Rock Hudson (who was just starting out) with 328, Anthony (Tony) Curtis with 1,434, and Audie Murphy with 2,217. That put him second only to Ann Blyth. In May 1951 the top three were Blyth (3,039), Audie (3,019), and Curtis (2,382). By November 1951 Blyth was still tops, with 3,502, Curtis had pulled into second place (2,955), and Audie had dropped to 1,272. These numbers reflected current reactions to the release of films and fluctuated according to that rhythm. Audie was to remain a popular figure for fan-letter mail all during the fifties. He averaged six hundred letters a month and by the mid-fifties was rated among the top ten stars for three years in a row by *Motion Picture*'s annual poll. Contrary to the fan mail received by such rising idols as Tony Curtis, much of Audie's came from "serious minded adults" rather than bobby-soxers, reported Universal. His war record was the explanation.

Promotion for *The Cimarron Kid* was extensive and focused on middle America, the Southwest, and the Midwest. In January 1952 Audie, Beverly Tyler, Yvette Dugay, John Hudson, James Best, and Tommy Turner barnstormed through Kansas City, Oklahoma City, Tulsa, Dallas, Houston, San Antonio, and Fort Worth. The itinerary for Kansas City shows the staggering amount of work required in such publicity campaigns. Audie got star treatment—a large hotel suite compared to smaller rooms for supporting cast members—but he had to do tons of work, too. On January 4, in Kansas City, for example, he began the day at 9:30 a.m. with a radio interview at the Hotel Muehlebach, followed by another radio interview at 11:10, an appearance at the R. J. Delano Home for Crippled Children at 1:00 p.m., and three more radio interviews at 2:00, 3:00, and 4:00 p.m. On Saturday there was a reception at the Chamber of Commerce, a luncheon, a tour of the Veterans Hospital at nearby Leavenworth, Kansas, and a visit with veterans. Sunday they rested; but on Monday he did two radio interviews and a luncheon, and on Tuesday a luncheon and three stage shows. At midnight the troupe left for Oklahoma City to do it all over again.

From Universal's viewpoint, the *Cimarron Kid* tour was an important manifestation of Audie's seriousness and of his value to the studio. Frank McFadden, the honcho on these trips, made a detailed report to his bosses at Universal:

Whenever or wherever he appears, he is a perfect gentleman and when he leaves a room each and every person there has something very nice to say about him. In Kansas City, for instance, the Superintendent of Schools called up and asked if we could remain in the city for two more days, and if so, a school holiday would be declared throughout the city so that the students could attend a huge mass meeting which Audie would address. They consider Audie a modern Horatio Alger and a prime example of what a young man can do in America, starting from nothing. Audie maintains an air of humility which pleases the young fans and actually thrills older people. From time to time we are asked to send someone out to represent the industry rather than the studio. I would not hesitate to recommend this job for Audie at any occasion . . . and although he is not a great orator, he delivers his lines in such a sincere and forthright manner that he is quite reminiscent of a young Will Rogers.

McFadden didn't report everything that happened on these tours. On one of them, there was a foul-up in hotel reservations and Audie said, "Well, what the hell, we'll stay at a motel." So, says Frank, "He and I wound up in a room together. Couple of beds. He took his coat off and this was the first time I ever knew he carried a gun with him. He carried a gun with him all his life. A small revolver.

"So, he gets ready for bed, puts the gun under the pillow. About two o'clock in the morning, I hear this goddamn noise and hitting. Audie's hitting the wall physically—with his fists. Nightmares. His hands are bleeding. And I thought, 'O, shit, here I am with a guy that's got a gun in here.' And I wasn't sure how to handle it. I said quietly, 'Audie, Audie.'

"He went in the bathroom, ran the water. He said, 'I had a dream.'

"And that was all. So I know he had those recurring nightmares. But I never slept in a room alone with him again."

McFadden and Audie became good friends. Frank says, "Audie either liked somebody or he didn't." Audie trusted Frank because he "kinda liked the way I handled things. I wasn't rude to people and yet at the same time we got in and out of places as fast as we could and did everything we had to do and kept on schedule." Because Audie wasn't wild about the tours, he wanted to get them over as efficiently as possible. He'd say to Frank, "Oh, shit, let's go." Much of Frank's job was to keep things moving. Audie "didn't like bullshit," Frank says, "he just didn't like bullshit of any kind. And when people started to give morals or something, he'd say, get on with it. He didn't like people who were hangers-on, the kind of people who tagged along."

He couldn't abide pretentiousness. Yvette Dugay, a sweater-girl starlet with a small role in *The Cimarron Kid,* rubbed him the wrong way. At an airport "in some goddamned Midwest place," they missed an airplane and had to wait. She wanted something to eat, and, Frank continues, "what do you eat at a little tiny airport? She wanted a caviar sandwich." Audie said, "What the hell! She'd throw it up if she ate one."

There were diversions on the road—women and pranks. Frank knew about the women. He says, "Women liked him. I'd go on the road with him, everybody wanted to mother him. Every woman would grab him. He was such a baby face and well known, and a lot of young girls were always chasing him, and he didn't shy away from them."

The pranks were a constant, too. "Audie had a weird sense of humor," says Frank. He liked to do stuff like put a match stem in a can of shaving cream so it would spurt out. Practical jokes. Frank remembers one time in New York, "I was walking with one of the girls from our New York office and was coming back and crossing in the middle of a busy street, and a goddamned apple core hit my shoe, and Audie was up on the seventeenth floor and he'd thrown that apple and it hit just where he wanted to, and he was up there waving. There wasn't twenty inches between myself and everybody else. He put it right where he wanted it. He could do uncanny things, with slingshots, with throwing. It was just natural to him. He had a sense of humor on things like that."

Sometimes Audie's humor took a distinctly male tone. One time in Dallas, he played a joke on the piano player sent along with the troupe. Audie liked him. Frank remembers the setup in detail: "There was a stripper down there. She had the biggest boobs I've ever seen. They ran her picture in the paper all the time, on the entertainment page. The girl with the biggest boobs."

So Audie got the stripper to come up to his room, and he telephoned the piano player and said, "Tommy, my sister's here from Farmersville, and I'd certainly like for you to meet her."

"Oh, sure, I'll come down and meet your sister."

When Tommy walked in, there the girl was, stripped to the waist. "Tommy, this is my sister." Tommy fell right over on the couch, dropped his pipe.

"That was Audie's sense of humor," says Frank. "Anything to shock you or do something so out of the ordinary that you'd not expect it."

There were other diversions, especially in Texas where Audie was "everybody's boy." When they had a little time on their hands, Audie and Frank would stay at somebody's ranch and go hunting for gophers. "He had the goddamndest eyesight," remembers Frank. "That son of a bitch could see and hit a gopher I couldn't even see. Audie was happy down there. He was happy when he was around horses and he was happy on a ranch and when he was around ranch people. That's when he was really Audie."

Audie's unfailing generosity remains vivid in Frank's memory, too. On one trip Frank said, " 'Hey, that's a nice suit.' It was hanging in my closet at the end of the trip." When Frank loaned him some money one time, Audie repaid him with a beautiful watch.

Audie was "never a completely happy young guy," says Frank; so does nearly everybody who ever knew him. One time in Dallas Frank got a glimpse into why. Audie's father showed up one day, at the Adolphus. The man said he was Audie's father, and Frank told Audie, "I ran into a man downstairs who said he's your father." He was rather old and rather fat. Audie said, "I don't have a father." The old man did not come up to the room.

Despite the fact that *The Red Badge of Courage* had flopped, the reviews bolstered Audie's standing in the studio. Universal hoped to devise a campaign for, *The Duel at Silver Creek* (1952), that "while holding his Western fans, would also appeal to the larger following that appears to be in store as a result of his performance in his current picture, *The Red Badge of Courage*." *Duel* was the first picture in which he played a good boy from start to finish. But one thing hadn't changed; again Audie played a kid, this time the Silver Kid.

Don Siegel, one of the best genre directors in American cinema, the man who made *Invasion of the Body Snatchers, The Line-Up*, and *Dirty Harry,* directed this actioner, but there wasn't much even he could do with the script, which he despised. When he complained to the producer about being too rushed, the producer said this was the nineteenth film he'd made that year, so hurry up. Siegel said later, "The only way to do it and keep my sanity is to have fun, and everybody cooperated including Audie. I could put my arm around him and coax some acting from him."

Though there was nothing new in *Duel at Silver Creek* in the way of story line or character development—it was a routine shoot-em-up about a boy who is deputized to help prevent claim-jumpers from stealing the good guys' land—there was something new in the way Audie carried off the part. More reviewers than ever before noted a new relaxation, a growing confidence, and, best yet, an injection of "dry, saturnine wit." One reviewer had a little fun at the expense of Audie's prior reputation: "The killers don't know this act will bring them up against Audie Murphy, who is later to distinguish himself as a hero of WWII."

Gunsmoke, which began shooting in June 1952, under the title "Roughshod," was the first of three taut westerns that Audie made with director Nathan Juran over a period of two years. Nathan Juran, or "Jerry" as everybody calls him, is a wispy-haired, gentle, retired, self-proclaimed workaholic who lives in a fine home on a hilltop in El Monte, south of L.A., overlooking the ocean. Nobody has asked him about making westerns in a long time, and he warms to the memory of those days. An Oscar-winning set designer (for *How Green Was My Valley*, 1941), Juran became a director in the early fifties and had to learn the ropes on the run. His credits include *Hellcats of the Navy* with Ronald Reagan and Nancy Davis, and the camp classic, *Attack of the Fifty-Foot Woman*. The Juran-Murphy westerns were the best of Audie's apprentice work in the period of his growth into full-fledged stardom, and like all B westerns, they were made under less than ideal circumstances. Juran's recollections are a tribute to a now moribund form:

"The terrible thing is that when you make these sort of B class pictures it's a terrible struggle because you get a B class director and you get second-rate actors and you get lousy music, and you get a cutter that's on his way down. All around you're surrounded with the sort of ball players from a team that's down there in Albuquerque or something, and it's tough to get out of that circle. What you really need is a good star, or a hell of a story, but you get poor writing and you get poor everything. Costuming is whatever they had on the shelf and the sets are somebody else's old sets, and it's pretty tough."

The limitations imposed by a restricted budget and a cost conscious studio were always a factor: "You never reshot anything. When you finished it, that was it. Also you didn't dare take too many takes of any particular shot because you didn't have time, it would be at the expense of the show. So most often if the scene was okay, and the part that you knew something was wrong with it, you'd say, well, I'll cover that in the close-up and fix it with a close-up, and very often you'd settle for a scene that's really not good and in the projection room it looks terrible and it's got some holes in it. But then you cover pieces that need to be covered, and there's no options for the cutter except to use those pieces and bridge the gap and usually it would work out fine."

Against this background of hurry, economy, and slapdash film making Audie was a superb action player. To Juran, he was not so much an actor as "a national hero, a unique personality that they— the studio—were trying to cash in on. . . . When I knew him, Audie wasn't an actor, he was a personality." But Audie had physical skills that redeemed his other limitations and that made these hurried productions viable.

Juran remembers one extraordinary incident in particular, a telling bit of action from the glory days of the Bs: "Audie just had an instinct of coordination in everything he touched and everything he did. Physical coordination. The kind of thing I mean is that we did a scene one time, it was a dry kind of fall of the year, and that grass on the hills at Universal was just like glass instead of grass. It was slick and you could hardly walk up these hills because your feet would slide on that grass, and the scene we had to do was Audie coming riding over this hill to the bottom where we were waiting with the camera, to tell the guy that's off camera, 'The whole valley's on fire, get those cattle across the river, move!' My big concern was that this grass was so slick we could never run a horse on it, especially downhill. So I said, 'Audie, I don't know whether we're in the right place to make this scene. This is something you can tell me. It's a hell of a thing. If you stop short it's no good, and if you go too far you're gonna hit the camera because you're supposed to come in to a close-up.'

"So Audie kinda took a little scratch at it with his foot and said, 'Hell, I think I can do it all right.'

"So he went around and got to the top of the hill, and gave him a whistle and the cameras running, here comes Audie over the hill and just as he got over the brow I could see him pull his horse up and the horse puts its front legs up and slid down the hill right up to the close-up in the camera where the mark was and Audie says, 'The whole valley's on fire, get those cattle across the river!'

"Great scene! This guy who knew his horses, guns, knew his own physical . . . he was just super that way. I can't remember Audie ever not knowing his lines, ever making a mistake; he was a sure-shot guy."

The only people Audie felt comfortable with on these shoots were wranglers and rodeo types, guys who didn't work in the movies, guys who "belonged to Audie." They hung around and talked with Audie during slack moments and practiced fast draws and twirled their guns.

Starting with the Juran westerns, the studio tried to expand Audie's audience. Because Audie was a "valuable property," they wanted to "break him in in the East and determine as best as possible what his potential is in this market." So for *Gunsmoke* they adopted a two-track campaign: one stressing romance, the other old-time shoot-em-up entertainment. The appeal to romance was something new, a calculated attempt to draw in more women fans. The studio stressed the "man-woman relationship" in *Gunsmoke,* a focus "considerably different from that normally used on Audie Murphy pictures." Audie's flirtation with a rancher's pretty daughter (Susan Cabot) was played with an adult edge. When he threatens her with a pistol, she says, "You can put your gun away. I'm not dangerous."

"You could be," he says. "You've got the equipment for it."

Different, too, was the style of clothing. For the first time Audie wasn't duded up in all-black outfits or buckskins. Instead he wore practical, working cowhand clothes marked by the dust of the trail. During this period Audie, in a studio press release, reflected upon his concern for realism. In contrast to the glamorous "two-hundred-dollar Stetson hats, expensively-tailored Technicolor shirts and solid gold buckles" worn by other western players of that era, and the kind of fancy clothing Audie himself had worn in earlier westerns, he preferred to "look as near 'natural' as possible in the sartorial line." The gritty new look would become part of his trademark style. The worn, sweated-through hats were a particularly effective touch. Stuntwoman Polly Burson said, "Audie always wore perfect hats."

In the end, though, the studio decided to stick with Marlboro country for the premiere of *Gunsmoke,* and the film opened in Great Falls, Butte, Helena, and Billings, Montana.

Tumbleweed, Juran's own favorite of the three films he made with Audie, featured an amiable horse named Tumbleweed who helps Audie out of several scrapes. In this likable little western Audie played a good guy, a wagon train guide, who is falsely accused of duplicity. Publicity ideas for *Tumbleweed* reflected the old themes grafted onto the concept of Murphy's star status. A feature article called "Guns Have Been Good to Me" was planned. As laid out by the publicity staff, the proposal traced the influence of guns throughout his life, from gunning rabbits to Germans to badmen and redskins: "And now he's a star, what's he gonna gun next?" Reviewers liked the simplicity of Audie's portrayal, his "doggedly honest style" and his "realism."

By now theater exhibitors knew they could depend on Audie Murphy westerns to pull in the fans. Said one Maryland theater owner: "Everybody believes Audie. Another kid that young-looking, handling those guns, and they wouldn't. But when Audie looks out of that smiling Irish face with those clear, calculating eyes, everybody believes him. I can see the show four times, and believe it every time, myself." A nationwide poll of theater exhibitors, conducted in 1953, predicted that Audie would be one of the top male stars of the future.

Press-book copy for theater owners stressed Audie's uniqueness among the big male western stars of the era. John Wayne, Jeff Chandler, Rock Hudson, Jimmy Stewart, and Gregory Peck were all tall men. Only Audie, whose height the press releases stretched to 5′ 10″, could "give the screen skyscrapers a run for their money." And when anybody called him, as sometimes happened, a "pint-sized Gary Cooper," Audie reacted, "I'd rather be a full-sized Audie Murphy."

Drums Across the River, Juran's third Audie western, was released in 1954. A pro-Indian film of the type common since the success of Jimmy Stewart's *Broken Arrow* in 1950, this rousing actioner showed the change in Audie from an Indian-hating youth— they killed his ma—to someone who learns to recognize the common humanity shared by Indian and white alike. In a Technicolor outdoor setting with a strong supporting cast that included Walter Brennan and Lyle Bettger, this film had strong action values and gorgeous scenery, plus a simple pattern of psychological conversion enacted in the great outdoors.

Reviews confirmed what was now a consensus opinion: Audie had arrived as a dependable western star. In the three Los Angeles newspapers, for example, there was mention of his "steadily improving," his "great show of action in his role," and his "grim, unsmiling manner." Each film etched a bit more deeply the recognizable style.

Audie's other westerns from 1952 through 1954 included one that didn't match up to his emerging standard—a cavalry film called *Column South*—and *Ride Clear of Diablo*, which did. In *Column South*, a confusing, overly complicated, and slow-moving pre–Civil War story directed by Frederick de Cordova, Audie played a cavalry officer who struggles to prevent an outbreak of hostilities between a U.S. cavalry splintered by North-South factionalism and Navajos led by Dennis Weaver (later famous as Chester on "Gunsmoke" and McCloud on "McCloud"). In his recent memoir *Johnny Came Lately*, de Cordova, executive producer of Johnny Carson's Tonight Show, remembers that Audie had such "frightening eyes" that camera angles had to be changed in a scene involving anger in order to avoid a close-up for fear of frightening the audience. De Cordova also relates an off-camera incident of some interest. One day during filming Audie learned that General Mark Clark was going to visit the set. Audie told de Cordova to watch what happened when the general approached. Military protocol required all soldiers, including officers, to salute a Medal of Honor winner, and when Clark came into view with his entourage, Audie said nothing, waiting till Clark realized the gaffe and saluted Audie first. Later Audie told de Cordova why he had one-upped the commander of American forces in Italy in World War II: "Too many soldiers, who didn't have to, died at Anzio."

Unlike the assurance and humor he showed in most of his films during this period, he looked ill at ease in *Column South,* stiff and wooden. Even so, *Variety* considered him the "most believable of the players."

Ride Clear of Diablo, on the other hand, was the equal of the Juran westerns. It also brought Audie together with Jesse Hibbs, who would direct Audie in his greatest popular success and in a couple of other films as well. Released in 1954, *Ride Clear of Diablo* presented Audie as a young hero who sets out to avenge the deaths of his father and brother. To the standard revenge plot he brought modesty, quiet effectiveness, and a convincing determination. *Newsweek* summed up the effect of Audie's realistic persona in a remark that would not have been made just a few years before: "It is very difficult for Murphy to appear unnatural in anything he does, whether it be a first-class motion picture like *The Red Badge of Courage* or the present routine job." For someone always at war with phonies, both on and off screen, such a review must have offered some vindication, some degree of secret pleasure.

The new, relaxed cowpuncher on the screen reflected a composed and happier private citizen. One interviewer said she had never seen such a marked change in anyone. When he made *Bad Boy,* he was so tense and unsure of himself he could only answer in monosyllables. Now he was mature and mellow, no longer tense, and "this has let the humor that's in him come out." The new Audie was a "big boy now . . . thoughtful, considerate, kind-hearted."

If in his films Audie had finally become a good boy, the same was true in his home life. The publicity campaign in the fan magazines laid to rest the image of the troubled veteran, the neurotic hero tormented by nightmares, the lonely Joe who couldn't fit in in peacetime America, replacing it with a new good-housekeeping version. Audie played along: "I still have touches of my wartime nightmares, a fact which I've concealed from Pam, but they're gradually diminishing and will probably disappear entirely."

The domestication of Audie underwent its second phase. Now he was the paterfamilias brought to the threshold of middle-class security and happiness by a happy marriage, rising stardom, and impending fatherhood. The fan magazines fairly twinkled with the delights of middle-class bliss.

After Pam became pregnant, with the baby due in March 1952, the young couple moved out of the four-room bungalow into what Audie called "probably the oldest house in L.A.," perched on a steep hill. They would need to move again before the baby got old enough to walk; the incline was simply too dangerous.

The baby was born on March 14, 1952, a boy. They named him Terry after Audie's friend Terry Hunt. Having a boy meant a lot to Audie. Coming from a large family as he had, he liked children and said many times that he hoped to have a big family himself. In a ghosted fan magazine piece entitled "Audie Gets His 'Man,' " his sister Corinne took the occasion of Terry's birth to review Audie's life. She concluded, "Audie hasn't changed at all really, other than to be happier than he's ever been before." His younger sister Billie also felt that Pam was the difference. Said Billie, "Pam understands him better than anyone I know. His idea that a quiet evening at home is fun happens to be hers as well. She's for everything that the guy wants, and doesn't care one whit whether it's the conventional Hollywood or not."

The fan magazines were chock-full of Audie and Terry and Pam—Audie wrestling with Terry, taking him to the studio for his first haircut, discoursing on his hopes and dreams for the child, being picked up late at night at the airport by a happy wife and infant. Audie spent about half of his time on the road, either making films or promoting them. Three or four times a week he spent considerable time with his quarter horses. He still went hunting and fishing. Pam went on some of these outings, but because she was highly susceptible to poison ivy she preferred not to.

In 1953 they moved into their own home in Van Nuys, a redbarn Early American with white shutters and trim sitting on a lot that used to be a walnut grove. The developers had left several trees to create shade and a pastoral effect. One of the sappiest quotes ever attributed to Audie in a fan magazine said: "Perhaps you think this house is built of stone and wood and mortar. But it isn't. It's built of dreams, a tangible creation of a child's dream." Having a home did mean something to Audie. It was part of the package of normality, a way to have what his own father had never been able to achieve: "I only want the things that any man wants: a wife, lots of kids, enough money for security, and a nice home."

The house had two bedrooms, a den, a living room, two baths. Everything was Early American. There was a rack in the den for his sizable gun collection. Here, with "Little Squaw," his nickname for Pam, they would be happy.

He turned the garage into a home-made gym where he worked out. He proved handy enough around the house to pour a concrete driveway. He had little Terry leave handprints in the hardening cement. The fan magazines called it Murphy's Chinese Driveway, after the famous Grauman's Chinese Theater. He would sometimes baby-sit when he wasn't on the road, giving Pam a break to go to church or lunch or shopping or a movie.

They had little social life. Audie didn't like Hollywood nightlife—a source of constant friction in his first marriage. Pam, however, did. She enjoyed the company of celebrities, but Audie found such gatherings awkward and boring—"I don't drink or smoke and there is nothing for me to do at those affairs but sit somewhere like a wet owl and watch."

They didn't entertain much, except for close friends in small groups. Audie continued to keep company with friends he'd formed in the late forties: Spec McClure, Willard Willingham, Perry Pitt and his family. The Murphys' new house was just five blocks from where the Pitts lived. Pam fit right in, and the two families became close friends. They got together for backyard barbeques. The Pitts were there for Pam if something came up when Audie was on the road.

From his marriage to Pam through the mid-fifties, story after story stressed domestic and fatherly images: Audie showing two-year-old Terry around the stables, Terry behind the steering wheel of a car, Terry riding with Audie on the champion quarter horse Flying John. They had titles like "Man Stuff" and "Father Knows Best."

Audie and Pam didn't always agree on child raising. Pam went by the book, Audie by "common sense." Audie thought Pam was too fussy; he wanted to make sure Terry was treated like a boy. He liked to toss the baby into the air, but such roughhousing made Pam wince.

Money was a more serious matter. Audie had never been very good with money, and he hadn't managed it very well to date. All he had to show for the past few years was a new two-toned green Oldsmobile. To give Audie his due, he had elected to take care of his kin back in Texas. He'd bought that house for Corinne and his younger brother and sisters, and he'd continued to send money back to Texas to aid the struggling family. Said Corinne, "His heart's always been bigger than his body—and usually it exceeds his pocketbook, too." But Audie hadn't done so well on the coast. His friend Terry Hunt said Audie had been taken by sharpsters: "When Audie arrived in this town you could've sold him five thousand shares of Atlantic Ocean Preferred. He'd sign anything. Not that he wasn't bright. He's very bright. It's only that he was very trusting. There are a lot of sharp operators in this city. Audie thought they were all men of goodwill.

"One morning he woke up and much to his surprise, he found out differently. He owed one studio two picture commitments, another producer three, and so on down the line. Everyone had a cut of the kid except himself."

Audie himself freely admitted his cavalier disregard for money. "When I was single," he said, "I was usually good for a guy needing a quick dollar, and whenever I had time off with nothing to do I fluffed away my money on things. Also, I made some poor business investments."

Now, with Pam as partner, the fan magazines saw a new management policy introduced into Audie's chaotic financial affairs. It didn't take long before things were turned over to her. Audie wrote a number of hot checks the first two weeks they were married. He neglected to record them, and so Pam took over the family accounts. Said Audie, "She's in charge of our bookkeeping at my request. I've a dream of eventually owning a cattle ranch in Texas, but if we're ever going to save enough for that we'll have to stick to our budget very closely. I'm too impulsive. Pam's more logical, so she takes care of keeping us on the beam financially." Pam was very careful and knew how to stick to a budget, how to cut corners. She got into the habit of using meat substitutes to save money, but Audie, a devout meat eater, retaliated with a birthday present, a cookbook entitled *1000 Ways to Fix Meat.*

By Hollywood standards, the Murphys lived frugally. They didn't have a swimming pool, already the *ne plus ultra* of status symbols, and they didn't have a butler or nursemaids. WHO NEEDS A MINK-LINED SWIMMING POOL? headlined one fan magazine article in which Audie was quoted. "Pam and I live very conservatively—not only from necessity, but also from choice." A girl came in twice a week to help with the cleaning, but the rest of the household management was handled entirely by Pam. They might have been any young married couple living in Iowa or Texas.

Audie specialized, though, in bending the budget with gifts. He wanted a .45 revolver for his birthday and bought it and thanked Pam for the gift. He bought her an expensive vicuña coat for her birthday. He couldn't resist lavishing gifts upon his children. He'd go to a store to buy a 10-cent toy and come back with a $35 item. It happened all the time.

For himself, he liked to dress well and he spent a lot of money to stable and feed his quarter horse, Flying John—at least $200 a month. Audie knew from the first how much trouble and expense horses were, but he loved them and he couldn't resist buying and training more horses. He said in 1954, "The first thing to do is get a promise from your wife that she won't leave you while you train the horse. Because you aren't going to have much time at home."

His sympathy for animals got him and Pam into financial difficulty the first year of their marriage. Audie bought a Doberman pinscher for $125, then in the course of a year spent $1,500 in veterinary bills, only to discover that the dog had distemper. It died, a total loss. The outlay cut into their savings in a drastic way and hurt their plans for new home furnishings.

Another expensive habit was making long-distance calls to Texas. Too impatient to write, he'd call family and friends instead, and the bills mounted up. Pam didn't like that, and she wasn't crazy about his practical jokes, either. Once he put a snail in her bathwater; another time, a green turtle in her bed. In a fan magazine article signed by Pam, she said there were two Murphys: "One of them is a sober and serious young man who is steadily building himself a fine career in motion pictures. The other is a pixie, a prankster, a player of practical jokes."

Despite the touches of potential discord, the overwhelming message of fan magazine copy in the mid-fifties told the story of a happy, domesticated hero turned actor. So it was perfectly fitting that the image of the domesticated gunfighter/husband/father formed the basis for Audie's tenth western, a handsomely mounted film with a solid supporting cast and one of Hollywood's most experienced directors at the helm. *Destry*, which began shooting on May 10, 1954, was George Marshall's second version of Max Brand's story of the shy, non-violent deputy sheriff. In 1939 he'd directed the celebrated *Destry Rides Again* with Jimmy Stewart and Marlene Dietrich. The new version bespoke Universal's confidence in their leading western player. A sunny, warm-hearted film, it brought out the best of Audie's emerging good-guy persona. Here he was required to play an unassuming baby-faced hero possessed of quiet, dry humor—bland, easygoing, non-threatening, yet capable, under stress and with provocation, of lightning-quick violence to set things right. The Murphy image received its most beguiling dramatization in this engaging film.

Destry was the logical fulfillment of the new Audie Murphy the fan magazines had been selling to the public—father, husband, citizen. A triumph of the intricate cultural exchange that took place between studio-generated fan magazine mythologizing and the image that appeared on the screen, it was the perfect cinematic corollary of the domesticated and happy Audie Murphy seen in the fan magazines from 1952 to 1955. One fan magazine photo story entitled "The Murphy Boys" captured this theme perfectly, with shots of Audie, Pam, and the boys on the set of *Destry*, Audie in costume.

A comedy about domesticity, *Destry* outlines the competing claims of an irresponsible masculine world, the saloon, where men foolishly gamble away their hard-earned ranches and lose gifts for their wives to the saloon girl Brandy, a woman who hates other women and who recovers her own femininity through the gentle courtesy of Destry. Destry himself makes several jokes about women—"You'll probably never get old enough to understand a woman," he tells a little boy—but at the end, the gentle town-tamer is walking the streets of Restful with the boy by his side, the brother of the girl Destry will marry.

The formula for Audie in all his westerns was that he would never use violence until forced to do so. In the outlaw films, he was forced early in the film and then could not break out of the cycle of violence. Thus the bad-boy pattern. In *Destry* the film knowingly played upon the audience's expectations, so that when Destry-Audie says, "I don't believe in guns," the audience is disbelieving. What? The kid from Texas not believe in guns? Later, in the demonstration of his gunplay, he says, as though he were a spokesman for the National Rifle Association, "You can have a lot of fun with a gun." The contrast between Audie's shy, self-deprecating gentleness and his remarkable capacity for quick, decisive action achieved its definitive expression in *Destry*. As he says humorously, "We don't want any more promiscuous shooting around here."

Audie's Destry is such a nice man that even the villains grow to like him. With very few exceptions, reviewers did too; there was a chorus of acclaim for Audie's performance. *Variety* went so far as to say that Audie "probably better fits the original Brand conception than his predecessors," high praise indeed. The *Hollywood Reporter* called Audie's role "an amazingly apt bit of casting" and explained: "The audience's knowledge of Audie's war record, both as a fighter and a marksman, gives his mild scenes a remarkable suspense. And as an actor, the young fellow seems to have come into his own. With a sure ease, he underplays Tom Mitchell . . . and Edgar Buchanan."

Already among the top ten in *Movie Life*'s poll of most popular stars—others included, for example, Doris Day, Robert Wagner, Liz Taylor, Dale Robertson—Audie in *Destry* was at the top of his genial form. By now he was so widely identified with the western that J. V. Edson, a writer of formulaic western fiction, based his novel *The Small Texan* (1956) on Audie's persona.

If Audie had been able to achieve in real life the confident self-assurance and healthy wholesomeness of his screen counterpart in *Destry*, he would have been a happy, settled, and *grounded* person. But he wasn't Destry, except in brief moments; he was Audie Murphy, who was ten times as complex as Destry and who held within himself, in uneasy solution, like nitroglycerin, paradoxical and unresolved tensions that could ignite to destroy his hard-won and temporary equilibrium. Destry, it must be said, has only a public life; we always see him as a sociable creature, never alone, never in the dark watches of insomniac nights. The gun that he keeps among his possessions, legacy of his slain father, rests securely in a valise; he doesn't sleep with it loaded under his pillow.

10.
THIS IS YOUR LIFE

"I want this picture [*To Hell and Back*] to be a success, and I'm not sure the public will accept me in the role. I don't think I'm the type—maybe Tony Curtis would do."
—*Audie Murphy*

For as long as Audie had been in Hollywood there had been talk about making a movie based on his military exploits, and the success of his book back in 1949 had made such a project only more tantalizing. Given Audie's growing popularity, it was hardly surprising that by early 1954 Universal thought the time was right for filming *To Hell and Back*. The idea still made Audie apprehensive: "It was a lousy book because it was a lousy war. Once I thought I didn't want to act it out again—because I had been through it and written about it—but now U-I wants to do it as a movie."

He had many fears about the undertaking. He didn't want the film to be a tribute to one soldier, but to all infantrymen: "I've always felt their story should be told. I just play a part in it. This isn't just my story—it's the story of all our company and of the infantry. There's going to be one hell of a jury looking at this film and reviewing it out front." He also felt he owed something to the Army, and this would be a way of paying back part of that debt. "I have to admit," he said, "I love the damned Army. It was father, mother, brother to me for years. It made me somebody, gave me self-respect."

Still he hesitated, and it took old friends like Frank McFadden, no longer at Universal, to help persuade him to make the film. According to Frank, Audie thought the film was "too self-eulogizing" for him to do it. But Frank told him, "Audie, you still look young. This is an historic film. From a publicity standpoint, how many actors ever made their life story? Nobody can portray you better than you can." Audie listened and finally he said okay.

Usually cavalier about preparing for a new film, he threw himself into preparations for shooting the most difficult film of his career to date. His off-screen duties included approval of script and of casting. For the crucial role of his friend Lattie Tipton, he chose Charles Drake, a seasoned actor who appeared, all told, in half a dozen of Audie's films. Said Audie, "I'd known Drake for some time. I liked him—and he has the same quality of quiet dependability Lattie had." Audie also personally recommended the young woman who played the Italian girl that he meets in Rome. After Audie and director Jesse Hibbs had interviewed scores of actresses, Audie suggested they try Susan Kohner, a nineteen-year-old UCLA student and daughter of his agent, Paul Kohner. She got the part. Hibbs said he "found Audie a man of exceptional taste in all matters including casting." Another bit of personal casting was Audie's son Terry, who appears as Audie's younger brother in one of the early scenes from the hero's childhood.

Paul Picerni, a veteran character actor who plays the role of the American-Italian Valentino, landed the part after an interview with Audie. "I remember the first day I met him, at Universal. That was before Universal became all towers and things as it is today. Just a little office in a wooden building. I think Jesse Hibbs was there, and Audie just sat there. We chatted for about five minutes, and he said, 'You've got the part. I'll see you on the set.' "

Picerni remembers vividly the impression Audie made on him: "To me he was a strong actor. He had the same quality that Brando had, or has; he had that inner intensity, that inner strength, because he was a strong little guy. I mean, if you get in a poker game with Audie and he calls you, you'd think about it, or if he raises, you'd think about calling him because . . . just something about him. I was bigger than Audie, but I would hate to be in a fight with him. Because you just had the impression . . . he had that inner strength and it came across as an actor, as far as I could see."

With the exception of Audie there were no name actors in the cast. Universal was a bit worried about that, but what they were more worried about was the grimness of the story itself. An internal U-I memo written early in 1954 described the book as a "series of bloody, graphic incidents" that revealed "mostly hate, frustration, horror, futile courage and terror" and that ended "on a definitely depressing downbeat." The memo concluded that more warmth, humor, and "a more encouraging conclusion" were necessary to lift the film out of the slough of despair.

Both director Hibbs and producer Aaron Rosenberg were acutely aware of Audie's difficulty in approaching the subject of his own life. Hibbs, a convivial man's man and former USC All-American football player who had already directed Audie in *Ride Clear of Diablo,* said that "just getting Audie to talk . . . was like pulling teeth for the first three months when we were planning the picture." He understood the reasons for Audie's reticence: "Audie had come out of grinding poverty to become the most publicized war hero in history. He was understandably sensitive about both of these factors in creating the picture. He knew he was sticking his neck out trying to recreate the war as he saw it."

Audie confirmed such difficulties when he told a reporter, "I was definitely on the spot. I didn't want to do the picture at all at first because I couldn't possibly analyze my own character like I could a fictional one. Ever try to re-enact, even in your own mind, something that happened to you ten years before? It's real tough."

Aaron Rosenberg, like Hibbs an All-American football player at USC, was also worried about Audie's deep resistance to exploring his past. The decision to frame his war exploits with scenes from his impoverished growing up in Texas proved especially difficult for Audie to overcome. "The problem of getting it out of Audie I turned over to Doud [scriptwriter Gil Doud]," said Rosenberg, "and Doud was weeks talking Murphy out of a deep mood which settled over him as he tried to recall the details of a childhood which was spent hunting rabbits for a twelve-place dinner table which knew no other sustenance but bread and molasses." Rosenberg called the whole experience the "equivalent of a psychoanalyst's couch." But Audie had good reason to be worried. During the pre-shooting phase, Rosenberg called Spec McClure in for a conference, and Spec asked him how they intended to portray Audie. "Like a young Abraham Lincoln," said the producer. "Goddamn it, Rosie, you can't do that to Audie," said Spec.

Stuntman and friend Bobby Hoy (he'd doubled for Audie in *Destry*) and the rest of the cast and crew were ready to leave for location shooting in Tacoma, Washington, but there was a delay and they didn't leave.

Hoy says, "I was working out in the gym and Murph came in. And after we worked out, we'd all go in the steam room. And I said to him, 'Audie, what the hell's going on? We're all ready to go and why the hell aren't we going?'

"He said, 'Well, Bobby, there's a sequence in there that I think people are going to laugh at me when I do it.'

"It was a sequence where his best friend is killed and in the film that best friend was played by Charles Drake. The Germans had their machine guns zeroed in during the day and could fire at night in crisscrossing patterns. It was where Charlie was killed by a grenade. Audie reached down and picked up a German machine gun and held it by the barrel. He picked it up and he dispatched about twenty-two or twenty-three Germans.

" 'I think that people will laugh because it's almost a parallel to what Victor McLaglen did in a movie called *Under Two Flags*, where he walked into the fort and picked up the water-cooled .30 and shot all the Arabs off the parapets,' said Audie.

" 'Jesus, Murph, did you do it or didn't you do it?'

" 'Of course I did it.' "

"Fuck 'em," said Hoy.

As production got under way, for both professional and personal reasons Audie continued to assume a bigger role off camera than he had in any previous picture. He wanted to learn, he said, the details of production because in the future "I'd like eventually to be a director." But the personal nature of the film created the overriding impulse to be involved. He said of his contribution to the film: "It would have been tough if I hadn't been so busy all the time. I was sort of an assistant technical director on it and I was helping out with these things. If I'd had nothing to do but sit there and do my little part—I'd have gone nuts."

Once on location, at the Yakima Firing Center, 140 miles from

Fort Lewis, Washington, Audie threw himself into the making of the film with an attention to detail and a concern for authenticity that impressed everybody. Hibbs was struck by the difference between making a western with Audie and making this film. In the western, "he had little to say about the script or the action and did exactly as he was told. In his own story of World War II I found him tenacious about every point." Rosenberg also found Audie totally absorbed in getting things right. One day on the set he watched Audie advise a painter how to color the sides of a crater to show that a fresh artillery blast had just taken place; he checked the uniforms and weapons of GIs and Germans; and he worked side by side with the special-effects crew to create explosions exactly as he had known them in Italy and France. Throughout the shooting, Audie stayed by Hibbs's side, checking details, reviewing dialogue for the next day's shooting, taking part in every phase of the film.

Despite Audie's intimate involvement in every phase of the picture, once they began shooting, he let Hibbs direct the film. Audie, said Paul Picerni, "never tried to step on Jess Hibbs's toes." Nor did he in any way let his personal involvement affect his relationship with others in the film. "Audie on that picture was friends with everybody. I never heard him raise his voice or have an argument. He had a good relationship with everybody on that film." Rosenberg said the same thing: "Never once did I get a report that he had been hard to handle, yet he had more right to be than any star I've known."

Recreating the battle sequences, Audie said, made him feel uneasy. Though it was a "powder-puff battle" and not a "real war," still, "what I felt now was a different uneasiness—the kind you feel when your mind plays back something that you don't want to hear or see or feel again." In recreating the fighting at Anzio, Audie got caught up in the action and had to recover his sense of reality when the director yelled "Cut" because there was too much smoke to photograph the battle. For a while Audie had forgotten that this was a war "being run not by the U.S. Army, but by Universal-International," a war in which "you have to do a retake because a tourist's dog ran across the field in the middle of the battle." In the real war, he reminded Hibbs, "there were no allowances for retakes." Whole fire fights lived again in his memory: "I can remember some of the battle highlights vividly. Especially was this true when I got a gun in my hands and smelled powder during the making of the picture. Smells, I believe, serve as the best reminders." Hibbs noted a powerful sense of verisimilitude coming over Audie in such scenes: "He didn't seem to think about acting. There was a primitive alertness about him all the time. And though it had been eight years since his honorable discharge, it seemed that his training still came to the fore. He reacted to every explosion and every sound of machine-gun fire instinctively."

Those scenes requiring intense emotion were difficult for other reasons. There were two that touched Audie deeply—the death of his mother and the death of Lattie Tipton. Hibbs said that one of his greatest problems was getting Audie to cry: "When we shot the scene in which his mother dies it was such a moving thing for Murphy that he could not weep. The tears were there but they would not spill over. He had sworn, after crying three days over the death of his mother, that he would never shed a tear again." The same thing happened during the second painful episode. Reliving the death of Lattie Tipton bothered Audie the most: "This was the toughest scene for me to do. It should have been easy. I had had to think through[out] the picture, 'This isn't me. I'm somebody else,' so I wouldn't worry about underplaying it." But, said Audie, "I found myself backing away from shooting the scene where Brandon gets killed. I made so many excuses and little criticisms that Hibbs quietly called off the scene and postponed it a day. It finally was shot much as it had happened while we were storming a hill in France." They made one change, however: "When we shot the scene, we changed the part where Brandon died in my arms. That was the way it had really happened, but it looked too corny, they said. I guess it did." According to Hibbs, "Audie wasn't doing much acting in this. He played it as he felt it. His lips were quivering and his eyes filled. Audie had been nervous that day, knowing the scene was coming up. He knew what I wanted from him. I wanted tears. Still, it was a hairline scene and we couldn't go overboard. When Charles Drake was hit and cried out 'Murphy!'—Audie wasn't acting from there on."

Audie's desire to avoid any hint of self-aggrandizement or self-posturing made him particularly alert to such moments in the script. The famous Colmar Pocket action worried him. "Rosie," he said, "I hope we're not going overboard on this hero business. I'm being a lot braver in this war than I was in the other one." Humor came to the rescue. When Audie mounted the burning tank destroyer and the machine gun jammed, he climbed down to wait while the gun was repaired. He told Rosie, "If that had happened in France, you wouldn't have had a picture." Rosenberg was relieved because he knew Audie had a tendency to brood.

Filming the heroic scenes exactly as they were described in the official citations documentation would have resulted in a pre-*Rambo*-like exhibition. The War Department record, said Audie, "looks to most people like some Wild West story." For that reason, he said, they "played down some scenes out of necessity. Truth is realistic to read about, but when seen on the screen it can look exaggerated."

The scene he most objected to was the tag scene, at the end, when he is decorated with the Medal of Honor. In his book, as many reviewers noted with amazement, there was not a single mention of any medals. Now the script called for a big decoration scene, and Hibbs felt it was absolutely crucial. For weeks, Audie refused to let the scene stay in the script. Audie "did not want to glorify himself and above all he did not want the picture to demonstrate how to become a hero." His position was simple: "I think it's kind of silly to show me getting the medals at the end of the picture. Those who know I got the medals will understand. And for the others the events will speak for themselves." Finally, Hibbs and Rosenberg prevailed: "We argued with Murph two solid days on that point. And we won. We had to. How could we shoot the story of the soldier who won more medals than any other combat veteran in history and not show him being awarded the greatest honor this nation has to give?"

In the end the filmmakers won in other respects, too. *To Hell and Back* cleaned up World War II, repackaged it, and made it seem like anything *but* "to hell and back." It sold a sanitized Cinemascope trip through the war zone. You can see this most clearly in the spick-and-span treatment of battles such as Anzio and the Colmar Pocket. Anzio was rain, mud, trenches, and trench foot, but in the film the weather is hardly noticeable. The Colmar Pocket was snow, bitter cold, and frostbitten feet and hands; in the film the battle sequence takes place as though in a sunny park.

The film altered certain facts in the book to refocus our attention away from cynicism and psychological wounds. The result is an American success story. If a completely innocent and ignorant viewer had to guess entirely on the basis of this film what happened to Audie once the war ended, the most reasonable assumption would be that he went to West Point and became a career officer. The movie constantly stresses his promotions, and during one scene at midpoint, just before the invasion of southern France, Audie's commanding officer wants to pull him out of the line and send him to West Point. "You'll never find a better break than this," the officer says. By moving up to a much earlier date this tentative possibility that actually occurred in the summer of 1945, *after* Audie was back in the States, the film creates a very strong impression of such a career. The ending confirms this impression. Audie receives the Medal of Honor—the film says on August 9, when the real date was June 2 (changed, perhaps, to fall after the Hiroshima bombing) and, again, inexplicably, "shortly after his nineteenth birthday"—and watches a parade of soldiers marching past in review. Other changes and omissions include moving Audie's wounding and stay in hospital to *after* the Colmar action, not months before, and the omission of duels with snipers, the action at Cleurie Quarry, and almost all of the horrors of living conditions and the sight of maimed and bloody soldiers.

Audie himself didn't like the final product. He told a reporter it was just a "western in uniform." To his old friend Spec, he confided, "I don't give a damn if this movie makes seventeen million dollars. You were right. We missed by a mile."

Not surprisingly, Universal liked it a lot and went all out promoting *To Hell and Back*. Fearful that everybody had forgotten Audie Murphy's war exploits, they set out to reeducate the public. Wrote Clark Ramsey, a U-I executive, "Audie Murphy's fame as the most decorated hero of World War II had received little attention in the public press since 1947. In fact, Audie Murphy, himself, went out of his way to avoid that type of publicity since he was anxious to establish himself as a motion picture star on his acting ability alone." Obviously Ramsey was thinking about national publications, not fan magazines which were sodden with Audie stories. For U-I the first goal, said an internal memo, was to "make the public aware again that Audie Murphy is the most decorated hero of World War II." So the studio plotted a five-track pre-release campaign featuring national television spots, national billboards, ads in national magazines such as *Life* and *Look*, newspaper and radio ads, and biographical articles in national magazines.

There was also, of course, an extensive promotional campaign featuring Audie. Before the film's official premiere, special screenings were held in Washington, D.C. The Army, which had enthusiastically cooperated in the making of the film, realized full well its value as a recruiting vehicle. Besides personal endorsements by officials such as Franklin L. Orth, Deputy Assistant Secretary of the Army, the Army saw to it that Audie was presented to dignitaries like Secretary of Defense Charles Wilson, General Maxwell Taylor, Chief of Staff, and Vice-President Richard Nixon. Perhaps the most thrilling moment in Washington occurred when Audie visited Congress, meeting in combined session. His old buddy Frank McFadden, who had been hired to handle publicity at Audie's insistence, was moved by what happened: "Here was this little kid, and we were in this front row of the gallery. Teague [Olin Teague, Representative from Texas] interrupted the proceedings and said he wanted to present a very special young man. And I saw the whole Senate arise and applaud this young man." It was also on this trip that Audie visited Arlington National Cemetery. He did so, he told McFadden, because, "Frank, I want to see where I'm gonna end up."

Other promotional activities were more familiar. By now a veteran of such tours, he was philosophical about the necessity of public appearances. U-I premiered the film in Texas, where Audie had always done well. Audie called it "a lucky break for me since it's my home state and I've been back there often enough since breaking into pictures that I feel perfectly at ease—even when I have to get up on a theater stage and talk." And talk he did—many times on that tour he made seven separate stage appearances a day. In Dallas he rode atop a tank in a parade to the theater. In San Antonio he laid a wreath at the Alamo and inducted fifty young men into the Audie Murphy Platoon of the U.S. Army. In all the Texas cities, the film shattered opening-day records. In San Antonio, at the splendid Majestic, it even broke the record set earlier that year by *Davy Crockett*. One newspaper account, probably invented but indicative all the same, turned Audie's arrival in San Antonio into pure myth. A small boy wearing a coonskin cap asked his dad, "Is that Davy Crockett?"

"No," said the father. "It's Audie Murphy. But they're made of the same kind of stuff."

Universal thought they had a solid film, but they soon learned they had a blockbuster. A U-I press release in September 1955 announced the news: *To Hell and Back* was on its way to becoming the studio's all-time box-office champion, ahead of *The Glenn Miller Story* and *Magnificent Obsession*.

For the first time Audie received rave reviews. Reviewers praised his "quietly natural performance," his "magnificent simplicity," and his "magnetism." "Magnificent" and "magnetism" were words that had never appeared in reviews of Audie's work before.

Other reviewers analyzed the effect of his performance in depth. The *New York Times* said his screen presence lent "stature, credibility and dignity to an autobiography that would be routine and hackneyed without him." *Time* caught another element in Audie's portrayal, something just beneath the surface: "And just for a nervous instant, now and then, the moviegoer glimpses, in the figure of this childlike man, the soul-chilling ghost of all the menlike children of those violent years, who hovered among battles like avenging cherubs, and knew all about death before they knew very much about life."

In every sense, critically and commercially, *To Hell and Back* was a smashing success. Nor was its or Audie's success confined to America. The British film magazine *Pictuegoer,* an influential popular weekly, named Audie among the ten best actors of the year, putting him in such company as Yul Brynner for *The King and I*, Laurence Olivier for *Richard III*, Marlon Brando for *Guys and Dolls*, and James Dean for *Rebel Without a Cause*. Even in such a far-flung corner of the world as Australia, Audie and his story were a hit, making the Aussies suspend their widely held opinion that "The Yanks give you a medal if you cut yourself shaving."

In the United States the film came out at exactly the right time for a nation which, having just fought its first war of attrition, the "police action" in Korea, was ready to be reminded of a better time, just ten years before, when the victories had been clear-cut and unmistakable. *To Hell and Back* was the answer. It made Audie Murphy into a "modern folk hero," said a film historian. Audie rivaled Davy Crockett, Fess Parker's folksy Disney hero, in popularity, and became, wrote one reviewer, "truly the Sergeant York of WWII conquering everything in sight." A generation of American kids, born since the war, many of them the sons of combat veterans of World War II, absorbed Audie Murphy into their collective consciousness, so that when some of them came of age and were drafted and sent to Vietnam, one of their models of heroism was the kid from Texas. But it also spoke to their parents, Audie thought. "It had a lot of appeal for a cross section of World War II vets and Korean vets. Women went to see it and said it's like my husband talked about and thought it was real—that's why it had lots of appeal."

The success story of *To Hell and Back*, both on and off screen, paralleled the general public's perception of Audie Murphy in 1954–55. The birth of a second son, on April 5, 1954, seemed to confirm the image of domestic bliss. James Shannon Murphy, named after Audie's Dallas friend James Cherry, quickly became "Skipper" to his parents and to readers of fan magazines.

Further proof of Audie's success and status could be seen quite vividly in his appearance on Ralph Edwards's popular TV show, "This Is Your Life," which gave a kind of official cultural imprimatur to worthy lives of the era. As in his earlier appearance on the radio version back in 1949, people from his past and present were brought forward to offer testimonials. His sister Corinne reported how Audie's mother was fond of saying, "If Audie just had a chance he'd make something of himself some day"; soldiers from B Company were there to give witness to his bravery on the battlefields; Terry Hunt, his old pal at the gym, told about Audie's early struggles; and Pam told about their romance. Edwards's schmaltzy peroration at the end defined Audie in the same glowing language of the fan magazine articles about his newfound maturity and happiness: "Yours is a full life now, Audie Murphy. You have two handsome, healthy sons, a charming early American home and a mansized career. Today your own son, Terry, plays soldier in your back yard. He shoots a trusty water pistol. He sings 'The Star-Spangled Banner' and salutes everything—including the family washing machine. . . . Because of you, life today for Terry Murphy—and all the Terrys—is a happier reality."

The film's success underscored and made real all the promises celebrated in the rhetoric of the era. It did a lot of things for Audie personally. It gave him more money than he'd ever had. It gave him prestige and the chance to break out of the western straitjacket. In less than a decade he had risen from a shy, awkward, nervous youth to the position of a star. Audie was at the top, poised to achieve a measure of security undreamed of just a few short years before. The film grossed around $10 million, and his take was right at a million. He had more money than he'd ever imagined possible growing up on a cotton farm in the Depression. In a 1955 interview he counted up his success, and it looked good and it smelled sweet. "I average about $2,000 a week now and have a six-year contract. In another five years I should be independent. By that I don't mean I'll be a millionaire. But I'll be able to have a ranch or a farm and enough put by to send my children to college." And many of these things did happen. He was able to own a plane, buy two ranches—one near Tucson, one near Perris, California—and to buy a new $75,000 house in North Hollywood, just up the hill and less than half a mile from Universal. The new house didn't mean that Audie had gone Hollywood, though. There would be no housewarming, he told Hedda Hopper. "Never. My wife and I lead a quiet life, have a few people in for dinner now and again. We'd both be terrified of a big party."

On Audie's part, there was incomprehension as to how he'd won such success. "You figure it out," he said in 1957. "I couldn't act worth a zinc cent when I got into this work. I'm not much better now." There was also some resentment in industry circles. "There's only one thing sells tickets to Murphy's horse operas and war epics. The twenty-three ribbons they pinned on him and the Congressional Medal of Honor," said one envious film person. And, overheard at Romanoff's bar, a producer complained, "It irritates me to see a guy who deserves it so little making so much money."

Some of the resentment would have been natural enough in such a competitive atmosphere, but Audie's relations with a certain element in Hollywood—especially producers and some actors—had not always been diplomatic, to say the least. Stories surfaced in the fan magazines about such moments of friction. One time a producer invited Audie to lunch, a business meeting—a good time to be cooperative and engaging. But when another film mogul walked by and the producer with Audie said, "There but for the grace of God go I," Audie retorted, "Name-dropper." Audie liked to puncture pretense, always a bad habit in any professional setting. On a radio show, Audie and some other actors were asked to name their favorite all-time stars. The usual names were put forward—Laurence Olivier, John Barrymore, and so on. Audie's answer: "Gene Autry and Harpo Marx."

Sometimes, too, there was a distinct note of aggression in Audie's relations with studio types. Sitting at a table in the commissary with a couple of directors, a writer, and a producer, he looked over at another table where a bunch of executives were having lunch. Quiet, he was roused from his silence when one of his companions said,

"A penny for your thoughts." They weren't pretty. "I was just thinking that with one hand grenade, a person could get rid of all these no-talent bastards at one stroke."

There were quips reported in the fan magazines that wouldn't make studio people happy. When a certain producer accidentally ran his car into a publicist's car, Audie said, "It's the first hit that producer's had since he's been on the lot." And there were practical jokes that sent up the studio system. In one script assigned to him Audie had to play opposite a boy and a dog, two sure scene stealers. He had a writer friend revise the script so that Audie *killed* the boy and the dog, changes that provoked outrage at every rung of the studio ladder.

One day on the backlot at Universal a contract player saw Audie's resentment flare up in an unforgettable manner. Audie, who had just come back from a meeting at the front office, sat down beside Frank Chase and said, "You know, there are some guys I would *really* like to do in." It wasn't bravado, he *meant* it, and Chase suddenly realized, "Here is a guy that means what he says."

Audie's basic hostility was such that close friends tried to protect him from himself. One day at the gym on the Universal lot, Audie remarked out of nowhere to his friend Bobby Hoy, "I'm gonna kill that son of a bitch."

"Who?" asked Hoy.

"That contract actor. I just happened to be going by the producer's bungalow and I heard the kid say, 'I guess the only way to get on this picture is to win the Congressional Medal of Honor.' "

"Audie, he's a kid! He's twenty years old. He's under contract. Of course he wants his career to go."

"Yeah, I guess you're right."

At the very crest of his popularity and newfound affluence, there were troubling tendencies that threatened everything, home, family, his hard-won, fragile happiness. Undercurrents of marital difficulty surfaced now and then in the press even in these halcyon years. The birth of their second child, it was hoped, would alleviate some of their problems by keeping them from too intense an absorption in each other's shortcomings. The new addition to the family would help forestall a threatening impasse of moods, nightmares, and stony silence. Together, the children, said one fan magazine, "cemented the temporary breaks in the domestic dam."

But real trouble in their marriage hit the press not long afterwards, that same year, 1954. Louella Parsons broke it nationally; more detailed accounts followed. The trouble had begun before the birth of Skipper, slackened off for a few months, then flared up again. NOW IT CAN BE TOLD, headlined one article. There was nothing to be unduly alarmed at, the writer assured his readers, but "the fact is, the Audie Murphys have been out of tune for some time." There were several danger signals. One was Audie's tendency to criticize Pam unmercifully, just as he had Wanda. Only the dynamics were different: Pam rarely cried, and Audie, instead of blowing up at her, clammed up and walked away. He gave her the silent treatment. Another echo from the past was irritability and nervousness on Audie's part; he wasn't sleeping well, and he was still having nightmares.

In September, after location shooting on *To Hell and Back* was completed, Hedda Hopper asked Audie point-blank if he and Pam intended to separate. Said Audie, "I hope not. We've quarreled, yes, but we both love our kids. It started about the time I went to Fort Lewis, Washington. I thought the studio had invited Pam to go, and they thought I had. Since we weren't speaking at the time, neither of us did. But I'm home, and I hope to stay." Columnists were skeptical. There were rumors the Murphys intended to sell their home. Said one columnist: "Don't count on this marriage lasting forever."

Audie said the right thing in a fan magazine interview, but he never really stuck to this position. He said, "The stakes are a lot higher when you're married and have children than when you're footloose and fancy-free. I don't take chances anymore. And that's been the hardest thing for me to learn—not to accept every challenge that comes along. I got away with a lot of things during the war. I could justify the chances I took then. But I couldn't justify them in civilian life now."

At the same time he was saying this, he had taken up skin diving, a dangerous sport for somebody who, like Audie, was a poor swimmer. He'd bought a boat, dubbed the *African Queen;* once, what he hoped would be a get-away three-day trip with Pam to Balboa turned into a full-scale operation when she insisted on taking the children. She spent two days packing for the trip, and when they got there there were problems with feeding, sleeping, and so on. They had to hire a baby-sitter. The tension between safe domesticity and risk taking was nothing new in Audie's life.

The most accurate fan magazine piece of the mid-fifties used secondhand pop Freudian psychology to analyze "Murphy's Other Self." Ross Taylor, writing in *Motion Picture*, described an Audie who was "as complex a bundle of nerves as ever stretched prone on a psychiatrist's couch." Taylor saw in Audie's present marriage the same patterns that had broken up his first. There were, Taylor argued, "certain aspects of his life and make-up [that] draw him to the brink of disaster as a husband." These included reckless disregard for money, nightmares, and constant criticism. Pam could deal with these tendencies better than Wanda, who by her own admission had not been smart enough to realize that "Audie wasn't ready for marriage, at least not to me."

Taylor concluded his article by imaginatively placing Audie on the couch of a "famed Beverly Hills psychiatrist." The verdict was predictable: Audie, deprived of his father at an early age, forced to assume the role of family provider before he himself was grown, had a "mother complex." In his marriages he was searching for a mother instead of a wife. Equally predictably, he had an "inferiority complex" based upon his short stature—here he's whittled down to 5' 6", an inch and a half shorter than he in fact was—and the resultant need to overcompensate led him to be hypercritical of others because, seeking perfection in them, he was actually seeking it in himself. Despite the oversimplified dramatics of poolside psychoanalysis, some of the insights were accurate. Audie was a perfectionist, he was deeply attached to his mother, and if he didn't hate his father, he hated what his father had done.

The difficult task of raising children was beginning to take an emotional toll on the Murphys. When Pam visited Audie on the set of *To Hell and Back*, one observer saw signs of conflict and tension between the two. Tom Shaw, a friend and production manager on several pictures with Audie, recalls what happened when Pam and the children came to Fort Lewis during the filming. "One of 'em, she wasn't holding the kid or some damn thing. They were on their way to the damn airport to come to the set, and the little boy cut his eye and Jesus, she was scared shitless. I happened to see her before Audie . . . you couldn't explain that to Audie. She was scared shitless, trying to explain to him how it happened. He had no patience for anything like that."

So things were not as peaceful within Audie or within the family as they could have been. On the one hand, those qualities of Pam that had drawn Audie to her in the first place were still appealing: patience, optimism, quiet religious conviction, thriftiness, and motherly skills—attributes that were presumably what he was looking for in a wife. At the same time he resisted these qualities. Gradually he resumed a familiar strategy of keeping things to himself. It was a way to do what he wanted and avoid unnecessary conflicts. The privatization of his emotions led him to conceal injuries. When he came home from the studio with a bad rope burn on his hands, Pam fussed over him so much that the next time he got hurt, an elbow in the throat from a fight scene, he kept quiet about it. He also didn't talk about his dealings with the studio, preferring to wait until there was good news before telling her. It saved her from worry, he reasoned.

But there was a much more dangerous tendency in Audie's make-up that threatened his family's well-being. All of his friends knew about it, knew that he was pursuing a potentially disastrous course. That course was gambling—serious, heavy, and ruinous gambling. In their ceaseless analysis of Audie's public and private life, the fan magazines never talked about gambling directly. When the magazine writers talked about money problems, it always had to do with Audie's profligate generosity, but not with the real drain— the gambling losses. They did use gambling as a metaphor, however. Audie had once been a gambler, they said, in the war, but no longer. Now the "only gambles Audie takes today are for their future." These gambles were real estate investments such as the ranch he purchased near Addison, north of Dallas, and resold within six months for a sizable profit. Audie did pull off some good deals of that sort, but the real gambling was the other kind, the kind that could finish you off if you weren't incredibly skilled and incredibly lucky.

Among his friends and the people he made movies with, his gambling was certainly no secret. He often gambled on the set, playing poker or gin, shooting craps, whatever, just as many actors and crew members gambled to pass the time during the long periods of boredom that moviemaking entails. Audie would bet on anything: which of two birds would fly first, what color car the next one to come by would be. But he was not, most friends believed, a good gambler. John Huston, whose poker-playing skills were so admired by Audie that he thought Huston should be made Secretary of the Treasury, said: "He was a most unlucky gambler. He'd pick up a pair of dice and he'd crap out immediately. Always unlucky, *always*. Not unskilled, just unlucky."

Audie sometimes won, sometimes lost, but it was rare for card games to add up to real money. One reason he sometimes won is that he had more money than the crew members he was playing against and could bet big and bluff because of a big wad. Audie wasn't above using intimidation at any time. At a friendly poker game at boxer Joey Barnum's house, Audie pulled out his pistol and put it on the table, friendly like, and said, "All right, this is gonna be a square game." Everybody laughed.

"You know what," Joey remembers, "that's the first time he won."

But he could also take pity on somebody who was losing. Casey Tibbs saw him get to feeling sorry for a guy who never won. He owed Audie several thousand dollars and couldn't pay. He wanted to cut high card for the whole debt, and Audie agreed. When the guy cut a five or a six, a sure loser, Audie went through the deck till he found a deuce and flipped it over. He told him, "I really don't want to gamble with you no more."

But it was at the track where Audie got into trouble, where the big money went down. When he wasn't working on a film or on the road doing publicity, he was at the track. He spent much of his time and money fooling with horses, buying them, breeding them, racing them, betting on them. Owning horses was, as John Huston said, "an awful good way to lose money if you aren't very lucky."

Audie liked to take his friends to the track with him; that's how you knew you were a friend. Jay Fishburn, a jockey, horseman, and friend, says Audie would "rather go to the races than eat," says he would go six times a week if he wasn't working. Fishburn considered Audie very knowledgeable because he really studied the racing forms and knew the horses. Unfortunately such knowledge didn't always pay off. "I seen him have quite a bit of money—[but] by the end of the night it was like, 'Does anybody have enough money to eat on?' "

Polly Burson, stuntwoman and a big fan of Audie's, remembers how Audie operated at the track. She says he was a "hell of a gambler." One time she saw him and a wrangler each bet $5,000 on a horse to win. Not to place or show, but to win—that's the way Audie always bet. He said, "Polly, we are betting to win." When they'd lost the $10,000, Audie told Polly, "All right, mother, we won't do it again."

On Sundays when there weren't any races in California, Audie and Casey Tibbs would drive down to Tijuana. One time they won $29,000 between them from an initial investment of about $2,000, but the next race day they didn't have enough money left for a daily double. "So that ain't bad luck; that's just dumb gambling," remembers Casey.

John Hudkins, nicknamed "Bear," a big burly stuntman with a gravel voice, became friends with Audie and went to the track with him a lot. Bear says that "money had no home with Audie, no home. He'd as soon bet $200,000 on a horse as he would $20." One day when Bear was with Audie, a guy said to him, "We're not gonna bet today," and Audie said, "What do you mean we're not gonna bet. I've bet twenty thousand already." When Audie was gambling, "You could walk by there in your birthday suit and he wouldn't pay any attention to you. If he was gambling." One time at the track with Bear, Audie had a little run-in with a stranger.

"We were sitting in a box, and John McKee, another actor, was there. And Audie was reading the form, before this race. And up comes a couple of gals walking up, and Audie just happened to look up, and went right back to the form; he didn't pay any attention really. So about five minutes later here comes a big Dago guy about two hundred and something pounds and he says, 'Hey, next time my wife ever comes by here again and you makes eyes at her . . .'

"And Audie says, 'Are you through?'

"And the guy says, 'No, I'll tear your head off.'

"So Audie just leaned back and pulled out his gun and laid it right here and said, 'I killed three hundred fifty of you guys; one more wouldn't make any difference.'

"And the guy couldn't leave go of the rail, he was so scared. He thought he was going to kill him. And then Audie just put the thing back and went back to reading the form like nothing happened."

Nobody fooled with Audie when he was gambling for high stakes. One morning at Universal, production manager Tom Shaw saw Audie place a winning bet with a bookmaker. Later that morning when the bookie came by to pay off Audie, the amount was thousands of dollars short of what Audie thought it should have been.

"Where's the rest of my money?"

The guy thought Audie was kidding.

"I want my money, goddamnit! Listen, you Jew son-of-a-bitch, you get that goddamn money here by twelve o'clock or I'll kill ya."

Though Audie was dead wrong, the guy paid off. He didn't think Audie was bluffing; neither did Shaw.

The amount didn't matter. Audie could be just as insistent about a handful of dollars. Frank Chase, an actor who didn't like to gamble, didn't like to lose twenty cents, recalls: "He'd play me, I remember, and I'd lose sixteen dollars and he'd want that right *now*. I had to go and borrow it."

Oscar-winning actor Ben Johnson (*The Last Picture Show*) often went to the track with Audie and Casey Tibbs. He and Casey'd bet a little, two or three dollars, but Audie'd bet two or three thousand. Johnson saw how Audie's habit of betting on his own horses when all the expert advice said not to got him into a lot of needless trouble. Audie owned good horses—Johnson and his father-in-law bred a world's champion from a brood mare they bought from Audie. Says Johnson, "The horse business was probably Audie's downfall, because he would go and bet four-five thousand on one, and them [his trainers] telling him he ain't gonna win with it, and therefore he thought they was trying to skip him and win a bet with his horse, and he wasn't gonna be left holding the sack." Shaking his head, Johnson says, "I seen him bet ten thousand on one one time, and the trainer saying we're not going to let him run. He goes and bets ten thousand on it." Audie was always afraid somebody was going to turn him around. Audie "was the kind of guy who was always on guard. He always had an old gun with him." He approached life that way because "he had a kind of inferiority complex, I guess you'd call it. He had the feeling that he had to be protected all the time, and he'd always carry an old gun or had somebody around him that was sort of security or something."

The sporting life might be all right for a single man, but it was tough on a marriage. The constant lure of the racetrack, of horses, betting, big-time gambling—all of this lay just beneath the surface of the seemingly placid married life, a kind of personal San Andreas Fault that could shake the foundations of family stability at any moment. There were telltale signs of duplicity at the heart of his marriage. Audie ran a kind of black-market economy that Pam didn't fully know about. He often had lots of cash on hand that she never saw; but it was highly liquid cash and could vanish in twenty-four hours. It was gambling money, and when you bet $10,000 a race, three races a day, as he came to do in his last years, a lot of money can turn over fast. Spec McClure said Audie was the worst compulsive gambler he'd ever known—he figured Audie ran through about $3 million in all.

One night Bear Hudkins and his wife and two other couples met at the Murphys' home before going out for a quiet night on the town. Later Bear's wife remarked that Pam had apologized to the other wives for their frayed divan; they were saving money until they could have it upholstered, Pam explained, "soon as Audie got hold of a little money." But that very night (Bear knew, because he saw it) Audie had $25,000 cash in his pocket.

Thus in the years of his greatest success, Audie was constantly pulled more and more toward the kind of life antithetical to a settled home and marriage. He kept his old friends and he made new ones, but rarely from within the motion picture industry. Most people in the industry felt they never really knew him. After being in Hollywood for more than a decade he said, in 1961, "I'm not an actor. I don't even like actors. By that I mean I have nothing in common with them. They're dedicated souls with just one driving goal in life, and I'm not. I don't malign them—I just don't spend any time with them." There was an inviolate circle of closed-off space surrounding Audie.

Increasingly Audie had friends in different levels of life and the levels rarely or never came into contact with each other. Audie liked it that way. He could move up or down the scale, in or out of all kinds of groups. He could deal with wranglers and starlets, a filling station owner or a U.S. congressman. He could talk ideas with a doctor of psychology or the metaphysics of betting odds with a bookie. Audie Murphy's America was a place of infinite democratic fluidity where there were no boundaries. Everything was possible if you had the guts and the savvy. Audie thought he had both.

11.
FADING
STARDOM

"If Audie was born in 18– something, that would have been his era. The gunfighters and all that. He was a courageous son of a bitch."
—*Bobby Hoy*

After the great success of *To Hell and Back* Audie's career stalled badly. From 1956 to the end of the decade he kept trying to find good roles in strong films, but nothing that either he or the studio came up with made any real difference or brought him any nearer to matching the glory of 1955. While Universal had done an excellent job of bringing him along slowly, letting him build up confidence, skill, and a faithful audience, then putting him, at just the right moment, into a hit film, they didn't do so well in keeping the momentum going. The bromide in Hollywood then, and now—"You're only as good as your last picture"—applied to Audie in spades. He knew it as well as anybody.

In the fickle and volatile world of filmmaking where nothing ever remains constant, he would have had a difficult time maintaining his star ranking under the best of conditions. Even Universal's big stars of the 1950s, Rock Hudson and Tony Curtis, couldn't stay at the pinnacle. Hudson eventually made a comeback on TV, but Curtis never did. To remain on top, Audie needed a strong follow-up after *To Hell and Back*, and naturally the studio was interested in a sequel, a story about Audie's return from the war and his subsequent "readjustment" to civilian life. In early 1956 Spec McClure was hired to do research and Richard Collins to write a screenplay. The result was a script entitled "The Way Back," which portrayed Audie being cured of his war neuroses by reliving the experiences shot during the filming of *To Hell and Back*. In other words, Collins tried to dramatize a catharsis that in fact had not occurred. Although both Jesse Hibbs and Aaron Rosenberg had thought they saw a kind of psychoanalytic process going on as Audie reenacted certain painful scenes, the evidence of the years ahead suggests no significant change; indeed, it suggests the opposite, a weakening of such bonds as would seem to hold Audie together, help him create a coherent, unified, and stable adult married and family life. Audie was too complex to be "cured" by a film. He refused to make such a picture because it wasn't true and because it was, he told Hedda Hopper, a "lousy script."

Next, Spec tried his hand at the screenplay. He spent ten weeks writing, but there were no story conferences with Rosenberg or Hibbs. "The Way Back," dated October 29, 1956, was a 199-page treatment, a meditative, repetitious, but always intriguing combination of fact and fiction. In a prologue listing the cast of characters, Audie is described as having "the swiftly changing moods of the Irish, a phenomenally bright mind, and a first-class set of 'war nerves,' of which, like most veterans, he is unaware." Other characters featured in Spec's version were Carolyn Price, Perry Pitt, Volney Peaveyhouse, Jean Peters, Terry Hunt, Wanda Hendrix, Pamela Archer, and himself. Spec's idea was to end with "a note of uncertainty and faint optimism." His solution was a scene with Audie, Pam, and the boys at the ranch in Arizona, near Tucson, finding comfort and peace in the sight of a newborn colt. "The Way Back" was really neither wholly a treatment nor a script; it consisted of the raw materials of a possible script. Audie didn't think it should be filmed in that version.

Spec left the studio after that, but there was still another version by another writer. This time out, Audie lost his war neuroses by discovering a purpose in life. The process of rehabilitation was getting more and more ridiculous. In this version Audie saved Spec from alcoholism and the gutter. None of this was true, and Spec threatened to sue the studio if they went ahead. The whole project was dropped.

In 1961 Audie expressed a strong interest in seeing "The Way Back" filmed. He told reporter Bob Thomas, "To me, the postwar story is more interesting than *To Hell and Back*. I'd like to buy it from them and make it with my own company." According to Spec, however, Audie never intended to make such a film in the first place. But through clever maneuvering he bought one screenplay for a pittance, sold it to Universal for $100,000, then repurchased the screenplay for $20,000, leaving a profit of $80,000. Spec got $18,000 for his research and script. Only years later did Spec realize that Audie never intended to make a sequel.

Then, in 1965, Desi Arnaz wanted to back Audie on the same project. Audie asked Spec to write a treatment, a "springboard" for a screenplay to be titled "Helmets in the Dust." Spec threw himself into the project and wrote a twenty-one-page treatment that he said might be called "Back from Hell." In a cover letter to Audie, Spec was hopeful, calling it "perhaps . . . the truest and most dramatic . . . variation on a theme we've tried." "Helmets in the Dust" is a curious document. It reveals almost as much of Spec as of Audie. Spec's rather florid analysis uses the metaphor of a tiger to symbolize the eternal restlessness, loneliness, and sometimes savage anger that tormented Audie. "There was a tiger prowling in his soul," writes Spec. The tiger preys especially on women, leading Audie to lash out against those who love him. The only thing that promises to calm the tiger is marriage to Pam and the birth of his two sons, but even those blessings are not enough to tame the tiger forever. In the end, all Spec can imagine for Audie is resignation. The tiger of wrath will never leave him. The best he can hope for is a quieting of its presence.

In 1972, still obsessed as always with the enigma of Audie Murphy, Spec wrote that Audie had looked over "Helmets in the Dust" and offered no challenges to anything it contained. In fact, said Spec, Audie himself had given the last two lines of the treatment to Spec. They read: "But the man knew that it would never go away. So he accepted the thing as a truth of his life that found its final answer in staring back into that ancient zoo, that crypt of bones called history, the dust of civilization, the cold ashes of eternity." Neither *To Hell and Back* nor any of the unfilmed sequels told the whole complex truth about Audie Murphy.

What Audie got for his next film was something altogether different from either a sequel or a western—what he got was a disappointing programmer, a modestly budgeted black-and-white boxing picture, *The World in My Corner*, which again teamed him with Rosenberg and Hibbs. The supporting cast was headed by veteran character actor John McIntire and Barbara Rush as the romantic lead, a calculated attempt by the studio to attract women viewers, who were said to be part of a growing audience of fight fans as a result of TV boxing matches.

Audie threw himself into the role, happy to have a shot at something besides a western. After getting his cheekbone cut in one scene, he told a reporter, "I would take all kinds of beatings for a part like this one. Not a horse in sight. But don't get me wrong—I've enjoyed doing westerns." He trained hard, lost some weight, and generally toughened up physically for the part. This might have been the one time in his screen career that he let himself be taken in by the illusion of his screen persona. His opponent in the film was a real boxer, Chico Vejar, the number-one ranking welterweight in the world. According to friend Tom Shaw, Audie "actually thought he could whip Chico. Audie was not that good a fighter at all." Another professional in the film, Cisco Andrade, admired Audie's guts, though: "That Audie. He really isn't faking. He's the first actor I ever saw who wasn't afraid of getting hit hard in a prize fight scene."

Although Universal hyped the realism of the fight scenes, *The World in My Corner* didn't do anything at the box office. Audie knew why: "People can sit home and see four or five fights a week on TV. Why would they go to the movies to see a phony fight and skimpy story?" He did all right in the reviews, but nobody thought the film was anything but routine.

After the boxing film, Audie made another western. In *Walk the Proud Land* he effectively portrayed Apache agent John Clum, a pacifist who tried to treat Apaches like humans; but the film lacked vitality. A critic for *Saturday Review* was right when he called it an "earnest, dreary exercise in naive anthropology." The best notice on Audie reckoned that "Murphy is probably one of the few actors who could successfully carry off this part. Although he is not a big man, he never implies weakness and the connotations of his name and career effectively underscore his determinedly mild behavior." Because of the film's lackluster showing at the box office, Universal shelved another true-to-life western project that especially appealed to Audie, a film biography of the Western painter Charley Russell. A very promising subject, it could have been one of his best westerns. Audie liked this project so much that he later considered producing it himself and starring his friend and Russell-look-alike, singer Guy Mitchell.

By 1957 Audie was chafing under a contract with Universal that called for two pictures a year. What had seemed like a good deal a few years ago was now a chain around his neck. Although he could still command fourth place in a poll of international stars conducted among British theater exhibitors and owners, he complained to his old friend Hedda Hopper about the "bread and butter stories U-I's been putting me in. . . . The pictures I make there are cheapies— but that's the kind of thing I have to do until I finish my contract. I have eight more pictures to make under contract for them—and two of them can be done outside." He was afraid, he said, that if U-I kept putting him in cheapies, he'd wind up as a replacement for Hugh O'Brian in "Wyatt Earp." Audie wanted to do other, better films, but that wasn't in the cards. The reasons lay partly in the industry, partly in himself.

Exercising his contract option to make films outside Universal, Audie had formed, back in 1955, a production company with producer Harry Joe Brown and bought three film properties. *The Guns of Fort Petticoat*, shot for Columbia in 1956 and released in '57, was their first and only effort. George Marshall, who had done a fine job with *Destry*, was brought in to direct, but this film never fulfilled the promise of its innovative plot line. The premise was intended to pull in women viewers by building a western out of a predominantly female cast. Audie plays a Texas cavalry officer during the Civil War who returns to Texas, where he teams up with a group of defenseless women whose husbands are away fighting. In a press release he claimed, "[my] rugged role in the film was nothing compared to the tedious job of training forty-two women how to become soldiers." But there was little of interest for either women or men in what, for his first outing as a producer, proved to be a disappointing effort.

After the one picture Audie and Brown had a falling-out. In September 1957, Brown brought suit against Audie for a million dollars. The reason: Audie had exercised a clause in their contract that gave him the right to choose which film to make next. Because he wanted out of the deal, he chose, hilariously, two impossibly high-brow works: Ibsen's *Peer Gynt* and Dostoyevsky's *The Idiot*.

Brown asserted that "these characterizations would be wholly un-suited to Murphy's talents and that his choice of them was made only to comply with the technical terms of the agreement." The suit had more than comic implications for Audie, however. He objected to Brown's characterization of him as a "specialist" in "outdoor, western, and Army pictures." Audie told the press: "I resent Mr. Brown's attempt to dictate my future in the industry by relegating me to the role of a 'specialist' in westerns. I completed one western picture for Mr. Brown, under our agreement, but it is my belief it has always been the American way for one to try and better oneself as you go along, and this is exactly what I am trying to do."

During this same period another movie-related suit was brought against Audie. Such suits are a way of life in Hollywood. In this instance Paul Kazear, an expert in underwater spear guns, skin-diving equipment, and photographic techniques, sued Audie in 1958 for $37,750. At issue was a dispute over Audie's alleged failure to complete his half of a movie deal with Kazear. Orally commissioned to write a script about skin diving (Audie's favorite hobby at the time), Kazear did so, producing a script entitled "Skin Diver with a Heart." At issue also were some photographs of Marina Orschel, a contestant in the Miss Universe contest for 1957. She was supposed to play opposite Audie in this film to be shot in Mexico. Audie refused to pay Kazear for the script and refused to turn over the photographs. The case was finally settled in 1962: Audie was ordered by the court to return the script and the photos.

Audie's other attempts to choose projects that interested him were no more successful. In 1957 Universal preempted him out of a picture that he wanted to do with Robert Mitchum called "Night Riders" for which he'd have gotten a big salary plus a commitment from Mitchum to do a picture for Audie's company.

There was also the case of *The Woods Colt*, a novel by Thames Williamson that Audie had been interested in filming since his days with Paul Short. Now Audie himself tried to bring the project to fruition. He acquired the rights to the novel and, through his agent Paul Kohner, met writer Marion Hargrove, who was trying to break into screenwriting. Audie hired Hargrove to write a script and in-stalled him in his bungalow on the Universal lot. Audie and Spec were in and out of the bungalow, and Hargrove got to know them both.

Hargrove understood why Audie was drawn to Williamson's

novel. "You can see an awful lot of Audie just from reading the book. It's about a kid, around twenty-one, a bastard, and a hillbilly, and a loser. And it's just the story of the scrapes he gets into and the people he runs up against; you know he's not going to come out in the end alive, and he doesn't. The character is believable, you know—rural and provincial and distrusting of outsiders."

In story conferences, says Hargrove, "Audie was good. He knew what was there and I never could figure out whether he was doing an awful lot of homework or Spec was doing an awful lot of homework, and it didn't really make much difference. Those two were very close."

But for many reasons the film never got beyond the script stage, and eventually Audie sold the rights.

Audie's next film for Universal was a complete departure for him. *Joe Butterfly*, originally conceived by Jack Sher and Sy Gomberg and rewritten by Hargrove, was a service comedy set in occupied Japan. It dealt with the misadventures of a Japanese servant (played by Burgess Meredith) who becomes attached to the staff of the GI magazine *Yank*. For the first time Audie was cast in a comic role—as Private John Woodley, a scamp, con man, and expert photographer described in a studio treatment as "one of those blithe people who go through life with a small storm cloud following in their wake." Although capable of humorous moments in his westerns, of a dry, understated wit, Audie was not at home with an out-and-out comic role. He told Sy Gomberg he "didn't feel comfortable with *Joe Butterfly*," and Gomberg concurs—"Audie shouldn't have been playing comedy." Actors like Frank Chase saw a man out of his league: "When you were around a guy like Burgess Meredith or Keenan Wynn or Fred Clark, you were in very fast company. Nobody ever tried to steal scenes from Audie, but I just don't think he ever got into the flow of the humor of it."

Reviews were better than the film's two-star rating today might lead one to expect. If Audie's performance didn't win kudos, at least it wasn't universally knocked. *Commonweal* said he exhibited "quite a flair for casual comedy"; and the *Hollywood Reporter* praised him for contributing "his own special brand of disarming persistence."

In Japan, however, the film was an enormous hit. Hargrove explains why: "For two reasons. First of all, Audie, the war hero. And secondly: the story is about the *Yank* magazine staff coming into Tokyo with the occupation of troops and they manage to steal a house that really should go to the generals, and they find they have inherited a Japanese house boy who runs things very well and has eighty-five servants waiting on him hand and foot, and they are all his relatives, whom he's taking care of. And this had a very profound impact on the Japanese; he was a very sympathetic character and he honored his family and he took care of his family, and there was an awful lot of that in the beginning of *To Hell and Back;* he's out shooting rabbits [to feed his family], so Audie had very high stock among the Japanese." *To Hell and Back* was in fact still playing at Japanese theaters when Audie and the *Joe Butterfly* company were in Hong Kong on location.

For his third film of 1957, back to the western. In *Night Passage,* Audie took second billing to James Stewart. Scripted by Borden Chase, the film originally was intended to team up Chase, Stewart, and director Anthony Mann, a threesome that had already made such acclaimed box-office westerns as *Winchester '73* and *Bend of the River.* But Mann pulled out at the last minute because he thought the script was weak. Audie didn't like the script either and protested loudly about his part until some changes were made. First-time director James Neilson took over, and it showed in a slackly paced, undistinguished film that did nothing for Audie's career.

Reprising the outlaw-kid role from his early days, Audie played good-guy Stewart's antisocial younger brother with menacing sureness. Ironic, humorous, mean, dressed in black leather, he deadpanned his lines with a murderous, laconic edge. At one point he makes a remark that could stand as a kind of coda to his whole film career: "One day I tried a gun. It fit my hand real good. Suddenly I wasn't a kid anymore." By now he had completely mastered the Kid style: the baby face, the humor, the irony, the soft voice, and the politeness beneath which violence flickered like heat lightning.

Audie's portrayal of a "dew-dappled, boastful little tough," as the *New York Times* described his role, earned him, as usual, favorable notices from the two leading trade papers, *Variety* and the *Hollywood Reporter. Picturegoer,* the highly regarded British magazine, liked his performance here much better than in his most recent film: "You never can tell about Audie Murphy these days. Just recently he turned in the worst comedy performance of the year—in *Joe Butterfly.* Now he has been cast as a villain and the new look suits him a lot better."

The next year, 1958, saw the release of two more films. The

first was a routine western, *Ride a Crooked Trail*, the kind of oater Audie could make in his sleep. Nothing new there.

The other was *The Quiet American*, a loan-out with United Artists, a serious and ambitious work that was an altogether different kind of film for Audie. He made nothing like it before or afterwards. Based on Graham Greene's novel by the same title, *The Quiet American* brought Audie together with another director of stature, Joseph L. Mankiewicz. Originally Mankiewicz wanted Montgomery Clift for the role of Pyle, the American, and Clift wanted to do it, but for various reasons did not. Audie, an excellent second choice, was regarded by many as a bold bit of casting. Laurence Olivier didn't agree. Tentatively slated to play the second lead, he declined to play opposite Audie. That left Michael Redgrave, who turned in an Oscar-level performance, though he did not receive a nomination.

Audie and Redgrave did not hit it off. Stories circulated among the cast about Audie's nightmares and his ever-present loaded .45s. Redgrave loathed Audie's pistols, and Audie, who had never appeared with an actor as polished and skilled as Redgrave, was so tense that his stiff manner bothered Redgrave. The English actor asked Mankiewicz if he would command Audie to blink now and then. Despite the distance and tension, what got on the screen is what counted, and there are critics, then and now, who believe that Audie held his own, that his kind of self-enclosed composure struck just the right note in this ironic film about an American innocent.

The Quiet American began shooting on location in Saigon on January 28, 1957. Two weeks into the eight-week shooting schedule, Audie had a sudden health problem when, on a weekend shopping trip to Hong Kong, he felt a sharp stitch of pain in his abdomen and had to be hospitalized for acute appendicitis. The operation went fine, but the doctor stung him for $4,500, U.S. money, which the studio did not reimburse. He lost 15 pounds and was slow in fully recovering. He wrote Spec, "My operation is still draining. If this keeps up, it will have a longer run than most of my pictures."

Saigon was seething with political unrest. There was one intelligence report that detected an attempt by the Viet Minh to disturb the American film company by assaulting Mankiewicz, but it proved to be merely rumor. On another occasion a scene depicting a religious ceremony involving a Cao Dai pope was mistaken for the real thing by a mob who thought a new pope was actually being installed. Audie took precautions. He said later, "The first thing I did was go to the nearest army post and draw a .45 and 500 rounds of ammunition, which I kept in my hotel room. The commies were only sixteen miles from Saigon at that time, and you never knew what was going to happen. I figured if they were going to get me, I'd give them a good fight first."

If Audie seemed tense, withdrawn, and difficult to people like Mankiewicz and Redgrave, he was a big hit with fans, who flocked to the Majestic Hotel where he was staying. They often waited hours to get a glimpse of the great war hero.

Shot in black and white, *The Quiet American* has the feel and look of an art house production. In that sense it was rather like *The Red Badge of Courage*—doomed to fail commercially. It was also exactly like the *Red Badge* in another sense: a daring but flawed film ahead of its time and out of sync with the mood of Cold War America. Aware of how his film might fare, Mankiewicz said in a postproduction interview: "I can't produce blockbusters. I don't want to make safe, ordinary little pictures, and I'm worried as hell about how the public is going to take to my *Quiet American*. How many of them ever heard of Michael Redgrave? And what will Audie Murphy fans think when they find their hero dead in the mud in the very first shot?"

Although the highly regarded French critic Jean-Luc Godard rated it the best film of 1958, no one else agreed. Not Mankiewicz, who later called it "the very bad film I made during a very unhappy time in my life." (He was referring to his wife's decline into poor health and eventual suicide.) And certainly not the author of the novel, Graham Greene, who attacked the film even before it was completed, calling it "a piece of political dishonesty." Greene felt Mankiewicz had turned his novel upside down, making it into a pro-American apologia rather than preserving the anti-American tone that had made the novel something of a *scandale* upon its appearance in 1956. Greene's public attack on the film hurt its chances to succeed in Britain very badly.

Although Mankiewicz felt that Greene's novel was too aggressively anti-American, the film itself was a work far less consolatory to American self-satisfaction than one might believe is the case from reading Greene's strictures. The reason, as much as anything, is Audie Murphy. Mankiewicz himself had said before shooting began that Audie was "the perfect symbol of what I want to say." Audie plays a Harvard-educated Texan named, as in the novel, Pyle.

Greene named his character Pyle because he considered the American do-gooder a pain in the ass. Despite changes in characterization, the Pyle of the film is essentially the Pyle of the novel. The Englishman Fowler (Michael Redgrave) describes him in the novel as "determined . . . to do good, not to any individual person but to a country, a continent, a world." In the novel, Pyle is the advance guard of terrorism in the name of the Four Freedoms—he helps smuggle plastique explosives into the country. In the film, this is changed to plastics for the manufacture of toys. Though the change would seem to make Pyle less sinister, it also serves to make him even more naive. His do-goodism in the film, however well intentioned, seems absurd, even arrogant.

Intentionally or not, Audie *did* play Pyle as a pain in the ass: he is confident, sunny, committed to fair play in all things, ingenuous, almost hopelessly impenetrable in his relentless American optimism, a sort of non-intellectual rather than an anti-intellectual. He is also not a little insufferable in his zealous devotion to his naive brand of Americanism. In a very convincing manner he is a prototype of the American innocence that led us into Vietnam. Playing a cold warrior with "spooky sincerity," Audie created a memorable portrait of the American as Boy Scout, a salesman for democracy, a true believer. He is the kind of CIA operative who keeps winding up on network news and in congressional hearings, an Ollie North type.

Reviews reflected a very mixed and divided response. The *New York Times*'s Bosley Crowther called it a "very interesting and mettlesome performance." John McCarten of *The New Yorker*, however, could only give Audie an A for effort, not for accomplishment. Numerous other reviewers felt that Audie paled by comparison with Redgrave. So did Graham Greene, who observed in retrospect: "The late Audie Murphy's limited acting ability looked even more inadequate than usual in the company of such seasoned performers as Sir Michael Redgrave . . . and Claude Dauphin."

For most critics, *The Quiet American* was disturbing, challenging, and perplexing. No wonder, then, that the film would fulfill Mankiewicz's fears and self-destruct at the box office. *Variety*, which prided itself on predicting what would appeal to the popular mind, had some astute things to say about this film's box-office prospects: "There are likely to be an awful lot of people who'll come out of this film saying [about Indo-Chinese problems], 'Who gives a damn?' " In the light of subsequent history, that question reverberates still. Appearing just four years after the United States's initial probes into Southeast Asia and seven years before the full commitment of ground troops, *The Quiet American* has an air of eerie prophecy about it. The location filming is part of it, too: seeing the film today, one sees a vanished old colonial Saigon, a city of gracious hotels, polyglot cultures, and charming cafés.

Audie also made another loan-out that year, a medium-budget adventure film, *The Gun Runners*, for the major independent Seven Arts Production, with Don Siegel. It was based on a Hemingway short story, "One Trip Across," itself the starting point for the novel *To Have and Have Not*. Hemingway mounted a legal protest that producer Clarence Greene easily fought off.

Siegel, frustrated by the task of making, as he says, a "sea movie on a 'C' budget," found Audie "a lot different" now than six years before when they'd made *The Duel at Silver Creek*. Recalls Siegel, "Audie didn't drink, was on time, and caused very little trouble as long as you didn't tread on his temper. He was incredibly shy and strange and there was a problem reaching him to get a good performance. Something was bothering him. He carried a loaded gun and one time jumped across the boat at a member of the crew. I had to pull him off. Even the tough guys on the set, the stuntmen, would take detours so they didn't have to walk past him. But he was always polite to me."

Audie's portrayal led one reviewer to a capsule description of his trademark screen persona: "a stubborn innocence, taciturn and firm character, an uncommunicative bravery, and suddenly a tight-lipped whirl of violence and vengeance."

For the first time Audie also got some favorable mention for his scenes with the female lead, Patricia Owens. One reviewer spoke of a "tongue-tied, believable domesticity"; another said he brought "an unexpected playfulness to the bedroom scenes that is very winning"; still another said that he conveyed "a good deal of love in his portrayal." Surprising words indeed for an Audie Murphy romantic portrayal.

Then came another western, *Cast a Long Shadow*, still another attempt by Audie to co-produce. He and Marvin Marisch put together a routine picture for United Artists, from a novel by veteran pulp western writer Wayne D. Overholser. There was nothing new in *Cast a Long Shadow*.

But Audie's next film for Universal, *No Name on the Bullet*, ostensibly just another oater, was actually the best western he ever made. Shot in 1958 and released in '59, it remains a fine example of the B + western at the top of its form. Production values—glossy Technicolor and Universal lot settings—are so predictable, so familiar, that in the opening moments one is at first lulled into thinking all this has been seen a thousand times before: A lone horseman, a gunman, rides into town, and people start getting nervous. A formidable reputation precedes him. He has killed many men, and the townspeople are afraid he's here to add another notch to his fame. The lonely, feared gunslinger who wants to escape his past was a staple figure in fifties westerns. Alan Ladd's Shane was the high romantic version; Gregory Peck's Johnny Ringo (in *The Gunfighter*) the realistic version. But Audie's John Gant likes his role; he likes killing people. He does it for money and with a kind of philosophical detachment. He is so detached he's unearthly; John Gant (i.e., "Gaunt") is Death personified. Originally entitled "Stranger from Nowhere," this grim little fable prefigured the spaghetti westerns that Clint Eastwood brought to perfection.

The script by Gene Coon, a talented scenarist who wrote for "Star Trek" and other TV series, describes a persona that fit the real Audie Murphy to a T, a character who is the flip side of the genial, law-abiding Destry. Gant, the script states, wears a "wellworn Colt .44 . . . in a shiny holster at his left side. He is calm, serene, untouchable by externals." This description might have come from the lips of many friends of Audie's who were struck by both his unnerving calm and his aloofness. John Huston recognized this side of Audie's character: "It wasn't his temper that sustained him, but a coolness of temper. I mean you don't do the things that Audie did in a fit of temper; you do it with detachment, like an angel."

The description of Gant's face is even closer to the mark: "Although Gant is expressionless, we become aware of his eyes, of the fact that nothing escapes them. Perhaps his face might appear dead, but his eyes are always alive, always on the alert, searching, watching . . . careful eyes." Those who knew Audie never forgot his eyes. Actor Morgan Woodward (Punk on TV's "Dallas"): "His eyes almost seemed to dance. They had a deadly gleam, a deadly wild look. I would not have wanted to cross him." Gant has Audie Murphy eyes.

Soon we learn why everybody is so afraid. Each person who has committed a crime or done some secret bad thing believes that he is Gant's intended victim. Paranoia and fear sweep the town. People come to Gant to tell on their neighbor. He watches them with Olympian aloofness, as the script states: "Gant already knows what is going to happen, and he's already bored by it. . . . Men afraid, who come to him under the drivings of their secret guilt, to make a deal. He is contemptuous of them." His contempt bespeaks a chilling cynicism. He carries on philosophical discussions with a physician named Luke (well played by Charles Drake, a familiar actor in Audie's films). Luke, a healer, tries to save men's lives, while Gant, a killer, sees no point in prolonging such diseased existences. And by disease Gant means moral decay; the dialogue cleverly trades upon patterns of disease and healing. Gant considers himself a kind of physician, too: "They're going to die anyway. Best you can do is drag out their worthless lives. Why bother?" In a conversation with Luke he makes his point explicit:

> LUKE: Gant, I'm a healer. I've devoted my life to it and I intend to continue. Right now I've got one big public health problem, and I'm looking at it.
> GANT: I like you, physician. You're like me. Why, you and I may well be the only two honest men in town.
> LUKE: Don't compare us, Gant. We've got *nothing* in common.
> GANT: Everybody *dies*.

Gant and Luke carry on many of their debates while playing chess, making *No Name on the Bullet* a sort of western version of Ingmar Bergman's *The Seventh Seal* in which Death plays chess with the protagonist.

The film's resolution is startling to anybody who believes that Audie always played misunderstood kids or good guys. Gant's target, the man he has been hired to kill, is an old, corrupt judge dying of consumption. His pretty daughter discovers Gant's intentions and tells him her father will thwart his murderous plan by refusing to take arms against him. But Gant will not be stopped. He rips her bodice and shows her father a piece of his daughter's dress, as though Gant had raped her. Enraged, the father attempts to kill Gant but dies of natural causes just as Gant is about to shoot him. At this moment Gant wears on his face "a terrible smile, insinuating anything . . . everything."

Audie's portrayal of a bored, cynical, world-weary gunfighter caught perfectly the flavor of his off-screen personality. Here was the man who wrote in his autobiography of killing his first two men: "I feel no qualms; no pride; no remorse. There is only a weary indifference that will follow me throughout the war"; the man who said in an interview in 1967, "With me, it's been a fight for a long, long time to keep from being bored to death"; the man who described himself as an "executioner"; the man Budd Boetticher called "deadly, absolutely deadly."

It's doubtful that anybody involved in the making of *No Name on the Bullet* understood the quality of what they had accomplished. Besides Coon's taut and intellectually stimulating script, Jack Arnold's direction should be given much credit. An underrated genre director of such B classics as *Monster on the Campus, It Came from Outer Space*, and *The Incredible Shrinking Man*, Arnold said of his star's performance, "Audie Murphy played a very good Audie Murphy," a statement that confirms the strong autobiographical impression left by Gant's character. The rest of the cast, Warren Stevens, Whit Bissell, and others, gave solid performances, but it was all in a day's work. Stevens, a veteran character actor who played a craven townsman, barely remembers the film at all; it was just another studio assignment. Audie, preoccupied with mounting personal problems, would hardly have felt anything special for this film either. To him, it was doubtless another shoot-em-up role, number seventeen in a long line of westerns.

The Wild and the Innocent, also shot in '58 and released in '59, was another U-I cheapie but a sweeter film, totally different from the mordant darkness of *No Name on the Bullet*. Together the two films bracket Audie's abilities to play startlingly different heroes in the western genre. The cast included teen star Sandra Dee, Joanne Dru, and Gilbert Roland in a script co-authored by Jack Sher and Sy Gomberg, with Sher directing. According to Gomberg, Audie "liked the subject of this picture because it had to do with a purity engrained in a kid from the mountains who had never been to a big city, and he comes to a place like Dodge City, and he sees the venality, the amorality, and the viciousness of the big city, and he's bewildered, but he has to call upon what he is, to survive, and yet to come out still being a human being."

Though *The Wild and the Innocent* did nothing at the box office and garnered only so-so reviews, it stands up quite well today. Audie is solid in his role as a naive mountain youth who falls in love with a prostitute. The film has a gentleness about it and offers a sympathetic treatment of changing times that is quite appealing. But there is one scene that deserves to be placed among the best in Audie's body of work. Again, the off-screen resonance is part of the scene's power. After Audie has unwittingly consigned a little tag-along mountain girl (Sandra Dee) to a brothel, he goes there to rescue her when he learns what the nice lady who hired her really is. Primed to stop him is corrupt sheriff Gilbert Roland, and Audie is forced to shoot him. Then, rushing to the stricken man's side, Audie says, "You can't die. I can't kill no human being." As the sheriff dies, a bystander says, "That was great shooting, fellow," and Audie says, "I'll be living with that for a long time." It is a very fine moment.

In the four years following *To Hell and Back*, Audie made eleven films. They included a boxing movie, a service comedy, a serious literary film (*The Quiet American*), an action-adventure movie (*The Gun Runners*), and seven low budget westerns. None of them were hits. He couldn't have been very happy about the way things were going with his career, and he wasn't.

But he was also unhappy in other matters, in his private life, too, or if not unhappy, then deeply restless. Those imprecise public barometers, the fan magazines, sentimentally registered the emotional fallout from otherwise unrecorded troubles. There was nothing one could quite put one's finger on, but there was something amiss.

Articles in the fan magazines were not as confident as they had been in 1954–55. The Audie Murphy who was described in "Journey Into Light," which appeared in *Photoplay* in 1957, was still a troubled man. Success had not calmed him as much as earlier writers had reported. He still suffered from physical problems such as nose bleeds and a delicate stomach. Nervous, irritable, still impatient with the world's imperfections, Audie, in this scenario, had to learn to accept, had to stop being so critical. His preternatural quietness was punctuated by a flippancy that belied a deep inner seriousness. Both attributes continued to cause him personal unhappiness. As a result, his and Pam's was a marriage always to be watched. Audie, it was agreed, needed to change in some fundamental way if he were ever going to lay to rest once and for all the ghosts of unrest, discontent, and angry impatience.

Ever ready to concoct a happy ending, the fan magazines cast

Audie's story in the form of a conversion narrative. His lengthy five-month trip abroad to film *The Quiet American* from January to May of 1957 provided an occasion for such narrative invention. Based partly on facts, partly on soapy sentiment, articles such as "Thank God I'm Home" told a story of renewal. During April, when the company had moved from Saigon to Rome to shoot interiors at Cinecitta, Audie invited Pam to fly to Rome to be with him for a second honeymoon. They stayed in a suite at the Grand Hotel, quite a difference from Audie's first visit to Rome in 1944 when he slept in an Army tent in Borghese Park. As often, he got in dutch with the local press when he said what he thought. He wrote Spec, "I made a big hit with the Italian press here in Rome the other day, told them I was very grateful to the Italians for fighting on the side of the Germans during the war . . . figured it shortened the war by at least eight months . . . nothing like good public relations I always say." His letter showed other signs of high good humor. Referring to Easter Sunday, he wrote, "Big things are happening in the Vatican . . . I can hear the beads rattling from here, and the bells have been ringing so long I'm getting a bit punchy. They say that a hundred thousand people have gathered to see the Pope . . . wish I had the spaghetti concession."

One day he and Pam drove down to Anzio, much changed now, "a sleepy little beach resort," Audie said. "To look around, it didn't seem like there had ever been a war there. Only an occasional piece of fighting equipment on the beach recalled its past history." But there was "one thing that makes you stop and remember . . . the cemetery. Seeing those miles of white crosses, and knowing what they stand for takes away the holiday spirit."

Audie's return with Pam on the liner *United States* in late May marked—the fan magazines would have us believe—a rekindling of their marriage and a reversal of Audie's tendency toward depression and pessimism. Something that happened in Saigon caused the conversion. Audie, touched by the sight of hungry children, burst into "uncontrollable tears," only to find himself consoled by a friendly priest who took him aside and told him about the foster-parents plan. Audie acted on behalf of these poor children (as he had earlier in Tokyo during *Joe Butterfly*). He adopted several under the plan, writing a large check on their behalf. In this instance children provided the means to engender soapy sympathy for Audie Murphy, the hero who could only find the meaning of life in the pages of a transparently hokey fan magazine article. Now Audie knew where he belonged, at home with his family.

In point of fact, Audie kept on the move when he came back to the States. He was hardly home before he was on his way to Denver to check up on some of his quarter horses. He bought good horses at every opportunity, and what with making films, racing and betting on horses, and restlessly seeking adventures amorous and otherwise, Audie was never going to be much of a homebody.

In June 1957 he received a slightly ironic honor. He was named "Picture Pop of the Year" and would receive the citation on Father's Day, June 16, from the Midwestern Fan Club Association, an organization of some 100,000 souls. Audie was thirty-three; his children were five and three. He was rich, or so thought the press. He had a 60-foot yacht that cost $35,000, two ranches, and a two-story house in Toluca Lake. Nice house, nice location, nice family. The fan magazines said so, and the award from the Midwestern Fan Club Association confirmed widespread approval of the benign image developed in the countless articles churned out in the pulps.

In reality Audie was leading a life that drifted further and further away from the safe moorings of marriage and home. Fretful as ever, bored, always in pursuit of excitement, he continued to seek a life outside the boundaries of work and family. Such life as he found tended always toward disruption of the safe, the routine, the normal.

There was, for example, his penchant for practical jokes. Some of them were harmless enough, but most of them were pretty crude. And some showed a fair degree of inventiveness, as in the time on the Universal lot when he and some pals spent hours rigging up Frank Chase's brand-new sports car so its back wheels would spin instead of catching hold, leaving Chase befuddled as to what might be wrong with his car.

Close friends tolerated the jokes; those not close to him did so only because they feared the repercussions of not being good sports. Anybody on a film set was fair game. His buddy Guy Mitchell, a singer and actor, said, "Audie's jokes never hurt too much once the bones got set." Audie liked physical humor. Director Jack Sher found Audie's brand of humor very primitive. So did Warren Stevens, a character actor who appeared in two films with Audie. "He used to dangle rubber monsters and spiders and stuff over the girls. He'd scare the hell out of them and then he'd laugh like hell when they screamed. He thought it was funny. He was the only one who thought it was funny." Other jokes were similarly juvenile. "He was the kind of guy if you were fast asleep he'd stick matches in your goddamned foot," remembers one friend. Or he'd throw a stink bomb in a trailer as he did once to comedian and actor Jesse White (known today as the lonely Maytag repairman in the TV commercials). Or he'd loosen the nails in a wooden set, causing it to collapse when the butt of the joke entered the building, as happened with Guy Mitchell. Or he'd undo the cinches on a saddle (Jesse White again), or, worse, when they were on location in desert country he'd toss rattlesnakes in people's living compartments. (On one set in Arizona in the sixties he kept a live rattler in the back of his station wagon, along with guns, handcuffs, and chains.) Such humor had an aggressive, dangerous edge to it. Audie's need to scare people that way, to trick them, to make them appear ridiculous or inferior in comparison with his super-cool demeanor, was a throwback to a childhood of hostile play, when such adolescent humor is often vented once and for all.

Audie's constant need for action found outlets, too, in his loose affiliation with certain law-enforcement agencies. During the mid-fifties he took to hanging out with the LAPD. Detective Frank Hronek, now dead, sometimes took Audie along with him on his rounds. Budd Boetticher knew about this side of Audie's interests. "All the police loved him. He had all the new gadgets. He had things that you wouldn't believe. They asked his opinion. Audie was a one-man army." One of his girlfriends who knew he hung out with policemen wasn't surprised one day when he came to her house, accompanied by a policeman buddy, and said, "I have something for you." It was a pistol. "I want to show you how to protect yourself because you're living alone." He showed her how to shoot through the door of the house and gave her sound legal advice, "Be sure if somebody is attacking you, that they fall out of your house, rather than in it."

Audie liked cops because they were men of action and because he hated certain kinds of criminals, especially dope dealers. According to Joey Barnum, Audie saw himself as a "crime fighter. If Audie was alive today, he'd be one of your top Angels. He would have loved that."

Joey's remark about Audie's crime-fighting activities was not a figure of speech. Nor were Audie's crime-busting activities confined to L.A. He carried an honorary deputy sheriff's badge in Dallas, given to him by Sheriff Bill Decker, who had a picture of Audie and Wanda on his office wall. In those days it was not unusual for the police to take a pretty casual attitude toward such matters, and Audie rode with Dallas policemen on their rounds at night. In 1956 a story made the papers in Houston concerning Audie's role in a drug bust. He accompanied a customs agent, Clarence N. Durham, on a raid that resulted in the arrest of one Felix Stone Ramirez on charges of a narcotics conspiracy. In those pre-Miranda kick-the-door-down days, law officers had a lot more latitude in such cases. Interviewed on the set at Tucson where he was filming *The Guns of Fort Petticoat* in 1956, Audie said, "I have been accompanying officers on similar cases in various cities because I am interested, as every citizen should be, in stamping out the narcotics traffic and combating juvenile delinquency." He also said such ventures were a way to develop "authentic background" for a film about the "menace of narcotics."

Tucson was one of Audie's favorite cities for such undercover work in the fight against narcotics. In 1956, not long after the bust in South Texas, he took part in an undercover operation for Pima County. Appointed as auxiliary deputy sheriff, he worked with Arturo Carrillo Strong of the Pima County Narcotics Office. Audie posed as a buyer, and according to Strong, he was an absolutely first-rate agent. He had a "deep hatred for drug dealers."

It was very dangerous work. Unarmed, Audie prowled the streets at night seeking contacts to purchase heroin or marijuana. (There was no cocaine coming down in Tucson in those days.) His "baby face and inner toughness" made a perfect front, and in a two-week period he made fifteen to twenty contacts that resulted in arrests—an amazing record.

When the Houston story broke, Audie was very upset because he was afraid it might jeopardize the Tucson cases, but that didn't happen. Every Tucson case resulted in a conviction. Audie Murphy, Crime Fighter, might have been the title of still another private movie in the secret life of Audie Murphy.

And there were, always, the women. There were generic girls and there were girls with names—he pursued both categories. How many women there were is impossible to say, but there were certainly many. In the loll-around time when he wasn't shooting a film or at the track, Audie frequented places where girls were plentiful. In the mid-fifties he and Casey Tibbs liked to hang out at the notorious poolside haunts of the Chateau Marmont Hotel. Perched just above Sunset Boulevard, on the strip, the Marmont was the place where the rich and famous came to play. Franchot Tone, Zsa Zsa Gabor, Peter Finch, and Christine Jorgensen were all regulars; so were Audie and Casey. The real attraction, though, was those who wanted to be rich and famous, the starlets who came hoping to catch somebody's eye. One way to do that was to sunbathe topless at the pool. Audie and Casey always found something worth seeing at the Marmont.

That side of his life remained a constant. Casey Tibbs never saw it slacken in the twenty years he knew him. "He was always chasing some," Casey remembers. "He was a worse chaser than I was, I think. Oh shit, he would lay them old sad eyes on them, he'd pull a little-boy act, and they'd feel sorry for him and they'd have to let him have some."

Among the famous beauties of the era, one who caught his eye was Natalie Wood. Audie wanted her to co-star in *The Woods Colt*, the film project that he was never able to get off the ground. Scriptwriter Marion Hargrove believed "she would have been very good casting for it, as the second character in there, the loyal, very young neighbor girl who traipses along with him." But Audie was interested in Natalie for personal reasons, too. He asked Hargrove what he knew about her, which wasn't much. Hargrove was well aware that Audie liked women a lot. "You got a sense of that. And there's constant talk, and also he's checking out the girls, that sort of thing. Audie had the Don Juan complex, like he was going to find extra life in bed or something like that."

Natalie was interested in the part and probably in the other. A fan magazine reported that Audie interviewed her for the part and that she was as delighted with the script as he was with her. She told him she'd approach Warners herself about a loan-out, in order to keep her price down.

Given his penchant for brunettes, how could he not have been drawn to the stunning looks of this doe-eyed, sexy brunette? Audie and Natalie were seen going to boxing matches together, in a party that usually included Robert Wagner, whom she later married. Audie's name does not appear in Lana Wood's book about her sister, but then Audie's name does not appear in a lot of Hollywood biographies. Hargrove thinks Audie "probably connected with Natalie." Another closer friend is certain.

And there were romances with married women, wives of friends. One of these was a woman Audie fell for pretty hard. He met her through his boxing pals Art Aragon and Joey Barnum, both well-known welterweights in L.A. in the fifties. Audie liked the man's world of boxing, had liked it ever since his days at Terry Hunt's gym, where he still went to work out. For years he had been an ardent fight fan, and he began to hang out with fighters. He liked tough guys, and fighters were plenty tough.

Pam knew about the other women, some of them anyway. Friends of Audie's like Budd Boetticher noticed the tensions. He said Pam and Audie were "like oil and water."

Hurt, she retreated more and more into religious faith. Always a religious person, now she found refuge and solace in her church. Audie sometimes made fun of her. He took to calling her the "reverend" to friends. He'd say to Boetticher, "Oh, God, I had another problem with the reverend this morning." Audie himself never attended church and refused to accompany Pam. Casey Tibbs thought theirs was "a strange marriage. Because she was a very religious girl, and I was a drinking man then, I used to clean up my act to go over there, but it was very strange. Audie'd come home and play with the kids and mess around, but they didn't have everything going."

Trouble came to a head in December 1958, when they separated for a time, Audie moving into an apartment. He used to bring girls there, "scragglers," one pal at Universal called them. After a while he moved back home, returning for the sake of his children.

12.
TRAIL'S END

"Yeah, the face is the same—and so is the dialogue. Only the horses
are changed. Some of them get old and have to be retired."
—Audie Murphy

A udie's career situation at the end of the decade was quite symptomatic of industrywide problems. The movie business was undergoing another economic crisis, and the chief cause, predictably, was television, which was proving to be as formidable a force as a *Saturday Evening Post* article had announced it would be back in 1946: "Prophets of television see the new medium putting a stadium, amusement park, theater and university into every home. They forecast a modern home built around the television room. Interior decorators have already designed furniture to arrange the family in concentric half-circles in front of the television screen." Now, millions of Americans sat hunched before their sets watching "Wyatt Earp," "Have Gun Will Travel," "Gunsmoke," ad infinitum.

Universal met the enemy by joining them. In 1958 it sold its 367-acre backlot with sixteen sound stages to MCA and Revue Productions in a deal that would permanently alter the direction of the studio. Revue Productions, long a subsidiary of MCA, was at that time the world's most successful producer and distributor of television series. Among its productions in the fifties were "Wagon Train," "This Is Your Life," and "Leave It to Beaver." From now on, television productions and blockbuster films (in the 1970s, *Airport*, *Jaws*, and *E.T.*) would be the main thrust of what would become, in 1962, Universal Pictures and Universal-Television.

Under the new regime the "three-button suit guys," as Audie called them, were pressuring contract players to do TV series. Audie wasn't completely opposed to TV; he could see the writing on the screen, and he had already done one TV dramatic role before the MCA-Revue merger. Earlier that year he starred in a Civil War drama, "Incident," on General Electric Theater (it aired on February 9, 1958). He played a Rebel soldier, opposite Dwayne Hickman, a reversal of an earlier stand that he would not make any further war movies. Audie liked the G.E. Theater drama because of its simplicity and its fidelity to basic human emotions. It showed pity for both the man killed and the man doing the killing (played by Audie).

In 1959–60 he made two more bids to adapt to television, appearing in a couple of serious dramas. "The Flight," produced for Suspicion Theater, aired on July 5, 1959, on NBC. "The Man," for Ford Startime Theater, aired on January 5, 1960. It was unlike anything else he ever attempted, casting Audie in an offbeat role. He plays a sickeningly ingratiating young man who worms his way into the household of a widower (Thelma Ritter) who has lost her only son in the war. He strangles the lady's dog and is just barely stopped from murdering her. This chilling little NBC drama about a psychopath is available today through a VideoYesteryear cassette recording.

But the new crowd running Universal insisted on a series. Naturally they wanted to exploit his war record. What they had in mind was a series entitled "Medal of Honor," but he wouldn't do it; he was tired of playing war parts, saying, "It's too hard to be realistic because audiences associate me with what I've done personally." So they turned to a western concept, which he agreed to do only "because it doesn't capitalize on my war record."

"Whispering Smith"—the title reprised an old Alan Ladd western from 1948—required Audie to play a cowboy detective in 1870s Denver who uses all the latest up-to-date police methods to solve crimes. A "kind of 'Dragnet' on horseback," Audie called it. Casting included familiar faces from Audie's westerns such as Marie Windsor (*Destry*) and James Best, who played in half a dozen Universal westerns with Audie and later starred as the sheriff on TV's "The Dukes of Hazzard"; and good young newcomers like Clu Gulager and Robert Redford.

Audie signed on for eighty-six episodes, but the production was troubled from the beginning. Rehearsals began in late May 1959. At a cost of $45,000 per episode, delays continued to mount up. After seven episodes had been completed by that summer, co-star Guy Mitchell, whom Audie had brought into the show, suffered a broken shoulder that closed down production for six weeks. By the next year internal memos reflected concern over the quality of the show. One dated March 3, 1960, reads: "NBC hasn't yet scheduled this. I've seen two episodes & NBC here wants me to screen additional shows. I'm not high on this show & feel Audie Murphy is too wooden & too young for the part."

There were headaches with "Whispering Smith" at every turn. Four different producers worked on the project. Costs soared. Even Audie's prize horse, Joe Queen, was a problem. Joe Queen was so fast he outran all the other plugs, until finally the director told Audie they'd have to use a double for his horse to avoid making the scenes ludicrous. One cast regular committed suicide. Audie believed he knew why. "I guess he must have seen the rushes," Audie commented wryly in a 1961 interview.

The starting date for the series kept getting changed, and the first show, finally set for May 8, 1961, was bumped to the next week by an NBC News Special on astronaut Alan B. Shepard, Jr. By then Audie was completely disgusted with the whole project. He cracked to an interviewer, "I'm glad that it didn't take as long to get Shepard off the ground as it's taken this series. I'd begun to think the Congo would be ahead of us in the space race before 'Whispering Smith' ever got on the air."

Audie's remarks about the series infuriated NBC officials. He criticized MCA and the network for taking too long to put it on the air. "It's like the Redstone rocket—obsolete, but they're going to fire it anyway." As for himself, he just hoped he wouldn't have to fulfill the rest of his contract. "I've decided that a TV series is sort of like World War II. You think you have enough points to get out, but then you find out you don't." He couldn't imagine having to complete the eighty-six-episode contract.

Audie also complained about the slipshod way a TV series got made. He wanted to see that "some quality got into a few episodes" and guessed that maybe that happened in about two out of twenty-six episodes. Haste overrode any artistic considerations. One bit of sloppiness was so bad Audie threatened to sue MCA over it. The main title—a trade term for the opening scene over which is super-imposed the series title and credits—showed a period scene, the American West in the 1870s, with Audie, Guy Mitchell, and a wran-gler wearing sunglasses who had accidentally wandered into camera range, then bolted off when he realized his mistake. Audie joked, "It wouldn't have been so bad if he had just stood still. The viewers might have thought he was just a horse with blinkers." He said, "That's the compromise of TV—little chance to do anything again [to smooth out errors]. You do something, get it out and they're happy with what they get. It's funny, though. People seem to like it. But they like everything like this. It's there, it's free and hyp-notizing. If people really watched it, I don't see how they could like it." Audie himself didn't like TV at all: "I never watch TV. It gives me a stomach ache," and he refused to watch the first episode of his own show.

By the time "Whispering Smith" made it into America's dens and living rooms the TV market was glutted with westerns, and the series bombed after a short run. It would probably have bombed at any time. One critic said it was "a bad show in practically all de-partments." The show also drew blasts from other quarters. Senator John Carroll, Democrat from Colorado, and a member of the Senate Juvenile Delinquency Subcommittee which reviewed the first epi-sode, said the series was "not only bad for children, it's bad for adults."

Audie issued a statement defending the show against charges of excessive violence, the only time he said anything positive about it. It read in part, "Apparently some people were shocked by what they considered violence in the first episode of 'Whispering Smith.' My feeling is that this episode had an extremely high moral value, which has been overlooked. The story was about a policeman who was willing to risk his life in order to rehabilitate a juvenile delinquent. . . . Smith was interested in helping youngsters and avoided violence for violence's sake."

He continued by once again addressing the artistic compromises made necessary by TV: "In a half-hour TV show, the bad must be established fast and with impact or the entire show would dwell on this subject. If even extreme violence is part of good drama, it is never criticized. Unfortunately, I have learned that a half-hour TV program cannot present drama at its best."

Audie had also learned that he never wanted to do another TV series. When the show was canceled in November 1961, after a run of twenty-five episodes, he said it was the "best news I've had in two years." The delays had cost him about $250,000, he felt, and had put him "in a bad way financially temporarily—not drastic, just irritating." As for future TV projects, he'd like to do, he said, "maybe an hour show here and there on TV."

With his TV series a bust, movies remained Audie's best bet for rebounding from the downturn. But not the old roles in the Bs at Universal. There were things he wanted to do that he couldn't do at U-I. He wanted better roles and top-flight directors. Back in '57 he had told Hedda Hopper, "I'd like to do a picture for John Wayne and John Ford." Making a film with Ford might have given Audie a real boost. He looked good in a cavalry uniform, and Ford certainly knew about Audie because during the making of one Ford western the director kept throwing up Audie's name to Harry Carey, Jr. Carey remembered the ragging he took: "Any time I did something he didn't like, Ford would say, 'I should have got Audie Murphy to play this part. You're not giving it any guts.' He was constantly throwing Audie Murphy at me. It was Audie Murphy this and Audie Murphy that."

A possibility of linking up with Wayne surfaced in 1958–59 when news stories circulated in Hollywood and Texas indicating that Audie might get the chance to play in John Wayne's next film. Wayne was going to film *The Alamo* in Texas, and well before the cast was announced, friends of Audie's urged Wayne to find a role for Audie to play. Despite receiving hundreds of letters from Texans stirred up by the idea of seeing Audie defend the Alamo, Wayne in the end felt there was no role left uncast that was large enough to accommodate Audie's standing in the industry.

In 1959, another great director came to the rescue, Audie's old friend from *Red Badge* days, John Huston. Audie was fond enough of Huston to accept a secondary role in a picture Huston was making down in Durango, Mexico. *The Unforgiven*, a big-scale western that dealt with the clash of Anglo and Indian culture on the Texas frontier, started out bright with promise. It sported a superb cast headlined by Burt Lancaster and Audrey Hepburn. Supporting players were equally impressive, including Lillian Gish, the legendary star from silent movie days; new talents such as John Saxon; and Audie Murphy, in a role originally intended for Tony Curtis, or rather improbably, Richard Burton. Huston, who for once and to his lasting regret had no hand in the script, wanted to turn the tale of a swash-buckling western hero into "the story of racial intolerance in a fron-tier town." Though there were things he liked in the film—such as the performances of Joseph Wiseman and Audie—in the end he considered it the only one of his pictures he actively disliked.

As usual with a John Huston film, the filming itself had the air of an event. Durango, Mexico, which they chose over Texas because the countryside around Durango was wilder, untouched by the dis-figuring marks of industrial America, was remote and dangerous-feeling. Armed bandits still roamed the countryside. Stuntman Chuck Roberson, who was there a few years later to film a Robert Mitchum western, said, "Murder was common in Durango. There was one whorehouse, five blocks from where we were staying, that had five murders in one month." John Saxon, twenty-three at the time of *The Unforgiven*, remembers that Durango was "really wild, like being in some exotic foreign country." People were packing guns; it was a "very live atmosphere"; the payroll on the film was robbed from the office at gunpoint, probably by somebody working on the film; the pilots, Saxon believes, were probably smugglers. Emilio Fernandez, the legendary Mexican actor who "shot some-body during or right after the movie," was on hand, employed to supervise outdoor action and play a Kiowa.

Locals weren't the only ones packing guns. Audie was armed to the teeth, and he shot up the landscape. Doug McClure (no relation to Spec), a young actor at the beginning of his career, re-members: "One day he yelled 'Get down!' and Audie shot over my head and hit a rabbit." John Saxon recalls a similar episode: "He shot at a bunch of us, in front, in jest, a long .22 marksman automatic that he had down there, across a small river and we were in cars or something, and I remember bang, bang, he was just shooting over our head for fun." Audie's gunplay particularly bothered Lillian Gish. According to one observer, "Audie had that damn rifle with him all the time, in the car, and he'd shoot on the way to the location . . . whatever the hell he saw move out there. It used to drive her crazy. She'd tell him to please stop it and the more she'd tell him to stop it, the more he'd do it. Just to provoke her."

Audie's behavior during the making of this film seemed edgier, more neurotic than usual. Doug McClure got a taste of that unsettledness when he went to call on Audie one night at the house where Audie was staying in Durango. After the kid banged on the door several times, Audie opened it and stuck a .45 right in his face. His eyes were telling the kid, "This is no joke."

The production manager got a taste, too, when Audie, who had his own plane, was going to fly over from Mazatlán to rejoin the company after having made a quick jaunt to L.A. The production manager told the assistant manager, who stuttered, to tell Audie he couldn't do it because of insurance; to tell him he had to fly in on commercial instead. "You go tell him that."

When the assistant returned, the production manager said, "Okay, what did Audie say?"

"Audie . . . Audie told me to tel . . . tell you to go fuh . . . fuh . . . fuck yourself."

When Audie flew in the next morning, about seven-thirty, everybody laughed his ass off. He landed right beside where they were shooting, and they used the propellers to kick up dust in some of the scenes that day.

Huston believed that Audie was "bordering on having a neurosis. One night Audie was ill in Durango, and I thought they hadn't got a doctor in quickly enough, and raised a little hell, and then discovered there was nothing really wrong with Audie, just a neurotic episode." More telling is Huston's recollection of the deep depression Audie admitted to at one point: "During the making of the picture in Mexico he had periods of depression. He was never withdrawn with me. Audie would turn to me, and he told me about himself. Feeling the way he did, [when] he was flying an airplane—he had his plane down there—he was tempted to go out to sea, and turn around and come back and run his plane into a mountain."

There were several near disasters during the making of that film. First, Audrey Hepburn suffered a severe fall from horseback, leaving her prostrate with four broken bones, torn muscles in her lower back, and a badly sprained foot.

But what happened to Audie was nearly fatal—he almost drowned in a boating accident. One afternoon when the day's work was over, Audie, pilot Bill Pickens, Huston, and a number of wranglers went duck hunting on a lake near Durango. Audie and Pickens went out in a small rowboat; Huston and the others stayed on the shore, Huston quite a distance away. Also around the lake that afternoon, but not of the hunting party, was the still photographer for the film, Inge Morath (now married to playwright Arthur Miller). She was there to try out a new telephoto lens. As the evening grew dark, Morath peered through the lens of her camera toward the lake and spied two heads in the water, but no boat. "I could see that they were very close together, and they didn't move." An expert swimmer, she stripped to her bra and underpants and swam out to them. Pickens was exhausted from keeping Audie afloat. Morath told Audie to lie on his back and he did, holding onto her bra for support while she towed him safely to shore. She remembers that "none of the other gentlemen ever came into the water."

As Huston learned later, the boat had sprung a leak and finally sunk down to the soft mud on the bottom of the lake. For a time Audie and Pickens were able to stand on the boat, but as it burrowed deeper into the mud they were forced to try to stay afloat by swimming. Audie wasn't a good swimmer, and Pickens, who refused to abandon him, was nearing the limits of his ability to keep the two of them above water when Inge Morath spotted them.

"*Time* magazine," Huston remembers, "thought this was a publicity gimmick. Anything but. They were at somebody's house, and Audie and Bill were both frozen to death. They both had blankets around them, and hot water bottles and everything to unfreeze them, and they both came out of it, thanks to Inge Morath."

Back at the compound, after Audie recovered—he had taken in a lot of water—he gave his rescuer a "very precious possession," a German watch that he had acquired during the war. Typically, Audie joked about the whole episode and said it was a good thing that Huston, with that hunting rig he wore, wasn't there or he'd have "succeeded in drowning us all."

Despite all these difficulties, the film got made in due time, and Audie gave one of his best performances ever. He grew a mustache to harden his appearance and give him less of a baby face; as a result he looks terrific in this film. He plays Cash, the hot-tempered Indian-hating brother of a large and boisterous family headed by his older brother (Burt Lancaster) and their sister (Audrey Hepburn), rumored to be part Kiowa. Cash calls the Kiowas "red niggers"; he would cheerfully exterminate them from the face of the earth.

He was also able to express emotion to a degree seldom seen in his other films. Perhaps being cast as a member of a large family and not having to carry the lead made him relax a bit. He seemed to take part in the made-up dynamics of the family. For Doug McClure, who plays his younger brother, Audie developed some real feeling based in part upon McClure's skillful ability to ride and rope well, feelings that were reciprocated by hero-worshipping McClure, who "actually felt like Audie was my brother."

Perhaps another reason Audie warmed to this role is that it required him to draw upon his roots in a racist culture. There is one extraordinary scene in which he gives in to his emotions, something he almost never did in films. Audie sees a spear hit the door, thrown by a Kiowa warrior who had killed their father. In a passionate fury Audie starts shooting at this galloping Indian and he won't, or can't, stop. According to McClure, "Audie was showing this emotion and crying and hitting, and Burt Lancaster gets up and says, 'That's enough, he's gone, he's out of range,' and Audie keeps shooting, and finally Burt slaps Audie, and he really slaps him, which breaks up Audie's emotion and Lancaster says, 'He's gone, Cash, he's gone.' "

Huston had to calm Audie down after the scene, walking back and forth with him, talking to him. McClure was certain that "if that had happened in real life, Audie would have killed him." Huston later explained to Spec McClure how he was able to get such acting out of Audie: "Audie is afraid of making a fool out of himself in front of the camera. So he tightens up. I assure him that I'll protect him. He believes me and gives his all."

When the film was completed and Burt Lancaster saw the final cut, he sent Audie a telegram of congratulations. Lancaster believed that for once Audie felt like he was a man acting instead of someone being exploited for his fame.

In the end, this alternately moody and hysterical western received mixed reviews. Since he had such a small part, many reviews mentioned Audie only in passing. But *Variety* pronounced his performance "surprisingly good," and the *Hollywood Reporter* made the most prescient observation: "Murphy, whose chief film characteristic until now has been a kind of stoic cheerfulness, uncorks a toughness and maturity that is a powerful aid to the story." On the other hand one critic felt that Audie "was mis-cast as a none-too-bright hot-head. I do hope he won't let Hollywood ill-wishers convince him he should play villains and off-beats. There are many who would like to see him ruin his career in just that way."

The Unforgiven would be Audie's last association with a big-budget A-level film. Thus both of his ventures with one of the era's great directors were personal triumphs but commercial failures. In fact Audie regarded Huston as the most successful failure in Hollywood. He told Spec once, "I'm just a mediocre failure; so everybody notices it. John is such a colossal failure that nobody can possibly believe it. He's like a gigantic slot machine into which people keep feeding millions of dollars, figuring that eventually he must pay off."

No matter how impressive his performance might have been, a backup role in a failed picture wasn't going to do anything for Audie's career. So in 1960 he returned to the corral at Universal where, once again, the studio's plans matched his needs. Realizing that a program of a few big pictures a year wasn't enough to support a large sales staff, the studio decided to get back in the feature western business in a modest way. Veteran producer Gordon Kay, who had cut his teeth at Republic in the 1940s, was brought on board to make small-scale Audie Murphy shoot-em-ups. From 1960 to 1965, Kay made seven Audie Murphy westerns, *Hell Bent for Leather* (1960), *Seven Ways from Sundown* (1960), *Posse from Hell* (1961), *Six Black Horses* (1962), *Showdown* (1963), *Bullet for a Badman* (1964), and *Gunpoint* (1966). Audie was enough of a studio pro to see the value of putting the best face he could on the downturn his career had taken. In 1961 he offered a rationale for the genre: "I think there's still a market for them. Westerns are still a good escape from everyday life, and we can give them color and scenery that they can't get on TV. And Westerns are still steady sellers in Europe and Japan, where they don't get so much TV." Yet it must have been discouraging to have to make films like *Gunpoint* which, as everybody in the cast was fond of saying, had "lots of guns and not much point." During that decade he made fifteen movies; thirteen of them were westerns.

The films for Kay were shot in eighteen to twenty days, at locations like Lone Pine, California, or St. George, Utah, and cost right at half a million, just like the Universal products of the early fifties. Kay, long since retired, recalls the pleasure he took in being able to deliver a product. He knew how to bring a picture in on budget, how to flip things around to make the best of weather situations. Universal executives Ed Muhl and Ed Tucker were happy to leave things up to Kay, who remembers, "They wanted to know what the basic story was. Generally they were satisfied with a synopsis. They'd read the screenplay and have some suggestions. We'd incorporate their suggestions, and after that do the principal casting. It got to the point where I had to ask the fellows to at least look at the picture. They said, 'We know it's good.' "

Kay also knew how to tailor a western to fit the Murphy persona. His production team wanted "to get good action going all the time and a story line that would hold the audience's interest and also a character that pretty much worked to Audie. I was looking for properties that worked for Audie; there was no point in trying to turn him into a gray personality. . . . He was fundamentally the hero." Kay traced the essential pattern to *To Hell and Back*: "You could push him just so far and then he'd explode. But in that, hopefully, there wasn't a sameness."

Clair Huffaker, western novelist and scriptwriter who adapted two of the Kay-produced films from his own novels, *Seven Ways from Sundown* and *Posse from Hell,* thinks "Audie fit in well with the two characters I wrote in those two books. In both scripts he was a young guy with a sense of humor, a wry quality about him, and put in a situation where he has to do something bigger than life. So it really kind of fit him in a way."

Like Kay and the scriptwriters, the actors in these films recognized Audie's strengths and limitations and responded accordingly. Jan Merlin, a veteran of some forty-odd films and over two thousand television shows, appeared in *Hell Bent for Leather* (1960). Contrary to how some actors felt, he liked working with Audie: "I knew a lot of people who said shit, they wouldn't work with him. They hated him. They didn't like him. Because he wanted things done his way. My attitude was he's the star of the fucking picture. What do you mean you don't want to do it his way? If he's not working, you're not working." Thoughtfully, Merlin considers two great difficulties Audie had to overcome: his height and, most of all, his baby face. He explains what it was like to be on the receiving end of dialogue delivered from such a person: "So when he's acting with you and he's being tough and he's trying to get over a point, he's saying it through this baby face which he couldn't help, and it was a hard thing to overcome. I'll give him a hell of a lot of credit, he was believable, he would do his parts, and you bought it. That's hard; that's damned hard." Merlin continues: "Audie learned his craft within his own limitations. He knew he couldn't be Quasimodo, or Romeo; he knew he couldn't stretch that far. But what he did was okay; it was always an extension of Audie, not Audie Murphy the hero because he didn't think of himself as Audie Murphy the hero. Over the years Audie became a very sincere performer."

Kay was keenly aware of the importance of proper casting in showing Audie off to best advantage. The most important role was the lead villain, usually a very smooth professional who gave the film, Kay says, "a little plus value." Although "Audie could pretty much carry the whole thing by himself, there was a value to a Dan Duryea, a Steve McNally, a Barry Sullivan." Warren Stevens, who played the bad guy in *Gunpoint* (1966), thought the villains had it over the hero in such films: "They were always the best parts. Audie as a hero is restricted, predictable right down the line."

The female leads in the Kay-Murphy westerns were contract players, starlets, and their roles never amounted to much. The starlets ranged from Venetia Stevenson, who by her own admission hated acting and got out of it as soon as she could, to Zohra Lampert, a method actress whose method gave Audie trouble. Kay remembers that in *Posse from Hell* (1961), Lampert took "liberties with the dialogue particularly with emotional things; she'd get carried away and the cues would go flying by and poor Audie was trying to catch his cues, to know what he was supposed to say in his next line." Audie said to Kay, "I don't know what to say. Can I talk to her?" So he went over and had a discussion with her. He told Kay, "She sure is different." But he didn't get angry with her.

Love scenes were always a problem, and Kay and company, recognizing the fact, went ahead on that basis. "He was uncomfortable. And it was best to play him as an uncomfortable guy in a love scene. I don't think we ever forced him to do things. Tried to make him a cowpoke who wished he could disappear. It was the only sensible thing to do. You can't force someone."

During Audie's five-year association with Kay there were very few problems. Audie was a professional and always on time and always knew his lines; he was very businesslike and did his part to keep production moving at the swift pace the budget required. Except for once, near the beginning. During the making of their second film, *Seven Ways from Sundown*, Audie had a major flare-up with director George Sherman. Sherman was something of a legend in the industry, having directed, it is said, over four hundred movies in a career stretching back to the late thirties. He was also a nice man, well liked by everybody. He had directed Audie without incident in the first Kay-produced film, *Hell Bent for Leather*, shot in

August 1959. But with *Seven Ways from Sundown,* which began shooting in May 1960, there was a big blow-up.

Two days after returning to the studio from location shooting near Las Vegas, Audie and Sherman had a run-in over how to say a line. They were very much alike in one respect; both took a "what-the-hell, let's-shoot-this-junk" approach; both knew they weren't making *Macbeth.* But on this particular occasion Sherman was sitting in his director's chair and Audie came up to him and said, "Yeah, I ought to read the line this way," and Sherman said, "Well, no, it ought to be read this other way," and Audie said, "No, I'll read it the way I think it should be read," and Sherman said, "Oh, for Christ's sake, just go out there and read it!" Sherman was "out-Audieing Audie" is the way Kay explains it. In any case Audie exploded; he pushed Sherman's chair back and said, "I'm gonna kill you." Sherman was really scared; after all, as he later told a friend, "So I'm looking at like, geez, this guy's killed eighty-six Germans, and me, all I've ever done was run over a cat on the San Diego Freeway."

Both men immediately left the set. Audie told Kay, who by now had heard the news and was trying to calm both parties down, "I'm not going back while that man's there." Sherman didn't want to finish the picture either, and the solution was to bring in a new director, Harry Keller, a friend of Kay's and a journeyman Universal director, to take over the remainder of the film.

In 1963 Audie had a beef with Kay himself. It was Kay's fault, he says. To save money, he went along with an associate's advice and decided to shoot *Showdown* in black and white instead of Technicolor. But he neglected to tell Audie, and when Audie found out he said, "I'm not gonna act." Kay said, "Come on, Audie, let's finish up the day." And he said, "Okay, but I'm not gonna act tomorrow." Kay urged him to talk to his agent and lawyer, and nursed him along. Audie calmed down and agreed to do one more day. Things died down, and Audie said, "This is the last picture I'm gonna do in black and white." He felt it was cheapening the thing. In Kay's view, the lack of color didn't make any difference. *Showdown* made just as much money as the others.

In fact the films Kay produced with Audie all made money. Kay set up a profit-sharing arrangement with Universal and still receives income from those pictures. He talked to Audie's agent about the advantages of Audie coming in for profit sharing and even showed

Audie his first check from the first picture. But Audie couldn't wait. He needed the money right then, not later.

Eventually, Audie's need for money led to a serious problem, from Kay's point of view. Audie began to make the same kind of picture for other companies. In '63 he made *Gunfight at Comanche Creek* for Allied Artists; in '64, *The Quick Gun* for Columbia and *Apache Rifles* for 20th Century Fox; in '65, *Arizona Raiders* for Columbia. Kay explains the problem: "Audie did one or two pictures [actually several more] for other companies than Universal and I wished he hadn't. They were spending less money and they had less action.

"What was happening was that people go to the movies, they go to see Audie Murphy, they don't look at the trademark. So it was assumed these were all made from the same aegis, and I think that's one of the things that kind of ran us out of time with Audie, and if he'd kept doing ours and hadn't done those we could keep going on for a couple of years."

During their five-year association the standoffish actor gradually warmed up to his producer. Kay thinks it might have been "erosion." He told a friend of Audie's, "I think Audie has decided I'm not out to assassinate him." And the friend said, "Yeah."

The films that Kay thought hurt his product were undistinguished, every one. They included a war film and four westerns. The war film was a low-rent combat picture for 20th Century Fox written by Richard Maibaum and Willard Willingham (Audie's friend and double). The script's description of the hero of *Battle at Bloody Beach* (1961) sounds as if it were tailored to Audie's specifications: "The SUB COMMANDER is a ruggedly handsome veteran, Benson, in his early thirties. . . . Except for a touch of premature gray at his temples, he is still youthful, and there is an unmistakable air of purpose about the set of his chin and the expression in his widely-spaced eyes." The cast was budget basement: Alejandro Rey, Gary Crosby, and Dolores Michaels.

The westerns were decidedly minor. Everything was smaller-scale than the already modest pictures with Kay. First there was *Gunfight at Comanche Creek* for Allied Artists in 1963, a dreary mostly-indoors affair about Pinkerton detectives that grafted onto the western a narrative voice filched from "Dragnet." The only interesting moment in the picture is in the first two minutes when we see Audie as a womanizer holed up with a cheap dame in a hotel room. Somewhat better in production terms were the four pictures that Audie made from 1964 to 1966 with independent producer Edward Small. Budgeted at around $400,000, Small's pictures were about $100,000 under the Universal budgets, and much of that came out of Audie's salary, down, for example, from the $125,000 range of the mid-fifties to $45,000 for *Arizona Raiders* (1965) and $50,000 for *40 Guns to Apache Pass* (1967). For *The Quick Gun* (1966), a B programmer for Allied Artists, he was paid a paltry $37,500.

The shooting time for these films was cut from eighteen to ten or eleven days. Despite the reduced circumstances of these ventures, Audie comported himself well with management. Small's office reported that he was a "pleasant and poised gentleman who displayed a good sense of values" and had a good professional grasp of the essential fundamentals of a script. He knew how to make films efficiently—there was hardly higher praise that an independent producer could give.

In these recyclings of a hoary genre all that Audie was required to do, he said, was "ride a horse, shoot straight, and look somber." By 1967 he felt himself a burnt-out case. "You make a success in westerns," he said, "they milk it dry—until you're dry." At the same time that Audie went through the motions in the genre he was growing sick of, he kept trying to turn up non-western scripts for better and different films. The movies he didn't make during this period were potentially far more promising than the ones he did.

There was "Impulse," for example. Audie's description of its plot line, in a 1961 interview, sounds absolutely terrific: "It's sort of a post-war thing involving me, and it's supposed to be true. A doctor—psychiatrist—brought the idea in, and it involves some German who's supposedly been stalking me, actually tried to look for me on a movie lot. He's stalking me, according to the script, because of my war record. He had some psychopathic thing about the war. He fought on the German side, came over here as a machinist, and when he gets a couple of drinks in him, he reverts back to his wartime days and feels I'm the guy who should get killed. As I say, it's supposed to be true." The same story was reported by at least one other newspaper columnist as true.

True or not, it had the ingredients of a great psychological thriller. The idea was so good, said Audie, that he would love to make it even though "the war thing is worn out and past." Unfortunately, it never got made.

In 1964 his own Terrania Production Co., another Murphy venture that was more a paper operation than anything else, announced plans to produce an "authentic cloak-and-dagger drama" about American and Soviet comrades during World War II who become adversaries in the pursuit of rocket scientists in Germany following the close of the war. The film, starring Audie, would portray the human interest side of scientific developments that resulted in the Ranger 7 moon landing. He hoped to use his contacts in the Army to provide him with documentary material. Like a million other projects announced in *Variety*, this one never got off the ground.

Repetition, undeveloped ideas, and some great missed parts—such were the facts of Audie's foundering career in 1960–65. The missed parts were the role Red Buttons won an Academy Award for in *Sayonara*, and the role that launched Clint Eastwood into international stardom as the Man With No Name in Sergio Leone's spaghetti westerns, which began coming out in 1964.

During this period Audie, starting in 1962, developed a new interest that offered more satisfying personal pleasure than any of the work he was doing in films. He began to write lyrics for country-western songs. Such creativity had its roots in the poetry he'd written years before. Those balladlike poems he'd penned in the forties offered evidence of a real talent for simple lyrics and effective rhythm that was confirmed by his efforts now as he channeled the need to express himself into the similarly congenial form of c/w songs. He had long been a fan of country-western music, and his friendship with Guy Mitchell stimulated his interest. Mitchell, one of the most popular pop and country-western artists of the fifties (he's still popular today in England), had some huge hits in his time, including "Singing the Blues" and "Heartaches by the Number." Audie liked to hear Mitchell "sing all the old songs that I sang from when I was a kid and worked on ranches. I mean things that go way back like 'Cowboy Jack' and all those things. The sadder it was, the better." Audie had several guitars, but he didn't play them and he didn't sing.

The songwriting came out of a collaboration with a third friend of both of theirs, Scott Turner, a professional country-western musician and songwriter. He had taken up the guitar when he broke his back playing college football, played backup for Buddy Holly on a record called "Maybe Baby," and went to Hollywood to get rich. It didn't happen. He stuck it out, though, and eventually played backup for singers such as Tommy Sands, Eddie Fisher, and Guy Mitchell. It was Mitchell who introduced Turner to Audie. They knew each other for several years before they wrote their first song together.

In the early sixties Audie spent a lot of time at his ranch near Perris, south of L.A., and one weekend night when Turner was there and the kids were in bed, Audie said, "Hey, let's write a song." Turner said, "Hey, you don't write songs," and Audie said, "I know, but I love putting things together." So Turner picked up a guitar, struck a chord, and sang, "Shutters and boards over the window," and Audie liked it and said, "Hey, that's good, let's write that." So they did. They finished it and Turner took it back to L.A. with him. That Monday Audie called and said, "Scotty, there's two lines that I think can be better. What do you think of this, 'If you open the shutters I'll tear down the boards/'Cause I drove every nail by myself."

The result was "Shutters and Boards," a simple lament about romantic loss symbolized by the boarded-up house "we used to live in." It became a medium-level hit that was eventually recorded by Jimmy Dean, Teresa Brewer, Dean Martin, and over sixty other artists.

Their second song took its cue from a remark of Audie's. They were sitting around Audie's home at the ranch one night and the wind was whipping around outside. Audie said, 'Boy, when that wind blows I sure get lonely," a line that evolved into the song "The Wind Blows Cold in Chicago," recorded by Roy Clark, among others. Audie and Turner eventually wrote eleven songs in all.

Audie continued to write songs all through the sixties. In 1969, with Terri Eddleman, he wrote a wonderful country-western song called "Was It All Worth Losing You?" Recorded by Charley Pride, it has an authentic mournful ring to it in the classic c/w manner. In all Audie cowrote six songs that were released (demo records of several others were recorded but not released). He remained interested in the country and western scene the rest of his life. In 1969 he and Turner discussed bringing out an LP of Audie's songs, but they never did.

In these same years something was going on in Audie's inner life—disruptions that threatened home, hearth, and hope for happiness. The blow-up on the set of *Seven Ways from Sundown* was one sign. There were others. He and Pam separated twice more, in

1959 and 1960, and came back together, uneasily as always. The separation in 1960 was announced in a Louella Parsons headline in March; it might in fact have been partly the cause for the explosion on the set in May. It was the most serious separation yet. This time both retained lawyers. Friends hoped for a reconciliation. "The Case of the Disappearing Daddy," a fan magazine called it, when Audie left and moved to his ranch near Riverside. Thirty-five years old, married nine years, he seemed more restless than he had ever been.

Right after the separation, in May, again in connection with *Seven Ways from Sundown*, Audie began an affair with his co-star, Venetia Stevenson. "It was one of those movie friendships, movie romances, that happens," she says today. One afternoon on location they were late reporting for shooting. The reason—a noontime tryst with Venetia in his trailer. An independent producer whose credits include *Southern Comfort* and *Take This Job and Shove It*, Venetia recalls the Audie Murphy she knew: "I really liked him. I would imagine that most women he was involved with would say the same thing. He was just a very nice, sweet, gentle kind of guy. A super guy."

They met for the first time in the office at Universal. He had veto power on casting and he approved of her partly, she believes, "because Audie was very short, and they didn't want to cast a taller woman. I'm 5' 5½".

They became close through horses. Venetia's knowledge of horses, gained from her experience with show jumpers on the California circuit, made her different from Audie's typical leading ladies. Polly Burson, the stuntwoman friend whom Audie and all the wranglers liked, says: "He always got some gal who couldn't tell which end of a horse drank out of a trough." But Venetia was an expert rider, which established an immediate bond between them. They'd talk about horses and he'd take her down to his ranch near Riverside.

Audie's protective, gentlemanly air reminded Venetia of another Southerner she knew at that time, Elvis Presley. She liked his voice, his delicate hands; she found him adorable. What she liked most was his sweetness. To Venetia, he "didn't seem macho at all." Her theory is that in a macho era, a man like Audie had to hide his sensitivity. But not with her. He had "a kind of gentle quality about him."

During the year she knew him, he was living at home, sleeping in the made-over garage at the house in Toluca Park.

Seven Ways from Sundown turned out to be her last film. In 1962 she married singer Don Everly of the Everly Brothers. A few years later she ran into Audie at the airport. She had her children with her. He was the same, sensitive and sad. He came up to her and her three children, two of whom were girls, and he said, "I'll trade you a jumping horse for one of your girls."

Besides the separations, the affairs, the blow-up with a director, the disclosures of inner turmoil, there was, in 1962, another of those bizarre public eruptions of violence that landed Audie in the headlines. The story broke the first week in June. Two teenagers, Edward L. Mayer, eighteen, and Robert T. Beasley, nineteen, were sitting in a parked car on Curson Avenue in Hollywood, a bad part of town. It was around ten-thirty on a Sunday night. According to their testimony delivered the next morning to Hollywood policemen, Audie Murphy came up to their car, flashed a badge, and pointed an automatic at them. Then he punched one of them, Mayer, on the side of the face. Audie's version, told to the same police the same morning, went this way. He was visiting in the apartment of Miss Judy Pope, twenty-four, a secretary for a photographer. He was there, he said, to discuss the fact that she had been receiving lewd letters, pictures, and threatening phone calls for the past two weeks.

That night, while he was there, she got another phone call telling her there was something in her mailbox. There was—another lewd picture. That was when, Audie explained, "I looked across the street and saw these two guys sitting in a car. I went over and identified myself and showed them my deputy sheriff's badge (courtesy of the LAPD). They could see the pistol which I had put into my belt.

"One of them got belligerent and slapped at my flashlight. Almost automatically I gave him a little punch in the face." He said he had no reason to believe the youths were responsible for the phone calls and mail drops, but wanted to know why their car was parked where it was. He thought it was a "simple thing." "If I'd considered it serious," he said, "I would have called the police. But they're busy enough in this area." He also said that although he had not pulled his gun on them, he was authorized to carry one, explaining, "I would rather get caught in South Viet Nam without a gun than in this neighborhood."

Mayer, a vacuum cleaner salesman, denied any connection with the obscene harassment. He said he and his friend were just sitting in the car talking. He also said he planned to press charges against

Murphy. Later, the D.A.'s office confirmed that Audie, two weeks earlier, had brought some of the lewd documents to its office, and the case was under investigation.

The story in the *Los Angeles Times* carried photos of Mayer pointing to a black eye; Audie, in suit and tie, displaying his sheriff's badge; and Judy Pope, a very striking woman pretty enough to be a model, a movie star, or a movie star's girlfriend. Audie explained that she was a friend of some of his friends who lived in the Hollywood apartment building where she lived. A blonde with a Sandra Dee, early sixties bouffant hairdo, Judy Pope must have been another liaison of Audie's, had to be—he was there at ten-thirty on a Sunday night—though the papers didn't say so and none of Audie's friends recall the incident.

Conflicting views of what happened were never resolved. One local newspaper, calling it a "mysterious row," quoted dialogue that sounds more convincing than what appeared in the *Times*. According to this account, Audie said to the youths, "I'm a sheriff. Get out!" Then, when one asked to see his badge, he said, "What are you, a wise guy?" and hit him a glancing blow on the cheek. Then he said, "Now if you still want to be a wise guy I'll let you have it." He questioned them at length, then let them go. Audie said in this account, "I didn't hit them or pull a gun." He insisted that they became hostile and there was a scuffle when one of them pushed him, but that he struck no blows.

Mayer, the one with the black eye, turned out to have a substantial juvenile arrest record. He had been arrested twelve times going back to 1959. The charges included burglary, narcotics, hit-and-run, auto theft, possession of alcohol, and lack of supervision. The case was closed and forgotten, another of those episodes in which Audie's tendency toward swift, decisive action with fists or guns brought him to the edge.

13.
A TIME FOR
DYING

"He didn't really like things when they was going good."
—Casey Tibbs, 1987

In the mid-1960s an aging B western actor like Audie Murphy was quite possibly the most anachronistic figure in Hollywood. With the days of factory-produced low-budget westerns doomed, familiar stars of the genre stabled their horses and decamped to the hills above L.A. Joel McCrea and Randolph Scott retired in 1962, and children's sagebrush heroes such as Gene Autry, Roy Rogers, Wild Bill Elliot, Sunset Carson, and all the rest had long since hung it up. Only Audie remained. "I seem to be the only one left," he said in 1963. "I'll keep on making them [westerns] until they get wise to me."

The western was changing as fast as the country. After the introduction of the rating system in 1967, families ceased to attend films together. When everybody started talking dirty in the movies, grown-ups were too embarrassed to hear such language in the presence of their children. By 1970 small-town and urban neighborhood picture shows were either boarded up or running *Deep Throat*. For cleaner family western fun at home, families could always watch

"Bonanza" on TV. But TV's capacity for saturation and overexposure of western settings, themes, and stereotypes meant that the genre, always a repetitive form, was becoming so completely exhausted that for many young people *Blazing Saddles* in the next decade laughed the traditional western off the stage of cinematic history once and for all.

A-budget westerns, though, were still viable in the sixties, provided they fit in with the country's mood of deep cynicism about America's past or were violent enough to catch the spirit of the war abroad and the domestic violence rippling through the home front. Audiences would still go see westerns if they were controversial (and great) like *The Wild Bunch* (1969), or hip like *Butch Cassidy and the Sundance Kid* (1969), or if they had John Wayne in them, or that rising new star, the only young actor of the decade to infuse new talent and energy into the genre, Clint Eastwood.

But Audie Murphy was neither John Wayne nor Clint Eastwood, and he was not bankable in a big-budget western. Trade reviewers, who knew exactly what he was, doffed their hats at his steady, gritty performances in the well-grooved genre. Said one: "Audie Murphy has carved a niche for himself in the standard Western field comparable to that held by Randolph Scott a few years ago. While Murphy does not make such films as frequently as Scott did, the effect of their appearances is the same: the fans always know exactly what to expect and are thus seldom, if ever, disappointed." And in 1966, when Audie was forty-two, a reviewer paid homage to his long career: "Despite the dozens of Westerns he has starred in, and the thousands of dusty miles he has traveled on horseback, Audie Murphy still looks good in the saddle." Such reviews, however, had the feel of premature eulogies. Only repetition and diminishment awaited him.

In 1965 his contract with Universal was not renewed, thus ending a fifteen-year relationship.

For several years Audie had regularly received offers from overseas to make movies, mostly war pictures. He turned them down, he said, because "it doesn't seem right for me to do one of those 'runaway' pictures. This town has been pretty good to me, and I want to work here as long as I am able." But once he was no longer under contract with Universal, economic necessity forced him to do what he said he didn't want to. Picking up some cash for a runaway film was better than not working. In September 1965 he went to

Spain to make a cheapie western, *The Texican*, with Broderick Crawford and a largely Spanish cast. *The Texican* was so cheap Audie
had to do all the stunts himself; in fact, he said, "I had to do
everything except pack my own lunch." The film was badly dubbed
and in every respect a sad falling off from the days of the Universal
Technicolor glossies.

In 1967 he went abroad again, this time to Algeria, to make
another independent cheapie, *Trunk to Cairo*, produced by a young
Israeli named Menahem Golan, destined for bigger and better
schlock in the next two decades. It was bargain-basement moviemaking. Said Audie, "We didn't have any skilled Hollywood stuntmen on our foreign location. So all of us pitched in and performed
most of the action ourselves." This lame story of international intrigue proved hopeless. "Try to imagine," wrote one reviewer, "Audie Murphy playing the part of a German scientist in an Israeli
production about foreign intrigue in Egypt."

Apart from his sinking career, in the mid-sixties Audie was in
trouble on all fronts. His marriage was a strained compromise. In
spring 1964, he moved out again. Pam was quoted in the press, "He
wants a divorce, and I will abide by his wishes." In those years he
would leave, come back, leave, take an apartment, come back. Eventually there wasn't any place to go except back, provisionally, to his
marriage. He scrambled to put together deals for films, crisscrossed
the country on promotional junkets, took the favors that women
conferred upon him, pursued girls, wives of friends, anything in
skirts, really.

Compounding his problems was insomnia, the old affliction from
right after the war that had come back to ravage his nights from, he
said, 1959 to 1966. He moved into his garage, made over into a
bedroom, so that he could be farther away from noises. Hypersen-
sitive to sound, he was bothered by any kind of noise. That, too,
he traced back to combat: "In combat, you see, your hearing gets
so acute you can interpret any noise. But now, there were all kinds
of noises that I couldn't interpret." Sometimes when he did sleep,
the old nightmare returned. He was on a hilltop and faceless people
were charging at him. He had his Garand rifle, but every time he
shot one of these people a part of the rifle fell off. Finally all he had
left was the trigger guard. Then he'd wake up. He kept the lights
on so that when he woke up from the dream, he'd know where he
was. Then, to cure the insomnia, he started taking a prescription

drug, Placidyl. One pill would buy him three or four hours' sleep; not enough but better than nothing. Before he knew it, he was hooked. He said he was "half dazed" and "the furniture in my room would take on odd shapes." The Placidyl made him look drowsy, bleary-eyed, as though he were drunk, and led some people to think he had a drinking problem when he didn't.

He started taking more pills and he began to lose weight. By now, he said, "I was a zombie. I dissipated all my money. I gave it away. I was not interested in anything. If a bus got in my way while I was driving on the freeway, I'd just force it to the side of the road." Audie wasn't kidding. His friend Al Jank, a wrangler and animal manager at Universal, was riding with Audie to the racetrack one day when a guy cut them off on the freeway. Audie threw his new Olds into high gear and raced after the guy at 100 miles an hour.

"Jesus, what are you doing?" asked Al.

"I'm gonna catch that son of a bitch and run over him and shoot him." Then he reached under the seat and brought out a Luger, but the guy ducked down a side street and got away, much to Al's relief.

Sleepwalking through the last two or three years of the addiction to Placidyl, Audie finally realized, in 1966, that he had to do something to get the monkey off his back. So he locked himself in a hotel room in Florida and went through withdrawal pains and convulsions, just like a junkie, he said. He broke the habit cold turkey. In 1967 when he told this story to writer Tom Morgan, he was confident: "This past year, I feel like I've been starting my life all over again. I've been sleeping lately—most nights, anyway. But I won't take any more pills. Not one."

Boredom was the keynote of his inner life, as he told Morgan. "You see, with me, it's been a fight for a long, long time to keep from being bored to death. *That's what two years of combat did to me.*"

Sex was still one of the few reliable methods for holding boredom at bay. But sex was very transitory: the pursuit, the conquest, a tremor in the loins. In 1966 he even sought out the services of a pro, and did so on a number of occasions.

And there were wives. Casey Tibbs, as good a friend as Audie had, never could approve of Audie's sexual ethics on this score: "That's the one thing I didn't have no respect for Audie about; he had no scruples about taking somebody's wife out or best friend's wife. I think it was kind of a challenge to him almost." In the case of one friend who had a beautiful wife, Audie used to go over to their house and just camp until he and the wife were left there alone. The friend was so gullible that he used to say to others, wonderingly, "Audie, he just really likes to come to my house and watch television." This went on for years.

From the mid-sixties on into 1968, when there was a climax, and beyond, the overriding issue in Audie's life wasn't marriage, career, Placidyl, or anything else except money. Although he had made a lot of money with the studio, he had little to show for it. The peak years of 1956–57 were long gone. He told an interviewer in 1970 that his cut from *To Hell and Back* had been $800,000. "I have no idea where it went," he added. Gone too were many of the tokens of his Hollywood success. He still had the house in North Hollywood, still under mortgage; but the plane was gone, and so was the ranch outside Tucson, purchased in 1956, sold in 1960; and, what hurt worst, the ranch at Perris, sold to Bob Hope in 1963. Audie said he was going to buy a smaller place, but he never did. When he sold that ranch, he told Hedda Hopper, "I feel better than I did ten years ago. I owed so much money it got where it didn't hurt anymore." The money from the Perris ranch, estimated by friends at between half a million to over a million, was gone almost as soon as he received it, to pay off gambling and other debts.

Suits filed against Audie from 1951 through the 1960s reveal a depressing pattern of indebtedness. He borrowed from banks and private individuals. A laundry list of contested loans shows the kind of financial jam he was in by the mid-sixties:

- A promissory note for $12,544.44, due December 31, 1949, plus another for $2,600, due on January 1, 1950; neither was paid. Dismissed with prejudice against Murphy on November 5, 1951.
- A promissory note for $21,525 was executed on July 1, 1961. Plaintiff filed against Murphy on October 19, 1962. Dismissed with prejudice against Murphy on December 24, 1962.
- Suit brought against Murphy, January 14, 1963, for $6,000 (personal check). Debt reduced to $900 and finally dismissed with prejudice against Murphy, May 19, 1966.
- A promissory note for $25,000, due on September 9, 1964; a

claim for $20,691.66 plus interest was filed February 23, 1965. Judgment found against Murphy on February 11, 1966, in the amount of $17,853.44. Murphy had paid $11,000 on the original note.

- A promissory note for $11,000, on November 13, 1964, due March 25, 1965. Complaint filed on May 26, 1965. Bench warrant for Murphy's arrest for non-payment eventually issued on May 19, 1967; total amount owed, $13,259.53.
- Suit in amount of $20,691 (promissory note) on December 19, 1965; satisfied May 28, 1966.
- A promissory note for $14,000; complaint filed on April 10, 1967. Murphy defaulted for non-appearance in court.

There were other loans that surfaced in court proceedings, too. In March 1964, Audie testified at bankruptcy hearing concerning a friend from whom he had borrowed a total of $60,000 and paid back $25,000. Asked where the money to pay back the loan came from, Audie snapped, "It might have been in my mattress." Then he asked the judge whether he had to answer that question, and the judge said he could keep his money in "a mason jar under a peach tree in the backyard" if he liked, and no, he didn't have to answer the question.

In addition, federal or state tax liens were brought against Murphy in 1959, 1960, 1963, 1964, and 1965. The judgments ranged from $4,687 to $27,787. He satisfied each of these.

Also during this period there was another suit over a disputed movie deal. A company called Famous Players Corporation, headed by Albert Zugsmith, filed suit against Audie on May 25, 1965, alleging that Murphy had reneged on a deal with Zugsmith to make a film in Israel. Zugsmith asked for $30,850 in damages, but the case never went to court.

Full ruin came in September 1968, when, under court order to pay the $13,260 balance due on a note that he signed on November 13, 1964, for the First National Bank of Dallas, Audie had to admit that he couldn't pay it. He explained that he had lost $260,000 in Algerian oil holdings as a result of the six-day Israeli-Arab War of June 1967. Also, he said, residuals from films and television reruns were attached by the state for past income taxes. At age forty-four, he didn't have a dime. One recourse was to declare bankruptcy, but he never did.

But the real story of Audie's finances is a story of that secret life, of gambling. Audie's gambling habit was eating him up. Even casual acquaintances on the set knew about Audie's increasingly intense gambling. One time Audie mentioned to William Witney in passing that he'd won $65,000 at the track. Win or lose, it was the same story. One day at Allied Artists Ben Cooper said to him, following a day's shooting, "Well, it's been a good day," to which Audie replied, "Yeah, I only lost nine hundred dollars; that's not bad."

Casey Tibbs and Audie's other friends "hated," says Casey, "to see him bury himself. He'd get in so deep and then he'd get mad 'cause he couldn't get more money to bet." Audie "saw snake-eyes all the time, and he never bet on the right ones at the right time with the right amount." He "just wanted the action. He just wasn't happy; he was more satisfied with himself when he would lose, somehow." He was "never happy with a big score. He'd bet a bunch for the trainer, the jockey, and all the stable help. The way he gambled, there was no way he could come out with money." According to Casey, "he was the greatest money-destroyer of all time."

Audie's well-known disregard for money "drove his accountants and agents and everybody crazy," says Casey. The way he tells it, "they'd get Audie in a room and they'd try to straighten things out. So one time he calls 'em all in, and he was that close to being suicidal almost. He wants to figure out how much insurance he's got, and what he can leave his family, and now he's trying to figure out how much more insurance he'll have to take out, and in order to be even he'd have to take out $750,000 more insurance and live another two years or something. He had them guys crazy all the time."

Audie himself said of his gambling habit, in a 1967 interview: "I got so that four hundred dollars was a minimum bet. Even that was boring. I didn't care whether I won or lost. It was as if I wanted to destroy everything I had built up. I got irritable. I hated everything and everybody." Clearly, Audie was presenting a defense of his actions; clearly, he was ignoring the fact that the gambling had been a problem for a long time. By Audie's lights, the boredom and the loss of sources of pleasure—plane, boat, ranch—made him turn to gambling. The other version, which, understandably, he didn't offer, was that the gambling cost him the plane, the boat, etc. Now, he said, he was through with gambling altogether.

Nineteen sixty-eight was the first year Audie hadn't made a film since he'd got started in the business in the late forties. But making films was what he knew how to do best and they offered the best shot at a financial comeback. He was a fighter, and he wasn't giving up. "I'm too tough for this town. It can't break my heart," he said in his old tough-guy style. In 1969 he formed a new production company, FIPCO, with his old friend Budd Boetticher. The groundwork for a partnership had been laid three years before when Audie walked into a hospital room in Mexico City in June 1966, where Boetticher lay very ill with pneumonia, his robust 180–190 pounds shrunken to 140. A former bullfighter himself, he'd come down with the illness while trying to complete a film about his favorite subject, bullfighting, a biography of the great Arruzo, who had died from wounds suffered in the ring in May.

He was dead broke and he hadn't seen Audie in a couple of years, but there he was, at the door of the hospital room.

"What the hell are you doing in here?"

"They think I'm dying."

"You're not going to die."

"What are you doing here?"

"Well, I have a horse at the track." (Which, it turned out, wasn't the case.) They talked for a few minutes.

"When are you getting out?"

"As soon as I can. You know me and hospitals."

"How much do you owe?"

"I don't owe anything, but I don't have anything."

"Well, of course you do. I checked at the studio. You owe the secretaries, mimeographing."

"Oh, hell, that doesn't even count, Audie. Probably five thousand dollars."

"You do? Well, I'm going out and get a bite to eat. I'll be back in a couple of hours." So Audie came back at four o'clock in the afternoon, and he had a cashier's check for $5,500, made out to Boetticher.

"Here you are."

"I can't take this."

"Here, you want me to tear it up? It's made out to a Mexican bank. Take it."

"What's the five hundred for?"

"Well, you gotta eat." And he started out the door, and Boetticher said, "Audie, what do you want?" (meaning a percentage).

"Oh, maybe just a sixteen-millimeter print if you ever get around to it."

Now, in the spring of 1969, Audie called in the chit. He asked Boetticher, "Do you have a western?" "You're damn right," said Boetticher. The script was *A Time for Dying,* and the creative pairing of Boetticher and Murphy called to mind the earlier Boetticher-Randolph Scott collaboration that had produced the great series of films they made together from 1955 to 1960, including such classics of the genre as *Ride Lonesome* and *Comanche Station.* Boetticher, whom a friend of his calls "the poor man's John Huston," possessed great directorial and writing talent, but he had always had a strong independent streak that prompted him to drop out of the studio system and live in Mexico for many years. Now, like a couple of aging gunfighters returning from the past, he and Audie were ready to take on all comers. They planned to do several more films, including "When There's Sumpthin' to Do," a Boetticher script that would be shot in northeastern Mexico in October, and "A Horse for Mr. Barnum," which would be shot in Spain, scheduled for April 1970.

A Time for Dying, which was shot on location near Tucson in April–May 1969, featured Victor Jory as Judge Roy Bean and the unknown Richard Lapp as a naive youth who wants to become a celebrated gunfighter. In this very dark western, however, the youth finds only comic incongruity and, finally, death at the hands of a sadistic young gunfighter named Billy Pimple. Audie, wearing a short, scruffy beard, appears in a small cameo role as an aging Jesse James. In his last turn as an outlaw, the final reprise of the type with which he had begun his six-gun film career twenty years before (and the second time he had played Jesse James), Audie gives the youth some sardonic, practical tips about how to survive as a gunfighter.

The production was something of a family affair, with Audie's two sons, now seventeen and fifteen, playing speaking parts, and with old friends such as Casey Tibbs and Jay Fishburn on hand for stunts and management of the livestock. Tibbs remembers how tight the money was. "I had a pretty good check coming, and I knew he was having trouble making the payroll, so I told him, 'Hey, I got too much money when I took the job. I don't need nothing.' He appreciated something like that. Not too many people really tried to do it; they all tried to stick it in him." The money was so tight, in fact, that the film came in several minutes short, and Audie had to spend the next year and a half trying to find additional financing for completion and distribution.

Boetticher and company made the film with all the integrity they could, although Boetticher came to despise Richard Lapp. According to him, Lapp pretended to be a great Audie Murphy fan and wormed his way into the role, then proceeded to play the big star. "The second day he was Clark Gable," says Boetticher, who remembers the last day of shooting with relish:

"The last day of the picture when he [Lapp] was dying there and I had my whole crew, Lucien Ballard and all the great guys from Hollywood making this picture, 'cause we all loved Audie, this guy, the little schmuck, says to me, 'I'm not gonna do it that way.' I said, 'Richard, let me tell you something. I've put up with you for eighteen days, and I said, you're gonna do it this way if I have to stay here all night, and one more word out of you, the minute we say wrap, I'm gonna beat your fucking brains out.' And everybody applauded."

Boetticher was very pleased with Audie's work: "He was excellent even if he didn't think of himself as much of an actor." He says today, "I just couldn't believe the performance he gave in *A Time for Dying*. Audie was good, and he was gonna get better and better and better."

The film received foreign release in France in November 1971, at which time *Variety* pronounced it a "terse, compact western" and praised Audie's "fine cameo." In the United States it was not screened until 1981, when it played briefly at several film festivals in New York. Vincent Canby lavished praise on Victor Jory's portrayal of Judge Roy Bean and said, "It's good seeing Mr. Murphy turn up in a cameo role as Jesse James."

For Audie, making the picture was a frustrating task. Even more frustrating was the task of raising more money to get the film completed and released. Audie naturally turned to old friends for help. Like George Putnam, for instance. A flamboyant television/radio announcer, Putnam had been on the L.A. scene for many years. He started out in radio, and during the war pinch-hit for Lowell Thomas on the Fox Movietone Newsreels. For many years he had been a highly prominent local TV personality and always rode the Golden Palomino in the Annual Rose Bowl Parade. In the sixties he began to proclaim himself a super-patriot, an old-fashioned flag-waver, and he and Audie became friends. So now Audie went to him and said, "George, I'm just absolutely flat. I've got to raise money." Putnam didn't have any money that wasn't tied up, but he knew a wealthy conservative, one of the richest men in the world, that he could go to and seek financial backing for Audie.

So Putnam took Audie to the rich man's lavish office and asked to see Mr. So-and-So. There they waited for a while, sitting together at a huge conference table until the rich man came in and was, Putnam says, "so thrilled to meet this wonderful hero of World War II, our Hero, our Patriot, Audie Murphy." And Putnam said to him, "You know, we all come upon hard times, and I like to do what I can, but it isn't enough. Audie's got to have about $250,000, but just a minute, he doesn't want that as a loan, he has two unfinished products here, has a couple of movies that aren't finished but they can be finished very easily, and there's enough here you can salvage enough out of this to guarantee your $250,000, but he's absolutely flat; could you help us?" Then, as Putnam tells it, "Mr. So-and-So left to think it over, and when he came back, he said, 'George, I think the best way to handle this is to have Audie call my banker and maybe you'd like to co-sign a note.' Here's a man who could have written a ten-million-dollar check if he had wanted to and never missed it, and he refused to help our hero." To Putnam this is a story of how easily people forget, of how a great hero, the most decorated hero of World War II, was "treated very shabbily by a multi-, multi-billionaire. Dammit!"

All through the fall of 1969 and into the spring of 1970 Audie kept trying to hustle up money. In January 1970, when a reporter dropped by the FIPCO office for an interview, Audie had been on the phone all morning talking to people, trying to drum up some financing. It was tough going, but he still had hope. Alternately buoyant and gloomy, he was optimistic about *A Time for Dying* and the other westerns he was going to make. They were "sure-fire," he said. He didn't want to make any war films because they "glorify death," or political films, "which preach," or love stories, "which are nothing but sex orgies." He also had in mind a TV series about a boy who befriends a war dog. It would star his son (he didn't say which one) and "just might make it, like *Lassie*, 'cause you never know." He'd written some songs and poems; he was going to launch a music publishing and recording firm; he hoped to get into the investment business. "We have big dreams," he said. Like most

Americans who get into trouble, he was beginning to sound like Willy Loman.

Still obsessed with the war, he drew a parallel between combat and Hollywood: "There, everyone understood the rules: You either killed or got killed. Here, the rules are much more complicated. A person gets mixed up in contracts and talent and no talent and big egos and phonies and it is hard to live, let alone have a decent marriage and raise a decent family."

He said he was ready to leave his marriage for good. "I've been living this strange life, like a watchman, for a long time, but my boys don't need a watchman much longer. I want to find a decent place to live and do decent work and get decently out of debt and forget the war and the hero stuff and the past goddamn ten years and make a new life for myself."

Then he ended with a final note of hope: "It was good for me being broke flat. It was good for me being hurt. It rekindled my spirit. It made me want to fight back. It made me want to begin living again." Brave words, but the question remained: where and how was he going to get enough money together to get back on his feet? Audie had to have money if he was going to regenerate any kind of career in the motion picture business.

What happened later that spring, in May, didn't help. Audie became embroiled in a deeply bizarre and widely publicized assault case that gave him the worst black eye in public relations he'd ever had.

The headlines blared: AUDIE MURPHY HELD FOR ASSAULT; WAR HERO MURPHY: I DIDN'T HAVE A GUN. His temper and anger and, perhaps, his sense of personal justice had finally landed him in big trouble. On May 18, 1970, he and a friend, a huge barkeeper named John Tuell, 6' 7", 270 pounds, became involved in a fracas with a dog trainer named David Gofstein. Everything about the incident was embarrassing to Audie. What happened remains a matter of some confusion, but the basic outline of the episode goes like this:

Audie was visiting at the apartment of his girlfriend, Maria D'Auria, when she became involved in a heated argument on the telephone with Gofstein, who had contracted with her to train her German shepherd. According to Gofstein, he told the woman, from whom he had collected $165 for obedience training, that she would have to pay an additional fee for guard training. "Then," said Gofstein, "a gentleman got on the phone and said, 'Hey, you . . . you better train that dog one way or another.' " Audie's version, of course, differed from Gofstein's. According to Audie, "I went over to his [Gofstein's] place to settle the differences after this man used the most vile and profane language to Mrs. D'Auria and myself." According to another newspaper version, Audie said, "I felt I had to resolve the matter, and it was after that [profanity] that the physical action took place."

Whatever words were said over the phone, Audie and John Tuell went to Gofstein's kennels and confronted him. Here again there are differing versions of what happened. Gofstein said that Audie said a few words to him, then followed him into the backyard and beat and kicked him. He also said Audie had a pistol and fired a shot at him. In another account, Gofstein said Audie knocked him down with a trash hand truck, punched him, and knocked him down again. Then, said Gofstein, when he panicked and ran, a shot was fired. His wife Judy said that Audie slapped her twice. She was inside calling the police when the shot was fired. Treated at a hospital for minor injuries, Gofstein said he didn't know who his assailant was until ten days later when the license plate number, which Gofstein's wife recorded, was traced by the police and Audie was arrested at his home. The arresting officer reported finding "all kinds of weapons" at Audie's home. Audie's version was in direct conflict with Gofstein's claim about not knowing the identity of his assailant. According to Audie, the dog trainer—who at 6' 1", 195 pounds, was a big man—called him a "pipsqueak and a phony movie tough guy."

The charges were deadly serious: assault to commit murder, assault with a deadly weapon, and battery. And they didn't surprise some of Audie's friends. Tom Shaw said, "I always thought Audie was gonna kill somebody." Casey Tibbs recalls that once when he invited Audie to go hunting with him, Audie replied ominously, "I don't like to hunt animals. But if you want to hunt some people, I'll go with you." In any event Audie moved quickly to defend his name. He hired a top-notch lawyer, Paul Caruso, and Caruso promptly called a press conference in early June. It was natural that Audie would turn to someone like Caruso. A well-known celebrity lawyer, he was also well connected with the fight game in L.A., having managed at one time, among others, Audie's friend Art Aragon. At the press conference, which featured liquor and food ("These make a good press conference," says Caruso), he used the opportunity to set the tone of his defense. Until May 28, he said,

Audie Murphy had been known by "most of the citizens of this country" as a "reputable name" and the "most decorated war hero in the nation's history." Now "that image was unfairly tarnished." Caruso went on to say that he and his client "do not want to try the case in the press but we do want equal time to rebut the charges."

Trying the case in the press was exactly what he was doing, a good strategy because, as Caruso had learned from an earlier case, back in 1965, "You can turn public opinion." Audie understood the strategy well, and his remark to the press that day, repeated over and over in subsequent accounts, was perfectly in character. When asked about Gofstein's statement that Audie had shot at him and missed, the war hero grinned and said, "I am embarrassed that anyone would think that I had taken a shot at a target as big as Mr. Gofstein and missed. Had I done so, he would not be among us now." To jaded reporters accustomed to weird press conferences of the rich and famous, Audie's remark, according to an account in *Motion Picture*, "altered" and made "eerie" the whole atmosphere. To the reporter, "Murphy seemed not upset primarily because of the serious charges against him. Rather he appeared to be disturbed because anyone—anyone—would dare imply that he, the man often called 'the fightingest man in World War II,' could take a shot at somebody and miss."

Audie pleaded not guilty at a hearing in July. He also predicted a happy outcome: "This charge against me has affected my career. I'm a producer of movies and financial backers wonder what kind of man they are doing business with. I expect to be completely exonerated."

To get ready for the trial, which because of delays did not take place until October, Caruso prepped Audie as though he were directing a performance. "We worked on everything—his appearance, his speech, his attitude on the witness stand, just like it was a part. I think he would have snapped." Audie responded well to direction. "Paul, I love watching you work; you're a bigger ham-bone than I ever knew." Caruso gave exact instructions about how to answer questions. He didn't want any free-lancing by Audie. He considers his advice to Audie valid today: "There are four perfect words for answers. 'Yes, sir,' 'No, sir,' and then if necessary, you employ a third series of four words, 'I don't know, sir.' That covers most situations."

At the time of the trial Audie continued to handle the press well.

He called the charge against him "the most glorified misdemeanor that's ever taken place in California." Caruso pronounced the charges "much ado about nothing."

Maria D'Auria was called to testify by the prosecution, but she proved invaluable for the defense. Phil Ochs, the folksinger and an Audie Murphy fan, attended the trial the day Maria D'Auria testified. He declared her "absolutely beautiful." Her version of what happened was the best yet. According to her, the German shepherd, named Rommel, was a gift from Audie, intended to guard her and her property. To do that, the dog would need to be trained, and the Yellow Pages yielded the name of Gofstein. He came to her house to administer the first lesson, and, by the terms of her contract, it was free, with fixed rates set for subsequent lessons. Gofstein then ripped a thorny branch from a cherry tree and began striking the dog in the face with it. Maria told him to leave at once, they struggled, and Gofstein squeezed her left breast. As soon as Gofstein had left, she called Audie, who came over immediately with his friend the bartender. Audie dialed Gofstein, said, "This is Audie Murphy," and Gofstein said, "Never heard of you."

Under oath, Audie's version of what happened went like this. Claiming self-defense, he said that he and Tuell went to Gofstein's kennels where Gofstein asked, "What are you doing here?" and shoved a trash cart into Audie's hip. Audie then punched Gofstein, and Tuell tried to break up the brawl. They heard someone say, "Go get the dogs," whereupon Tuell fired the shot. Audie denied hitting Mrs. Gofstein or having a gun. "Audie told it the way it was," said Caruso.

The way Audie told it to a friend later was a little different still. In this version Audie cased the place first and discovered that Gofstein always came out of his house every evening at five to feed his dogs. He carried the food in huge cans so big that he had to wrap both hands around them. So Audie waited that afternoon till the dog trainer had his hands full, then walked by him (the dog trainer not suspecting anything) and leveled him. The dog trainer never knew what hit him. That would be Audie's way, the friend felt. He never lost; he figured this big guy could whip him, so he cut the odds in his favor and just destroyed him.

An English journalist named Andy Wickham, urged to attend the trial by his friend Phil Ochs, provides the best picture of what the trial itself felt like. Audie, dressed in a "natty blue suit," conveyed a presence that evoked awe in the journalist: "His skin is golden, his white teeth are perfect, and his hair is full and shining with barely a streak of grey. His eyes are sparkling grey, a strange, faraway grey, unforgettable eyes which are beginning to wrinkle at the corners when he smiles, and he has a little nervous tic which contorts his face, for his are eyes which have seen much pain. There is something unmistakably haunting about him. He is 46 now but he has hardly changed at all." He was a "study in impassive dignity."

Caruso was something, too. Dressed in "an elegant grey silk suit" and wearing rings that sparkled, he "exuded the air of one whose life has been spent in expensive restaurants and luxury penthouses, in Cadillac limousines and presidential yachts." During cross-examination of the arresting officer, Caruso was a master of courtroom theatricality.

Audie took the stand that afternoon, and Wickham found his testimony most compelling when he was questioned about guns. The one that fired the shot was a Magnum .38 and was in Caruso's possession. What about the other one, pressed the prosecution; where was it? Over Caruso's objections, Audie was required to answer. He waited a spell, and then said, "The police were unable to locate the weapon because I gave it to President Boumedienne of Algeria for a Christmas present last year." To Wickham, Audie was truly the Quiet American, a war hero and Cold War operative whose confidantes included the presidents of distant nations.

The trial that pitted a handsome war hero and celebrity against a man who had been found guilty, in June, of cruelty to animals was not much of a contest. "A first-year law student could have won that case," says Caruso. "How could you sit in a jury box and say America's number-one war hero was a bad guy?" Still, Caruso took no chances. Once, pointing to his client and to Gofstein, he exclaimed, "This five-foot-seven tiger is supposed to have assaulted this . . . six-foot-one, 195-pound helpless victim!" But those who knew Audie well, like Budd Boetticher, knew that indeed he was a tiger. According to Boetticher, Audie "believed that if he couldn't lick you, he had to figure another way to win. He never lost a fight. His attitude was, if you can lick me I get a shot at you with a brick." Caruso also kept Tuell off the witness stand. He would have been a "terrible witness," says Caruso. Tuell was conveniently out of town during the time of the trial.

Audie was acquitted on all counts by a jury of ten men and two

women, after four hours of deliberation. Following the verdict, several jurors shook his hand and asked for autographs. But the judge
was not so impressed. He lectured Audie: "You sit there. You are
a great war hero but you're a spoiled brat." Afterwards, in the
corridor outside, the press asked Audie if he had learned anything
from the episode. He said yes, stay out of Burbank.

Caruso saw behind the glamour that dazzled the English journalist. During the trial, which was held in seedy downtown L.A.,
Audie and Caruso would lunch together at a cheap Mexican joint.
"One day Audie said, 'Let me pay for lunch,' and he got his wallet
and he had one one-dollar bill. He was too proud. He would never
admit he was broke." Caruso's fee of twenty-five grand was
never paid.

Legally, Audie wasn't out of the woods yet. The search of his
home by the Burbank police, back at the time of his arrest, had
unearthed two blackjacks. Guns were okay, but blackjacks were
another matter, and charges were brought against him for possession
of unlawful weapons. Audie and Caruso won this case easily when
the chief of police of Port Hueneme, a suburb north of L.A., testified
that Audie had been made a "special police officer" in 1969. Audie
carried on his person a card that gave him "all the privileges of a
special law enforcement officer," said the chief, thus entitling him
to "have certain weapons for self-defense . . . and to help in case of
a riot or other special conditions." Testimony also revealed that
Audie held a special deputy's card from the Sheriff's Department
in Dallas. (Similarly, an FBI background check in 1968 showed that
Audie had received a permit to carry weapons from the Los Angeles
Police Department in 1955.) The judge, the same one who'd presided
over the assault case, dismissed the charges, saying, "Mr. Murphy
has a mercurial temperament, but he's not on trial for that."

In the wake of the notoriety created by the assault case Audie
struggled to keep his foundering career as a producer going. He still
needed post-production money for *A Time for Dying*, money to live
on, and money to fund other film projects. Among his uncompleted
works, one was the strangest film Audie ever proposed. He made
the announcement during the summer of the dog-trainer incident,
in 1970. Whether he was serious or not is impossible to tell. If
serious, then it was another sign of Audie's being caught up in the
apocalyptic craziness of the era. If joking, it was vintage Audie.
What he proposed, he said, was to make a film about the "multi-

million-dollar rubbish collection and disposal crisis." He said, "I intend to bring the true story of a garbage man's rise to power to the screen." He was looking for an actor to play Neji, "an American youth who begins life in America as a humble collector, but eventually becomes one of the richest and most powerful men in the state." The plot would reveal "how politicians and ambitious civic leaders scheme to get kickbacks on the award of the garbage collection contract." And Audie had a great title for it: "Empire of Rodents."

On the other hand, he was truly interested in threats to the environment. And because he was a man who met all threats head-on, he set out personally to do something about smog. In September 1970, in the midst of that very troubled year, he found time to submit, on his own, a proposal to Governor Ronald Reagan concerning smog control. Audie had been doing a little research for the past two years, he told a friend. In his cover letter to the governor, he reviewed various measures that had been taken to combat smog, but urged that none of them got at the "real culprit, Nitrogen Oxides." To Audie, defender of justice, nitrogen oxides were like outlaws that had to be arrested and eliminated from society. There followed a ten-page document entitled "Attack on Smog—A New Approach for the Seventies," by Audie Murphy. The data, he said, were taken from documents secured through a private security organization. Audie, a true Southern Californian, distrusted the government and found the "true facts" through a private connection, Challenge Security Services. The document is fascinating for what it reveals about Audie's many-sided interests and his level of energy even in the midst of personally devastating problems like being broke.

Of the possibilities for acting jobs that came his way, the most intriguing was proposed by Don Siegel, who'd directed him in two undistinguished B efforts. Now in 1970 Siegel was lining up the cast for what would become the stylish and controversial *Dirty Harry*. Clint Eastwood would play the free-lance police officer, and Siegel was looking for someone to play the killer, a psychopathic assassin who uses a telescopic rifle to gun down innocent women and children. He recalls how he got the idea of casting Audie in the role: "I hadn't seen him for a while and I met him on the plane on the way back from a Dallas film festival where I had been with *The Beguiled*. He seemed genuinely happy to see me, as I was to see him; he didn't want to bother me because he could see I was reading a script.

"I told him to sit down. We started to talk and I suddenly realized, my God, I'm looking for a killer and here's the killer of all time, a war hero who killed over two hundred fifty people. He was a killer though he didn't look it. I thought it might be interesting. He had never really played a killer." (Presumably Siegel had not seen *No Name on the Bullet* or the TV drama "The Man.") Siegel has a knack for offbeat casting, for it was he who, back in 1964, cast Ronald Reagan as a sleazy gangster-businessman in *The Killers*.

Playing a psychopathic killer would have been the most radical departure in Audie's acting career. At 2 percent of the gross, which is what Siegel was offering, Audie stood to make in the neighborhood of $600,000 for such a role. He could have used the money.

14.
INTO THE
DARKNESS

"And since a dead man has no substance unless one has actually
seen him dead, a hundred million corpses broadcast through
history are no more than a puff of smoke in the imagination."
—*Albert Camus, The Plague*

Audie's life from 1969–70 on got crazier and crazier, as though
he were taking on the colorations of madness and violence
that marked a period of personal and cultural tailspin. Audie,
who had always liked the edge, out where the nihilist walks,
began to move closer and closer toward some final apocalypse. With
few or no prospects open to him on the movie front, he began
increasingly to look about for other sources of income.

One source he turned to was that old malady, gambling. Not
only had he not quit gambling as he said he was going to in 1967,
the habit had grown worse and worse, the stakes higher and higher.
By the fall of 1969 Audie was once again gambling compulsively at
a desperate level, the activity running concurrently with his efforts
to raise money for *A Time for Dying*. And the people he was gambling
with, off-track bookmakers in Chicago and Miami, were not exactly
nice company. Somehow the FBI, which was trying to put together

a gambling conspiracy case against the Chicago mob, headed by Fiore Buccieri, got word of Audie's involvement and interviewed him at his FIPCO office in September 1970. The story he told them affords a fascinating glimpse into the seamy, distrustful, paranoid sub rosa world in which Audie was deeply immersed.

About five years earlier, at Santa Anita where he went to the races all the time, Audie had met a man from Chicago who was, among other things, a convicted burglar. In the fall of 1969 this man, who was well connected with the mob in Chicago, told Audie about a bookmaking operation in Chicago which was guaranteed to pay. It was operated by Fiore Buccieri and Chicago hoodlums. Because Audie liked to bet with off-track bookmakers to avoid reducing odds in the para-mutual machines, he said fine. One of his contacts in Chicago was, as the FBI file puts it, his "Chicago girl friend." Using the code-name of AM, he began betting three or four times a week. Typical bets were "ten dimes" ($10,000) per race, and the understanding was that the account would be settled at the end of each month. At the end of the first month Audie owed a cool $37,000. Putting together a patchwork of loans from a California bank and friends in L.A., Washington, D.C., and Salt Lake City, he flew to Chicago on November 2, 1969, where, in a hotel near O'Hare Airport, he paid the thirty-seven grand in cash to a man dressed in an overcoat with a hat pulled down over his face. On that same trip Audie was also guest speaker at a convention of the National Hardware Association. He also doubtless spent time with his "Chicago girl friend." Later he made two more payments, one for $26,000, on December 9, 1969, and another for $30,000 sometime later. In both these cases delivery was made by an associate of Audie's. The payment was always in cash, and Audie's total loss for that fall was $93,000.

In late 1969 and early 1970 the heat was on in Chicago and the operation shifted to Miami—same game, different town. Audie's telephone contact in Chicago had left the organization, a new voice in Miami said, and Audie continued to place bets three times a day when he bet, at the usual "ten dimes straight" per race. "I like your business. You give me action. . . . I like a man like that," said the voice in Miami. Only now Audie started winning, and in one streak he won a total of $120,000. The problem was, he couldn't collect.

Possibly for reasons of protection or leverage, Audie taped a number of his conversations during that spring and summer. In

September he turned over cassettes of these conversations to the FBI. The voices on the other end were those of an "unknown clerk" in Miami and various other "unidentified males," including two brothers. Audie sometimes wasn't even sure who he was talking to. The one thing he did know was that he wasn't getting his money.

The conversations reveal a man out of his depth. Audie comes across as a man who believes in "honor" and "trust" who is being duped by skillful con men and racketeer gamblers. Using a code name that sounds like it comes from a James Bond movie, MA-5 (his initials reversed), Audie pursued the elusive trail of the $120,000 he was owed. All he wanted, he said, was his money. "I never got paid nothing. I never got nothing, don't you understand?" he told them. Later, more emphatically: "I've never seen a dime. I swear on my dead mother's eyes for Christ's sake, I haven't seen a dime." The debate went on from telephone conversation to telephone conversation, unresolved, infuriating, and deeply frustrating.

Things were further complicated by the actions of Audie's associate, the ex-con who'd told him about the operation in the first place. He had turned Audie around before—a $5,000 loan one time, $1,500 another time, $2,500 to pay for a kidney operation his girlfriend needed, none of it paid back. Passing himself off to the Miami operation as Audie's trusted friend, he caused most of the trouble and suspicion. The Miami brothers were ready to pay, they kept insisting, but they also said they didn't know who to believe—Audie or the man who presented himself as his associate. The brothers believed, or so they said, that Audie had in fact received partial payment, believed that the associate, following their instructions, had delivered "28 large [$28,000] plus some rocks" to Audie in L.A. Audie said none of it had showed. Now one of the brothers claimed to have the "rock" (jewelry) in his possession and estimated its worth at $150,000. He wanted to set up a meeting between Audie and a woman in Vegas who would give him the jewelry. Audie scoffed at first, "What the hell is it, snuff boxes and old junk like that?" "Man o' man, are you kidding? There is one Lapel watch in here worth twenty thousand from France, all handpainted with a key that winds it and it hangs down on a chain, all baked enamel." Audie preferred "bread" to hot jewelry, even if it had been lying around for ten years as the voice on the telephone swore. Audie's main point was that he'd paid bread, "37 large myself to Chi," but had himself "never collected a dollar." He told the guy, "People get paid . . .

they don't cry. You know I'm not a God [profane] crybaby. I never cried in my life."

Eventually, the brothers called Audie and said they wanted to get some things settled. His associate was with them; they put him on the phone to Audie, and he said he had paid Audie and wanted to know what was going on. Audie said he hadn't been paid. Audie told the brother again how the associate, acting as courier, had come to Las Vegas on the way to L.A. to pay Audie and had gotten thrown in jail and how Audie had bailed him out for $200. "They shook him down there and all he had on him up there, according, I got the police report on him, all he had was some old phony paste, ya know?" "I'm just a soft touch, a sucker," said Audie. Audie and the two brothers argued over the phone about this guy. Who could believe him? Audie said he was "like a seagull, I mean he eats everything in front of him and [obscene] on everything behind him."

The brothers wanted to arrange a meeting in Chicago with somebody "big" who could arbitrate and decide who was lying, who wasn't. Then, in the summer, Audie learned that Buccieri, kingpin of the Chicago operation, was staying at the Beverly Rodeo Hotel. Audie made an appointment with him; he had something he wanted Buccieri to hear, the tapes of telephone conversations with the Miami group. Buccieri refused. A Caporegime (underboss or lieutenant) in La Cosa Nostra, Chicago branch, "Fifi" Buccieri was the real thing, an authentic Italian mobster. His dossier suggests a very busy career: "arsonist, bomber, terrorist and professional assassin, he has been identified with labor union rackets, juice and gambling." In 1966 the feds named him the "lord high executioner of the Chicago syndicate." A prime target of the Crime Task Force, Buccieri was eventually run out of the Chicago rackets.

But Audie couldn't deliver Buccieri, who had moved on to Palm Springs. In the last conversation recorded (or turned over to the FBI), he and the brothers agreed to meet at the O'Hare Sheraton where, they said, Audie was "going to be weighed out." There the file ends. Audie never did get the money. He had paid when he lost, and he hadn't been able to collect when he won. It was the story of his life.

His mood in those days could be very grim. One Sunday Boetticher walked into their FIPCO office in a hotel on Franklin Street right above Hollywood Boulevard to pick up some stationery. Audie was sitting there with a bottle of wine and had had a couple of drinks (although he wasn't really a drinker), and his pistol was lying on the desk beside him and he looked really terrible. Boetticher asked him, "What's the matter?"

"You know, I lost a couple of hundred thousand dollars yesterday at the track."

"What are you talking about?"

"I was way ahead at noon."

"Audie, you owe the government; what's the matter with you?"

"I figured I could get the whole damn thing, and I blew it all in the end."

Another time, one night, Audie telephoned Boetticher and said: "Look, everything is in order, and I've got my .45 here and I'm gonna stick it in my mouth and blow my brains out. I've had this Hollywood shit."

"Why don't you do that," said Boetticher. There was a pause, and Boetticher went on, "That would be a wonderful goddamned thing to do, Audie, for all the kids of the United States and all over the world who really worship you. Why don't you stick your fucking gun in your mouth and blow your brains out." Then Boetticher hung up on him, and they never discussed it again.

The question that presumably neither Audie nor Boetticher pondered was whether in fact kids in the United States, in 1970–71, still "worshipped" Audie Murphy. One who did, by his own testimony, was Lieutenant William Laws Calley, Jr., who told his biographer, John Sack, "We learned one thing at OCS we had been taught through childhood was bad: killing. We came to believe that we would go to Vietnam and become Audie Murphys. Run in the hooch, kick in the door, give it a good burst—kill. We would get a big kill ratio there—get a big kill count."

The trial and court-martial of Calley, covered extensively in the national press all through 1970 and 1971, troubled Audie as it troubled the nation. For Audie it seemed to symbolize the ambiguous course America had pursued since 1945. There had been the no-win war in Korea; now it seemed clear Vietnam was going down the drain, too. All through the postwar era, from 1948 on, when Audie had clarified his views amid the confusing movements of Hollywood's pre-McCarthy political skirmishes, through his years with the National Guard from 1950 to 1956, he had been a consistent cold warrior. In the early sixties this meant occasionally lending a hand to military-related projects. In 1961 he received an Outstanding

Civilian Service Medal for his work on an Army-produced film called *The Broken Bridge*, which dealt with the missile program. Audie took the occasion to offer some humorously belligerent remarks about Cuba: "All I would like is a weekend in Cuba with the Third Infantry Division. And I'll take the barber concession." And in 1963 he lent his prestige to a hard-hitting low-budget film about Korea called *War Is Hell*. In the opening frames Audie makes a recruitment pitch for the Army. The film itself has accidental historical interest for two other reasons. It was the first to deal with the disturbing problem of "fragging" (U.S. troops shooting their own officers) which would become an issue in Vietnam. By pure chance, it was also one of the films playing at the Texas Theater in Oak Cliff on November 22, 1963, where Lee Harvey Oswald was captured by the Dallas police. Did Oswald, who once posed for an armed Billy the Kid-like photograph of himself, see on the screen that day America's most famous war hero, the kid from Texas?

As Vietnam heated up and as Audie's private affairs turned more and more futile, he looked outward and saw complexity, change, and frustration. Deeply mired in its third war in as many decades, the country seemed to be rapidly turning away from traditional concepts of military valor toward pacifism and protest. Like many Americans, Audie felt we should go all out and win the war and bring the troops home. Naturally he didn't like the protesters marching in the streets of the nation's cities. He told an interviewer in 1967, "Gee, I'd hate their guts if they had any." His idea about how to win was simple, but costly, and nobody knew the cost better than he: "It'll take one million troops! But I say—we go in, we do the job, then we get out! There's no other way."

Describing himself as "something of a super-patriot," Audie now seemed more inclined to risk the charge of exploitation of his war record than he had been before. In May 1968, for example, *Variety* announced that he would host 260 four-and-a-half-minute radio segments on military heroism, with an option for another 260. "Beyond the Call" would relate the heroics of Medal of Honor winners. The idea fell through, however.

In places where traditional patriotic fervor was still in fashion, Audie was still in demand—in Alabama, for example. On July 20, 1968, at the Alabama War Memorial Ceremony in Montgomery, he read a poem of his own composition, "Dusty Old Helmet." The poem's sentiments were those of familiar patriotic themes—a will-

ingness to die for flag and freedom, etc.—but what was more eloquent was the thoughtful and moving speech that he delivered. Of
the war he had fought in, he said, "More than half the population
of this nation was born since the beginning of World War II. That
ancient conflict, which still seems very close to some of us, is as
remote to the young people today as the War of the Roses is to their
elders." He also saw the difference between his war and the present
one: "Our country has never in its history been involved in a war
as controversial and as frustrating as the bitter struggle in which we
are now engaged in Southeast Asia." To those young people who
were asking "hard, penetrating questions," he proposed providing
"good answers." For Audie, the war offered a supreme test of what
the American experience meant: challenge and response. In this
formulation he gave expression to one of his deepest beliefs. His
whole life, he felt, had been a fight to overcome challenges.

Like many parents, Audie felt the war personally because his
two sons, both in their teens, weren't that far from draft age if the
war dragged on. He told an interviewer in 1970, "It's not right to
ask young men to risk their lives in wars they can't win. Anyway,
war is a nasty business, to be avoided if possible and to be gotten
over with as soon as possible. It's not the sort of job that a man
should get a medal for. I'll tell you what bothers me. What if my
sons try to live up to my image? What if people expect it of them?
I've talked to them about it. I want them to be whatever they are.
I don't want them to try to be what I was. I don't want dead heroes
for sons." Audie sounded like a dove on occasion: "I don't think
we ought to be over there."

Now, in the winter and spring of 1970–71, the Calley case intensified the national debate. Nobody, conservative or liberal, could
ignore it. What Calley did in that peasant village that day, eyewitness
testimony revealed, was to lead his twenty-five-man squad in a massacre unprecedented in U.S. Army annals. In all, approximately one
hundred fifty unarmed citizens were killed and thrown into a ditch.
Calley himself, testimony revealed, smashed in the face of a Buddhist
priest with an M-16, then blew his head half off, after which he
tossed a baby into a ditch and shot it. He was officially charged with
the murder of twenty-two civilians.

In December 1970, Audie expressed publicly his first reaction
to the Calley episode. He remembered his own training and the
imperative to kill: "I'm not saying Calley's innocent or guilty, but

there's no excuse for the kind of behavior he's accused of unless he was following orders. If orders came from above, then he's guilty of nothing. That's what a soldier is supposed to do—follow orders." From his own experience he understood the difficult roles required of a soldier: "It's exasperating to the military mind for a man trained to be a good soldier, to be a statesman, politician, judge and executioner all at once."

After an unprecedented length of over four months, the court-martial reached its judgment on March 26, 1971: Calley was found guilty of the murder of twenty-two Vietnamese citizens. "Distressed and shocked" by the finding, Audie expressed his strongest defense of Calley yet: "I'm not so sure that in those days, having been indoctrinated to a fever pitch, I might not have committed the same error—and I prefer not to call it an error—that Lt. Calley did." Nor was Audie alone in his defense of Calley. Shockwaves were felt throughout the nation, and President Nixon, already sympathetic to Calley and bowing to mounting public pressure, on April 3 ordered that Calley be removed from the stockade and confined to general quarters. A few days later, he announced that he would personally review the case and make final judgment. But Nixon eventually backed off from intervening in the case. In August, Calley's life term was reduced to twenty years; later it was reduced again, to ten years, and after serving one third of that term Calley was released on parole in March 1974 with a dishonorable discharge.

Audie's public comments on the Calley case were but one sign of his increasing investment of energies in the unsettled political atmosphere of a most tumultuous decade. Privately he was engaged in a complicated political scheme that he hoped would have a big personal payoff. In this instance politics and self-interest were the same, and both had a very unsavory odor. Audie's last bizarre scheme to raise money grew out of his association with businessmen, politicians, and an assortment of hard-to-classify types interested in securing a pardon for one of the nation's best-known, most powerful, and most feared labor leaders. What Audie wanted to do was nothing less than free Jimmy Hoffa. He wasn't alone. Ever since the Teamsters official had entered prison on March 7, 1967, people had been trying to spring the still-powerful labor boss: an "incredible cast," said Budd Schulberg, "of governors, federal judges, Louisiana Mafiosi, Chicago gangsters, pension fund lawyer-grafters, senators, congressmen, administration officials, con-men, sleazy go-betweens."

And Audie Murphy. Audie and his associates figured that anybody who could spring Hoffa would be made for life. That was the word on the street, and Audie wanted to be the one.

Richard Nixon, nearing the end of his first term with what he thought was going to be a tough reelection ahead (he couldn't have been more wrong on that one), wanted Hoffa released, too. He needed the Teamsters' endorsement and contributions. Audie indicated in a telephone conversation to Senator George Murphy, who he hoped would be his pipeline to the administration, exactly how much money might be involved. When Senator Murphy said the case was "hot as a deep-bowl stove" and that "nobody wants to touch it," Audie said, "I told him somebody'd better touch it . . . he agrees, he says—hell, that means like six million for the man— you know . . . they count them, you see." In these conversations, published in Walter Sheridan's *The Fall and Rise of Jimmy Hoffa,* the "man" means the President. So whether Audie was exaggerating or not, he and all the others involved in the pardon Hoffa deal, from bottom to top, believed the issue was big money. So it was that Audie plunged into the Hoffa quagmire with tireless energy—a typical late Audie Murphy operation involving much travel, telephoning, and enough deception and braggadocio on all sides to stimulate the most jaded sensibility.

The complicated trail of the Hoffa connection begins, it would seem, with Audie's friendship with D'Alton Smith, whom Audie had met sometime in 1969. Smith had had a checkered career. He had entered the fray on behalf of Hoffa early on, the year Hoffa was jailed. He had close ties to New Orleans Mafia boss Carlos Marcello (and two of Smith's sisters had married Marcello associates Joseph Poretto and Nofio Pecora). Marcello in turn was a good friend of Hoffa's and very interested in seeing his friend released from prison. A "wheeler-dealer swindler" and fixer for Marcello, Smith had had several brushes with the law. In 1970 he was indicted by a federal grand jury in Los Angeles for transporting stolen securities. In early 1971 he was convicted on that charge. He was also indicted by the state of California for his alleged part in the theft of securities there. In the meantime he had moved to Denver, formed a plastics company, bought a big house and an airplane, and was looking around for other investment opportunities.

In this period, 1970–71, Audie turned to Smith for financial help. Smith was going to help him raise money, and Audie became increasingly interested in business possibilities generated by Smith. And, of course, there was the ongoing Hoffa business. At issue was the testimony of Edward Grady Partin, a Teamster official in Baton Rouge, Louisiana, and a former associate of Hoffa. It was Partin's testimony concerning jury tampering in a trial in Nashville in 1962 that provided the key to the Justice Department's eventual conviction which resulted in Hoffa's being sent to the slammer. From the time he testified against Hoffa, Partin was under intense pressure to recant. Smith, Partin once claimed, offered him a million-dollar bribe to recant. There were other bribe offers, and after the election of Richard Nixon, increasing harassment by legal means. There are so many claims and counterclaims by so many parties in the Hoffa case that it's sometimes impossible to know what or whom to believe. Walter Sheridan, special assistant to Attorney General Robert Kennedy and the man who bird-dogged Hoffa for fifteen years, kept a close watch on Partin and his book provides an intricate account of the Smith-Murphy efforts.

Partin met with Smith several times, including a visit to Smith's home in Denver in March 1971. Smith and Partin also met a new player, Pat Willis, who described himself as a good friend of Audie Murphy. Although this wasn't entirely true, Audie did know Willis and had, in fact, he later told Partin, helped Willis out on an investment deal in the Philippines. "I don't do those kind of favors for many people," said Audie. (Partin taped this and many conversations during these years. The government had provided the equipment.) Willis, described by Walter Sheridan as a "private investigator, professional informant and con man," assured Partin that if he produced an affidavit saying that he had committed perjury in Chattanooga, the President would have a reason to pardon Hoffa. Partin, he promised, would not have to sign the affidavit until the President had provided written immunity against indictment for perjury.

Later Partin talked by phone to Audie, who was hoping to meet with him in L.A. and was setting in motion plans to deliver the affidavit to the Western White House at San Clemente. Against Sheridan's advice, Partin went to L.A. and, in a session with Smith and Willis presided over by a lawyer, he answered questions that indicated he had been pressured by the government in the jury-tampering case and had played along with the government's scheme to nail Hoffa. His answers were mostly vague, however, and since it was neither signed nor notarized, the document was worthless. Over the years there were dozens of bogus affidavits floating around Washington, each purporting to be Partin's true story of what happened, of how he lied in the jury-tampering trial and so on, but the one Audie, Smith, and Willis were betting on was a thirty-one-page document typed up from the answers Partin gave that day, March 27, 1971. Said Partin, "I gave 'em nothing. Sure, I said some words, and they wrote them down. But they were accusing me of doing everything, including being involved in the Kennedy assassination. So I just told them what they wanted to hear and refused to sign anything."

Now Partin got in touch with Willis and told him that he had perjured himself in that affidavit, that nothing he had said was true. Willis was very upset and agreed not to use it. Then Partin talked to Audie, telling him the document was a phony and that Willis wasn't going to use it. But Audie had already arranged for Willis to visit the Western White House. Time was running out; Hoffa's parole board would meet on March 31. The day of the hearing, another player in the Murphy–Smith–Willis deal, Arthur Egan, flew to Washington to deliver the document to Hoffa's attorney. Egan was a reporter for the Manchester *Union Leader,* the rabidly conservative New Hampshire newspaper run by William Loeb, a tireless Hoffa supporter and liberal-baiter. His mission that day was fruitless because the lawyer, recognizing the spuriousness of the document, declined to submit it to the board. Hoffa's appeal was denied, thus reigniting the efforts of Audie and the others to carry on their campaign.

Audie and Smith got back in touch with Partin and told him they were dropping Pat Willis. He was the one, they said, who had screwed up the whole deal. They had a new plan and, they believed, a new backer: wealthy conservative ideologue Gordon McClendon of Dallas, owner of radio station KLIF and a man who had dabbled in everything from cheap exploitation films (*The Killer Shrews* and *The Giant Gila Monster* were two of his) to conservative political causes. The plan was to get the parole board to reopen the hearing. Partin was still the key. Audie and Smith hoped to bring Partin together with McClendon in Dallas where Partin would produce a new affidavit. Audie said, "We don't want another piece of junk around . . . because we got one more shot at this and that's all." He was a great believer in Partin's recanted story, saying, "I have met several times with Ed Partin, I'm convinced he's telling the truth and it is a shame the government won't allow the truth to finally come out in the open."

On April 10 Audie and Smith flew to Baton Rouge to meet with Partin. Audie said he had good connections in Dallas, with Lester May, Gordon McClendon's brother-in-law and a former U.S. Attorney. Audie thought he could get millionaire Clint Murchison's help, too. Audie also explained to Partin what was going on with Senator George Murphy. The day before, the senator had acknowledged that about ten days earlier he had been approached by Audie Murphy to deliver a package to the San Clemente White House. The senator claimed he didn't know what the contents of the package were, but Audie told Partin the senator certainly did know. Audie also told Partin that he and others were orchestrating a campaign, centralized in the White House, to generate a favorable atmosphere for a pardon, just like in the Calley case. Off the record (he thought), in one of those taped conversations with Partin, Audie compared the publicity campaign to free Hoffa to what had happened in the Calley case. If it happened with Calley, it could happen with Hoffa, reasoned Audie and his associates. Here the intersection of right-wing politics of self-interest takes on a particularly odiferous quality.

Egan, who sort of filled the gap left by Willis, saw the distinct advantage of having Audie Murphy on their side. He told Partin, "Let's face it—the guy's a Congressional Medal of Honor winner and you know that still carries a hell of a lot of weight when this guy is on your side." On April 14, Audie talked to Partin again by telephone. He said he'd had another talk with Senator Murphy and told him the original document delivered to the Western White House should never have been submitted. A meeting with Partin in Dallas could, he said, "nail things down."

Audie and his friends never did, however, get Partin together with McClendon. Said Partin later, "But when it came down to doing business, McClendon wasn't involved. Instead I was dealing with Audie Murphy, Arthur Egan from the Manchester *Union Leader*, and McClendon's brother-in-law, Lester May." All that resulted was another unsigned and worthless document.

Egan continued to apply pressure in Washington, visiting with senators, and trying to exploit his boss William Loeb's influence with the President. What Egan, Smith, Audie, and the others wanted was for Attorney General Mitchell to investigate Walter Sheridan and everybody associated with the Kennedy Justice Department. As Audie put it in a conversation with Partin, "It's just going to be a battle between which one's got the biggest dogs. . . . After they run that Epstein [Mike Epstein of the Kennedy Justice Department] out of there—then Walter Sheridan is the only one they got to worry about it looks like."

Egan's next move was to break the story of the Partin affidavit in his paper, the Manchester *Union Leader*. Audie's role in the negotiations was described, as were those of Pat Willis and, of course, Partin. Egan also disclosed that he and Audie and attorney Lester May had met in Dallas on April 22 to discuss plans for getting a new affidavit from Partin. When the wire services chose not to pick up Egan's "exclusive," the movement was dealt a setback. Time was again running out. The Teamsters' International Executive Board would be meeting soon, and tops on its agenda was the selection of a candidate for the presidency of the union, a job that Hoffa wanted badly to keep, but of course that would be difficult as long as he was in prison. (Ironically, one condition of his presidential pardon was that he would have to relinquish the top job.)

On May 13 Audie called Partin and invited him to Las Vegas the following week, ostensibly to see one of the fighters that Audie managed in a match at the Silver Slipper. D'Alton Smith would be there too. Obviously the real reason for the invitation was to try once more to obtain a new affidavit from Partin. On May 19 Audie was in Vegas, at the Desert Inn. He was looking for Partin, but Partin never showed. On through May efforts to meet with Partin by Egan and James Hoffa, Jr., continued. Although Audie's efforts all proved futile, he was right about his prediction of what the President would do. On December 23, 1971, Richard Nixon commuted Jimmy Hoffa's prison term, thus ensuring the high-dollar support of the Teamsters' Union in the upcoming election. In 1978 Jimmy Hoffa disappeared in a famous and as-yet-unsolved case; in 1982 he was declared legally dead.

Audie's closest friends didn't know about the Hoffa negotiations. His old friend and patron in Dallas, Skipper Cherry, for example, saw Audie that May, and when he heard later about the Hoffa connection, he said, "I would be surprised at him being involved in anything like that." There were many reasons not to tell Cherry, but one of them was characteristic of Audie throughout this period— a passion for secrecy. He operated on several different levels and, as before, moved freely in and out of different sorts of groups without the one knowing about the other. There was Hollywood; there was the boxing world, intertwined with the Vegas world; there was the domestic world of wife and children; there was the world of sexual affairs; there was the off-track gambling world; there was the police world; there was the underground political world of intrigue and influence; there was the world of business investments; and so on. So many worlds, and increasingly Audie was in command of none of them.

Powerless, broke, and on the down slope to that crucial watershed of fifty, he had begun to show signs of aging. Time and strain were beginning at last to mark the man who had never looked anything but incredibly youthful. The baby face was getting a trifle jowly. The films from the mid-sixties on reveal a tiredness and slight puffiness. Friends back in Texas noticed something different about Audie during a visit in 1968 when he had returned to Hunt County to attend the funeral of one of his brothers, Joe Preston, thirty-two, a policeman killed in a car wreck. His father, Emmett, was there, and according to Audie's neighbor and long-time friend, Mrs. Cawthon, Audie "put his arms around his daddy's shoulders and talked to him nice." To his brother Eugene, Audie seemed nervous, depressed, and melancholy. Helen Woods, widow of Ray Woods, whom Audie called "the only daddy I ever knew," saw him in the fall of 1970 and thought he looked bloated, old, and depressed. Old friends in California thought the same thing. Casey Tibbs, who had always been aware of this tendency in Audie, says, "Another thing about Audie, he was almost a hypochondriac. He'd want to wake up sick; it was almost like he wanted to feel sorry for himself. . . . Audie was a fine-looking guy for a long time; then he got to looking like a little old man."

A photograph of Audie at his desk taken in mid-May 1971 shows an amazing transformation. The face is that of a man aging fast. There was a Dorian Gray quality to Audie now, as if the forever innocent baby face was finally beginning to reveal a life far different from the one implied by all the photographs in all the years, as though Huck Finn were turning into a puffy version of Pap, or Audie into his father, an overweight Irish drinker.

He remained as combative as ever. Casey Tibbs was on a commercial flight with him that spring and saw Audie become furious with a man sitting behind him who made some flip remark. Casey told him, "Audie, goddamn, forget it. For Christ's sake, it ain't worth it. This is some punk, don't pay any attention to it." But when the plane landed, Audie tracked the guy to the baggage area where the guy realized how things were and broke and ran. The whole thing was "over nothing, really," says Casey. "But it just burned him; it was just in his mind." Audie remained as relentless in the rectification of real or imagined wrongs as any gunfighter in the third reel. It was a good thing he didn't drink, says Casey. "If he'd have drank, as hyper as he'd get sometimes, he'd have been impossible." Casey concludes with a shake of his head, "Audie was one of my best friends and I really loved the guy and he was a great guy, but I think he was the closest man to self-destruction I ever knew in my life."

That spring of 1971 as Audie shuttled back and forth across the continent pursuing chimeras of financial redemption, a business opportunity led him in late May to Atlanta, to act as a go-between for parties interested in investing in Modular Properties, Inc., an Atlanta-based company. The plan was to meet with a small group in Atlanta, then fly to Martinsburg, Virginia, to look over a plant that constructed prefabricated buildings. After that Audie had a heavy round of celebrity appearances and political functions lined up. He was going to Tennessee to take part in the Chet Atkins Invitational Golf Tournament. His friend and songwriting buddy Scott Turner would be there. Then he was scheduled to take part in a George Putnam "Selling America" telecast back in L.A.

In an Aero-Commander, a two-engine plane, Audie and five others left Atlanta on the morning of May 28. The pilot, Herman Butler, had a spotty record—he'd had his license pulled once for running out of gas and having to crash-land and he was not instrument rated. Butler got into trouble about sixty miles from their destination when he flew into foggy, rainy weather. Observers in the area saw and heard the plane flying low and erratically, apparently looking for a place to land. After groping through the low-lying clouds, Butler made contact with Roanoke, where the ceiling was high enough for him to land. But he never got there. Just past noon, the plane flew straight into a mountain. The date was exactly one year from the day Audie was arrested in the dog-trainer incident. It was also Memorial Day weekend.

Because of the rugged, mountainous terrain the crash site was not located by search parties until four days later, on the afternoon of May 31. Near the summit of a heavily wooded mountain twelve miles north of Roanoke lay the wreckage. Three bodies were badly burned inside the fuselage; three were thrown clear. Audie's was one of these. He died of "massive total body injuries." As Spec McClure said later, "He took a lot of killing. It took a plane diving into a mountain."

On May 31 the three major networks each carried a twenty-second spot announcement near the end of the half-hour, saying only that Audie Murphy was among six people killed in a light plane crash.

The minute he heard it, Bobbie Hoy thought, "It wasn't Audie flying. Murphy wouldn't have done that. He'd have filed a flight plan; he'd have checked the weather; he'd have done all that."

Casey Tibbs was in South Dakota shooting a documentary, "Born to Buck," when the call came. It was Vernon Scott of the UPI. "Casey, are you standing up?" he asked. "You'd better sit down." When Scott told him Audie Murphy was dead, Casey says, "It hit me really hard."

Tom Willett, a former radio announcer turned movie extra, never knew Audie, but when he heard the news in Las Vegas where he was living at the time, he wanted to do something. He called the local radio station and requested they play "Shutters and Boards." Then he called the local VFW to see if flags could be put at half-staff. The man who answered asked, "Who's Audie Murphy?"

We read in the remains of plane crashes all kinds of signs—hints for our own possible escape from a similar destiny, hints of forewarning, last-ditch heroism, salvation, signs of life. Since there was plenty of advance warning in this disaster—officially, nineteen minutes—Audie and the others knew they were imperiled. His widow looked for revelation in the final minutes of his life. Pam believed that in those last moments Audie had time to come to Christ. She said later, "So Audie had some warning that he was in trouble and he had time to make the decision with God that he had not made before."

Others read a sinister meaning into the event. There was something troublesome about the circumstances of the plane crash. Men involved in the Hoffa business wondered about it. Grady Partin said Audie had told him he was worried about both the condition of the plane and the pilot's skill. Arthur Egan believed the crash had something to do with Audie's involvement in the Hoffa case. Said Egan:

"Murphy played a very prominent role in trying to free Hoffa. And I think it cost him his life. That's my firm opinion and I got to know Audie pretty well." But Egan's opinion seems to be simply a theory derived from a penchant for conspiratorial plots, the "web of conspiracy" view of America in the 1960s.

In December 1971, Pamela and their two sons filed a suit for $10 million, alleging negligence in the operation and maintenance of the plane. Herbert Hafif, a top lawyer in the field of wrongful death suits, handled the case when it finally came to trial in 1975, in a Denver court. He proved pilot error as the cause of death. His strategy also involved a reconstruction of the life of Audie Murphy, and in his presentation to the jury he sought to prove Audie's potential earning power. Hafif mounted convincing arguments to show Audie's proven capacity to earn money as actor, producer, songwriter, and businessman. The jury agreed with him, awarding $3.2 million to the plaintiffs. Unfortunately, however, they never received any money from the judgment.

At the time of his death several close friends—Casey Tibbs, Budd Boetticher, Guy Mitchell, George Putnam—felt that Audie, who would have been forty-seven the next month, was on the comeback trail. Congressman Ray Roberts, from Audie's old home district in Hunt and Collin County, believed Audie was on his way to becoming "as rich as Croesus." Perhaps so, but the cold-as-death records at the L.A. County Courthouse Archives Building suggest no comeback, no pattern of change, no change of luck. Audie was burrowing deeper into debt as 1971 unrolled. That spring he had written three hot checks for $600, $750, and $750. These were peanuts compared to the recent outstanding loans: promissory notes of $12,000, $20,000, and $50,000 from 1970. His financial picture, reads one entry in the archives, had "become extremely complex."

The body was returned to L.A., and a memorial service was held at the Church of the Hills at Forest Lawn Memorial Park, in Hollywood Hills, on June 4. (There was also a memorial service at the First Baptist Church in Farmersville the same day.) Over six hundred people attended, including six Medal of Honor winners. It was not a "Hollywood" event. Almost none of the glittering film community came, only the "little" people, grips, crew members, and the like. His old agent Paul Kohner was there. The only stars in evidence, both much faded now, were Ann Blyth and Wanda Hendrix. Wanda left the church in tears, saying to the press, "He was a great soldier. No one can ever take that away from him. May he rest in peace."

Then the body was taken to Arlington National Cemetery for burial with full military honors, on June 7. A caisson drawn by six black horses brought the flag-draped coffin to the burial site, only a short distance from the Ampitheatre of the Tomb of the Unknown Soldier. There was something odd about the coffin, the gravedigger remembers: "It was surprising to me that a man like Audie Murphy was buried with no outer casing, just a casket." (Today Audie Murphy's grave is one of the announced sites on official tours of Arlington National Cemetery.) Among the hundreds of mourners were some forty-odd members of the 3rd Infantry Division, General William C. Westmoreland, the Army chief of staff, and George Bush, at that time Ambassador to the United Nations. General Westmoreland later issued a statement that sought, through Audie, to link two wars: "His example to fellow Americans served as an inspiration to all persons during World War II—Americans and allies alike, at the front and at home. Today, also, his example should be an inspiration to all Americans—in or out of uniform—at home or overseas—who serve in support of the policies of our country." There were also representatives at graveside of other facets of Audie's life, one of the most striking of whom was John Tuell, towering in a tuxedo and black brogans.

Pamela bore herself with great dignity, clasping the flag that covered his casket. His sons stood by her, their longish hair a token of the Vietnam era. The sound of "Taps" played by a military band reminded those in attendance of all wars. The sound of "Dogface Soldier," the 3rd Division anthem, reminded them of Audie's war.

President Nixon's Army aide, Lieutenant Colonel Vernon Coffey, issued a statement on the President's behalf: "As America's most decorated hero of World War II, Audie Murphy not only won the admiration of millions for his own brave exploits; he also came to epitomize the gallantry and action of America's fighting men. The nation stands in his debt and mourns at his death."

Audie's death threw into high relief the extent to which he belonged to an earlier era. In 1971 the nation, deeply suspicious of traditional military valor, was sick of a war that refused to go away, sick of Kent State, the Calley trial, and a decade of upheaval, assassinations, and burning cities. It had little time for heroes of the past and none at all for those of the present. There were no garlands for grunts in Vietnam. Nobody can name the most decorated hero of that war. Over half the American public felt very keenly that it wasn't our war in the first place.

The state of the western in 1971 further underlined Audie's irrelevance. The smash hit of the year, released at the time he died, was *Little Big Man*, an allegory about Vietnam that dramatized startling parallels between the massacre of a Sioux village and My Lai. General Custer, the romantic figure who "had died with his boots on" as played by Errol Flynn back in the 1940s, was in this film a raving madman. And the anti-hero, Dustin Hoffman, was a goofball, a schlemiel, an ugly little guy who was half-hippie, half-Indian—a far cry from the old days of Gary Cooper, Randolph Scott, and Audie Murphy.

All in all, Audie Murphy's death did not occasion as much national media attention as one might have expected. The evening news on the day of his funeral offers a time-capsule collage as to why. The relentless pastiche of events shown to the American public on June 7 included two reports of commercial airline crashes, one in Maine, one in California; a traffic gridlock in New York City brought on by a strike; pictures of a Soviet satellite making a successful docking in space; a disturbing report of a secret military campaign being waged in Cambodia by mercenaries hired by the CIA; brief mention of the fact that the North Vietnamese had completed their seventeenth straight day of attacks along the DMZ; and a detailed description of the dresses to be worn by bridesmaids for the impending marriage of Tricia Nixon in the White House.

Amid the calamity and detritus of daily history, neither CBS nor NBC found time to mention the funeral. For an American hero who had given two and a half years of unprecedented valor in combat for his country, the only recognition Audie Murphy received from these two networks was twenty seconds the day his body was found. ABC did better. In a two-and-a-half-minute story headlined "Audie" featuring shots of the graveside ceremony at Arlington, the narrator concentrated on his war record, quoted his remark about being a "fugitive from the law of averages," and at the end said (erroneously) that he had given away all of his medals to children. There was no mention at all of his film career.

In all the tributes, editorials, and commentary, Audie Murphy in death as in life represented a variety of symbolic meanings in the nation's consciousness. Among conservatives he stood for the Past, Americanism, and the Good War. In L.A. George Putnam memorialized Audie's passing in both a personal and political sense. He ran footage of Audie reciting the Alabama speech of 1968 (recorded at Putnam's insistence three years before); then he read Audie's last poem, "Dusty Old Helmet."

In Dallas, tributes stressed Audie's ties with a treasured past, one that now seemed threatened on every hand. Roy Edwards, a sports columnist for the Dallas *Morning News*, turned Audie's life into a kind of Merle Haggard song, a time when "smoking a cigarette or drinking a beer was fast living for a youngster," when "officers of the law" weren't called "pigs or fuzz," when young men from all over "these United States went to war without a backward glance." Gordon McClendon, on June 1, delivered a radio editorial every hour on the hour on station KLIF. McClendon painted Audie as "the hard luck kid" who paid for his naivete in a world of promoters and sharpsters, and concluded by placing him in a characteristic Dallas political context: "Is there not to be a day of national mourning for Audie Murphy? Or was John Kennedy a greater hero?" The answer to the first question was no; there would be no day of national mourning. (In Texas and Nevada, though, flags were flown at half-mast in honor of the fallen hero.) The answer to the second depended on which side one belonged to in what was, in 1971, a nation divided against itself.

For the national press Audie also evoked the past, but not in a nostalgic way. *Time* magazine recounted his heroics but concentrated on the arc of failure in the postwar years. *Time* (whose reviewers had in the past given some of his films quite good reviews) now dismissed his movie career and focused instead on his private war on drug dealers and the dog-trainer incident. According to *Time,* the sixties "left Audie farther and farther behind"; he belonged "to an earlier, simpler time, one in which bravery was cardinal and killing was a virtue." *Newsweek,* in a much briefer piece, rehearsed his war record and said that except for his film *To Hell and Back,* "most of his roles were best forgotten."

The *New York Times* article, which gave a full but more neutral account of his war record and postwar life, was the only American account to take his movie career seriously (though, like virtually every article, it too mentioned the oft-repeated story about Audie's telling a director that he had no talent for acting). Noting that *To*

Hell and Back had by chance been playing on early morning television in New York the day Audie's body was found, the article quoted several of his statements about the differences between the real war and the film. In England the London *Times* gave more space to his movie career than to his war record. This is not so surprising since Europeans have always held a much higher opinion of the western than have Americans. They believe, as noted French critic André Bazin has written, that the western is "American cinema par excellence." The *Times* mentioned in particular such films as *The Unforgiven, The Red Badge of Courage,* and *The Quiet American.*

The most prescient farewell anywhere belonged to Bill Mauldin. In *Life* magazine, which is where, after all, Audie Murphy's postwar life could be said to have begun, Mauldin described him as an anachronistic figure for whom "nothing came out right. His country got into wars it couldn't win." For Mauldin, Audie's greatness and downfall were both bound up in his refusal to "adjust, accept, tolerate, temporize, and sometimes compromise." "In him," he concluded, "we all recognized the straight, raw stuff, uncut and fiery as the day it left the still. Nobody wanted to be in his shoes, but nobody wanted to be unlike him, either."

EPILOGUE

I n Beverly Hills all the finest homes have signs posted on the front lawn that read: "Armed Response," beneath which appears the name of a security agency. This legend might stand as a symbol of Audie Murphy. He lived his entire life armed, physically and emotionally, against dangers real and imagined.

He came by such resistance naturally, shaped as he was by three major twentieth-century clusters of force: Depression, war, and Hollywood. The Depression made him lean, tough, and eager for experience; the war gave him all the experience he ever wanted; and Hollywood provided a complex, ironic, illusory sort of existence for a man of action.

The most important of the three, the one that bound everything together, was the war. What he accomplished in combat and the internal toll that battle exacted from him formed a permanent legacy. The war (and *Life*) made him famous; his memoir *To Hell and Back*, which tried to tell the disturbing truth about the war and its effects, clinched his fame; and the film version brought him his greatest critical and financial rewards. War both made and unmade Audie Murphy because, unlike all those veterans who were able to resume their lives and put the days of blood and killing behind them, he was never able to recover from the profound lassitude, the boredom, inscribed upon his inner life.

With the gradual shading of World War II into the remoteness of the past, Audie's name has dimmed, too. He can hardly be held accountable for that. Old soldiers, in America, really do fade away. One could see the erasure process clearly at work in a 1986 television homage to *Life* magazine on the occasion of its fiftieth anniversary. Host Barbara Walters stressed *Life*'s impact on Vietnam and hardly mentioned World War II. And in her review of all the famous people who had appeared in the pages of *Life*, there was no mention of Audie Murphy.

In contemporary America it is very hard to make a name last much beyond one's lifetime. Such seemingly imperishable stars of the cinema as Gary Cooper, for example, are blurring very fast; one generation's idol becomes trivia to successive generations. Who, among American film stars of the fifties, has truly lasted? Marilyn Monroe, James Dean, and, in westerns, though he is less known for his great films than for his bigger-than-life presence, John Wayne. So it is hardly surprising that Audie Murphy's film reputation has persisted only among a dwindling number of die-hard western fans. Randolph Scott is in a similar position; already young people have trouble understanding the allusion to Scott in an old Statler Brothers song (or to Joe DiMaggio in Simon and Garfunkel's "Mrs. Robinson").

Audie Murphy's reputation as a representative cultural figure has proved more durable, but it too has undergone steady erosion. One can see it in the war films that invoke his name. In 1956's *Pork Chop Hill* officer Gregory Peck questions a young GI in Korea who has just wiped out a machine-gun nest: "Who do you think you are? Audie Murphy?" The reference suggests grandstand heroics, old-time blood-and-guts glory. In *Platoon*, the 1980s thinking man's war movie, there is a darker reference. A lean, pinch-faced GI tells another soldier, just before the big night attack, "Stick with me. I'm a regular Audie Murphy." The allusion is already contaminated, though, because in an earlier scene we saw this kid lay waste to a helpless village—Audie Murphy crossed with My Lai. The invocation of Audie's name is the kiss of death, and sure enough, the young proletariat warrior does not survive the fire fight.

In books of the Vietnam generation, too, when Audie is mentioned at all, the tone is one of disillusionment. Julian Smith's *Look-*

ing Away: Hollywood and Vietnam recalls how the author felt when Audie died: "I had forgotten him, had seen none of his films since 1958, had left him as an all-American boy-faced hero. And there he was, splashed on the front page of a local paper, middle-aged, jowly, heavy-eyed, wearing the face of an outwardly successful auto dealer who might, any day now, be indicted for fraud." The title of Vietnam vet McAvoy Layne's 1973 volume of war poetry links Audie directly to that war: *How Audie Murphy Died in Vietnam.*

Audie Murphy's was not the kind of life that Americans like to emulate. It lacked the Iacocca curve, the continuously upward spiral toward the dizzying heights of great wealth, great power. From age twenty-one on, Audie Murphy's life was a postscript to battle; the success he enjoyed ten years later, in 1955, was actually the beginning of a long, slow decline that came only after much pain, much struggle, and a descent into the labyrinthine depths of America in the 1960s. In the end, at the personal level, Audie belongs with Elvis Presley, whom women thought he resembled in good-mannered shyness, and Howard Hughes, whom he resembled in his nocturnal paranoia. Audie, Elvis, and Hughes were all representatives of American dreams gone astray.

Maybe they were right, those friends of Audie's who thought he belonged in an earlier age, on the frontier, patrolling the streets of some flyblown Western town, keeping the peace. But he didn't live then; he lived in a time of change when the idea of heroism was itself open to challenge on every front.

Audie Murphy, impoverished child of agrarian America, trained executioner, champ soldier of World War II, B + movie cowpoke, husband, father, lover of uncounted women, poet, songwriter, compulsive gambler, friend of pugilists, grafters, jockeys, Mafiosi, and congressmen—what an extraordinary life he lived. On the edge, the way the Kid from Texas, the Quiet American, always preferred it.

FILMOGRAPHY

1948

BEYOND GLORY. Paramount. *director:* John Farrow. *producer:* Robert Fellows. *screenplay:* Jonathan Latimer, Charles M. Warren, and William W. Haines. *cast:* Alan Ladd, Donna Reed, George Macready, George Coulouris, Harold Vermilyea, Henry Travers, Luis Van Rooten, Tom Neal, Conrad Janis, Margaret Field, Paul Lees, Dick Hogan, Audie Murphy, Geraldine Wall, Charles Evans, Russell Wade, Vincent Donahue, Steve Pendleton, Harland Tucker.

TEXAS, BROOKLYN AND HEAVEN. United Artists. *director:* William Castle. *producer:* Robert S. Golden. *screenplay:* Lewis Meltzer and Earl Baldwin. *cast:* Guy Madison, Diana Lynn, James Dunn, Lionel Stander, Florence Bates, Michael Chekhov, Magaret Hamilton, Moyna Magill, Irene Ryan, Colin Campbell, Clem Bevans, Roscoe Karns, William Frawley, Alvin Hammer, Erskine Sanford, John Galldet, James Burke, Guy Wilkerson, Audie Murphy, Jesse White, Tom Dugan.

1949

BAD BOY. Allied Artists. *director:* Kurt Neumann. *producer:* Paul Short. *screenplay:* Robert Hardy Andrews. *cast:* Lloyd Nolan, Jane Wyatt, Audie Murphy, James Gleason, Stanley Clements, Martha Vickers, James Lydon, Rhys Williams, Selena Royle, William Lester.

1950

THE KID FROM TEXAS. Universal-International. *director:* Kurt Neumann. *producer:* Paul Short. *screenplay:* Robert Hardy Andrews, Karl Lamb. *cast:* Audie Murphy, Gail Storm, Albert Dekker, Shepperd Strudwick, Will Geer, William Talman, Martin Garralaga, Robert H. Barrat, Walter Sande, Frank Wilcox, Dennis Hoey, Ray Teal, Don Haggerty, Paul Ford, John Phillips, Harold Goodwin, Zon Murray, Tom Trout, Rosa Turich, Dorita Pallais, Pilar Del Rey, Richard Wessell.

SIERRA. Universal-International. *director:* Alfred E. Green. *producer:* Michel Kraike. *screenplay:* Edna Anhalt. *cast:* Wanda Hendrix, Audie Murphy, Burl Ives, Dean Jagger, Richard Rober, Anthony (Tony) Curtis, Houseley Stevenson, Elliott Reid, Griff Barnett, Elisabeth Risdon, Roy Roberts, Gregg Martell, Sara Allgood, Erskine Sanford, John Doucette, Jim Arness, Ted Jordan, I. Stanford Jolley, Jack Ingram.

KANSAS RAIDERS. Universal-International. *director:* Ray Enright. *producer:* Ted Richmond. *screenplay:* Robert L. Richards. *cast:* Audie Murphy, Brian Donlevy, Marguerite Chapman, Scott Brady, Tony Curtis, Richard Long, Richard Arlen, James Best, Dewey Martin, John Kellogg, George Chandler, Richard Egan.

1951

THE CIMARRON KID. Universal-International. *director:* Budd Boetticher. *producer:* Ted Richmond. *screenplay:* Louis Stevens. *cast:* Audie Murphy, Beverly Tyler, Yvette Dugay, John Hudson, James Best, Leif Erickson, Noah Beery, John Hubbard, Hugh O'Brian, John Bromfield, Roy Roberts, William Reynolds, Palmer Lee, Rand Brooks, David Sharpe, Frank Silvera, David Wolfe, Richard Garland, Eugene Baxter, Frank Ferguson.

THE RED BADGE OF COURAGE. MGM *director-screenwriter:* John Huston. *producer:* Gottfried Reinhardt. *cast:* Audie Murphy, Bill Mauldin, Douglas Dick, Andy Devine, Tim Durant, John Dierkes, Royal Dano, James Dobson, Robert Easton Burke, Gloria Eaton, Smith Ballew, Glenn Strange. Narration by James Whitmore.

1952

THE DUEL AT SILVER CREEK. Universal-International. *director:* Don Siegel. *producer:* Leonard Goldstein. *screenplay:* Gerald Drayson Adams, Joseph Hoffman. *cast:* Audie Murphy, Stephen McNally, Faith Domergue, Susan Cabot, Gerald Mohr, Walter Sande, Eugene Iglesias, Lee Marvin, George Eldredge.

1953

GUNSMOKE. Universal-International. *director:* Nathan Juran. *producer:* Aaron Rosenberg. *screenplay:* D. D. Beauchamp. *cast:* Audie Murphy, Susan Cabot, Paul Kelly, Charles Drake, Mary Castle, Jack Kelly,

Donald Randolph, Jesse White, Chubby Johnson, William Reynolds, Bill Radovich, James F. Stone, Jimmy Van Horn, Clem Fuller.

COLUMN SOUTH. Universal-International. *director:* Frederick de Cordova. *producer:* Ted Richmond. *screenplay:* William Sackheim. *cast:* Audie Murphy, Joan Evans, Robert Sterling, Ray Collins, Dennis Weaver, Palmer Lee, Russell Johnson, Jack Kelly, Johnny Downs, Bob Steele, James Best, Ralph Moody, Rico Alaniz.

TUMBLEWEED. Universal-International. *director:* Nathan Juran. *producer:* Ross Hunter. *screenplay:* John Meredyth Lucas. *cast:* Audie Murphy, Lori Nelson, Chill Wills, K. T. Stevens, Roy Roberts, Russell Johnson, Ross Elliott, Madge Meredith, Lee Van Cleef, I. Stanford Jolley, Ralph Moody, Eugene Iglesias, Phil Chambers, Lyle Talbot, King Donovan, Harry Rarvey.

1954

RIDE CLEAR OF DIABLO. Universal-International. *director:* Jesse Hibbs. *producer:* John W. Rogers. *screenplay:* George Zuckerman and D. D. Beauchamp. *cast:* Audie Murphy, Susan Cabot, Dan Duryea, Abbe Lane, Russell Johnson, Paul Birch, William Pullen, Jack Elam, Denver Pyle.

DRUMS ACROSS THE RIVER. Universal-International. *director:* Nathan Juran. *producer:* Melville Tucker. *screenplay:* John K. Butler, Lawrence Roman. *cast:* Audie Murphy, Lisa Gaye, Walter Brennan, Lyle Bettger, Mary Corday, Hugh O'Brian, James Anderson, Jay Silverheels, Emile Meyer, Regis Toomey, Bob Steele, George Wallace, Lane Bradford, Morris Ankrum, Robert Bray, Howard McNear, Greg Barton.

1955

DESTRY. Universal-International. *director:* George Marshall. *producer:* Stanley Rubin. *screenplay:* Edmund H. North, D. D. Beauchamp. *cast:* Audie Murphy, Mari Blanchard, Lyle Bettger, Thomas Mitchell, Lori Nelson, Edgar Buchanan, Mary Wickes, Wallace Ford, Alan Hale Jr., George Wallace, Richard Reeves, Trevor Bardette, Walter Baldwin, John Doucette.

TO HELL AND BACK. Universal-International. *director:* Jesse Hibbs. *producer:* Aaron Rosenberg. *screenplay:* Gil Doud. *cast:* Audie Murphy, Charles Drake, Marshall Thompson, Jack Kelly, Gregg Palmer, Susan Kohner, David Jannsen, Felix Noriego, Richard Castle, Art Aragon, Bruce Cowling, Paul Langton, Rand Brooks, Gordon Gebert, William Bryant, Mary Field, Paul Picerni, Julian Upton, Terry Murphy, Denver Pyle.

1956

WORLD IN MY CORNER. Universal-International. *director:* Jesse Hibbs. *producer:* Aaron Rosenberg. *screenplay:* Jack Sher. *cast:* Audie Murphy, Barbara Rush, Jeff Morrow, John McIntire, Tommy Rall, Howard St.

John, Chico Vejar, Steve Ellis, Art Aragon, Dani Crayne, James F. Lennon, Cisco Andrade, H. Tommy Hart, Sheila Bromley.

WALK THE PROUD LAND. Universal-International. *director:* Jesse Hibbs. *producer:* Aaron Rosenberg. *screenplay:* Gil Doud, Jack Sher. *cast:* Audie Murphy, Anne Bancroft, Pat Crowley, Charles Drake, Jay Silverheels, Tony Caruso, Tommy Rall, Addison Richards, Robert Warwick, Victor Millan, Eugene Mazzola, Morris Ankrum.

1957

THE GUNS OF FORT PETTICOAT. Columbia. *director:* George Marshall. *producer:* Harry Joe Brown. *screenplay:* Walter Doniger. *cast:* Audie Murphy, Kathryn Grant, Hope Emerson, Jeff Donnell, Jeanette Nolan, Sean McClory, Ernestine Wade, Peggy Maley, Isobel Elsom, Patricia Livingston, Kim Charney, Ray Teal, Nestor Paiva, James Griffith, Charles Horvath, Ainslie Pryor, Dorothy Crider, Madge Meredith.

NIGHT PASSAGE. Universal-International. *director:* James Neilson. *producer:* Aaron Rosenberg. *screenplay:* Borden Chase. *cast:* James Stewart, Audie Murphy, Dan Duryea, Dianne Foster, Elaine Stewart, Brandon de Wilde, Jay C. Flippen, Herbert Anderson, Robert J. Wilke, Hugh Beaumont, Jack Elam, Tommy Cook, Paul Fix, Olive Carey, James Flavin, Donald Curtis, Ellen Corby, John Day, Kenny Williams, Frank Chase, Harold Goodwin, Tommy Hart, Jack C. Williams, Boyd Stockman, Henry Wills.

JOE BUTTERFLY. Universal-International. *director:* Jesse Hibbs. *producer:* Aaron Rosenberg. *screenplay:* Sy Gomberg, Jack Sher, Marion Hargrove. *cast:* Audie Murphy, George Nader, Keenan Wynn, Burgess Meredith, Keiko Shima, Fred Clark, John Agar, Charles McGraw, Shinpel Shimazaki, Reico Higa, Tatsuo Saito, Chizu Shimazaki, Herbert Anderson, Eddie Firestone, Frank Chase, Harold Goodwin, Willard Willingham.

1958

THE QUIET AMERICAN. United Artists. *director/producer/screenplay:* Joseph L. Mankiewicz. *cast:* Audie Murphy, Michael Redgrave, Claude Dauphin, Giorgia Moll, Kerima, Bruce Cabot, Fred Sadoff, Richard Loo, Peter Trent, Clinton Andersen, Yoka Tani, Sonia Moser, Phuong Thi Ngiep, Vo Doan Chau, Le Van Le, Le Quynh, Georges Brehat.

RIDE A CROOKED TRAIL. Universal-International. *director:* Jesse Hibbs. *producer:* Howard Pine. *screenplay:* Borden Chase. *cast:* Audie Murphy, Gia Scala, Walter Matthau, Henry Silva, Joanna Moore, Eddie Little, Mary Field, Leo Gordon, Mort Mills, Frank Chase, Bill Walker, Ned Wever, Richard Cutting.

THE GUN RUNNERS. United Artists. *director:* Don Siegel. *producer:* Clarence Greene. *screenplay:* Daniel Mainwaring, Paul Monash. *cast:* Audie Murphy, Eddie Albert, Patricia Owens, Everett Sloane, Gita

Hall, Richard Jaeckel, Paul Birch, Jack Elam, John Harding, Peggy Maley, Carlos Romero, Edward Colmans, Steven Peck, Lita Leon, Ted Jacques, John Qualen, Freddi Roberts.

1959

NO NAME ON THE BULLET. Universal-International. *director:* Jack Arnold. *producer:* Howard Christie, Jack Arnold. *screenplay:* Gene Coon. *cast:* Audie Murphy, Joan Evans, Charles Drake, R. G. Armstrong, Karl Swenson, Willis Bouchey, Whit Bissell, Jerry Paris, Charles Watts, Edgar Stehli, Virginia Grey, Warren Stevens, Simon Scott, John Alderson.

THE WILD AND THE INNOCENT. Universal-International. *director:* Jack Sher. *producer:* Sy Gomberg. *screenplay:* Sy Gomberg, Jack Sher. *cast:* Audie Murphy, Joanne Dru, Gilbert Roland, Jim Backus, Sandra Dee, George Mitchell, Peter Breck, Strother Martin, Wesley Marie Tackitt, Betty Harford, Mel Leonard, Lillian Adams, Val Benedict, Stephen Roberts, Tammy Windsor.

CAST A LONG SHADOW. United Artists. *director:* Thomas Carr. *producer:* Walter M. Mirisch. *screenplay:* Martin M. Goldsmith, John McGreevey. *cast:* Audie Murphy, Terry Moore, John Dehner, James Best, Denver Pyle, Rita Lynn, Ann Doran, Stacy B. Harris, Robert Foulk, Wright King.

1960

HELL BENT FOR LEATHER. Universal-International. *director:* George Sherman. *producer:* Gordon Kay. *screenplay:* Christopher Knopf. *cast:* Audie Murphy, Felicia Farr, Stephen McNally, Robert Middleton, Rad Fulton, Jan Merlin, Herbert Rudley, Malcolm Atterbury, Joseph Ruskin, Allan Lane, John Qualen, Eddie Little Sky, Steve Gravera, Beau Gentry, Bob Steele.

SEVEN WAYS FROM SUNDOWN. Universal-International. *director:* Harry Keller. *producer:* Gordon Kay. *screenplay:* Clair Huffaker. *cast:* Audie Murphy, Barry Sullivan, Venetia Stevenson, John McIntire, Kenneth Tobey, Mary Field, Ken Lyncy, Suzanne Lloyd, Ward Ramsey, Don Collier, Jack Kruschen, Claudia Barrett, Teddy Rooney, Don Haggerty, Robert Burton, Fred Graham, Dale Van Sickle.

THE UNFORGIVEN. United Artists. *director:* John Huston. *producer:* James Hill. *screenplay:* Ben Maddow. *cast:* Burt Lancaster, Audrey Hepburn, Audie Murphy, John Saxon, Charles Bickford, Lillian Gish, Albert Salmi, Joseph Wiseman, June Walker, Kipp Hamilton, Arnold Merritt, Carlos Rivas, Doug McClure.

1961

POSSE FROM HELL. Universal-International. *director:* Herbert Coleman. *producer:* Gordon Kay. *screenplay:* Clair Huffaker. *cast:* Audie Murphy, John Saxon, Zorah Lampert, Ward Ramsey, Vic Morrow, Robert

Keith, Rudolph Acosta, Royal Dano, Paul Carr, Lee Van Cleef, Ray Teal, Forrest Lewis, Charles Horvath, Harry Lauter, Henry Wills, Stuart Randall, Allan Lane.

BATTLE AT BLOODY BEACH. 20th Century Fox. *director:* Herbert Coleman. *producer:* Richard Malbaum. *screenplay:* Richard Malbaum, Willard Willingham. *cast:* Audie Murphy, Gary Crosby, Dolores Michaels, Alejandro Rey, Marjorie Stapp, Barry Atwater, E. J. Andre, Dale Ishimoto, Miriam Colon, Pilar Seurat, William Mims, Ivan Dixon, Kevin Brodie, Sara Anderson, Lloyd Kino.

1962

SIX BLACK HORSES. Universal-International. *director:* Harry Keller. *producer:* Gordon Kay. *screenplay:* Burt Kennedy. *cast:* Audie Murphy, Dan Duryea, Joan O'Brien, George Wallace, Roy Barcroft, Bob Steele, Henry Wills, Phil Chambers, Charlita Regis.

1963

SHOWDOWN. Universal. *director:* R. G. Springsteen. *producer:* Gordon Kay. *screenplay:* Bronson Howitzer. *cast:* Audie Murphy, Kathleen Crowley, Charles Drake, Harold J. Stone, Skip Homeier, L. Q. Jones, Strother Martin, Charles Horvath, John McKee, Henry Wills, Joe Haworth, Kevin Brodie, Carol Thurston, Dabbs Greer.

GUNFIGHT AT COMANCHE CREEK. *director:* Frank McDonald. *producer:* Ben Schwalb. *screenplay:* Edward Bernds. *cast:* Audie Murphy, Ben Cooper, Colleen Miller, DeForrest Kelley, Jan Merlin, John Hubbard, Damian O'Flynn, Susan Seaforth.

1964

THE QUICK GUN. Columbia. *director:* Sidney Salkow. *producer:* Grant Whytock. *screenplay:* Robert E. Kent. *cast:* Audie Murphy, Merry Anders, James Best, Ted de Corsia, Walter Sande, Rex Holman, Charles Meredith, Frank Ferguson, Mort Mills, Gregg Palmer, Frank Gerstle, Paul Bryar, Raymond Hatton, William Fawcett.

BULLET FOR A BADMAN. Universal. *director:* R. G. Springsteen. *producer:* Gordon Kay. *screenplay:* Mary Willingham, Willard Willingham. *cast:* Audie Murphy, Darren McGavin, Ruta Lee, Beverley Owen, Skip Homeier, George Tobias, Alan Hale, Bereley Harris, Edward C. Platt, Kevin Tate, Cece Whitney.

APACHE RIFLES. 20th Century Fox. *director:* William H. Witney. *producer:* Grant Whytock. *screenplay:* Charles B. Smith. *cast:* Audie Murphy, Michael Dante, Linda Lawson, L. Q. Jones, Ken Lynch, Joseph A. Vitale, Robert Brubaker, John Archer.

1965

ARIZONA RAIDERS. Columbia. *director:* William Witney. *producer:* Grant Whytock. *screenplay:* Alex Gottlieb, Mary Willingham, Willard Willingham. *cast:* Audie Murphy, Michael Dante, Ben Cooper, Buster Crabbe, Gloria Talbott, Ray Stricklyn, George Keymas, Fred Drone, Willard Willingham, Red Morgan, Fred Graham.

1966

GUNPOINT. Universal. *director:* Earl Bellamy. *producer:* Gordon Kay. *screenplay:* Mary Willingham, Willard Willingham. *cast:* Audie Murphy, Joan Staley, Warren Stevens, Edgar Buchanan, Denver Pyle, Royal Dano, Nick Dennis, William Bramley, Kelly Thordsen, David Macklin, Morgan Woodward, Robert Pine, Mike Ragan.

THE TEXICAN. Columbia. *director:* Lesley Selander. *producer:* John C. Champion, Bruce Balaban. *screenplay:* John C. Champion. *cast:* Audie Murphy, Broderick Crawford, Diana Lorys, Luz Marquez, Antonio Casas, Molino Rojo, Gerard Tichy.

1967

40 GUNS TO APACHE PASS. Columbia. *director:* William Witney. *producer:* Grant Whytock. *screenplay:* Willard Willingham, Mary Willingham. *cast:* Audie Murphy, Michael Burns, Kenneth Tobey, Laraine Stephens, Robert Brubaker, Michael Blodgett, Michael Keep, Kay Stewart, Kenneth MacDonald, Byron Morrow, Willard Willingham, Ted Gehring, James Beck.

TRUNK TO CAIRO. American-International. *producer-director:* Menaham Golan. *screenplay:* Marc Behm, Alexander Ramati. *cast:* Audie Murphy, George Sanders, Marianne Koch, Hans Von Borsodi, Jospeh Yadin, Gila Almagor, Eytan Priver.

1969

A TIME FOR DYING. [first released in June 1971, in France; American release, 1981] Fipco Production. *director-screenwriter:* Budd Boetticher. *producer:* Audie Murphy. *cast:* Richard Lapp, Anne Randall, Bob Random, Victor Jory, Beatrice Kay, Peter Brocco, Burt Mustin, Audie Murphy.

ADDITIONAL SCREEN APPEARANCES

1963

WAR IS HELL. *director-screenwriter:* Burt Topper. *cast:* Tony Russell, Baynes Barron, Burt Topper. With introduction by Audie Murphy.

TELEVISION

1954
THIS IS YOUR LIFE

1958
G. E. THEATER. (February 9). CBS. "Incident."

1959
SUSPICION. (July 5). NBC. "The Flight." *cast:* Audie Murphy, Dwayne Hickman.

1960
FORD STARTIME. (January 5). NBC. "The Man." *producer:* Robert Northshield. *director:* Robert Stevens. *screenplay:* James P. Cavanagh. *cast:* Audie Murphy, Thelma Ritter, Michael J. Pollard, Joseph Campanella, Joseph Sullivan, William Hickey.

1961
WHISPERING SMITH. (May 8–September 18). *producer:* Herbert Coleman, Willard Willingham. *cast:* Audie Murphy, Guy Mitchell, Sam Buffington. Twenty episodes.

NOTES

There is a great deal of archival information about Audie Murphy. My research carried me to a number of libraries and collections. They include:

1. The W. Walworth Harrison Library, Greenville, Texas. It contains extensive materials on Murphy. Anybody seriously interested in the subject must remain in debt to Col. Harold B. Simpson, who generously deposited here the eight file cabinets of materials that he collected during the research for his 1975 biography, *Audie Murphy, American Soldier* (Hill Jr. College Press). The materials include interviews with Murphy family members, citizens of Hunt County, officers and soldiers of the Third Division, and documents, papers, and records, touching upon many other phases of Murphy's life. The library also has an Audie L. Murphy Room with various momentos, documents, and photographs that are of interest both to a researcher and the hundreds of visitors a year who come to pay their respects to Murphy's memory. The ledger is filled with sentiments such as "God Bless America for giving us men like Audie Murphy." Oddly enough, many of these visitors hold an unshakable conviction that Audie Murphy was once married to Shirley Temple.

2. The Special Collections, Doheny Library, University of Southern California, Los Angeles. Contains extensive records of films produced by Universal-International, including budgets, shooting schedules, promotional campaigns, interoffice memos, and the hundreds of pages of written matter that go into the making of even the lowliest *B* film.

3. The Margaret Herrick Film Library, Academy of Motion Picture Arts and Sciences, Beverly Hills, California. A film researcher's heaven. Especially valuable for this study were the biographical and film files, and special collections such as the Hedda Hopper Collection and the John Huston Collection.

4. Theater Arts Library, UCLA, Los Angeles, California. It contains numerous film scripts, plus a clipping file.

5. The Texas Collection, Baylor University, Waco, Texas. Contains numerous indispensable unpublished materials about Murphy.

6. Additional clipping files on Murphy were examined at the research department of the Dallas *Morning News*, Dallas, Texas; and the Barker Texas History Center, University of Texas, Austin.

7. Finally, for fan magazine materials, I was fortunate enough to be invited to examine the extensive private collection of Claudette and Garnett Harris of Austin, Texas. Also helpful are the issues of the Audie Leon Murphy Memorial Fan Club, published in La Mirada, California.

I interviewed and talked with numerous people who knew Audie Murphy during his years in the film industry in California. Herewith, a list in no particular order: Budd Boetticher, John Huston, Harry Keller, John Saxon, Al Jank, Art Aragon, Joey Barnum, Marshall Thompson, Jane Wyatt, Burt Lancaster, Doug McClure, Bobby Hoy, Clair Huffaker, Marion Hargrove, Frank Chase, Jack Sher, Sy Gomberg, William Witney, Gordon Kay, John "Bear" Hudkins, Ben Johnson, Venetia Stevenson, Jack Arnold, Ken Tobey, Douglas Dick, Paul Kohner, Casey Tibbs, Guy Mitchell, Paul Picerni, Gale Storm, Barbara Rush, Sharon O'Neill, Nathan Juran, Paul Caruso, Polly Burson, Estelle Harman, Arvo Ojalla, James Lydon, James Pratt, Warren Stevens, Ben Cooper, Frank McFadden, Treva McClure, Jeff Donnell, Morgan Woodward, Tom Shaw, Jesse White, Caril St. John (interviewed by Betsy Berry), Jan Merlin, Nathan Juran, and George Putnam. Visiting and talking with these people was a very diverting and memorable experience, and it especially saddens me to think that since the time I began this book, several of those with whom I discussed the past have departed the scene, including Mr. Keller, Mr. Huston, Mr. Kohner, and Mr. Sher.

The notes below provide a fuller record of sources both written and oral consulted during the making of this book. In those instances where bibliographical information is lacking, the most common reason is that clipping files for newspapers, and especially for fan magazines, often contain incomplete citations.

1. You Have Seen Their Faces

Page

1 *The county was less:* sketch of Hunt County drawn in part from *The Handbook of Texas* (Texas State Historical Association, 1952) and W. Walworth Harrison, *History of Greenville and Hunt County, Texas* (Texian Press, 1976).

Page
3 *"the great open air slum":* Quoted in C. L. Sonnichsen, *From Hopalong to Hud: Thoughts on Western Fiction* (Texas A & M University Press, 1978).
4 *They named him:* Corinne Murphy quoted in Ralph Edwards, "This Is Your Life, Audie Murphy," *Photoplay,* June 1954.
4 *Later, the Murphys:* Monroe Hackney, interview with Harold Simpson, June 11, 1974; Neil Williams, interview with Simpson, July 27, 1974.
5 *"Every time my old man":* quoted in Richard G. Hubler, "He Doesn't Want To Be A Star," *Saturday Evening Post,* April 18, 1953.
   Not much is known: account of family antecedents drawn from Harold Simpson, *Audie Murphy, American Soldier* (Hill Jr. College Press, 1975); and Clara Stearns Scarbrough, *Land of Good Water, A Williamson County, Texas, History* (Williamson County Sun Publishers, 1974).
6 *"was not lazy":* Audie Murphy, *To Hell and Back* (Henry Holt, 1949).
   Emmett Murphy: details about father drawn from Eugene Porter Murphy, interview with Harold Simpson, November 7, 1974; Johnny Cawthon, interview with Simpson, July 1, 1974; Cleatis Hudson, interview with Simpson, June 11, 1974; Roy Lanier, interview with Simpson, November 12, 1974.
   One thing Pat did: Mrs. Dan Barnard, letter to Harold Simpson, November 24, 1974.
7 *On two occasions:* Mrs. John Cawthon, interview with author, May 2, 1985.
   "strapped like a papoose": Murphy, *To Hell and Back.*
   "If you want to fight": Murphy, *To Hell and Back.*
8 *"People know me for my record":* Audie Murphy, "You do the prayin' and I'll do the shootin,' " *Modern Screen,* January 1956.
   "sad-eyed, silent woman": Murphy, *To Hell and Back.*
   "I use to stand him": Corinne Murphy, letter to Harold Simpson, July 1974. For Corinne's general picture of their family life: Margaret Galloway, "Audie Murphy Leads Family Struggle For Food, Becomes Hero, Movie Star," Grand Prairie *Banner,* December 2, 1958.
9 *"You wouldn't call the place":* W. B. (Bill) Taylor, quoted in James Kerr, "Home Town Report on Audie," *Motion Picture,* March 1952.
   It was T-shaped: Al McGuire, interview with author, May 17, 1985.
   The Murphy home: Neil Williams, panel interview with Fred Tarpley, June 20, 1985.
10 *When the good ladies of the Methodist Church:* Dorothy Nickles Wehrung, interview with Harold Simpson, October 24, 1974; Mrs. Frank Barnard, letter to Simpson, December 10, 1973.
   Some people: Hunt County resident, interview with author, March 16, 1985.
   Some families: Josie Pierce, interview with Harold Simpson, November 13, 1974.
11 *Every time she came to work:* McGuire/Graham interview.
   The drugstore was everybody's library: Joe Goulden quoted in Lucy McDonald, Melva Geyer, and John Edminston, "Hunt Residents Recall Audie As Youth," Greenville *Banner,* February 19, 1973.
   One time when they were eating: Corinne Murphy, letter to Simpson.
   The only surviving report card: Audie L. Murphy Room, W. Walworth Harrison Library, Greenville, Texas.
12 *"Little Britches":* Murphy, "You do the prayin' and I'll do the shootin'."
   He didn't like being called: Hackney/Simpson interview.
   He did well in class: details of school years drawn from Ruth Rutherford, letter to Harold Simpson, January 20, 1974; and Mrs. Charles Dupre, letter to Simpson, January 5, 1974.

Page

On another Christmas: Ardith Davis, quoted in Kerr, "Home Town Report on Audie Murphy."

13 *His third-grade teacher:* Myra Vestal Schultz, interview with Harold Simpson, June 26, 1974.

"*I was a mean kid":* quoted in Hubler, "He Doesn't Want To Be a Star."

"*always a struggle":* Rutherford, letter to Simpson.

One good thing about living: Mrs. Cawthon/Graham interview. See also: Lucy McDonald, "Down Memory Lane With Mrs. Cawthon," Greenville *Banner*, February 17, 1973.

14 "*plumb to his ankles":* Mrs. Cawthon, panel interview with Tarpley.

"*Pat was little":* quoted in Simpson, *Audie Murphy: American Soldier.*

But the biggest risks: details about firearms and pranks drawn from Bob Cawthon, interview with Harold Simpson, September 11, 1974; Johnny Cawthon/Simpson interview; Neil Williams/Simpson interview; Bill Caldwell, interview with Simpson, July 1, 1974; and Hackney/Simpson interview.

15 "*There was also one instance":* Kerr, "Home Town Report on Audie Murphy."

"*agitating the black community":* Neil Williams, panel interview with Tarpley.

16 "*Hand me the shotgun":* Williams interview.

One summer day: McGuire/Graham interview.

17 *All of Audie's outdoor skills:* Hackney/Simpson interview; Weldon Glen Burns and Poland Burns, interview with Harold Simpson, July 3, 1974; and Everett Brandon, interview with Simpson, August 27, 1974.

"*When you grow up in the country":* Steve Fromholz, "The Texas Trilogy."

He lost his virginity: Spec McClure, letter to Harold Simpson, March 1, 1974.

18 "*simply walked out of our lives":* Murphy, *To Hell and Back.* Further details drawn from Corinne Burns, interview with Harold Simpson, July 17, 1974.

"*I suppose I hated him":* quoted in Hubler, "He Doesn't Want To Be a Star."

Over the years: details of father's later life drawn from Eugene Porter Murphy/Simpson interview; Jack Gordon, "Audie Murphy's Dad Works as Caretaker at Fort Worth Lake," Fort Worth *Press*, June 8, 1951; "Pardon Poppa's Pride," Abilene *Reporter-News*, August 7, 1962; "Father of Murphy Living in Abilene," newspaper article, 1971; and "Audie Murphy's Father Dies," Greenville *Herald Banner*, September 24, 1976.

19 *Informed of her condition:* details about mother's death drawn from Corinne Burns/Simpson interview, July 17, 1974.

"*The first thing I can remember":* Hubler, "He Doesn't Want To Be A Star."

"*Continued poverty":* Audie Murphy, "You do the prayin' and I'll do the shootin'."

The three youngest children: Details of the Boles home drawn from unpublished manuscript, "Where Children Have a Hope Because Christians Have a Heart, Boles Home, Quinlan, Texas, 1924–1974; A Few Impressions from Boles' Home's First Fifty Years." Levitt Library, York College (Nebraska).

20 *The first time Mrs. Lee:* Haney Lee and Mrs. Lee, interview with Harold Simpson, September 27, 1974. Other comments in letter from Haney Lee to Simpson, April 3, 1975.

"*sad type person":* Mrs. Snow Warren, interview with Harold Simpson, 1974.

His second job in Greenville: details of the radio repair job drawn from J. C. Bowen, interview with Harold Simpson, September 26, 1974; and William D. Bowen, letter to Simpson, January 22, 1975.

21 "*The humanitarian award of the century":* quoted in Wick Fowler, "Audie Murphy: Hunting Proved Valuable in War," Dallas *Morning News*, September 16, 1962.

Reagan's childhood: details from Gary Wills, *Reagan's America: Innocents At Home* (Doubleday, 1987) and Michael Paul Rogin, *Ronald Reagan, the Movie, and Other Episodes in Political Demonology* (University of California Press, 1987).

Page

22 *"one group of horsemen":* quoted in Laura Fermi, *Mussolini* (University of Chicago Press, 1961).

   It took the Axis powers: Charles B. MacDonald, *The Mighty Endeavor: The American War in Europe* (William Morrow, 1956).

   "the United States moved up": Geoffrey Perrett, *Days of Sadness, Years of Triumph: The American People, 1939–1945* (Coward, McCann, and Geoghegan, 1973).

23 *"like a few nice boys":* quoted in William Manchester, *The Glory and the Dream: A Narrative History of America, 1932–1972* (Little, Brown, 1973).

   Such uncertainty: Manchester, *The Glory and the Dream.*

   "I ran into": quoted in "Rising Hero At 20, Fading Star At 30," *Miami Herald,* June 1, 1971.

24 *The war had an immediacy:* Arthur M. Schlesinger, Jr., ed., *The Almanac of American History* (Putnam, 1983).

25 *"Had it not been for World War II":* Mickey Francis, interview with author, June 24, 1987.

2. The Pure Products of America

26 *The size of the U.S. Army:* Robert Leckie, *Delivered From Evil: Saga of World War II* (Harper and Row, 1987).

   "whose conceptions": quoted in William Manchester, *The Glory and the Dream. A Narrative History of America, 1932–1972* (Little, Brown, 1973).

   He came from the region: Lee Kennett, *G.I.: The American Soldier in World War II* (Charles Scribner's Sons, 1987).

   He also came: Eli Ginzberg, *Patterns of Performance,* vol. III of *The Ineffective Soldier* (Columbia University Press, 1959).

   And from a large group: Selective Service in Wartime (Second Report of the Director of Selective Service, 1941–1942 (Government Printing Office, 1943).

27 *In education, too:* Eli Ginzberg, *The Lost Divisions,* vol. I of *The Ineffective Soldier.*

   In age: Selective Service in Wartime.

   Over five thousand Texans: T. R. Fehrenbach, *Lone Star* (Collier, 1980).

   In a 1939 poll: Fehrenbach, *Lone Star.*

28 *By June 30, 1942: Selective Service in Wartime.*

   Because the United States: Max Hastings, *Overlord: D-Day & the Battle for Normandy* (Simon & Schuster, Inc., 1985).

   "wastebin for men": Hastings, *Overlord.*

   The lack of quality: Hastings, *Overlord.*

   The basic class structure: Leckie, *Delivered From Evil.*

   "most professional and skillfull": Leckie, *Delivered From Evil.*

   From June 6: Kennett, *G.I.: The American Soldier in World War II.*

29 *"lacked strong motivation":* Kennett, *American Soldier.*

   "so poorly educated": Ginzberg, *The Lost Divisions.*

   "at so little provocation": Leckie, *Delivered From Evil.*

   "Without American production": quoted in Leckie, *Delivered From Evil.*

   "unbelievable": quoted in Manchester, *The Glory and the Dream.*

   By 1944: Leckie, *Delivered From Evil.*

   "What was really amazing": quoted in Leckie, *Delivered From Evil.*

30 *Like the nation:* Hondon B. Hargrove, *Buffalo Soldiers in Italy: Black Americans in World War II* (McFarland & Co., 1985).

   In its experience: Kennett, *G.I.: The American Soldier in World War II.*

   And he was ready: John Ellis, *The Sharp End: The Fighting Man in World War II* (Charles Scribner's Sons, 1980).

Page

    Because Camp Walters: Kara Kunkel, "Lufkin Man Remembers Slovik As 'Tragedy of War,' " *Dallas Times Herald*, July 15, 1987.

31 *A shrimp:* Hastings, *Overlord*.

    "no bigger than a guinea": Corliss T. Rowe, quoted in Harold B. Simpson, *Audie Murphy, American Soldier*, (Hill Jr. College Press, 1975).

    "Came through with flying colors": Audie Murphy to Corinne Murphy, July 17, 1942; quoted in Simpson, *Audie Murphy*.

    "meek, mild, and reserved": Milton Robertson, quoted in Simpson, *Audie Murphy*.

    "particularly looked forward": Walter Black, quoted in Simpson, *Audie Murphy*.

    He loved the rifle range: Simpson, *Audie Murphy*.

32 *"always see":* Walter Black, quoted in Simpson, *Audie Murphy*.

    "When I first got": Audie Murphy to Corinne and Poland Burns, July 14, 1942; quoted in Simpson, *Audie Murphy*.

    "Always quick-witted: Simpson, *Audie Murphy*.

33 *Oddly, he did:* Simpson, *Audie Murphy*.

    "The crease in his trousers": quoted in Simpson, *Audie Murphy*.

34 *"In the Army":* quoted in Jane Wilkie, "Memoirs of a Small Texan," *Modern Screen*, July 1955.

    "I hate blabbermouth Texans": quoted in Wilkie, "Memoirs."

    At a shooting gallery: Simpson, *Audie Murphy*.

    The other incident: Wilkie, "Memoirs."

35 *"the soft underbelly":* quoted in Fred Sheehan, *Anzio: Epic of Bravery* (University of Oklahoma Press, 1964).

36 *The 3rd was:* Don Taggart, *History of the Third Infantry Division in World War II* (Infantry Journal Press, 1947); and, Simpson, *Audie Murphy*.

    General Lucian K. Truscott: Simpson, *Audie Murphy*.

37 *"loved to gamble":* quoted in Simpson, *Audie Murphy*.

    "didn't look sixteen": Robert O. Millar, quoted in Simpson, *Audie Murphy*.

    "You are going": quoted in Simpson, *Audie Murphy*.

    "hill just inland": Audie Murphy, *To Hell and Back* (Holt, 1949).

38 *The island was manned:* Leckie, *Delivered From Evil*.

    "almost childish": Ernie Pyle, *Brave Men* (Holt, 1944).

    "The south coast": Pyle, *Brave Men*.

39 *"We got pinned down":* W. Heard Reeves, quoted in "Wichitan 'Gave' Murphy Promotions," Wichita *Times*, June 1, 1971.

    "Ten seconds": quoted in Wilkie, "Memoirs."

    "I can remember": quoted in Bob Thomas, "Audie Recalls Told To Kill," Greenville *Banner*, December 2, 1960.

    "The fear of aggression": S. L. A. Marshall, *Men Against Fire: The Problem of Battle Command in Future War* (William Morrow, 1964).

40 *"My next actions":* Raleigh Trevelyan, *The Fortress* (Collins, 1956).

    "easy killing": John Keegan, *The Face of Battle: A Study of Agincourt, Waterloo and the Somme* (Jonathan Cape, 1976).

41 *"the best showing":* Marshall, *Men Against Fire*.

42 *"Fire wins wars":* Marshall, *Men Against Fire*.

    "All wars": Hastings, *Overlord*.

    "In the last analysis": Ellis, *The Sharp End*.

    "poor bloody infantry": Harold P. Leinbaugh and John D. Campbell, *The Men of Company K: The Autobiography of a World War II Rifle Company* (William Morrow, 1985).

    Ordinary riflemen: Ellis, *The Sharp End*.

    "For the infantryman it was": Charles B. MacDonald, *The Mighty Endeavor:*

Page

American Armed Forces in the European Theater in World War II (Oxford University Press, 1969).

"the infantry": Mauldin, *Up Front*.

"rabid one-man": Pyle, *Brave Men*.

43 "In World War II": Ellis, *The Sharp End*.

"the finest soldier": "Finest Soldier I've Ever Seen," *Army Times*, July 1964.

"Lines of soldiers": Murphy, *To Hell and Back*.

"One soldier": Norman Lewis, *Naples '44* (Pantheon, 1978).

44 "ideal country": Pyle, *Brave Men*.

"The front-line soldier": Pyle, *Brave Men*.

"poked fun at the enemy": Audie Murphy, "Why I Gave My Medals Away," *This Week*, May 29, 1955.

45 "On a man for man basis": T. N. Dupuy, *A Genius for War*, quoted in Hastings, *Overlord*.

"One cannot help thinking": Roger J. Spiller, "Man Against Fire: Audie Murphy and His War," unpublished essay.

"I am still": Audie Murphy to Corinne Burns, August 18, 1943; quoted in Simpson, *Audie Murphy*.

46 *But not the British:* analysis of strategy of British and Churchill drawn from W. G. F. Jackson, *The Battle for Italy* (Harper & Row, 1967); Sheehan, *Anzio: Epic of Bravery*; Martin Blumenson, *Anzio: The Gamble That Failed* (Dell, 1963); and Leckie, *Delivered From Evil*.

47 "bitterest, most heart breaking": quoted in Simpson, *Audie Murphy*.

"Another time:* Murphy, *To Hell and Back*.

48 "As a farm youngster": Murphy, *To Hell and Back*.

"I got to where": quoted in Wick Fowler, "Audie Murphy: Hunting Proved Valuable in War," Dallas *Morning News*, 9-16-62.

"The ground itself": Marshall, *Men Against Fire*.

49 "I am in Italy": Audie Murphy to Corinne Burns, October 28, 1943; quoted in Simpson, *Audie Murphy*.

"What I expected": John Guest, *Broken Images: A Journal* (Longmans Green, 1949).

50 "changed my outlook": Lewis, *Naples '44*

"astonish the world": quoted in Sheehan, *Anzio: Epic of Bravery*.

51 "trailor loads of corpses": Murphy, *To Hell and Back*.

"drinking some coffee": Audie Murphy, *American Weekly*, October 31, 1954.

"They came": MacDonald, *The Mighty Endeavor*.

"abcess south": quoted in MacDonald, *Mighty Endeavor*.

52 "Fear is moving": Murphy, *To Hell and Back*.

"Sometimes it takes": quoted in Jack Brown, "Price of Glory High for Audie Murphy," *Los Angeles Herald Examiner*, June 1, 1971.

"Wherever one surveys": Marshall, *Men Against Fire*.

"I do not": quoted in Ellis, *The Sharp End*.

53 "What you hate": Audie Murphy, "You do the prayin' and I'll do the shootin'," *Modern Screen*, January 1956.

"Audie was scared": Corliss T. Rowe, quoted in Simpson, *Audie Murphy*.

"I went where": James Jones, *World War II* (Ballantine, 1975).

"It was": Michael Paulick, "Commander Recalls Heroism of Audie's Trip to Hell, Back," *Dallas Times Herald*, August 25, 1975.

54 "The whole affair": quoted in Leckie, *Delivered From Evil*.

"We hoped": quoted in Hastings, *Overlord*.

"In many ways:" Trevelyan, *The Fortress*.

"As the months passed": quoted in Ellis, *The Sharp End*.

"At Anzio": Ellis, *Sharp End*.

"constant hellish nightmare": Mauldin, *Up Front*.

Page
55 *"People whose jobs":* Pyle, *Brave Men.*
   Hospital units: Blumenson, *Anzio: The Gamble That Failed.*
   "terror of every": Mauldin, *Up Front.*
   "doom like quality": Murphy, *To Hell and Back.*
   "learned to accept": Trevelyan, *The Fortress.*
   "He concluded": Paul Woodruff, *Vessel of Sadness* (Southern Illinois University Press, 1969).
   "sea of mud": Murphy, *To Hell and Back.*
   Albert Pyle: Albert Pyle, untitled, undated 17 pp. document, Texas Collection, Baylor University.
56 *Radio broadcasts:* Trevelyan, *Fortress*; Ralph G. Martin, *The G. I. War* (Little, Brown, 1967).
   Axis Sally: Pyle, *Brave Men.*
   All through February: Ellis, *The Sharp End.*
57 *"We left regulations":* Murphy, *To Hell and Back.*
   "looked much younger": Pyle, document.
   Another member: Robert Tubb, interview with Harold Simpson, February 6, 1975.
   "You don't fight": Mauldin, *Up Front.*
58 *"The question of killing":* S. Berlin, *I Am Lazarus* (Galley Press, 1961).
   "But you don't": Mauldin, *Up Front.*
   "He and men": Harold Bond, *Return to Cassino* (J. M. Dent & Sons, 1964).
59 *"Audie was selected":* quoted in Simpson, *Audie Murphy.*
   "If I discovered": quoted in David McClure, "How Audie Murphy Won His Medals," unpublished manuscript, October 10, 1969, Texas Collection, Baylor University.
   "were forever going": Pyle, document.
   "He had a boy": Bob Millar to Harold Simpson, February 3, 1975.
60 *"One thing about him":* Alex Sabatini, quoted in "Audie Murphy Buried With Full Honors," Dallas *Morning News*, June 8, 1971.
61 *"perfect Keats country":* Trevelyan, *The Fortress.*
   "good used car": Audie Murphy to Corinne and Poland Burns, March 22, 1944; reprinted in Simpson, *Audie Murphy.*
   "It rains": Audie Murphy to Mr. and Mrs. John Cawthon, ca. May, 1944; reprinted in Simpson, *Audie Murphy.*
62 *"like a pigeon":* Murphy, *To Hell and Back.*
   "The 200-yard interval": Don Taggart, *History of the Third Infantry Division in World War II* (Infantry Journal Press, 1947).
   The sergeant: "Audie Murphy Describes Feats That Won Honor Medal for Pal," Dallas *Morning News*, October 19, 1945.
63 *"You do not know":* Guest, *Broken Images.*
   "as if a giant rake": Mauldin, *Up Front.*
   "In terms": Ellis, *The Sharp End.*
   "All of my life": Bond, *Return to Cassino.*
   "Rome is most disappointing": Guest, *Broken Images.*
64 *"but another objective":* Murphy, *To Hell and Back.*
   "I have had two passes": Audie Murphy to Avery Dowdy, June 18, 1944; rpt. in Simpson, *Audie Murphy.*
65 *"is going very well":* Audie Murphy to Corinne Burns, July 15, 1944; rpt. in Simpson, *Audie Murphy.*

3. A Fugitive from the Law of Averages

67 *"the comedy of little men":* Murphy, *To Hell and Back.*
   "the best invasion": Mauldin, *Up Front.*
   "To a foot soldier": quoted in Ellis, *The Sharp End*, p. 271.

Page

    "People think I brood": David McClure, "The Way Back," unpublished manuscript, 1956, Texas Collection, Baylor University.

68 *"I brace myself":* Murphy, *To Hell and Back.*

    He told him: McClure, "How Audie Murphy Won His Medals," unpublished manuscript, Oct. 10, 1969.

    "nightmare": Murphy, *To Hell and Back.*

69 *"He was not":* McClure, "How Audie Murphy Won His Medals."

    "That was a personal": quoted in Richard Hubler, "Audie Murphy: The Man Behind the Medals," *Coronet,* August 1955.

    "Actual combat experience": McClure, "How Audie Murphy Won His Medals."

    "do anything that": Murphy, *To Hell and Back.*

70 *"Sir, a German":* McClure, "How Audie Murphy Won His Medals."

    "There was a time": Murphy, "Why I Gave My Medals Away," *This Week,* May 29, 1955.

71 *"a small car":* Pyle, document.

72 *"I don't suppose":* Walter W. Weispfenning, quoted in McClure, "How Audie Murphy Won His Medals."

73 *"embarrassed by his lack":* Michael Paulick, "Commander Recalls Heroism of Audie's Trip to Hell," Dallas *Times Herald,* August 25, 1955.

    Short of men: Paulick, "Commander Recalls."

    "I whet my bayonet": Murphy, *To Hell and Back.*

    Pyle saw the remains: Pyle, document.

    The fighting in eastern France: Michel Droulhiole, "France's Battle-Scarred Forest," *Manchester Guardian Weekly,* March 15, 1987.

74 *"all hell broke loose":* Millar to Simpson, February 3, 1975.

    "Coolness and calm fury": Murphy, *To Hell and Back.*

    "because the fates were kind": Pyle, *Brave Men.*

    Some of the new troops: Marshall, *Men Against Fire.*

75 *"I figured those gentlemen":* quoted in McClure, "How Audie Murphy Won His Medals."

    "Machine gun bullets": Paulick, "Commander Recalls Heroism."

76 *"I took my time":* quoted by David McClure in letter to Harold Simpson, January 27, 1974.

    "They say I killed": quoted in *Photoplay,* July 1956.

77 *"I heard three carbine shots":* Pyle, document.

    "crawled to the edge": Millar to Simpson, February 3, 1975.

    "This is the most lonely": quoted in McClure, "How Audie Murphy Won His Medals."

    "the near presence": Marshall, *Men Against Fire.*

78 *"cold, wet and scared":* quoted in Simpson, *Audie Murphy.*

    "alertness and coolness": quoted in Simpson, *Audie Murphy.*

    "You are now": Murphy, *To Hell and Back.*

    "In a fifty-day period": Lucian K. Truscott, Jr. *Command Missions: A Personal Story* (E. P. Dutton, 1944).

    They had: Ellis, *The Sharp End.*

79 *Then things began:* Roy L. Swank and Walter E. Marchand, "Combat Neuroses: Development of Combat Exhaustion," *Archives of Neurology and Psychology,* 55 (1946).

    "between June and November": Hastings, *Overlord.*

    "There is a condition": quoted in Ellis, *The Sharp End.*

    Eighty-seven percent: Ellis, *Sharp End.*

    "There is no such thing": quoted in Keegan, *The Face of Battle.*

    "granted no home leave": Keegan, *Face of Battle.*

    "Those who are left": quoted in Ellis, *The Sharp End.*

Page
80 *"The noise, the shock":* Leinbaugh and Campbell, *The Men of Company K.*
    "In such a shelling": Bond, *Return to Cassino.*
    The 88's: Leinbaugh and Campbell, *The Men of Company K.*
81 *Such bombardments:* quoted in MacDonald, *The Mighty Endeavor.*
    "For some reason": Murphy, "You do the prayin'."
    "For many men": Ellis, *The Sharp End.*
    "one of the great surprises": Hastings, *Overlord.*
83 *"somebody you wanted to hug":* Colista McCabe, interview with author, September 10, 1985.
    "He looked like": Perry Pitt, "To Me, He's Murph," fan magazine, ca. 1953.
84 *"had the fresh boyish":* Carolyn Price Ryan, letter to David McClure, February 12, 1973.
85 *"A lot of guys":* Mauldin, *Up Front.*
    "as equals": Keegan, *The Face of Battle.*
    "in the last analysis": Ellis, *The Sharp End.*
    "Say Gen. those Krauts": Audie Murphy to Haney Lee, November 3, 1944; rpt. in Simpson, *Audie Murphy.*
86 *"But thares work":* Audie Murphy to Haney Lee, ca. late December, 1944; rpt. in Simpson, *Audie Murphy.*
    "finest hour": Leckie, *Delivered from Evil.*
    "Battle of the Bulge": Glenn D. Kittler, "The Fighting Third," *Saga,* September 1954.
87 *"one of the toughest assignments":* Murphy, *To Hell and Back.*
    No thermal underwear: Paul Fussell, "My War," in *The Boy Scout Handbook and Other Observations* (Oxford University Press, 1982).
    "Every now and then": quoted in Al Stump, "G.I. in Hollywood," *Saga,* June 1957.
88 *"the white bones":* Murphy, *To Hell and Back.*
    "like a tired": Murphy, *To Hell and Back.*
    As at Anzio: Simpson, *Audie Murphy.*
    "the entire reenforcement pool": Marshall, *Men Against Fire.*
    "butt-end of a rough U": Murphy, *To Hell and Back.*
89 *"At that moment":* Murphy, *Hell and Back.*
    "I turned the machine gun": quoted in David McClure to Harold Simpson, February 10, 1974.
90 *"You know, he never":* Frank Chase, interview with author, May 28, 1987.
91 *"I saw hundreds of Germans":* Walter W. Weispfenning, "Medal of Honor To Officer Who Stopped Advance of Two German Companies," War Department News Release, May 24, 1945.
    "When a man is expecting": statement by Abramski, February 1945.
    "The German infantrymen": quoted in McClure, "How Audie Murphy Won His Medals."
    "no exhilaration at being alive": Murphy, *To Hell and Back.*
93 *"more peevish and defiant":* Murphy, *Hell and Back.*
    "There's only one way": quoted in Ellis, *The Sharp End.*
    "phantom body of troops": Murphy, *To Hell and Back.*
94 *"their bodies . . . frozen":* Pyle, document.
95 *"we have been":* Audie Murphy to Mrs. Cawthon, February 7, 1945; rpt. in Simpson, *Audie Murphy.*
    "it sure has been": Audie Murphy to Corinne Burns, February 7, 1945; rpt. in Simpson, *Audie Murphy.*
    "How I want": Guest, *Broken Images.*
    "seen too much": Murphy, *To Hell and Back.*
    "an almost fatalistic": Kenneth B. Potter, letter to Harold Simpson, November 5, 1973.

Page
96 *"the Cong. medal of honor":* Audie Murphy, letter to Corinne Burns, March 5, 1945; rpt. in Simpson, *Audie Murphy.*
   *"the only thing they":*Audie Murphy, letter to James Farber, April 24, 1953.
   "much to his disappointment": H. C. Auld, Jr., letter to Harold Simpson, January 29, 1974.
   "contact man": Murphy, *To Hell and Back.*
97 *"Once, on a patrol":* Murphy, "Why I Gave My Medals Away."
   "As you see in the paper": Murphy to Corinne and Poland Burns, March 20, 1945; rpt. in Simpson, *Audie Murphy.*
   "We are moving": Murphy to Corinne Burns, April 2, 1945; rpt. in Simpson, *Audie Murphy.*
   "We do not knock": Murphy, *To Hell and Back.*
98 *"this very self-possessed":* Martin Blumenson, interview with author, April 22, 1986.
99 *"Please, sir":* quoted in McClure, "How Audie Murphy Won His Medals."
   "Then one night in Lyons": quoted in Jack Brown, "Price of Glory High for Audie Murphy."
   "It works with buttered smoothness": Murphy, *To Hell and Back.*
100 *He sounded:* quoted in Simpson, *Audie Murphy.*
   Four hundred and thirty-three men: Taggart, *History of the Third Division.*
   "the best division": quoted in Simpson, *Audie Murphy.*
   Of the original 235 man roster: Hubler, "The Man Behind the Medals."
101 *"All of us knew":* Bond, *Return to Cassino.*
   A commander in North Africa: S. L. A. Marshall and Bill Davidson, "Do the Real Heroes Get the Medal of Honor," *Collier's,* February 21, 1953.
   "Homeric happenings": Marshall, *Porkchop Hill* (William Morrow, 1956).
102 *"Certainly there have been cases":* Murphy, letter to Farber.
   "I feel as if": quoted in Hubler, "Audie Murphy: The Man Behind the Medals."
   "They [the medals]": quoted in Wick Fowler, "Audie Murphy: Hunting Proved Valuable in War."
   "War is a nasty business": Audie Murphy, "Why I Gave My Medals Away."
   "All the Boches": quoted in David D. Lee, *Sergeant York: An American Hero* (University Press of Kentucky, 1987).
103 *Cheering crowds saw in him:* Lee, *Sergeant York.*
   Like Charles Lindbergh: see John W. Ward, "The Meaning of Lindbergh's Flight," *American Quarterly,* X (Spring 1958).

4. Soldier's Home

104 *"because I don't go":* quoted in newspaper clipping, "Texas Lieutenant Is One of Two," June 2, 1945.
105 *"stole the show":* William C. Barnard, "Determination To Do A Tough Job— Audie Murphy's Definition of Bravery," A.P. release, July 8, 1945.
   He was so shy: William C. Barnard, "Freckled Youth Poison in Battle," New Orleans *Times-Picayune,* July 8, 1945.
   "I sure wouldn't": quoted in "13 Generals," newspaper article, June 13, 1945.
   "every medal": Bishop Clements, "Farmersville Ready To Give Lieut. Murphy Welcome Fit For Hero," Sherman *Daily Democrat,* June 14, 1945.
   What really happened: Note by David McClure, June 17, 1972, attached to letter to Col. Red Reeder, March 27, 1964; Texas Collection, Baylor University.
106 *"every detail about":* Clements, "Farmersville Ready"; Barnard, "Freckled Youth."
   Finally, after much: Clements, "Farmersville Ready."

Page

"This is what": quoted in William C. Barnard, "Gala Farmersville Parade Bewilders Lt. Audie Murphy," A.P. release, June 14, 1945.

107 "most unique": Clements, "Farmersville Ready."

One headline read: "Home Front Is Tougher Than War for Bashful Texas Hero," Fort Worth *Star-Telegram*, June 15, 1945.

"If it takes points": William C. Barnard, "Celebration in His Honor Tougher Than Battle for Lieutenant Murphy," Greenville *Evening Banner*, June 15, 1945.

108 "We'll nab him": "Home Folks Say Audie Must Face Celebration," *Houston Post*, June 6, 1945.

"Shucks": quoted in Clements, "Farmersville Ready."

"I'm scared": quoted in "Welcome Is Given Heroes at San Antonio," newspaper clipping, June 13, 1945.

In town: "Farmersville Is Planning to Give Hero Big Welcome," newspaper clipping, June 9, 1945.

"He hasn't changed": "Farmersville's Biggest Hero Center of Parade," A.P. release, June 14, 1945.

"All this won't": "Home Folks Say Audie Must Face Celebration."

109 "I'm as shaky": Barnard, "Gala Farmersville Parade."

110 "About the best way": quoted in Lois Sager, "Little Town Shows Big Stuff," Dallas *Morning News*, June 1945.

"Now make yourself": C. S. Boyles, Jr., "Audie Is Home," *Saturday Evening Post*, September 15, 1945.

111 "I could talk": quoted in Lois Sager, "Modest Hero Relaxes Among Wounded," Dallas *Morning News*, June 19, 1945.

There is one photograph: Barnard, "Determination to Do a Tough Job."

"Aren't you Lieutenant Murphy": quoted in Lois Sager, "Lieutenant Murphy Has Hero Trouble on His 21st Birthday," newspaper article, June 21, 1945. Other details of experiences in Dallas drawn from this article.

112 "I feel like": Mauldin, *Up Front*.

"I should have on stilts": "Would you like me to tell you how I captured those 123 Germans?" "No, but I'd like to know how you went like a gobbler." Sager, "Lieutenant Murphy Has Hero Trouble on his 21st Birthday"; James Kerr, "Home Town Report on Audie Murphy," *Motion Picture*, March 1952.

113 "Are you kiddin' ": quoted in Dan MacIver, "Dear Tex," Dallas *Morning News*, June 24, 1945.

"His remarks were few": T. O. Perrin, "Rotary News, Greenville *Morning Herald*, June 28, 1945.

Some of them: "Lieutenant Murphy Can Sympathize With Sinatra; Bobby Soxers Mob Him," Greenville *Evening Banner*, June 28, 1945.

114 "Gee, it's really great": quoted in "Greenville Friends Honor Lt. Audie Murphy Wednesday," Greenville *Morning Herald*, June 28, 1945.

Melvin T. Munn: Munn letter to Harold Simpson, September 26, 1974.

"The sudden realization": "Greenville Ready For Celebration in Honor of Lieutenant Murphy," Greenville *Herald Banner*, June 1945.

All of it: "Veterans Arrive Here For Wednesday's Show," Greenville *Evening Banner*, June 26, 1945.

115 "Eddie, the real heroes": quoted in Kenneth Ayers, letter to Harold Simpson, March 11, 1974.

"Well, I must of": quoted by Mrs. Cawthon, interview with author, May 2, 1985.

McKinney held: "Lt. Audie Murphy To Lead Parade," newspaper clipping, June 29, 1945.

On July 8: "VFW Induct Lt. Murphy," Dallas *Morning News*, July 8, 1945.

116 "Well, he may be": Don McNeill, "Surprise for a Hero," *Coronet*, July, 1953.

117 "a great film": James Agee, "A Great Film," *The Nation*, September 15, 1945.

Page

118 *For a time:* details about Maurice Britt derive from interview with Britt by
   author, January 14, 1987.
   Later, when Audie: Front Line, March 20, 1945; May 26, 1945.
120 *was "the nicest":* Sager, "Little Town Shows Big Stuff."
   "So that is what": "Audie Recovering Town's Welcome," newspaper clipping, June 16, 1945.
122 *"complete defeat":* "Japan: An Opportunity for Statesmanship," *Life,* July 17,
   1945.
   They saw signs: Harold Simpson, *Audie Murphy, American Soldier* (Hill Jr.
   College Press, 1975).
   "shouting out the names": quoted in Simpson, *Audie Murphy.*
   "Audie would probably": quoted in David McClure letter to Harry Wilmer,
   August 6, 1985.
123 *"Sis, I didn't sleep":* quoted in Simpson, *Audie Murphy.*
   "kept drinking": quoted in Simpson, *Audie Murphy.*
   "When I saw": quoted in Poland Burns, interview with Harold Simpson,
   March 7, 1974.
   Another time: Burns/Simpson interview.
124 *It was one thing:* Frank Chappell, "Tears, Cheers And Fried Chicken, That's
   Audie's Homecoming," *Dallas Times Herald,* June 15, 1945.
   "They took Army dogs": quoted in Bob Thomas, "Audie Recalls Told To
   Kill," Greenville *Banner,* December 2, 1960.
   War robs you": quoted in Wick Fowler, "Audie Murphy: Hunting Proved
   Valuable in War," Dallas *Morning News,* September 16, 1962.
   "I don't think": quoted in Mary Blume, "Audie Murphy—A Wry Hero,"
   New York *World Tribune,* February 5, 1967.

5. A Beachhead in Beverly Hills

125 *The whole country:* William Manchester, *The Glory and the Dream: A Narrative
   History of America, 1932–1972* (Little, Brown, 1973).
126 *"A lot of men":* Harold P. Leinbaugh and John D. Campbell, *The Men of
   Company K: The Autobiography of a World War II Rifle Company* (William
   Morrow, 1985).
   "After being in the front lines": quoted by Guy Mitchell, interview with author,
   August 19, 1987.
   "an individualistic motivation": Samuel A. Stouffer, et al., *The American Sol-
   dier: Combat and Its Aftermath,* vol. II (Princeton University Press, 1949).
   Most men put the war: Lee Kennett, *G.I.: The American Soldier in World War
   II* (Charles Scribner's Sons, 1987).
   A study in 1951: Kennett, *G.I.: The American Soldier.*
   "of all the surprising": William L. O'Neill, ed., *American Society Since 1945*
   (Quadrangle, 1969).
   "I want to finish": quoted in Bishop Clements, "Farmersville Ready to Give
   Lieut. Murphy Welcome Fit For Hero," newspaper clipping, June 14, 1945.
127 *"study like [he'd]":* Hallett D. Edson to Audie Murphy, August 10, 1945.
   "At home, some wanted": quoted in Bill Libby, "A Different Kind of Hell,"
   Los Angeles Times Magazine, July 18, 1971.
128 *"We all fell in love":* quoted in "Dallasite Helped Audie Murphy Launch Ca-
   reer," *Dallas Times Herald,* June 1, 1971.
   Cherry became Audie's mentor: John Rosenfield, "Skipper Cherry Keeps Busy
   Both in the Theater and Out," Dallas *Morning News,* June 20, 1950.
   It was Cherry: James Cherry interview with Harold Simpson, April 26, 1975;
   July 28, 1975.
   "very reticent, freckled": Felix McKnight, interview with author, May 3, 1985.

Page

　　Several talent scouts: "An American Named Murphy," Universal-International biography, Special Collections, Doheny Library, University of Southern California.

　　"At that time": quoted in Ezra Goodman, "War Was Hell and So Was Hollywood," New York *Star*, December 12, 1948.

　　Finally he decided: "An American Named Murphy."

129 *"better able to adjust":* "Murphy Heads Parade Opening Livestock Show," Dallas *Morning News*, Sept. 19, 1945.

　　"I did like the idea": quoted in Libby, "A Different Kind of Hell."

　　"People don't realize": quoted in Jack Holland, "I've Learned My Lesson," fan magazine, November 1951.

　　"When I met him at the plane": quoted in Spec McClure, "Audie Murphy—the Actor," *New Castle* [Penn.] *News*, May 17, 1971.

130 *"I had all kinds":* quoted in Ezra Goodman, "War Was Hell."

　　"I saw Audie's picture": article by Gene Handsacker, quoted in Harold Simpson, *Audie Murphy, American Soldier.*

　　"I saw that Audie": quoted in "Little Audie Has Poise," Ft. Worth *Star Telegram*, October 10, 1945.

131 *"Jimmy. He's so":* quoted in "Most Decorated Movie Actor," *Picture News*, October 6, 1946.

　　"humorous, charming": Carolyn Price Ryan, letter to Harold Simpson, February 12, 1973.

　　Attendance was the highest: Andrew Dowdy, *The Films of the Fifties: The American State of Mind* (William Morrow, 1975); and Tina Balio, "Retrenchment, Reappraisal, and Reorganization, 1948—," in *The American Film Industry*, rev. ed. (University of Wisconsin Press, 1985).

132 *Just a year after:* Robert H. Stanley, *The Celluloid Empire: A History of the American Movie Industry* (Hastings House, 1978).

　　Every area of the industry: Balio, "Retrenchment, Reappraisal, and Reorganization, 1948—"

　　"The minute you refuse": Patricia Bosworth, *Montgomery Clift, A Biography* (Bantam, 1980).

133 *In Audie Murphy's case:* See Robert Dallek, *Ronald Reagan: The Politics of Symbolism* (Harvard University Press, 1984); and Michael Paul Rogin, *Ronald Reagan, the Movie, and Other Episodes in Political Demonology* (University of California Press, 1987).

　　"We tried to work": quoted in Doug Warren (with James Cagney), *Cagney: The Authorized Biography* (St. Martin's Press, 1986).

　　"I am fine": Audie Murphy, letter to Cawthons, March 7, 1946; quoted in Simpson, *Audie Murphy.*

134 *The Lab held its classes:* Material about the Actors Lab, both methods and politics, derives from Delia Nora Salvi, "The History of the Actors' Laboratory, Inc., 1941–1950" (unpublished dissertation, UCLA, 1969). Additional information on the political context of the times is derived from Robert Vaughn, *Only Victims: A Study of Show Business Blacklisting* (Putnam, 1972); and Larry Ceplair and Steven Englund, *The Inquisition in Hollywood: Politics in the Film Community, 1930–1960* (University of California Press, 1983).

135 *"even though the school":* Audie Murphy, interview with Hedda Hopper, June 22, 1957; Hopper Collection, Margaret Herrick Library, Academy of Motion Picture Arts and Sciences.

136 *"I mounted the holstered gun":* Ronald Reagan, with Richard G. Hubler, *Where's the Rest of Me?* (Duell, Sloan and Pearce, 1965).

137 *"Hell, I can't even":* Murphy/Hopper interview.

　　A Hollywood writer: Ida Zeitlin, "Lonely Joe," *Photoplay*, January, 1951.

Page
139 *Russell Johnson entered:* Universal-International biography, February 27, 1952, Margaret Herrick Library, AMPAS.

"anti-semitism": quoted in Salvi, "The History of the Actors' Laboratory, Inc., 1941–1950."

"so intelligent": Louella Parsons, *Los Angeles Examiner*, October 12, 1947.

Under contract to: 20th Century-Fox studio biography, Margaret Herrick Library, AMPAS.

140 *Audie told a close friend:* details related in letter from David McClure to Harold Simpson, March 1, 1974.

He would never: David McClure, "The Way Back," 1956. Texas Collection, Baylor University.

141 *In a wide-ranging interview:* "Most Decorated Movie Actor."

His expected first role: "Audie Murphy Signed For Films by Cagney," Dallas *Morning News*, July 13, 1946. Details of Cagney's company are drawn from Kevin Hagopian, "Declarations of Independence: A History of Cagney Productions," *Velvet Light Trap*, 22 (1986).

"believed that Audie": quoted in McClure, "Audie Murphy—The Actor."

"They're trying to teach": quoted in Perry Pitt, "To Me, He's Murph," fan magazine, ca. 1953.

"Doesn't drink or smoke": Cynthia Miller, "Rage in Heaven," *Screen Stories*, 1949.

142 *"I took one look":* quoted in Kay Poctor, "Love Is Young," *Photoplay*, April 1948.

"Ah know ah hev": Fredda Dudley, "Our Own True Love, *Movie*, March 1948. Details of Wanda's life drawn from Evelyn Mack Truitt, *Who Was Who on Screen*, 3rd. ed. (R. R. Bowker, 1983); and William Lynch Vallee, "Movie Life of Wanda Hendrix," fan magazine, ca. 1949.

"like making clothes": Production Notes, Universal-International; USC.

When Wanda arrived: details of their first meeting are drawn from the following sources: Dorothy O'Leary, "Oh Promise Me," *Movie Stars Parade*, April 1949; "Love Is Young"; Wanda Hendrix, "This Love Of Ours," fan magazine; Toni Holt, " 'Audie Murphy Was Destined To Die,' Says Wanda Hendrix, Soldier-star's First Wife," *National Tattler*, April 21, 1974; David McClure, "They Want To Get Married," fan magazine, ca. 1949; and Audie Murphy, "Why I'm Not Afraid to Marry Wanda," *Photoplay*, January 1949.

144 *"he backhanded me":* quoted in Ezra Goodman, "War Was Hell and So Was Hollywood," New York *Star*, December 12, 1948.

"LITTLE AUDIE MURPHY": Austin *American-Statesman*, December 12, 1946.

"unlike so many": "Hero and Actress," *Life*, November 17, 1947.

145 *"I was rather sensitive":* quoted in Holland, "I've Learned My Lesson."

146 *"Let's cut out":* quoted in Al Stump, "G.I. in Hollywood," *Saga*, June, 1957.

"public perhaps tired": *Hollywood Reporter*, June 15, 1948.

"part with-the kid": quoted in Goodman, "War Was Hell."

"Audie has as much": quoted in "Profile of Audie Murphy, the Kid from Texas," Paul Short Production, ca. 1949; Margaret Herrick Library, AMPAS.

"I had eight words": quoted in Hubler, "He Doesn't Want To Be A Star."

147 *"It turned out":* Warren, *Cagney*.

"decidedly egocentric": James Cagney to Harold Simpson, July 1, 1975.

"Bill Cagney told me": quoted in Bob Thomas, "There Are Some Things You *Never* Forget," *Movie Show*, September 1956.

148 *"He wouldn't do it":* Sy Gomberg, interview with author, March 27, 1987.

"guy with a long, scrawny frame": Jaik Rosenstein, *Hollywood Leg Man* (1950).

149 *"so young, so fresh":* David McClure, letter to Harold Simpson, January 27, 1974.

Page

They had several: David McClure, "Audie Murphy—The Man," *New Castle News* (Pennsylvania), May 11, 1972.

"voluble, hard-drinking reporter": McClure, "The Way Back."

"Cynicism is": Rosenstein, *Hollywood Leg Man.*

At one time or another: David McClure, letter to Harry Wilmer, June 13, 1985.

"usually drunk": McClure, "The Way Back."

As late as 1957: David McClure, "Helmets in the Dust," manuscript, Texas Collection, Baylor University.

150 *"moody, brooding":* McClure, "Helmets."

He would withdraw: McClure, letter to Wilmer, August 6, 1985.

"You take fifty": Quoted in "Reminiscences of Audie Murphy," George Putnam Television Transcript, KTTV (Los Angeles), June 1, 1971.

In Spec's view: McClure, "The Way Back."

"Then, my name": quoted in Paul Howarth, "Audie Murphy Is Nobody's Fool!", fan magazine, October 1, 1957.

"I had a shower": quoted in Bob Thomas, "From the Seeds of Poverty," *Screen*, August 1956.

"But it was": quoted in Thomas, "There Are Some Things You Never Forget."

151 *In the meantime:* McClure, "Audie Murphy—The Man."

"But can he": McClure, "The Way Back."

152 *A poll taken: Hollywood Reporter*, September 15, 1983.

"easily one of the": Frank Eng, *Daily News*, October 6, 1948.

"The shirts": quoted in McClure, "Audie Murphy—The Actor."

"When I was down and out": quoted in Ezra Goodman, "War Was Hell."

When Pine and Thomas: Spec McClure, "How Audie Murphy Became a Movie Star," fan magazine; and McClure, "Audie Murphy—The Actor."

6. Breakthrough

154 *A newspaper report:* Harold Heffernam, "Texas Hero Turns Author Of War Book," Dallas *Morning News*, December 8, 1947.

In February: David McClure, "Audie Murphy—the Actor," *New Castle* [Penn.] *News*, May 17, 1972.

155 *"German grabs":* David McClure, notes (one page), Texas Collection, Baylor University.

Spec would show: David McClure, note on Chapter 21 of *To Hell and Back*, Murphy—The Actor.

Sometimes Audie would say: quoted in note by David McClure attached to manuscript pages of *To Hell and Back.*

Spec thought: McClure, "The Way Back," unpublished manuscript, Oct. 29, 1956, Texas Collection, Baylor University.

"needed a lot": Ezra Goodman, "War Was Hell and So Was Hollywood," New York *Star*, December 12, 1948.

156 *"its funny how things":* Audie Murphy, holograph copy of *To Hell and Back.*

Audie wanted the book: McClure, "The Way Back."

Spec felt comfortable: McClure, letter to Harold Simpson, January 27, 1974.

"Often yet, when asleep": David McClure, manuscript of *To Hell and Back*, Texas Collection, Baylor University.

157 *Audie thought this material:* David McClure, headnote to first version of Chapter One of *To Hell and Back.*

He also said: Kate Holliday, "Still in Stride," *Screenland*, April 1949.

Audie received: McClure, "The Way Back."

"I requested the tour": Audie Murphy, in letter to Major Kenneth B. Potter,

Page

June 29, 1948. Hedda Hopper Collection, Margaret Herrick Library, Academy of Motion Picture Arts and Sciences.

158 *"publicity specialist":* McClure, "How Audie Murphy Won His Medals," unpublished manuscript, October 10, 1969, Texas Collection, Baylor University; McClure, "Audie Murphy—Man of Humor," unpublished manuscript, 1971, Texas Collection, Baylor.

In Paris the press: McClure, "The Way Back."

Spec got blind drunk: Frank McFadden, interview with author, June 11, 1986.

159 *The search began:* McClure, "How Audie Murphy Won His Medals."

"On the battlefields": "Profile of Audie Murphy, the Kid from Texas," Paul Short Productions, ca. 1949, Margaret Herrick Library, AMPAS.

Spec examined it: David McClure, in letter to Col. Red Reeder, March 27, 1964.

"Well, how did you": quoted in McClure, "Audie Murphy—Man of Humor."

"arranged in wobbly": McClure, "Man of Humor."

"It was still": Audie Murphy, "The Love That I Feel," *Motion Picture*, December, 1956.

160 *"fat-headed":* "Audie Rough on Diplomats," newspaper clipping, July 21, 1948.

"one of the better": quoted in letter from Doris Flowers to Audie Murphy, January 27, 1949.

Other reviewers concurred: Herald-Tribune Book Review, February 27, 1949; Gladwin Hill, *"To Hell and Back," New York Times*, February 27, 1949; Charles Poore, "Books of the Times," *New York Times*, March 10, 1949; A. C. Fields, *"To Hell and Back," Saturday Review of Literature*, March 26, 1949; *Christian Science Monitor*, March 3, 1949; and "Dogface Odyssey."

161 Bad Boy *had:* Production Notes, Allied Artists, USC.

162 *"teen-age, trigger-happy":* Cue, March 25, 1949.

Steve Broidy: Al Stump, "G.I. in Hollywood," *Saga*, June, 1957.

"No Murphy, no story": Paul Short, "Producer Voices Faith in Murphy," *Dallas Morning News*, February 26, 1950.

"Okay. Quit worrying": Stump, "G.I. in Hollywood."

"Finally, we cut": Robert Hardy Andrews, "Audie's Script Writer Remembers and Remembers," *Chicago Sun-Times Showcase*, June 20, 1971.

"I crawled down": quoted in Goodman, "War Was Hell."

"I didn't mind": quoted in "Top War Hero Makes Film Grade," *Boston Post Magazine*, October 10, 1948.

163 *"frightened young fellow":* James Lydon, interview with author, June 23, 1986.

"I along with others": Jane Wyatt, interview with author, June 5, 1986.

"very nervous, very upset": Lydon/Graham interview.

164 *"Unless you have been":* quoted in "Murphy Complains Film Fights Tough," newspaper clipping, January 8, 1949.

"What's wrong": quoted in McClure, "Man of Humor."

He does everything: Holliday, "Still in Stride."

165 *"Being an orphan":* Audie Murphy, "Why I'm Not Afraid To Marry Wanda," *Photoplay*, January 1949.

Reviewers were struck: Ann Helming, "Audie Murphy Gives Good Performance," newspaper clipping, March 16, 1949; *Cue*, March 29, 1949; Edwin Schallert, " 'Bad Boy' Would Assume . . . ," *Los Angeles Times*, March 16, 1949; "Story Essentially . . . ," *Hollywood Reporter*, January 1, 1949; *Variety*, January 21, 1949; *Cue*, February 4, 1949; Los Angeles *Daily News*, March 16, 1949; Bosley Crowther, *New York Times*, March, 1949; Robert Hatch, *New Republic*, April 11, 1949.

166 *"They are all so different":* Ruth Waterbury, " 'Bad Boy' Looks Like Hit," *Los Angeles Examiner*, March 16, 1949.

At the same time: Louella Parsons, *Los Angeles Examiner*, November 24, 1948.

Page

These included: "Audie Moves Along with Three Films," *Los Angeles Examiner*, July 12, 1949.

During the first half: McClure, "Audie Murphy—The Man."

Spec said Audie: McClure, "The Way Back."

To his later regret: McClure note on two holograph poems, July 16, 1972; Texas Collection, Baylor University.

167   Audie spent his days: McClure, "The Way Back."

Audie was always: Jalk Saltman, "Mooning Over Murphy?" fan magazine, ca. 1951.

These were his friends: Goodman, "War Was Hell."

168   "If it hadn't": Holliday, "Still in Stride."

"going steady": "Hero, Starlet Romance Bared," *Los Angeles Examiner*, June 9, 1947.

"money throw Cupid!": *L. A. Examiner*, July 7, 1948.

"I can't marry": Sheilah Graham, "Mr. Cupid," fan magazine, 1948.

"he would not": Wanda Hendrix, "Hero's Wife," *Photoplay*, December 1949.

"it'd have been ok": quoted in MacPherson, Dallas *Morning News*, November 3, 1948.

169   In the mid-fifties: Patrick Agan, *Is That Who I Think It Is?*, vol. 1 (NY, 1975).

She liked frilly: Dorothy Leary, "Oh Promise Me," *Movie Stars Parade*, ca. 1948.

"They accuse, deny": McClure, "They Want To Get Married."

One episode: McClure, "The Way Back."

170   "With the lights": McClure, "Way Back."

"I dislike the back-slapping": quoted in McClure, "They Want To Get Married."

"conscious of her career": quoted in Hyatt Downing, "What Makes Audie Run?" fan magazine, ca. 1949–50.

"I have seen too many": quoted in McClure, "The Way Back."

"They slap each other": Goodman, "War Was Hell."

"never bothered about": Budd Boetticher, interview with author, March 4, 1985.

He had a run-in: Shelley Winters, *Shelley Also Known as Shirley* (Ballantine, 1980).

171   "At that time": Lydon interview.

"I remember one night": quoted in Bob Thomas, "Audie Recalls Told to Kill," Greenville *Banner*, December 2, 1960.

"when I can afford": McClure, "The Way Back."

172   "Hello, Skipper": David McClure, "Happily Ever After," *Movieland*, April 19, 1949.

When Audie returned: "Murphy, Most Decorated Yank, Greeted by Fiancee," *Los Angeles Examiner*, July 25, 1948.

Then he bought: *Los Angeles Examiner*, August 5, 1948

"watermelon pink": *Los Angeles Examiner*, October 16, 1948.

"Maisonette Murphy": O'Leary, "Oh Promise Me."

173   "That's another thing": quoted in MacPherson, *Daily News*, November 3, 1948.

"Things look very good": quoted in Goodman, "War Was Hell."

"It's very refreshing": *Los Angeles Examiner*, January 20, 1949.

"the cutest couple": Lydon/Graham interview.

"own true love gift": *Farmersville Times*, June 1948.

"Anyhow, I'm pretty positive": Audie Murphy, "Why I'm Not Afraid to Marry Wanda," *Photoplay*, January, 1949.

"nothing wrong between us": quoted in McClure, "They Want To Get Married."

174   Audie forgot: "Hero Forgets License," *Los Angeles Times*, January 19, 1949.

Page

Some luminaries: "Happy Ending," fan magazine, ca. 1949.

"From the beginning": quoted in Ross Taylor, "Murphy's Other Self," *Motion Picture*, ca. 1954–55.

"Everything was going fine": quoted in Holt, "Audie Murphy Was Destined. . . ."

"If there's a God": McClure, letter to Wilmer, August 6, 1985.

"She had no more right": Richard G. Hubler, "He Doesn't Want To Be a Star," *Saturday Evening Post*, April 18, 1953.

175 *Audie had gone all out:* Leary, "Oh Promise Me."

"In Heaven, Texas": *Movie Life*, July 1949.

To Audie's Texas friends: James Cherry, interview with Harold Simpson; Mrs. Ray Woods, interview with Simpson, quoted in Harold B. Simpson, *Audie Murphy, American Soldier* (Hill Jr. College Press, 1975).

176 *"and for that clacking noise":* quoted in Fred Williams, "Modest Texas Hero Impresses Solons in Plea for Juveniles," Austin *American-Statesman*, Feb. 15, 1949.

"Not enough people": quoted in Steve Perkins, "Texas' Audie Murphy Speaks Before Legislature at 11 A.M.," Austin *American-Statesman*, February 15, 1949.

After Taylor's objections: "Audie 'Insult' Closed, Rep. Agrees," newspaper clipping, February 19, 1949.

"refreshing lack": Fairfax Nisbet, "World Premiere of 'Bad Boy' Greeted by Majestic Sellout," Dallas *Morning News*, February 17, 1949.

177 *"Everywhere Murphy's geniality":* "The Hero from Texas," *Newsweek*, February 28, 1949.

7. Kid with a Gun

*For a good overview of Murphy's Western movie career, see John H. Lenihan, "The Kid from Texas: The Movie Heroism of Audie Murphy," *New Mexico Historical Quarterly*, 61 (October 1986), 329–340.

178 *"Maybe everybody thinks":* quoted in Richard G. Hubler, "He Doesn't Want To Be a Movie Star," *Saturday Evening Post*, April 18, 1953.

179 *"I have been criticized":* Paul Short, "Producer Voices Faith in Murphy," Dallas *Morning News*, February 26, 1950.

"a kid caught in a web": quoted in "Fear Is For The Brave," *Movieland*, July–December, 1956.

"who might have gone": Audie Murphy, "The Role I Liked Best," *Saturday Evening Post*, January 13, 1951.

"When I was a youngster": quoted in "Fear Is For The Brave."

"as a quiet guy": Murphy, "The Role I Liked Best."

180 *"a still of Audie":* Herman Levy to Dan Green, October 18, 1949; Universal-International files, Special Collections, Doheny Library, University of Southern California. Hereafter cited as USC.

"We should be very careful": Clark Ramsey to Archie Herzoff and others, August 1, 1949; U-I files, USC.

"The feeling up front": Archie Herzoff to Hank Linet, September 28, 1949; U-I files, USC.

"in civilian clothes": memo on "Kid from Texas," U-I files, USC.

"he is very touchy": Frank McFadden to Bob Ungerfield, Dec. 19, 1951; U-I files, USC.

Premiere activities: notes on itinerary for "The Kid from Texas" World Premiere; U-I files, USC.

181 *"developed considerably":* Fairfax Nisbet, "Audie Measures Up as Emcee and in Film Desperado Role," Dallas *Morning News*, March 2, 1950.

Page

"*Audie is idol*": telegram to Universal from Frank McFadden, March 30, 1950; U-I files, USC.

"*Everyone was wonderful*": Murphy, "The Role I Liked Best."

The first hint: comments taken from "Sneak Preview Cards," August 19, 1949; U-I files, USC.

182 *For the most part the reviewers: New York Times*, June 2, 1950; *Variety*, March 1, 1950; "Complicated Story Slows Down Action," *Hollywood Reporter*, February 22, 1950; *Fortnight*, March 31, 1950.

"*What they missed*": Robert Hardy Andrews, "Audie's Script Writer Remembers and Remembers," *Chicago Sun-Times Showcase*, June 20, 1971.

"*It's strange*": review of *Sierra* in fan magazine, ca. 1950.

"*natural acting ability*": *Sierra* notes; U-I file, USC.

For the first time some reviewers: Bosley Crowther, *New York Times*, September 15, 1950; *Fortnight*, June 9, 1950.

183 "*greatly shaken*": Wanda Hendrix, "Hero's Wife," *Photoplay*, December 1949.

"*I may have killed*": quoted in David McClure, "The Way Back."

One photo showed Audie: Modern Screen Pictures, November, 1949.

184 "*treated members of the cast*": Production Notes to *The Kid from Texas*; U-I files, USC.

"*fights the war*": *Los Angeles Examiner*, August 1, 1949.

"*All I had to do*": quoted in Production Notes, *Sierra*, August 29, 1949; U-I files, USC.

"*Take it easy*": quoted in *Modern Screen*, December, 1949.

185 "*We can get a wire break*": Production Notes, *Sierra*, September 1, 1949; U-I files, USC.

Another time Wanda: Production Notes, *Sierra*, September 15, 1949; U-I files, USC.

What supposedly happened: Production Notes, *Sierra*, September 28, 1949; U-I files, USC.

"*It's all my fault*": quoted in Louella A. Parsons, "Audie Murphy, Wanda Decide to Live Apart," newspaper clipping, October 4, 1949.

"*He does not believe*": Maxine LaFarge, "Love Takes a Beating," *Movieland*, January–June 1950.

186 *One of the most thorough:* Cynthia Miller, "Rage in Heaven," *Screen Stories*, 1949.

187 *In a signed article:* Hendrix, "Hero's Wife."

"*Audie had made*": quoted in "They're Doing All They Can," fan magazine.

"*We decided to give*": quoted in "Wanda Back, Reconciled," *Los Angeles Examiner*, November 20, 1949.

188 "*Everything is still okay*": quoted in "Audie Murphy to Retry Marriage," *Los Angeles Examiner*, December 20, 1949.

"*Farmers are happier*": quoted in "The Hero from Texas."

"*steadily through the dark woods*": "They're Doing All They Can."

189 "*From the beginning*": Quoted in "Miss Hendrix Gets Divorce," April 15, 1950.

"*had the most beautiful smile*": Holt, "Audie Murphy Was Destined . . .".

"*Actually, I suppose*": Downing, "What Makes Audie Run?"

"*The only thing I did know*": quoted in Holt, "Audie Murphy Was Destined . . .".

"*Audie was so cold*": McClure to Wilmer, August 6, 1985.

"*What in the hell*": quoted in McClure, "The Way Back."

"*Okay. Bring up the emotion*": quoted in McClure, *The Way Back*

190 "*said that if he didn't*": quoted in Holt, "Audie Murphy Was Destined . . .".

"*went to see*": quoted in McClure, "The Way Back."

"*He never seemed to feel*": McClure to Wilmer, June 13, 1985.

"*The big thing in his life*": quoted in Holt, "Audie Murphy Was Destined . . .".

Page
    "She locked him out": Budd Boettecher, interview with author, March 4, 1985.
    "Physically and mentally": quoted in "Wanda Hendrix in Tears . . . ," *Los Angeles Times*, April 15, 1950.
191 *"I suppose ours":* quoted in Downing, "What Makes Audie Run?"
    "I was in no shape": quoted in Bob Thomas, "From the Seeds of Poverty," *Screen*, August, 1956.
    "the killing of enemy soldiers": Harry Wilmer, "War Nightmares: A Decade after Vietnam," in *Vietnam in Remission*, ed. James F. Veninga and Harry A. Wilmer (Texas A&M University Press, 1985).
    The nightmares of World War II combatants: Lee Kennett, *G. I.: The American Soldier in World War II* (Charles Scribner's Sons, 1987).

8. War and Peace

194 *"I think that World War III":* quoted in "Audie Murphy Joins Guard," *Los Angeles Examiner*, July 15, 1950.
    "I don't know anything": quoted in Jimmy Banks, "Audie Joins Up With Texas Unit," Dallas *Morning News*, July 15, 1950.
    "didn't make any fuss": Mickey Francis, interview with author, June 24, 1987.
    Movie Life *pointed out:* September, 1950.
    "war movie": "Cast, Production Excel in War Film," *Hollywood Reporter*, November 8, 1950.
195 *Reviews of* Kansas Raiders*:* Ann Helming, "Quantrell's Raiders Ride Again," Hollywood *Citizen News*, November 15, 1950; John L. Scott, "Quantrell's Villains Take Over Screens," Los Angeles *Times*, November 15, 1950; *Variety*, November 8, 1950; "Cast, Production Excel in War Film"; Scott, "Quantrell's Villains"; *Motion Picture Herald*, November 11, 1950; New York *Times*, November, 1950.
    "What I want": Spec McClure, "How Audie Murphy Became A Movie Star," fan magazine.
    "during the war": Jerry Wald to Ranald MacDougall, April 19, 1950, quoted in *Inside Warner Brothers*, ed. Rudy Behlmer (Viking, 1985).
196 *"nasty, ugly people":* quoted in Axel Madsen, *John Huston* (Doubleday, 1978).
    In the end: John Huston, *An Open Book* (Ballantine, 1980).
197 *"I called Dore":* Hedda Hopper, "War Hero Makes His Place Among Stars," Chicago *Tribune*, 1953.
    "She—in a way": quoted in George Ellis, *Hedda and Louella* (Putnam, 1972).
    "I regard this": Paul Short to John Huston, July 29, 1950; Huston Collection, Margaret Herrick Library, Academy of Motion Picture Arts and Sciences.
    "continue in the movies": quoted in A. H. Weiler, "By Way of Report," New York *Times*, Nov. 14, 1951.
    "I'd never have tried": quoted in "Movie News," New York *Herald Tribune*, October 27, 1951.
    "Murphy loved the classic": David McClure, "Audie Murphy—The Actor," *New Castle* [Penn.] *News*, May 17, 1972.
    "But he knew": quoted in Robert Hardy Andrews, "Audie's Script Writer Remembers and Remembers," *Chicago Sun-Times Showcase*, June 20, 1971.
198 *"I championed Audie":* quoted in Gerald Pratley, *The Cinema of John Huston* (A. S. Barnes, 1971).
    "He was in": quoted in pressbook to *The Red Badge of Courage*.
    "rare spirit": John Huston, interview with author, March 25, 1987.
    "They just don't see": quoted in Lillian Ross, *Picture* (Rinehart, 1952).
    "You sense it": quoted in Ross, *Picture*.

Page

According to one observer: Paul Kohner, interview with author, August 21, 1987.

But Huston was: James Lydon, interview with author, June 23, 1986.

"grizzled sonsobitches": quoted in Madsen, *John Huston.*

"glamorized too darn": quoted in Al Stump, "G.I. in Hollywood," *Saga,* June 1957.

"I didn't like it": quoted in Ezra Goodman, "Behind the Camera," Los Angeles *Daily News,* Sept. 18, 1950.

199 *"something I knew and felt":* quoted in Weiler, "By Way of Report."

"Physically and from": quoted in Goodman, "Behind the Camera."

"inquisitive little lady": Kohner/Graham interview.

200 *"Anything I do":* quoted in Goodman, "Behind the Camera."

"This sort of acting": quoted in "Picture Gallery," *Photoplay,* ca. 1950–51.

"thought he could": Douglas Dick, interview with author, June 26, 1986.

"He needs your": quoted in Ross, *Picture.*

201 *"this was a day":* Kohner/Graham interview.

"I don't think": Dick/Graham interview.

202 *"had a host of admirers":* Huston/Graham interview.

203 *"There's something mighty":* Bill Mauldin, "A Tribute to Audie Murphy," 1955–56, UCLA.

Reinhardt's fears: following quotes are from Ross, *Picture.*

204 *"It looks, kid":* Dore Schary to John Huston, September 9, 1950, September 15, 1950; Huston Collection, Margaret Herrick Library, AMPAS.

"disastrous": Dore Schary, *Heyday, An Autobiography* (Little, Brown, 1979).

"the reaction of that audience": quoted in Pratley, *The Cinema of John Huston.*

"absolutely no Commie": Ellis, *Hedda and Louella.*

"accepted by critics": quoted in Ross, *Picture.*

205 *"All that violence":* quoted in Ross, *Picture.*

But not before Schary: Ross, *Picture.*

"I guessed he": Schary, *Heyday.*

"It was while": quoted in Pratley, *The Cinema of John Huston.*

He wanted to shoot: Don Ross, "Audie Murphy's Personal Movie War," New York *Herald Tribune,* September 11, 1955.

"So, I am afraid": Gottfried Reinhardt to John Huston, January 28, 1957; Huston Collection; Margaret Herrick Library; AMPAS.

206 *"must not appear":* quoted in Ross, *Picture.*

"The story, actually": quoted in Lowel E. Redelings, "The Hollywood Scene," Hollywood *Citizen-News,* August 18, 1950.

"It was at the time": quoted in Pratley, *The Cinema of John Huston.*

"war picture": clipping from fan magazine.

Audie himself received: The New Yorker, October 27, 1951; *Newsweek,* October 15, 1951; *Time,* October 8, 1951; *Saturday Review of Literature,* "SRL Goes to the Movies," September 29, 1951; Bosley Crowther, *New York Times,* 1951; Philip T. Hartung, "Pasted in the Sky," *Commonweal,* November 2, 1951); Robert Hatch, *New Republic,* September 24, 1951; Manny Farber, *The Nation,* October 10, 1951.

208 *"For a kid":* quoted in Arthur L. Charles, "Just Married!" *Modern Screen,* ca. 1951.

"He's got the ability": quoted in "Mr. and Mrs. Murphy: It was . . . ," clipping from fan magazine, ca. 1951.

"splendid, beautiful": Huston/Graham interview.

"I'd read just about": Mrs. Audie Murphy, "The Day He Proposed," fan magazine, ca. 1951.

209 *"There were lots of people":* quoted in Arthur L. Charles, "Just Married!"

"how he was": quoted in Charles, "Just Married!"

Page
"*I still see Wanda*": quoted in "Picture Gallery," *Photoplay*.
"*Look, I've got*": quoted in fan magazine, ca. 1950–51.
"*Few women could*": McClure, letter to Harry Wilmer, June 13, 1985.
"*When I first met*": Ida Zeitlin, "Lonely Joe," *Photoplay*, January 1951.
210 *Another girl:* Production Notes, *Kansas Raiders*, 1950; U-I files, USC.
"*From now on*": quoted in Harold B. Simpson, *Audie Murphy, American Soldier* (Hill Jr. College Press, 1975).
"*Hey, you two*": Mrs. Audie Murphy, "The Day He Proposed."
"*The first time I saw*": quoted in Charles, "Just Married!"
211 "*The day before*": quoted in Charles, "Just Married!"
"*You might have changed*": Maxine Arnold, "His Love Wears Wings," *Photoplay*, May 1951.
212 *In fact, her name:* details from Sharon O'Neill, interview with author, April 23, 1987.
213 "*The first time I met*": quoted in Alyce Canfield, "When You're In Love," *Motion Picture*, ca. 1952.
"*There were many things*": quoted in Jack Holland, "I've Learned My Lesson," fan magazine, November 1951.
In her postmarriage reflections: Wanda Hendrix, "If I Love Aain," *Motion Picture*, April 1951.
214 "*beauty, but she's*": quoted in "Something Wonderful," fan magazine.
"*Pamela Archer sounds*": quoted in Arnold, "His Love Wears Wings."
"*Pam's a wonderful*": quoted in *Movie Life*, June 1951.
215 "*same walk, same grin*": "Reminiscences of Audie Murphy, II," June 2, 1971; George Putnam.
"*Wait until she*": quoted in Canfield, "When You're In Love."
"*Expensive? It's downright*": quoted in Pamela Murphy, "Forever Audie," *Photoplay*, August 1951.
She asked what: Mrs. Audie Murphy, "The Day He Proposed."
216 "*My mother always*": quoted in Pamela Murphy, ibid.
"*Pamela: If you marry*": quoted in Maude Cheatham, "We Belong Together," *Movies*, June 1952.
On their wedding night: fan magazine.
217 "*dares to dream*": "Audie Dares To Dream Again," fan magazine.
"*Her sole interest*": "Mr. and Mrs. Murphy: It Was," *Modern Screen*, October 1951.
"*The only career she wants*": "Young Married: Mr. and Mrs. Murphy," *Movies*, December 1951.
He gave instruction: "Audie Murphy Ends Duty Tour," Austin *American Statesman*, Sept. 30, 1951.
"*kids were walking*": Lt. Col. Mickey Francis, interview with author, June 24, 1987.
218 "*Audie was really*": quoted in Simpson, *Audie Murphy*.
"*Oh, I know*": quoted in Downing, "What Makes Audie Run?"
"*I expect they will be*": quoted in Weiler, "By Way of Report."

9. Quick-Draw Audie

220 "*I loved watching him*": Michael Dante, interview with author, June 18, 1986.
Once a picture editor: Dorothy O'Leary, "Audie's All Right," fan magazine, ca. 1952–53.
"*At one time*": Ben Cooper, interview with author, June 3, 1986.
220–221 *He later claimed:* Rona Barrett, newspaper clipping, February, 1976.
221 "*We used to meet*": *TV Super Shows*, December 1977.

Page

"we went into the steam room": Casey Tibbs, interview with author, March 29, 1987.

222 *"Ben Johnson is":* Don Page, "Tibbs Back On Trail," *Los Angeles Herald-Examiner*, August 23, 1976.

"Sure. I like making": quoted in O'Leary, "Audie's All Right."

"It has paid dividends": Thomas M. Pryor, "Studios Hang Out Help Wanted Sign," *New York Times*, April 16, 1956; Thomas M. Pryor, "Studio Advances Actors' Training," *New York Times*, June 8, 1956.

"clean up the diction": Estelle Harman, interview with author, May 28, 1987.

223 *"glorified and exclusive":* "Puttin' On An Act," fan magazine, ca. 1953–54.

224 *"Excessive slaughter":* Joseph I. Breen to William Gordon, May 3, 1951; Universal-International files, Special Collections, Doheny Library, University of Southern California. For information on Breen, see Larry Ceplair and Steven Englund, *The Inquisition in Hollywood: Politics in the Film Community, 1930–1960.* (University of California Press, 1983).

"unacceptable killing": Joseph I. Breen to William Gordon, May 10, 1951; U-I files, USC.

"Audie, who receives": The Cimarron Kid Production Notes"; U-I files, USC.

In February 1951: Veerlee Groos, in memos to David Lipton, February 1, 1951; May 1, 1951; November, 1951; U-I files, USC.

He averaged six hundred letters: Reba and Bonnie Churchill, "Murph and his Money," *Motion Picture*, p. 67.

serious minded adults": "The Cimarron Kid Production Notes"; U-I files, USC.

225 *The itinerary:* Duke Hickey, memo to Frank McFadden, January 4, 1952; U-I files, USC.

"Whenever or wherever": McFadden memo to David A. Lipton, January 21, 1952; U-I files, USC.

226 *"Well, what the hell":* McFadden, interview with author, June 11, 1986.

228 *"while holding his Western":* Archie Herzoff to Publicity and Advertising Staff, November 6, 1951; U-I files, USC.

When he complained: Alan Lovell, "Don Siegel—American Cinema," undated pamphlet.

"The only way to do it": quoted in Stuart Kaminsky, *Don Siegel: Director* (Curtis Books, 1974).

"dry, saturnine wit": "Lively Sagebrusher Loaded with Action," *Hollywood Reporter*, July 11, 1952.

"The killers don't know this": Philip K. Scheuer, " 'Duel at Silver Creek' First-Rate Horse Opera," Los Angeles *Times*, August 4, 1952.

229 *"The terrible thing":* Nathan Juran, interview with author, June 9, 1986.

230 *"valuable property":* Charles Simonelli to David Lipton, January 8, 1953; U-I files, USC.

231 *"man-woman relationship":* Clark Ramsey to Jeff Livingston, November 11, 1952; U-I files, USC.

"two-hundred dollar Stetson hats": "Production Notes to 'Ride Clear of Diablo,' " U-I files, USC.

"Audie always wore": Polly Burson, interview with author, March 23, 1987.

A feature article: Memo on "Tumbleweed" Campaign Ideas; U-I files, USC.

Reviewers liked: Library Journal, November 1, 1953; *Variety Daily*, November 17, 1953.

"Everybody believes Audie": Production Notes, "Tumbleweed"; U-I files, USC.

232 *A nationwide poll:* Richard G. Hubler, "He Doesn't Want To Be a Star."

"pint-sized Gary Cooper": Hubler, U-I files, USC.

Reviews confirmed what was now: S. A. Desick, " 'Drums' Sound Wester

Page
Film," *Los Angeles Examiner*, May 20, 1954; Edwin Schallert, "Scoundrels Give Hero Rough Time," Los Angeles *Times*, April 20, 1954; "Indian Adventure Breaks Tradition," Los Angeles *Daily News*, May 20, 1954.

233 *"Too many soldiers":* quoted in Frederick de Cordova, *Johnny Came Lately* (Simon and Schuster, 1988).
"It is very difficult": Newsweek, March 15, 1954.
"this has let the humor": Dorothy O'Leary, "Audie's All Right," fan magazine, ca. 1952–53.

234 *"I still have touches":* quoted in "Things I Don't Tell My Wife," fan magazine, ca. 1954.
"probably the oldest house": quoted in Helen Gould, "Audie Murphy—Hollywood Lone Wolf," fan magazine, ca. 1953.

235 *"Perhaps you think":* quoted in Maude Cheatham, "An Irishman's Castle," fan magazine, ca. 1953.
"I only want": quoted in "That Fadeout Kiss," fan magazine, ca. 1953.
The house had: Cheatham, "An Irishman's Castle."
"I don't drink or smoke": quoted in Helen Louise Walker, "I'm Not The Type," fan magazine, ca. 1953.
Audie continued to keep: Jack Holland, "If You Were Audie's Friend," *Movies*, August, 1952.
Audie and Pam: Pamela Murphy, "The Trouble with Murph," fan magazine.

236 *"His heart's always":* Corinne Murphy, "Audie Gets His 'Man,' " *Photoplay*, August, 1952.
"When Audie arrived": quoted in "Mr. and Mrs. Murphy," *Modern Screen*, Nov., 1951.
"When I was single": quoted in Jack Holland, "True To Himself," ca. 1953.
"She's in charge": "I Know Why I'm In Love," fan magazine, ca. 1951–52.

237 *"Pam and I live":* quoted in Reba and Bonnie Churchill, "Murph and His Money," *Motion Picture*, ca. 1952–53.
"The first thing to do": quoted in Reba and Bonnie Churchill, "Murphy to See Story in Film," *Hollywood Daily*, April 20, 1954.
Another expensive habit: "I Know Why I'm In Love."
"One of them": Pamela Murphy, "The Trouble with Murph."

239 *With very few exceptions, reviewers: Variety* December 18, 1954; Jack Moffitt, "New 'Destry' Should Ride Into Easy Boxoffice Favor," *Hollywood Reporter*, December 2, 1954.

10. This Is Your Life

240 *"It was a lousy book":* quoted in Hubler, "He Doesn't Want To Be a Star."
"I've always felt": quoted in Maxine Arnold, "The Personal War of Audie Murphy," *Photoplay*, October 1955.

241 *"I have to admit":* quoted in Richard G. Hubler, "Audie Murphy, the Man Behind the Medals," *Coronet*, August 1955.
"too self-eulogizing": McFadden, interview with author, June 11, 1986.
"I'd known Drake": quoted in Arnold, "The Personal War of Audie Murphy."
he "found Audie": Production Notes, *To Hell and Back*; U-I files, USC.
"I remember the first day": Paul Picerni, interview with author, June 6, 1986.

242 *"series of bloody":* Typescript, unsigned, undated; U-I files, USC.
"just getting Audie": quoted in Arnold, "The Personal War of Audie Murphy."
"Audie had come": quoted in Production Notes, *To Hell and Back*; U-I files, USC.

Page

"*I was definitely*": quoted in John L. Scott, "Audie Murphy, No. 1 Hero, Slogs Again," Los Angeles *Times*, September 4, 1955.

"*The problem of getting*": Aaron Rosenberg, untitled document; U-I files, USC.

243 "*Like a young*": David McClure to Harold Simpson, January 27, 1974.

"*I was working out*": Bobby Hoy, interview with author, June 3, 1986.

I'd like eventually": quoted in Jack Mullen, "Today He Is A Man," *Movies*, 1954.

"*It would have been*": quoted in Arnold, "The Personal War of Audie Murphy."

244 "*he had little to say*":quoted in Production Notes; U-I files, USC.

Rosenberg also: Production Notes; U-I files, USC.

"*powder-puff battle*": Audie Murphy, "A Soldier Relives Anzio," *Collier's*, September 2, 1955.

"*I can remember*": quoted in Scott, "Audie Murphy, No. 1 Hero."

245 "*This was the toughest*": Murphy, "A Soldier Relives Anzio."

"*Audie wasn't doing*": quoted in Arnold, "The Personal War of Audie Murphy."

"*Rosie*," *he said:* quoted in Production Notes; U-I files, USC.

246 "*looks to most people*": Richard Dyer MacCann, "Murphy Book on Way to Screen," *Christian Science Monitor*, May 17, 1955.

"*played down some scenes*": Arnold, "The Personal War."

"*I think it's kind of silly*": quoted in Bob Thomas, "Audie Murphy To Portray Audie Murphy in Movie," Austin *American-Statesman*, June 21, 1954.

247 "*a western in uniform*": quoted in Bob Thomas, "Audie Recalls Told to Kill," Greenville *Banner*, December 2, 1960.

"*I don't give a damn*": McClure to Simpson, January 27, 1974.

248 "*Is that Davy Crockett*": newspaper clipping, 1955.

Universal thought: " 'To Hell and Back' Heading For Top Gross of Any U-I Picture," U-I press release, September 27, 1955; U-I files, USC.

249 *For the first time:* Dick Williams, " 'To Hell and Back' Tells Audie's Amazing Army Career," *Mirror-News*, October 13, 1955; Jesse Zunser, *Cue*, September 24, 1955; Hazel Flinn, " 'To Hell and Back' Is Sincere Movie; Tops All U-I Grosses," Beverly Hills *Citizen*, October 12, 1955; A. W., *New York Times*, September 23, 1955; *Time*, October 17, 1955.

"*The Yanks give you*": Robert Larkins, "The Films of Audie Murphy," monograph, (Australia).

"*modern folk hero*": Douglas Brode, *The Films of the Fifties* (Citadel Press, 1967).

"*It had a lot*": quoted in interview with Hedda Hopper, interview transcript, June 22, 1957; Hopper Collection, Margaret Herrick Library, Academy of Motion Picture Arts and Sciences.

250 "*Yours is a full life*": transcript of "This Is Your Life," 1954.

250–251 "*I average about $2,000*": quoted in Hal Boyle, "Audie Murphy Finally Readjusted From War," Greenville *Banner*, August 3, 1955.

251 "*Never. My wife*": quoted in Hedda Hopper, *Motion Picture*, March 1956.

"*You figure it out*": quoted in Al Stump, "G.I. In Hollywood," *Saga*, June 1957.

Some of the resentment: Stump, *Saga*.

252 "*A penny for*": David McClure, "The Way Back."

The birth of their second: "Moods, Nightmares, and Stony Silence," fan magazine, ca. 1954.

"*cemented the temporary*": "Home of the Brave," fan magazine, ca. 1954.

253 "*The stakes are*": quoted in Arnold, "The Personal War of Audie Murphy."

254 "*One of 'em*": Tom Shaw, interview with author, March 28, 1987.

Page

> *So things were not:* Hubler, "Audie Murphy: The Man Behind the Medals";
> Ben Maddox, "I Know Why I'm In Love," fan magazine, ca. 1953.

255 *Gradually he resumed:* "Things I Don't Tell My Wife," fan magazine, ca. 1954.
> *"only gambles Audie takes":* Arnold, "The Personal War of Audie Murphy."
> *"He was a most unlucky":* John Huston, interview with author, March 25,
> 1987.

256 *"all right, this is":* Joey Barnum, interview with author, June 13, 1986.
> *"I really don't want":* Casey Tibbs, interview with author, March 27, 1987.
> *"rather go to the races":* Jay Fishburn, interview with author, June 24, 1986.
> *"hell of a gambler":* Polly Burson, interview with author, March 23, 1987.

257 *"money had no home":* John Hudkins, interview with author, June 9, 1986.
> *"Where's the rest":* Tom Shaw, interview with author.

258 *"He'd play me":* Frank Chase, interview with author, May 28, 1987.
> *Spec McClure:* McClure to Simpson, February 10, 1974.

259 *"I'm not an actor":* quoted in "Audie Not Exactly Shouting For Joy," *TV
> Guide*, July 29, 1961.

11. Fading Stardom

261 *"a lousy script":* Audie Murphy interview with Hedda Hopper, June 22, 1957;
Hopper Collection; Margaret Herrick Library, Academy of Motion Picture Arts
and Sciences.

262 *"To me, the postwar story":* quoted in Bob Thomas, "Audie Recalls Told To
Kill," Greenville *Banner*, December 2, 1960.
> *Audie asked Spec:* McClure, July 16, 1972; Texas Collection, Baylor
> University.

263 *"I would take":* quoted in *Movie Time*, March 1956.
> *"That Audie": Movie Time, Movie Time.*
> *"People can sit home":* interview with Hopper, June 22, 1957.
> *"earnest, dreary exercise": Saturday Review*, August 25, 1956.

265 *"that these characterizations":* "Audie Murphy Sued for $1,000,000 by Pro-
ducer," *Los Angeles Times*, September 18, 1957.
> *"I resent Mr. Brown's":* "Audie Bridles at Sagebrusher 'Specialist' Tag,"
> *Variety*, September 19, 1957.
> *In 1957 Universal:* Murphy/Hopper interview, June 22, 1957.

266 *"You can see an awful lot":* Marion Hargrove, interview with author, March
24, 1987.
> *For the first time:* " 'Joe Butterfly': Character Analysis"; Universal-Interna-
> tional files, Special Collections, Doheny Library, University of Southern
> California.
> *"didn't feel comfortable":* Sy Gomberg, interview with author, March 27, 1987.

267 *But Mann pulled out:* Phil Hardy, *The Western* (William Morrow, 1983).

268 *Audie and Redgrave:* Kenneth L. Geist, *Pictures Will Talk: The Life and Films
of Joseph L. Mankiewicz* (Charles Scribner's, 1978).
> *"My operation is":* quoted in David McClure, "Audie Murphy—Man of
> Humor," unpublished typescript; Texas Collection, Baylor University.
> *Saigon was seething:* Geist, *Pictures Will Talk.*
> *"The first thing I did":* quoted in Bob Thomas, "Texas Audie Making 29th
> Western," Dallas *Morning News*, November 27, 1963.

269 *If Audie seemed tense:* Reba and Bonnie Churchill, "The Return of the Native,"
Screenland, November, 1957.
> *"I can't produce":* quoted in "One Man's Movie," *Saturday Review*, January
> 25, 1968.
> *"the very bad film":* quoted in Gene D. Phillips, *Graham Greene: The Films
> of His Fiction* (Teachers College Press, 1974).

Page

"the perfect symbol": quoted in Thomas M. Pryor, "Producer Finds 'Quiet American," *New York Times,* December 14, 1956.

270 *Intentionally or not:* Bernard F. Dick, *Joseph L. Mankiewicz* (Twayne, 1983).

"spooky sincerity": Dick, *Mankiewicz.*

"The late Audie Murphy's": quoted in Phillips, *Graham Greene.*

271 *"a sea movie":* quoted in Stuart Kaminsky, *John Huston, Maker of Magic* (Houghton Mifflin, 1978).

"a stubborn innocence": Floyd Stone, *Motion Picture Herald,* September 20, 1958.

For the first time: Jack Moffitt, "Greene-Siegel Pic Sexy, Actionful," *Hollywood Reporter,* September 15, 1958; Ron., *Variety Daily,* September 15, 1958.

272 *"well-worn Colt. 44":* Gene Coon, "No Name on the Bullet," August 30, 1958. UCLA.

"His eyes almost": Morgan Woodward, interview with author, August 15, 1987.

274 *"I feel no qualms":* Audie Murphy, *To Hell and Back* (Holt, 1949).

"With me it's been": quoted in Thomas B. Morgan, "The War Hero," *Esquire,* December 1983.

"Audie Murphy played": Jack Arnold, remarks to author, June 8, 1986.

"liked the subject": Gomberg, interview with author, May 27, 1987.

276 *"I made a big hit":* Audie Murphy to David McClure, April 21, 1957.

"To look around": quoted in "The Return of the Native."

"uncontrollable tears": Jean Frazier, "Thank God I'm Home," *Modern Screen,* September 1957.

277 *"Audie's jokes never":* Guy Mitchell, interview with author, August 19, 1987.

"He used to dangle": Warren Stevens, interview with author, June 18, 1986.

278 *"He was the kind":* Joey Barnum, interview with author, June 13, 1987.

Or he'd throw: Jesse White, interview with author, August 17, 1987.

On one set: Ken Tobey, remarks to author, June 19, 1986.

"I have something for you": Venetia Stevenson, interview with author, June 5, 1986.

279 *"I have been accompanying":* "Murphy Has Role in Arrest," newspaper clipping, April 25, 1956.

"a deep hatred": Art Strong, interview with author, November 11, 1987.

In the mid-fifties: Raymond Sarlot and Fred E. Basten, *Life at the Hollywood Marmont* (Roundtable, 1987).

12. Trail's End

282 *"Prophets of television":* quoted in Charles Higham, *Hollywood at Sunset* (Saturday Review Press, 1972).

283 *Earlier that year:* Audie Murphy, "Taps Never Blow For War Stories," *Hollywood Reporter,* November 26, 1959.

"It's too hard": "Audie Murphy Finally Agrees To TV Western," *Dallas Morning News,* June 22, 1959.

284 *"NBC hasn't yet scheduled":* unsigned memo to Seymour in New York; Universal files, Special Collections, Doheny Library, University of Southern California.

Even Audie's prize horse: "Rapid Horse Creates a Dilemma," Los Angeles *Mirror,* September 9, 1960.

"I guess he must have": quoted in Hal Humphrey, "NBC Again Set to Launch Audie but He Isn't Happy About It," *Los Angeles Mirror,* May 15, 1961.

"I'm glad that it didn't": "Audie Isn't Exactly Shouting For Joy," *TV Guide,* July 29, 1961.

Page

"It's like the Redstone": quoted in Humphrey, "NBC Again Set to Launch Audie."

285 *"That's the compromise":* quoted in Rick DuBrow, "Close to the Earth," *Dallas Herald Magazine,* November 26, 1961.

"I never watch": quoted in Humphrey, "NBC Again Set to Launch Audie."

"a bad show": TV Guide.

"not only bad for children": TV Guide.

"Apparently some people": TV Guide.

286 *"the best news":* TV Guide.

"Any time I did something": quoted in Maurice Zolotow, *Shooting Star* (Simon and Schuster, 1974).

287 *"the story of racial":* John Huston, *An Open Book* (Ballantine, 1980).

Though there were things: Gerald Pratley, *The Cinema of John Huston* (A. S. Barnes, 1977); Huston, *An Open Book.*

"Murder was common": "Bad Chuck" Roberson, with Brodie Thoene, *The Fall Guy: 30 Years as the Duke's Double* (Hancock House, 1980).

"really wild, like being": John Saxon, interview with author, June 27, 1987.

"One day he yelled": Doug McClure, interview with author, July 1, 1986.

"Audie had that damn rifle": Tom Shaw, interview with author, March 28, 1987.

288 *"You go tell him":* Shaw/Graham interview.

"bordering on having": Huston/Graham interview.

289 *"I could see that":* Inge Morath Miller, interview with author, March 13, 1987.

"succeeded in drowning": quoted in Hedda Hopper, "Audie Murphy Tells of Unique Incident," *Los Angeles Times,* Mar. 27, 1959.

290 *"Audie is afraid":* quoted in David McClure, "Audie Murphy—The Actor," New Castle [Penn.] *News,* May 17, 1972.

When the film: Lancaster, remarks to author, September 19, 1986.

On the other hand: Albert ("Hap") Turner, *Films in Review,* May 1960.

291 *"I'm just a mediocre failure":* quoted in McClure, "Audie Murphy—The Man," New Castle [Penn.] *News,* May 11, 1972.

"I think there's still": quoted in Bob Thomas, "Murphy Story Remains Unfilmed," 1961.

"lots of guns": Warren Stevens, interview with author, June 18, 1986.

He knew how: Arthur Knight, *Saturday Review,* November 5, 1960.

"They wanted to know": Gordon Kay, interview with author, June 15, 1986.

292 *"Audie fit in well":* Clair Huffaker, interview with author, June 3, 1986.

"I knew a lot of people": Jan Merlin, interview with author, June 3, 1986.

294 *"So I'm looking at":* William Witney, interview with author, July 1, 1986.

295 *"The SUB COMMANDER":* Richard Maibaum and Willard Willigham, "Battle at Bloody Beach," January 6, 1961; UCLA.

296 *"pleasant and poised gentleman":* F.B.I. interview, August 5, 1968; F.B.I. file on Audie Murphy. In late summer 1968, the F.B.I. conducted a "full field investigation" of Murphy in response to a request from the Johnson White House. The reason was that Audie was being considered for appointment to a minor post, the Battle Monuments Commission. F.B.I. agents interviewed a few people in Texas and a good many more in the film industry in Los Angeles. There is nothing revelatory in these records; the impressions and information conform very closely with the picture of Murphy developed independently in this book.

"It's a sort of post-war thing": quoted in DuBrow, "Close to the Earth."

297 *"authentic cloak-and-dagger":* "Audie, Donning Khaki Again After 9 Years, to Help U.S. Defeat Reds in Filmization of Race to 'The Moon'," *Variety,* August 10, 1964.

Page

 "*[some] missed parts*": Don Safron, "Audie A Dove," Dallas newspaper, ca. 1970.

 He began to write lyrics: details on Murphy's ventures in country western songwriting derive from "Scotty Turner—Just Talkin'," Nashville trade publication; Kenny Meyers, "Is Scotty Turner 1000 Years Old?," magazine; Turner's letter and notes to Harold Simpson, September 1, 1974; Turner interview with Simpson, July 17, 1975; and Mitchell/Graham interview.

299 *The separation in 1960:* Louella A. Parsons, "Audie Murphy, Wife of 9 Years Separate," *Los Angeles Examiner*, Mar. 24, 1960.

 "*It was one of those*": Venetia Stevenson, interview with author, June 5, 1986.

300 *The story broke:* details of this incident are drawn from "Audie Murphy Admits Striking Youth," *Los Angeles Herald-Examiner*, June 4, 1962; "Check Police Record of Murphy Case Boy," newspaper article, June 5, 1962; "Audie Murphy Admits Punching Youth in Row," newspaper article, June 5, 1962; and "Audie Murphy, Teens in Mysterious Row," Hollywood *Citizen-News*, June 14, 1962.

13. A Time for Dying

302 "*I seem to be*": quoted in Bob Thomas, "Texas Audie Making 29th Western," Dallas *Morning News*, November 11, 1963.

303 *Trade reviewers:* Richard Gertner, " 'Arizona Raiders,' " *Motion Picture Herald*, August 4, 1965; Sy Oshinsky, " 'Gunpoint,' " *Motion Picture Herald*, March 30, 1966.

 "*it doesn't seem right*": quoted in Thomas, "Texas Audie Making 29th Western."

304 "*I had to do*": quoted in Thomas Morgan, "The War Hero," *Esquire*, December 1983.

 "*We didn't have any*": quoted in "Spy Dramas Rougher than Westerns Says Audie Murphy," Pressbook, *Trunk to Cairo*.

 "*Try to imagine*": Sy Oshinsky, " 'Trunk to Cairo,' " *Motion Picture Herald*, March 8, 1967.

 "*He wants a divorce*": Harrison Carroll, "Audie Murphys Split Marriage of 13 Years," Los Angeles *Herald-Examiner*, May 6, 1964.

 "*In combat, you see*": quoted in Morgan, "The War Hero."

305 "*Jesus, what are you*": Al Jank, interview with author, June 25, 1986.

306 "*I have no idea*": quoted in Bill Libby, "A Different Kind of Hell," *Los Angeles Times Weekly Magazine*, July 18, 1971.

 "*I feel better than*": quoted in Hedda Hopper, "Bob Hope Purchases Audie Murphy Farm," *Los Angeles Times*, July 22, 1963.

 A laundry list: financial details taken from records at Los Angeles County Courthouse.

307 "*It might have been*": quoted in John Kendall, "Audie Murphy Tells of Loan From Bud Suhl," *Los Angeles Times*, March 5, 1964.

308 "*I got so that*": quoted in Morgan, "The War Hero."

309 "*I'm too tough*": quoted in Vernon Scott, "Texan Audie Murphy Sets Dallas Premiere," Dallas *Morning News*, August 25, 1969.

 "*What the hell*": Boetticher/Graham interview.

311 *The film received: Variety*, October 6, 1971; Sam Sasoff, "Orphans of the Storm: When Hollywood Chickens Out," *Village Voice*, May 20, 1981; Vincent Canby, "Screen: 'Time for Dying,' Vintage '69," *New York Times*, June 2, 1982.

312 "*George, I'm just absolutely*": George Putnam, interview with author, October 17, 1987.

 Alternately bouyant, and gloomy: Libby, "A Different Kind of Hell."

313 *The headlines blared:* The Murphy-Gofstein incident is reconstructed from the following sources: Paul Caruso, interview with author, June 12, 1986; and

Page

newspaper articles contained in Mr. Caruso's personal scrapbook which he generously made available to me: "Audie Pulled Gun?" Los Angeles *Herald-Examiner*, October 7, 1970; "Audie Murphy Tells Story," Los Angeles *Herald-Examiner*, June 4, 1970; "War Hero Murphy: I Didn't Have a Gun," Miami *Herald*, June 5, 1970; "Not Guilty, Says Audie to Judge," Hollywood *Citizen News*, July 21, 1970; "Audie Murphy Held For Trial," Los Angeles *Herald-Examiner*, July 6, 1970; "Audie Murphy Held For Assault," *Sun-Sentinel*, May 29, 1970; "Audie Says Plaintiff Called Him a 'Phony,' " *Stars and Stripes*; "Audie Murphy's Private War Still Rages," *Motion Picture*, September, 1970; "Audie Murphy Denies Guilt in Assault Case," *Daily News*, July 21, 1970; "Trial of Audie Murphy Delayed; Witness' Son Ill," Los Angeles *Herald-Examiner*, October 5, 1970; Andy Wickham, "Return of the Quiet American: The Los Angeles Trial of Audie Murphy," *Coast*, June, 1971; "Audie Murphy Acquitted," Santa Ana *Register*, October 17, 1970; "Actor-Hero Audie Murphy Acquitted in Assault Case," Van Nuys *News*, October 18, 1970; "Found Guilty of Cruelty to Animals," newspaper article, 1970; "Complaint On Audie Belittled," Los Angeles *Herald-Examiner*, October 16, 1970; "Audie Murphy Is Found Innocent," Los Angeles *Herald-Examiner*, October 17, 1970; "Murphy Cleared by Police Chief," Los Angeles *Herald-Examiner*, January 6, 1971; "Audie Freed of Blackjack Charges," Los Angeles *Herald-Examiner*, January 5, 1971.

319 *"multi-million dollar":* Audie Eyes Garbage Film Expose," Hollywood *Citizen News*, August 21, 1970.

Audie had been doing: Audie Murphy to George Putnam, September 22, 1970.

In his cover letter: Audie Murphy to Ronald Reagan, September 21, 1970.

"I hadn't seen him": quoted in Stuart Kaminsky, *Don Siegel* (Curtis Books, 1974).

14. Into the Darkness

321 *By the fall of 1969:* the story of Audie's gambling in this period is taken chiefly from sixteen taped conversations contained in the F.B.I. file on Audie Murphy, made available through the Freedom of Information Act.

324 *His dossier suggests:* for details on Buccieri, see Virgil W. Peterson, "Fiore (Fifi) Bucciere," *A Report on Chicago Crime for 1966* (Chicago Crime Commission, 1966); Ovid Demaris, *Captive City* (Lyle Stuart, 1969); and Clark R. Mollenhoff, *Strike Force: Organized Crime and the Government* (Prentice-Hall, 1972); and Wayne Moquin, ed., with Charles Van Doren, *The American Way of Crime: A Documentary History* (New York: Praeger, 1976).

325 *"What's the matter":* Boetticher/Graham interview.

"We learned one thing": William Laws Calley, as told to John Sacks, *Calley* (Viking, 1971).

326 *"All I would like":* quoted in "Audie Would Like Special Cuba Duty," Los Angeles *Examiner*, November 8, 1961.

"Gee, I'd hate": quoted in Thomas Morgan, "The War Hero," *Esquire*, December, 1983.

327 *"It's not right":* quoted in Bill Libby, "A Different Kind of Hell," *Los Angeles Times Weekly Magazine*, July 18, 1971.

"I'm not saying": quoted in William Greider, newspaper article, Austin *American-Statesman*, December 25, 1970.

328 *"It's exasperating":* quoted in "Calley Receives Hero's Sympathy," Dallas *Morning News*, December 13, 1970.

"Distressed and shocked": quoted in "Audie Shocked," *New York Post*, April 1, 1971.

Page

"*incredible cast*": Budd Schulberg, "Introduction" to Walter Sheridan, *The Fall and Rise of Jimmy Hoffa* (Saturday Review Press, 1972).

329 *Smith had had:* For details on D'Alton Smith and Carlos Marcello, see Dan E. Moldea, *The Hoffa Wars: Teamsters, Rebels, Policians, and the Mob* (Paddington Press, 1978); and Sheridan, *The Fall and Rise of Jimmy Hoffa.*

"*wheeler-dealer*": John H. Davis, *Mafia Kingfish: Carlos Marcello and the Assassination of John F. Kennedy* (McGraw-Hill, 1988).

331–332 "*I have met several times*": quoted in Jack Nelson, "Audie Murphy Worked on Plan to Free Hoffa," *Los Angeles Times*, June 6, 1971.

332 *If it happened:* Arthur Everett, Kathryn Johnson, and Harry F. Rosenthal, *Calley* (Dell, 1971).

333 "*I would be surprised*": quoted in "Audie Murphy Struggled to Free Hoffa," newspaper article.

334 *Friends back in Texas:* "Actor's Brother Killed in Crash," Greenville *Banner*, January 3, 1968; Mrs. Cawthon, interview with author, May 2, 1985; Eugene Porter Murphy, interview with Harold Simpson, November 7, 1974; Helen Woods, interview with Harold Simpson, August 4, 1975; Casey Tibbs, interview with author, March 27, 1987.

336 "*massive total body*": "Audie Murphy, War Hero, Killed in Plane Crash," *New York Times*, June 1, 1971.

"*He took a lot*": McClure, quoted on radio broadcast, George Putnam, June 1, 1971.

"*It wasn't Audie*": Bobby Hoy, interview with author, June 3, 1986.

"*Casey, are you*": Casey Tibbs, interview with author, March 29, 1987.

He called the local radio station: Tom Willett, letter to author, July, 1987.

"*So Audie had some warning*": Pamela Murphy quoted in Ann Faragher, "Deep Faith Helps War Hero's Widow Meet Tragedy," Greenville *Herald Banner*, February 25, 1973.

337 "*Murphys played a very prominent*": quoted in Earl Golz, "Was Audie Murphy a Victim of the Assassination Conspiracy," *National Tattler*, June 8, 1975.

He proved pilot error: Herbert Hafif, tape of summation to jury, made available to me courtesy of Mr. Hafif.

337–338 "*He was a great soldier*": quoted in Dorothy Townsend, "Audie Murphy's Heroism Described in Final Eulogy," newspaper article, June 5, 1971.

338 "*It was surprising to me*": "Harold Hall, Gravedigger," *Washington Post Magazine*, November 13, 1988.

"*As America's most decorated hero*": quoted in "Audie Murphy Buried With Full Military Honors at Arlington," A.P. release, June, 1971.

340 "*smoking a cigarette*": Roy Edwards, "Of A Different Time," Dallas *Morning News*, June 2, 1971.

For the national press: compiled from following: "To Hell and Not Quite Back," *Time*, June 14, 1971; "Died: Audie Murphy," *Newsweek*, June 14, 1971; "Audie Murphy, War Hero, Killed in Plane Crash"; "Audie Murphy," London *Times*, June 1, 1971; Bill Mauldin, "Parting Shots," *Life*, June 11, 1971.

345 "*I had forgotten him*": Julian Smith, *Looking Away: Hollywood and Vietnam* (Charles Scribner's Sons, 1975).

INDEX